COLD FURY

COLD FURY

TONI ANDERSON

ALSO BY TONI ANDERSON

COLD JUSTICE® SERIES

A Cold Dark Place (Book #1)

Cold Pursuit (Book #2)

Cold Light of Day (Book #3)

Cold Fear (Book #4)

Cold in The Shadows (Book #5)

Cold Hearted (Book #6)

Cold Secrets (Book #7)

Cold Malice (Book #8)

A Cold Dark Promise (Book #9~A Wedding Novella)

Cold Blooded (Book #10)

COLD JUSTICE® – THE NEGOTIATORS

Cold & Deadly (Book #1)

Colder Than Sin (Book #2)

Cold Wicked Lies (Book #3)

Cold Cruel Kiss (Book #4)

Cold as Ice (Book #5)

COLD JUSTICE® – MOST WANTED

Cold Silence (Book #1)

Cold Deceit (Book #2)

Cold Snap (Book #3)

Cold Fury (Book #4)

Cold Spite (Book #5) - Coming soon

For Jodie Griffin — for her brilliant ideas and endless enthusiasm.

PROLOGUE

Today, Hope Harper had won the biggest victory of her life in the courtroom. After weeks of fiery and often brutal testimony, her client had been released. The problem was, Hope suspected Julius Leech was truly the vicious serial killer the police and District Attorney's office had accused him of being.

And now he was free again.

Her stomach clenched. She closed her eyes and laid her head against the warm steering wheel in the quiet parking garage attached to her firm's downtown building.

It wasn't her job as a defense attorney to make a judgment regarding her clients' guilt. Only for her to vigorously defend them and focus on the government's failure to legally prove their case.

The cops had fucked up.

Worse, they'd lied. Perjured themselves on the stand.

Last night, one detective had tragically taken his own life. His partner, a junior detective, was now under investigation.

She raised her head. Glanced at the text her husband had sent her a few hours ago.

We need to talk…

And didn't that sound ominous.

They hadn't spent a lot of time together recently, this case consuming every minute of her existence since Jeff Beasley had dangled a partnership in front of her like a carrot on a stick if she took on Leech as a client. She hadn't even needed a "Not Guilty" verdict. She'd only needed to show up.

Partner before thirty?

Amazing.

With a kid?

Unheard of.

Hope liked to win. Liked to prove she was as good as any of the arrogant, self-righteous prosecutors in the DA's office. Her goal had always been a partnership at Beasley, Waterman, Vander & Co., so she had job security and some say in what cases she handled in the future. Mainly, so she could spend more time with Danny and Paige, and they could think about adding to their little family.

Well, now she was officially one of the "Co."

And even though her insides churned with unease, she wasn't the one who'd screwed this up for the prosecution. The cop who'd planted the evidence was the reason Julius Leech was once again free to wander the streets. She was good, but she wasn't good enough to beat the wave of circumstantials the Boston Police Department had produced to back up their accusations.

And she was truly sorry about Detective Pauly Monroe. She'd known him personally via her brother-in-law, who was also a BPD detective.

She blew out a massive sigh. This trial had damaged her relationships on so many levels.

She couldn't bear to think about Leech any longer. She'd been forced to sit next to the guy for months and pretend he didn't make her skin crawl every time they accidentally brushed against one another. She'd had to pretend the obvious admiration in his pale blue eyes wasn't something that made her want to retch.

She was taking next week off. God knew, she'd earned it.

We need to talk…

Anxiety gnawed along her nerves. She missed her husband, and she missed her daughter. She started the car and began the drive out of the city. She contemplated calling ahead to see if they needed anything picked up from the store but dreaded the idea Danny might tell her not to come home at all.

They'd argued last night to the point where for the first time in their lives together she'd slept in the spare room and left before the sun was up.

She hated when they fought. Danny was her safe place, her rock, and usually backed her.

Not last night.

Last night, Danny had begged her to walk away. To walk away from the case and the firm.

It had been an impossible ask after she'd worked so hard and the trial was almost over. Why couldn't he have seen that? Instead, he'd said she was a workaholic who was selling her soul.

That had cut deep.

It was okay to work tirelessly on the Innocence Project and help get wrongly convicted individuals out of jail, but it wasn't okay to vigorously defend people the public had decided were guilty, whether the facts backed them up or not?

That was bullshit.

Criminal justice was not necessarily about right and wrong. It was a game of legalese chess, and she was damned good at it, even if her morals were a little bruised from some of the people her firm represented—but no more than the experienced detective who'd planted DNA or the rookie who'd let him.

Her jaw hurt from clenching her teeth together, but she had to let it go.

She loved Danny. Had loved him since the first day they'd collided. They'd figure it out.

Hell, she'd quit if it meant that much to him. Deal with corporate or entertainment contracts instead. Even though she loved trying cases in court, she'd quit for the man she loved.

It was after seven p.m., and the rush hour traffic had died

down. Getting out of the city only took twenty minutes. She arrived at their beautiful, leafy, suburban craftsman-style house and parked in the driveway. She stared at the building that Danny had turned into a comfortable home for them all. It was deep blue and had white-painted shutters. Flowers bloomed in the containers they'd set up that spring. That was the extent of her gardening prowess, but Danny enjoyed being outside. He'd planted a flowerbed at the side of the driveway and a small vegetable garden at the back where he and Paige were growing lettuce and carrots and a pumpkin to carve for Halloween.

He'd made the choice to stay home with Paige while Hope went out to work. He was a crime fiction author and managed to squeeze out pages in-between playdates and kids' movies. She and his brother Brendan served as technical advisors for his plots. One of his novels had been optioned for a movie, though Danny had told her not to get excited because most options expired before the movie was ever made. But Hope was secretly planning what to wear at the Oscars and mentally helping Danny prepare his acceptance speech for winning best adapted screenplay.

She smiled.

She loved her husband. She believed in him. Up until yesterday, she'd thought he believed in her too.

Lawyers often didn't like their clients. Clients were often bad people. They still deserved a solid defense.

Last night, they'd both said things in anger they shouldn't have, but maybe the real issue was the fact she'd been absent so much lately. She didn't want to be absent anymore.

She climbed out and met the muggy September air. The fact Paige didn't immediately throw open the front door and run to greet her was a bad sign. Aged four and a half now, her daughter was usually allowed to stay up late if she knew her mom was going to be home in time to tuck her into bed.

Hope stretched her neck to the side, working out the kinks before walking around to grab her heavy briefcase and suit jacket off the passenger seat.

The sun had started to drop in the sky, casting long shadows from the detached garage into the yard. It was unseasonably hot. A bird sang in the tree, and a kid rode his bicycle down the sidewalk followed by a girl on a skateboard. Cars were parked along the street. The house opposite was having an addition built on the back, and Danny had been cursing the noise and distraction from his writing. The workers were gone now, the dumpster at the front of the house full of sheetrock and rubble. Construction mud covered the sidewalk.

Hope brushed her hair from her forehead and went in through the side gate to see if her family were in the back yard.

It was so *quiet*.

Her heartbeat sped up in sudden apprehension.

What if he'd left her?

"Danny?" She hurried up the back steps and inside. "Paige?"

She dumped her bag and jacket on the kitchen island, pulled out her phone. No messages. She texted him before slipping it back into her pocket. Danny's car keys were hanging up beside the door, and the awful tension that had gripped her eased. No evidence of dinner being made though. Where the heck were they? Maybe they'd gone to pick something up. Or to grab an ice cream from the convenience store at the end of the street to celebrate the end of summer.

Perhaps they could all go out to that place on Field Street and eat on the patio. Celebrate her partnership and a week's well-earned vacation.

She kicked off her heels and absently leaned down to stroke the kitten, Lucifer, who'd come running through from the family room meowing for food as usual. Then she noticed blood on the floor.

"Did you cut yourself?" She picked up Lucifer and checked his paws. There were traces of crimson on his soft pads, but he didn't seem to be injured.

She walked through to the family room, clutching the kitty to her chest. Her heart stopped, vision tunneled. She dropped the cat. Ran toward her husband who lay on the floor in front of the muted TV.

"Oh, God. Oh, God. Oh, God. No."

Paige lay next to him. Still as a rock. They were holding hands and a chill stole over her.

"No, no, no."

She searched for Danny's pulse. Belatedly noticed the blood drenching his dark blue graphic tee that had a small hole in the center. The faint flutter of his heartbeat beneath her fingertips took her by surprise.

He was alive.

He was *alive*.

Thank God.

The slight rise and fall of his chest told her he was breathing. Just.

She fumbled for her phone and called 911 and put it on speaker, yelling her address and begging for help. She lifted his shirt to see the wound, used the material to wipe away the blood. The small puncture wound immediately refilled with dark crimson. She pressed her palm against the wound to staunch the bleeding, but she needed to help Paige. She grabbed a thin cushion off the sofa, arranged it over the gash before draping Danny's heavy arm over the material to apply pressure.

She turned to her daughter and frantically felt for a pulse, internally recoiling from her daughter's cool skin even as she checked to see if she was breathing. She wasn't.

"Baby, come on."

Danny's eyes flickered as she started CPR on their child. They couldn't lose her. Hope *refused* to lose her. She repeated the thirty compressions to two breaths, five times, ignoring the lack of response in Paige's blood-speckled blue eyes.

She turned to Danny to make sure he was still alive, still with her. She placed a kiss on his forehead. "I love you, honey. I'm so sorry we argued last night. I'm so sorry. I love you. Don't leave me."

He tried to open his mouth, but nothing came out. His eyes flicked to their daughter, and Hope began CPR again, knowing it was almost certainly too late and their beautiful, amazing daughter was gone. But she was called Hope for a reason.

She refused to give up.

The doorbell rang. The paramedics were here. Thank God. She stumbled to her feet and crashed into the coffee table on the way out of the room, barely registering the blow. She threw open the door, and suddenly, it was as if she'd slipped into a surreal dream. It wasn't the paramedics standing there, it was Julius Leech, and he held a bunch of flowers and a bottle of red wine and wore a big smile.

"I wanted to thank you—"

Hope ignored him. Blinked and looked around. An ambulance was racing down the street toward her, and she pushed past Leech to stand on the cool grass in her bare feet, frantically waving her arms.

The ambulance pulled to a stop.

"This way," she urged as they jumped out of their rig and grabbed their heavy bags.

"Quickly. My husband is alive. I did CPR on my daughter, but she isn't breathing." She broke off on a sob as she led the way inside. She eased into a space between Danny and Paige as the paramedics began to work on her family. Stroked her daughter's silky blonde hair. "Her name is Paige."

"What happened?" one of the paramedics asked.

"I don't know. I arrived home a few minutes ago and found them like this."

The paramedic avoided her gaze, but she refused to accept what she could see on the woman's face.

"Please keep trying." Terror strangled Hope. "Please don't give up. They are *everything* to me."

The paramedic nodded and began inserting an IV while another medic worked on Danny.

Hope stroked his black hair. "He was breathing and had a

7

pulse when I came home. His eyes were open and aware." She didn't know how coherent words were spilling out of her mouth when all she wanted to do was scream.

More medics arrived, and she was forced aside as the two teams worked side-by-side.

"Please help them. I don't know what I'll do without them." She'd die. She'd cease to exist.

She glanced up and saw Julius Leech standing on the threshold of the family room. A smile flickered around the corner of his mouth as his eyes shone with what looked like glee.

Realization hit her like a shotgun blast. "You son of a bitch."

Hope stumbled to her feet and launched herself at him. Leech looked startled. He scooted from the room and out through the wide-open front door, and she chased him, grabbing the neck of his suit jacket, jerking him off his feet. He lay there in the grass, staring up at her.

"What did you do to them? What did you do!" she screamed.

Another figure rushed over and threw himself on top of Leech and started pummeling the guy.

Danny's brother, Brendan.

"You bastard. You fucking piece of filth." Brendan slammed his fist into Leech's face, over and over again.

Hope wanted Julius annihilated. Wiped off the face of the earth. He'd come to her home and hurt her family—to toy with her, to torture her. The fact she'd gotten him released from jail would only add a nice twist for the sick bastard.

But Brendan wasn't stopping and none of the other cops who'd rolled up in their squad cars appeared to be willing to prevent her brother-in-law from beating Leech to death on her front lawn. As much as she wanted Leech to suffer, she couldn't allow that kind of mindless slaughter. Nor allow Brendan to risk his freedom.

She grabbed Brendan's arm. "Stop it. Stop. We need to go with Danny and Paige to the hospital. We need to be there for them."

"I want him to pay for what he's done," Brendan sobbed.

"He will. We need to be with our family, and they need our support." She dragged Brendan to his feet.

"They're alive?"

"Barely."

The guy looked shattered. News of the attack had spread fast through the Boston PD as every cop on the force seemed to have arrived.

Leech lay unconscious on the lawn, face battered and bloody. The medics came out of the house with two gurneys, and she dashed toward them, dragging Brendan with her.

"Reap what you sow, bitch," one of the cops snarled at her.

Ice flashed across her skin.

Was this her fault?

She tried to climb into the ambulance, but the paramedic blocked her. "No room."

Brendan grabbed her arm. "We'll follow. Come on."

She ran barefoot to his car and got into the passenger side. Brendan pulled away behind the ambulance, riding in the slip-stream with only a few feet between them. Hope stared at the back of the ambulance as it raced through the city, lights and sirens blaring, willing Danny and Paige to survive. She wrapped her arms around her middle, rocking back and forth.

"What the hell happened?" Brendan's knuckles were raw.

"I came home and found them inside. Danny was bleeding but conscious. Paige—" She sobbed. "Paige wasn't breathing." Her hands trembled as she raised them to cover her mouth. "I did CPR, but her lips were blue, Brendan…"

"She'll be okay. The EMTs have her now. What did Danny say?"

"Nothing. He didn't say anything." Hope's lungs seized, and she had to close her eyes and will her muscles to give enough to draw in air. "They were holding hands." The words forced out, their import not lost on the police detective.

Tears coated her cheeks. Blood smeared her hands.

"That fucking bastard," Brendan growled.

Leech.

Leech, who always left his victims in pairs, holding hands.

Crimes she'd persuaded a judge he wasn't legally guilty of. And he hadn't been. The cops had messed up. She'd done her job and won because those cops had messed up big.

But this, *this* was her fault.

"If I hadn't been his lawyer, he would never have targeted my family. Danny and Paige…"

"They'll be okay."

"Yeah." She needed to hold on to that thought. Modern medicine could accomplish miracles.

The ambulance pulled up outside the Emergency Room, and she threw open the door and jumped out before Brendan stopped the car.

She took Danny's hand as they wheeled him past her, heading inside through the glass sliding doors. She felt the warm skin and the faint pressure as his fingers squeezed her back.

"I love you, Danny. I love you so much. Please hold on for me. For us." They forced her away as they whisked Danny through the doors into the OR.

Hope looked around, grabbed a nurse. "Where's my daughter, Paige? The little girl who came in?"

The nurse led her to a small room. Hope saw her daughter lying on the stretcher as she pushed open the door.

Brendan sat beside her crying. He held Paige's hand.

"Why aren't you helping her?" Hope shouted at the doctors who looked as if they were already leaving. "I started CPR on her as soon as I found her. The paramedics worked on her the whole time. She can be resuscitated."

A female doctor shook her head. "I'm afraid it's too late to save her. She's already gone." The doctor looked at the clock and declared time of death.

"No!" Hope pushed past and closed her daughter's small turned-up nose and tilted her chin. Pressed her lips to her child's to fill Paige's lungs with air, willing her to start breathing on her own again.

No one said a word. They watched with tears in their eyes for what felt like hours. Eventually, strong hands gripped her arm, drawing her firmly away.

"Enough. Enough now." Brendan pressed her face to his chest. "She's gone. She's gone."

Hope sagged against him as her knees went.

She pulled back. "Danny?"

The terrible truth burned in Brendan's eyes.

Grief immersed her, submerged the denial for long enough for reality to finally penetrate. She'd lost them both. She'd lost everything. She gripped Brendan's shirt as emotion took over and simply gave in to it.

1

SEVEN YEARS LATER

Julius Leech sat half-frozen to death in the transport vehicle, manacled at the wrists and ankles. It was snowing outside, which he might have appreciated had his toothache not been excruciating and his extremities numb from cold.

Not only did his orange jumpsuit assault his eyes and sense of style, but it was also thin polyester that did nothing to keep him warm. His shoes were worn, grubby, old-fashioned tennis shoes that reminded him of his boarding school days. Socks that had once been white were now dishwater gray and full of holes. The strong smell of body odor that emanated from him and his fellow prisoners made him want to gag, but no one wanted to take too much time in the shower—especially if you happened to be a convicted child killer.

At least the constant death threats and beatings meant he had his own cell. His duplicitous, rat bastard of a lawyer had, at least, seen to that.

Rage seethed inside him at the unfairness of it all.

Who said he was a fucking psychopath who didn't have feelings?

Well, that bitch of a Forensic Psychologist for one. He laughed inside. The fantasies he'd had about getting her alone for a few hours...

He had plenty of feelings. Plenty of emotions. Just no way to express them in a manner anyone else would appreciate.

The freezing temperatures made him shiver violently, but he refused to be the first one to voice weakness. Weakness was exploited. Weakness could get him killed.

It was difficult enough to concentrate on staying alive when he was in constant agony. The searing pain from his tooth was incessant. Throbbing along every nerve, so bad he'd tried to extract it himself, but it wouldn't budge.

It was all that bitch's fault. Hope fucking Harper. If he hadn't been in prison, he'd have all the dental care he needed. He'd offered to bring in his personal dentist from Boston, but the warden refused. Instead, Julius had to rely on the Bureau of Prisons to provide someone and, for some reason, being a dentist to maximum security inmates wasn't high on most graduates' list.

He wondered if the guy he'd seen last week was even qualified. The moron had performed one root canal but had run out of time to conduct the second one. And the procedure had *hurt*. If Julius hadn't been shackled to the dentist's chair, he would have shoved that shiny stainless-steel drill right up the guy's nose—which was presumably why he, and the other prisoners, were all restrained.

It was a harmless fantasy, that's all. A way to get through the tedium of endless monotony. Every day the same. Every day as dull and gray as mud, stretching at infinitum into the future. It was enough to drive even a sane person over the brink, let alone the rest of them.

Scaring the bungling dentist was at least entertaining.

Observing people's fear gave him a buzz. Fear was power. Power was a drug.

He fantasized about seeing fear in Hope's eyes.

He fantasized about killing Hope every night before he closed his eyes and went to sleep. But even in his dreams, she plagued him.

Last time he'd seen her, she'd been staring at him across a courtroom, her strong jaw clenched. Her eyes cold with accusation and loathing.

The things she'd said…

Rage, his constant companion, burned inside his chest, even as his flesh felt as if snowflakes danced upon his skin. A shiver wracked him, and his teeth began to chatter.

Purgatory was real.

He was living it.

Sometimes he wished he was dead…but he wasn't ready yet.

"It's fucking cold back here," Perry Roberts complained.

Hallelujah.

"Turn up the heat. You ain't supposed to torture us this way," Michael Herbert yelled.

"Too right," mumbled Reggie Somack, sitting behind and across from him.

"Quit your whining." The guard at the front of the van was wearing a heavy jacket and decent boots. He fumbled with the heat settings, thank Christ.

"Blast it before we freeze to death!" Somack yelled.

It was early afternoon but looked almost dark out. Overcast, gloomy, the snow growing so thick Julius could barely make out anything outside the window. They were driving on a back road in rural Massachusetts, heading toward Worcester and the nearest medical clinic.

"That's the radio not the heater." The driver, Protection Officer Byron, took his eyes off the road for a fraction of a second to adjust the heat levels, and Julius watched everything unfold in slow motion. The minibus drifted across the divide on a corner, and the driver overcorrected. The minibus started to skid onto the other side of the road and there, out of the snowy darkness, came the faint glow of headlights. Byron jerked the wheel the other way and only succeeded in making the skid worse.

Everyone braced by holding onto the bottom of their seats. The irony of dying in something as mundane as a car accident made Julius laugh despite the situation.

Byron fought to control the vehicle as the other guard, Pedrós, was flung violently against the passenger door. An awful grinding impact seared the air as they hit the guardrail and went straight fucking through it, like a sharp blade through flesh. Roberts and Somack both screamed. Julius opened his mouth in horror, but no sound came out.

It felt as if they were flying through the snowy night—Santa's nightmare sleigh. Tree branches rushed past the windows, scraped the sides of the vehicle like giant, bony fingernails. Then the minibus smashed into the side of a hill with a jarring impact. The windshield shattered as they shuddered to a halt. The side of Julius's face bashed against the seat in front of him even as chains held him in place. His wrists and ankles burned from yanking on the restraints.

After the shock of the accident, the sudden frigid, silent darkness was strangely alien and overwhelming.

"Everyone okay?" asked the driver shakily.

Julius started to laugh.

"You are one messed-up motherfucker, Leech," Somack huffed out.

Metal groaned. Branches cracked. Someone cried out in pain.

The idiot driver, Byron, turned on the light from his cell phone and swung it over the prisoners. The other guard, Pedrós, was nowhere to be seen. Byron stared dazedly around as if looking for the missing man. Julius flinched when Byron shone the light in his eyes.

"E-everyone stay calm, and I'll call for help."

Herbert rasped out, "Got a problem here."

The cell phone's light swung back to the man, and Julius winced as he saw a tree branch had speared the guy through the chest.

Wow.

That had to hurt.

"I think my arm's broken." Reggie Somack cradled his right arm awkwardly as the remaining guard swung the light toward him while still trying to make a call.

Julius had no idea if Somack was telling the truth, but it was a miracle they weren't all dead.

"Goddammit," Byron bit out. "I don't have signal."

The vehicle gave a sudden, terrifying lurch, and they all screamed. The driver scanned his beam over to the right, and Julius realized the ground dropped precipitously away and into the icy river below. The minibus was propped against a group of large saplings that strained under the heavy load.

The minibus jolted again, metal grinding against wood.

"Get us out of here!" Reggie yelled.

Byron was sheet white with blood dripping from his forehead as he looked through the wire screen that separated off prisoners. He belatedly came to a decision and quickly unlocked the divider. "I'm going to come back there and release you all. Those that can will climb back up to the road with me, and I'll call for help. Get the emergency response team out for Herbert and Somack if they can't make it up the hill. Search and rescue team will have to come out here to look for Officer Pedrós."

Julius was pretty sure Pedrós was dead at the bottom of the ravine.

Byron unlocked the chain that looped through Perry Roberts's cuffs and undid the shackles so he could move. Byron stood back with his hand on the butt of his weapon. "Go on now. No funny business. People are hurting."

Roberts uncurled his large frame and staggered forward.

Byron unlocked Herbert next, though the guy wasn't going anywhere with the branch skewering his chest. Byron rested a hand on the injured man's shoulder. "Hang on, Michael. Help's coming."

"Hurry it the fuck up."

Byron unlocked Julius next. Julius scooted forward. A sense of hope pierced the shock of the accident and bloomed inside him with the same euphoria as a line of the finest coke.

Perry Roberts had his feet pressed against the buckled door, attempting to kick it open. "It's stuck."

Julius peered over the man's massive shoulder. "There's a tree in the way. Let me get out through the front window and pull from the other side."

Roberts shoved him aside with his handcuffed hands. "I'm going first."

Julius reined in his seething resentment.

Roberts cursed when the broken safety glass cut into him as he crawled over the steering wheel. Julius went to follow, but Reggie Somack knocked him aside and awkwardly maneuvered like a big orange caterpillar over the dash and across the hood. Nothing wrong with his arm now.

The minibus lurched and Julius launched himself out after Somack.

The wind stole his breath. It was so damned cold.

His numb fingers clung to frozen metal as he pulled himself urgently over the slippery hood and tumbled to the ground. He rose to his feet, then stumbled over the broken roots in the darkness and clung onto the sinewy trunk of a young sapling that threatened to snap under his weight.

Julius could make out the faint orange-clad figures of his fellow convicts through the falling snow. As Officer Byron began to climb out of the window, Roberts and Somack began to rock the bus.

"Stop that! Stop! Herbert's in there." Byron lost his gun as he used both hands to hold on.

Roberts and Somack didn't stop. The guard tried to pull himself through the window frame, but his equipment belt snagged just as the back end of the vehicle began to slide. A few seconds later, the sound of the minibus crashing into the water reached them, it had taken poor, pathetic Officer Byron with it.

The two convicts turned toward him, and Julius tried not to shrink away. Was he next?

"That never happened. Got it?" Roberts pointed his finger at him.

"I didn't see a thing," Julius agreed quickly.

"Don't follow us, you little freak," Somack warned.

They set off east, and Julius stood there frozen for a few seconds until he realized he was free. He was *free,* and this was his big chance. The fact he was more likely to freeze to death as snow immediately soaked through his pathetic shoes and the tangerine jumpsuit was more irony in play, but he wasn't about to sit here and die. He slipped and staggered up the rugged bank, heading toward the road. Terrain was steep, and he was breathing heavily. He took another step and tripped and landed on something bulky and warm.

His numb fingers reached out and found cloth beneath a thin layer of snow.

Shit.

It was a body.

Pedrós?

Was he dead?

Julius searched through pockets until he found the guard's cell phone. He turned on the flashlight and saw the man's head was bent at an unnatural angle, eyes staring. Those eyes made Julius pause for a second, but he didn't have time to contemplate death's mystique. He found the guard's keys next and unlocked the cuffs, rubbing his wrists as he removed the hated metal bracelets.

He leaned back for a moment as violent shivers overtook him. Then he decided fate had placed Pedrós in his path for a reason. Julius wrestled off the guy's coat, jacket, and shirt. He did the same with the man's boots, socks, pants. He skipped the underwear because he had standards. He stripped off his own hated orange jumpsuit, dancing in the cold, before he quickly slipped into the guard's warm clothes. They were too big, but that was okay.

Julius finished dressing, patted the gun he now wore on his belt and the cuffs resting in his pocket. It felt odd to be dressed like the men and women who'd controlled his every move for so many years. Odd, but good. He straightened his spine and rolled his shoulders. He gathered his jumpsuit under one arm because leaving it behind would be a giant orange flag.

Nothing he could do about the body, but the authorities wouldn't know who'd taken the guard's clothes. They wouldn't even know if Julius had survived the crash. It might give him a head start.

He kept the cell phone. He'd get rid of it as soon as he got his bearings.

Freedom.

He could taste it. It was as precious and desired as a baby to a barren couple, as food to a starving man.

He clambered to the top of the hill, breathing hard, cautious in case Roberts or Somack were also there, or in case the authorities had already missed them. When he got to the edge of the road, he peered through the trees.

Nothing.

No one.

He tried to check the map on Pedrós's cell, but it was passcode protected and useless to him. Frustrated, he flung it toward the river.

A car approached, and Julius took a risk. He stuffed the jump-suit under his jacket, stood at the edge of the road and flagged down the driver. He had to get away from here as fast as possible —that was the only way he'd escape for good. The car skidded to a halt, and Julius strode confidently to the passenger window and bent down.

It was a young man, mid-twenties.

Julius slipped the gun into his pocket.

"There's been an accident. I need a ride to the nearest town."

"Sure, man. Get in."

Julius got in. He knew suddenly that this was all meant to be.

This was fate. He finally registered something else too. He touched his jaw. His tooth didn't hurt anymore. He'd knocked it out during the crash.

The day got better and better.

He pictured Hope's face when she heard the news. She couldn't ignore him now, could she? *Bitch.*

She'd know he was coming for her. And she'd know why.

2

FEBRUARY 1

Mon., 4:15 p.m. FBI HRT compound, Quantico

Aaron Nash wrapped his arm around Ryan Sullivan's neck and, like so many people must often dream, squeezed. The two men lay grappling on the floor. Aaron wrapped his legs around the other guy and held the slippery bastard immobile. Sweat dripped into Aaron's eyes and his breath was hot in his lungs, but no way would he let Ryan out of this grip.

Aaron's moniker, a nickname he secretly hated, was "The Professor" because he was one of the few in the Hostage Rescue Team without a military or law enforcement background. Instead, he had an advanced degree in Biology and, except for a twist of fate, would have made that his life's work. Cowboy didn't have a military background either, but they could both hold their own on the team. And on the mat.

Ryan tapped out, and Aaron released the other man, and they rolled away from each other, panting hard.

"Who's next?" Ryan sounded hoarse but resigned. "Bring it on."

"Donnelly's the only one who hasn't kicked your ass yet today."

Ryan slumped onto his back, gym clothes dark with sweat. His face was flushed as he stared at the ceiling. "I'll concede now and avoid the humiliation."

Meghan Donnelly snorted.

Aaron pushed to his feet and held out his hand to the other operator. "Good idea. Save your energy for when Steel gets back from Maine."

Ryan grunted as he took his hand and let Aaron haul him to his feet. "Grady is gonna kill me. I was an asshole."

"Past tense?" Aaron arched a brow.

Ryan grinned but it didn't reach the man's eyes. "Probably not."

Aaron knew his friend was hurting. He wished he could help, but some people seemed to hoard their inner misery. Maybe it was what held them together.

He could hardly throw stones but, rather than dwell on the past, he preferred not to think about it. Unless it was shoved in his face, and then he had to grin and bear it.

Hunt Kincaid tossed them both a towel. Everyone on Gold team had taken a turn at hand-to-hand with Ryan this afternoon. Cowboy had held his own for a while, but after two hours he wouldn't be able to defend himself against a potato chip let alone highly skilled operators. Everyone had gained a little exercise and a lot of satisfaction. Ryan had gotten the message to keep his nose out of other people's business.

It might stick.

But Aaron doubted it.

They began heading toward the locker room when team leader Payne Novak strode in. "Who else is still in the compound?"

Aaron wiped the perspiration off his face. Gold team was comprised of two seven-person assault units, Echo and Charlie, plus one eight-person sniper unit. Most of the assaulters were in the gym or the locker rooms. "Everyone except the snipers who went home already."

Between serial killers, drug cartels and a rogue former FBI agent, Gold team had been run ragged since the turn of the year.

They'd lost two of their colleagues within a week of one another, and those losses had hit them all hard. Aaron still couldn't get his head around the fact Dave Monteith and Kurt Montana were both dead.

"What's up?"

Novak gave him a look that spelled trouble. "We may have a prison break."

"May?" Aaron raised a brow and smiled. "We don't know for sure?"

Novak's expression remained serious. "Overdue transport carrying two guards and four inmates from a Maximum-Security prison in western Massachusetts. Minibus went missing on the way to a medical facility during a blizzard."

That storm was sweeping down from the Canadian prairies and threatened to swathe half the continent.

Novak checked his watch. "It was due to arrive at the medical center around two-thirty p.m. After another hour went by with no prison transport, the medical facility called the prison, and the alarm was raised. State Troopers are out searching for the vehicle now. US Marshals are en route to the area and will be in charge of the incident should it prove to be an escape."

It was 4:30 p.m. now.

A pulse of excitement shot through Aaron. "Are we involved in the search?"

Novak shook his head. "Not yet."

The storm would make it too dangerous to get aircraft into the sky to look for heat signatures and also worked against personnel on the ground.

Aaron waited as Novak sent out the text alerting everyone to a crisis situation. Then he raised his voice for everyone still in the gym. "Wheels up in thirty."

"Where are we going?" asked Aaron.

They headed toward the locker rooms.

"DoJ got wind of who was on that transport and wants protection on several prominent figures related to their cases as a precaution." Novak stopped, his expression serious. "Apparently the BAU agrees."

"Who *possibly* escaped?"

"Reggie Somack, Michael Herbert, Perry Roberts."

Didn't ring any bells.

"And…Julius Leech," Novak finished.

"The serial killer?"

"Yeah. Although the other three are no angels. One high-level drug dealer, a guy who murdered his girlfriend and kidnapped her kid with intent to traffic her, and a serial rapist."

Aaron pressed his lips together. "You think Leech is going after the lawyer whose family he murdered?"

Novak shrugged. "Or the lawyer who failed to save him from prosecution the second time around, or the judge who sentenced him to life without the chance of parole, or witnesses who testified against him. I seem to remember he made a lot of threats in that courthouse when he was convicted."

"Where was that again?"

"Boston. The judge retired outside of the city. The lawyer who lost the case has a fancy private firm in the city, and Hope Harper is now an assistant district attorney for the Suffolk County District Attorney's office."

Aaron vaguely remembered her. At the time of the murders, he'd been doing his master's on an island in French Polynesia. The double homicide of husband and child had made sensational headlines even in that remote part of the world. Some people had called it divine justice after she'd defended an accused serial killer and gotten him released. Aaron didn't think the murder of two innocents should ever be acceptable collateral damage for someone else's choices. He was all for people paying for their own crimes.

Defense attorneys were a necessary evil, but having been

grilled numerous times on the stand as a field agent, he wasn't a fan.

"Seems unlikely Leech would head back to the lion's den simply for revenge. Unless he's innocent and looking for a one-armed man," Aaron scoffed, referring to the Harrison Ford movie.

Novak smiled, but the edges were strained. The guy had fallen easily into a leadership role, but Aaron knew he'd give it up in an instant to have their old boss back.

Wishful thinking. Montana's memorial service was in ten days despite them not having a body to bury.

"I guess we're off to Boston?"

Novak nodded. "ASAP. Even though it's unlikely Leech will go anywhere near Beantown. It'll be a good training opportunity and give the FNGs some experience with close-protection work."

The "Fucking New Guys" on Gold team were his equipment cage partner Hunt Kincaid, plus Will Griffin, and Meghan Donnelly—the first woman ever to make it through Selection.

"I'm putting you in charge of Echo squad for this one. Romano has Charlie. We'll get updates en route as to the exact location of our principals."

"Have they been informed yet?"

"Not that I'm aware." Novak strode away.

There was a lot to organize if they hoped to beat this storm. Aaron stripped for a quick shower.

"Where're we headed?" Ryan was already drying off.

"Boston."

Ryan's expression brightened. "What are we doing in Boston?"

"Probably freezing our asses off protecting people from a non-existent threat."

"Fun. I have friends in Boston." Ryan had *friends* everywhere. "Beats getting my ass kicked all day."

"We can still kick your ass in the field." Aaron gave him a look that told him all was not forgiven.

Ryan shot him a sardonic grin and drawled in his best Montana accent, "Well, Professor, you can certainly try."

3

"Get me the file on the Du Maurier case and chase the lab for the report on the fibers found at the Dutton apartment. They promised it for last Friday," Assistant District Attorney Hope Harper instructed her legal intern, Colin Leighton, as she packed up her leather briefcase with her laptop and a thick file she'd read tonight after she grabbed something to eat.

"You want the Du Maurier file emailed to you?"

"No, leave it on my desk. I'll read it in the morning."

This routine generally worked for them. Colin was a night owl, and she was an early riser. Not that she slept much.

"Don't forget we have court at ten," she reminded him.

"I haven't forgotten. You have dinner plans tonight?" he asked.

"No. Why?" Hope looked at the young man who was medium height and fit-looking with wiry brown hair that always seemed a little out of control. She'd heard some of the other interns saying he was hot, but to Hope he looked like a teenager. Considering that she felt as ancient as the Appalachians, everyone did.

"Just wondered." He shifted his feet as if suddenly uncertain.

The guy had graduated early, completing a three-year law degree in two and a half years. He'd worked for her for a couple of months, having interned for the DA's office the previous summer. She knew almost nothing about him beside the fact he was competent, efficient, and slightly cocky. But she'd also been cocky and, as he knew how to take orders without screwing up, she cut him a break.

"You have plans outside studying for the bar exam?"

He gave her a rueful smile. "I'm going for a quick drink with some friends."

Friends. What a concept. She'd pushed everyone away in the aftermath of Danny's and Paige's murders. Didn't particularly miss any of them.

She raised a brow. "Are you that confident?"

"It's only for an hour, and I've studied my ass off the last few years." He shrugged. "Plus, there's always next time."

As he was a great intern, she didn't care if he passed or failed the bar this time around. Failing might ground his ego. Plus, she hated training new people.

"Well, have fun." Had she really said that? "See you tomorrow."

It was 7 p.m. She slipped her arms into her thick wool coat. If she hurried, she could catch the 7:13 p.m. bus and be home by 7:30. She hurried downstairs and out the big glass doors onto Sudbury Street. The February wind coming off the bay hit her like shards of broken glass. *Holy crap.* She took a few steps and then pulled up short when a car crawled up beside her. She tensed.

Someone rolled down the window of a red Ford Thunderbird and leaned across the seat. "Get in."

Brendan.

She let out a relieved breath, opened the door, and slid into the warm interior. She wrinkled her nose at the slight scent of cigarette smoke that lingered in the air. He'd told her he'd given them up at Christmas.

"New ride?"

"Confiscated from a drug dealer."

Maybe it wasn't cigarettes she was smelling. "Figures."

"Headed home?" he asked.

"Yeah. You?"

"Yeah."

"Drop me at the transit stop on Congress or give me a ride back to Charlestown? I don't want to miss my bus." It was getting late, and dealing with Danny's brother always brought on a headache.

"I'll give you a ride home."

"Were you waiting for me, or was that a lucky coincidence?"

Brendan gave her a grin. He was a good-looking guy. She was grateful for the lack of close resemblance to the man she'd loved. Brendan was heavier. He and Danny shared the same blue eyes, but Brendan's hair was thinning, and gray threaded the brown. Danny had taken after his Irish mother with thick, almost jet-black hair.

Even after all these years, thoughts of Danny's smiling face brought a stab of sorrow.

"Ma was asking after you."

Hope huddled into her coat as the guilt piled up. "Tell Mary I'll come over when this case is finished."

Brendan shot her a look that held both understanding and censure. "There's always another case, Hope."

She looked away.

Her father-in-law had died three years ago, leaving Mary Harper alone in the small row house in South Boston where she'd raised her boys. Brendan lived in an apartment in East Boston with cheap rent and a million-dollar view.

"I'm going over for Sunday lunch. I can pick you up if you want. Two hours max. You gotta eat, right?"

It was Paige's birthday on Wednesday, and every year that passed without her child corroded Hope until her bones felt like nothing more than rusted strands of barbed wire.

Paige would have been twelve this year.

Every anniversary was religiously observed by Danny's family. Sometimes it helped. Sometimes the constant reminders hurt. Her own family were easier to deal with. Just her grandparents nowadays down in Florida, and they respected the loss without zeal. A phone call or a card with a brief message. It was all she needed. All she wanted.

Hope stared out the window at the Charles River as they crossed the North Washington Street Bridge. She was known as a fearless, relentless bulldog in the courtroom and at work, but when it came to Danny's mom, she was defenseless. Maybe if she hadn't cost the woman her youngest son and only grandchild it would be easier to loosen the bonds. Pull back enough so she could breathe.

But she couldn't.

So, she'd choke for two hours on roasted chicken and self-recrimination. Anything else would have disappointed her late husband and even after seven years without him, she couldn't do that.

"Fine," she relented, "but I'll meet you there. One o'clock?"

Brendan scratched his head. "I'll pick you up at twelve-thirty."

Hope pinched her lips together and breathed out via her nose. Fine. "How's Loretta?"

Brendan stared straight ahead. "We broke up."

"I'm sorry." Brendan had struggled with relationships since his brother's murder.

Hope had no desire to even try to find anyone else. What was the point?

"Working on anything interesting?" she asked. Work was the one area they never ran out of things to talk about and didn't have to pretend they weren't inherently broken.

"Nasty homicide in the Back Bay area. Looks like a hate crime."

"Any suspects?"

"Not yet but we have CCTV footage of someone leaving the apartment complex that might lead somewhere."

"DNA?"

"Still waiting on results."

Hope nodded. The labs were backed up and results took time. As long as the techs got it right, she didn't mind a few days wait but when the weeks dragged on, she got snippy. "You still working with Janelli?"

"Yeah." He shot her a look.

"How's he doing?"

Brendan shrugged. Grinned. "Good. Still bitching about the DA's office."

About her.

Lewis Janelli hated her guts, as did a few other Boston PD officers. Not that she cared, but she liked to keep up with whatever was happening in the police department.

Maybe that's why Brendan was still a constant part of her life.

Sure.

It was a lie but made her feel better about the lack of control she had over her and her brother-in-law's relationship. She'd managed to kick everyone else to the curb, but not Brendan or his mother.

Brendan gunned the engine and jumped a yellow light. He hooked a right and turned down Monument Avenue, speeding around the park that housed the Bunker Hill Monument, to the opposite side where Hope shared a large row house with a couple who lived on the bottom floor. She had the upper three levels and a rooftop garden. It was a little excessive for a single woman, but she liked the space. Needed the space.

And she had the money.

Not only had there been life insurance and a settlement from her old law firm when she'd left the partnership, but Danny's books had taken off after his death. The fact she'd taken over writing his series—which had been released under a pseudonym —was not something the rest of the world needed to know.

Brendan jerked the car to a stop.

She went to get out.

"Hope." Brendan grabbed her arm then quickly released her.

He wanted to come in for a drink and to talk. He did that a lot, but she didn't have time tonight. She didn't have the energy. She didn't want to hear him reminisce about his and his brother's often death-defying childhood antics. She didn't want to listen to Brendan pouring out his grief that, after a few beers, was as fresh today as it had been seven years ago.

She had her own sorrow to deal with. She wasn't into public displays of emotion, not even in front of the only person who really understood how she felt. Nowadays she kept everything locked into a tight ball, deep inside her. She didn't know what would happen if she let it escape.

Nothing good.

"I'd invite you in, but I have court in the morning and want to go over the case one more time and finish notes on my opening statement in case we progress faster than expected."

"I bet you know the facts inside out and back to front."

"Any good prosecutor would." She climbed out of the car and pulled her bag out of the footwell. She also wanted to plot her next novel.

"DA's office is lucky to have you, Hope."

She held his blue eyes in a direct stare that had him turning away.

They both knew the reason she worked for the DA. Luck had nothing to do with it.

She was hellbent on putting away as many killers as possible because that was all she had left. It was purely selfish. The fact she was as hard on the cops as the criminals didn't win her any friends in the Boston Police Department either.

He revved his engine loudly as she walked up the stone steps she shared with her neighbors, who were currently on a Caribbean cruise. She raised her hand in farewell as she unlocked the door and went inside.

She was disarming the alarm when the doorbell rang. She let out a heavy sigh and dumped her bag on the side table in the hallway.

Brendan was a senior detective and sometimes he didn't take

no for an answer. Subtlety didn't always work. Not that she'd been particularly subtle.

She gritted her teeth and prepared to be blunt. She really didn't have the time or mental energy to deal with him tonight.

She opened the door only to jerk back in surprise. A group of black-clad, heavily armed men with "FBI" stenciled on their front stood on her doorstep.

"Hope Harper."

It wasn't a question.

"How can I help you?" She blocked the doorway. Over their shoulders she noticed two black Suburbans pulling away.

The man flashed his credentials. "FBI HRT Operator Aaron Nash, ma'am. May we come in?"

Hostage Rescue Team?

"Why?"

"Why?" His tone was questioning. As if he couldn't imagine why she'd deny them entry and keep them on the doorstep unless she was guilty of something or had something to hide. He was tall with a short beard and inky black hair that reminded her a little of Danny's, but rather than blue, this man's eyes were a deep, rich brown, almost black. Pretty eyes. Too pretty for someone bristling with so many weapons.

Another man with blond hair and arctic blue eyes pushed past the tactical operators. He wore a suit and a cynical expression.

Lincoln Frazer.

She exhaled.

She'd met him originally during Leech's first trial when they'd been on opposite sides of the courtroom. She always listened to what Lincoln Frazer had to say. Of course, it helped that they were on the same side nowadays.

"Hope." He nodded in acknowledgement. "We need to talk, and you'd probably rather the media didn't see us all crowded on your doorstep like this."

Hope raised a brow as the FBI agents piled past her without waiting for any more permission than that.

Fine.

She closed the door after them, and they stood in loose formation along the elegant hallway. Nine agents, plus Frazer.

Something major was going on.

"We'd like to conduct a search of the premises." Agent Nash towered over her even though she was five foot ten in her boots. "Can I have your keys, or shall we use ours?" He indicated the breacher one of the men raised in salute.

"Funny."

The dark-haired man, Aaron Nash, seemed to be in charge.

"Are you going to tell me why, or do I have to guess?"

"We believe your life might be in danger."

"What's new?" Hope got death threats on a regular basis, but no one usually rushed to her defense. She was careful and had decent security. She even had a gun locked in her bedroom safe. "I'll need details—a lot more details than that, I'm afraid, before I let you into my home."

Those dark liquid eyes said he thought that should be enough for anyone. They questioned her intelligence, which immediately put her back up.

"Why don't you let me explain while HRT conducts a sweep?" Lincoln Frazer touched her arm in an unexpected gesture of comfort. "Make sure there are no unwelcome surprises waiting for you inside."

It took her a moment to mask the horror his words evoked. She knew what unwelcome surprises looked like in graphic detail, and no one could hurt her that much ever again, not even if they ripped her limb from limb.

"Apologies." Frazer pulled a face. "I didn't think."

That surprised her more than anything. Frazer wasn't the apologizing type.

Agent Nash held out his hand, palm up for her keys.

Telling herself that the sooner they did what they needed to do, the sooner they'd leave her alone, she dug into her pocket and reluctantly handed them over. He tossed the keys to another action-man wannabe, and four of them headed up the stairs—remarkably quietly for such over-sized, heavily armed human beings.

"Watch out for my cat!" Hope shouted after them.

One of the other agents knocked on the downstairs door.

"Who lives in the ground floor apartment?" Nash's voice was deep and resonant.

"My neighbors, Enrique Hernandez and Larry Langton." She knew her expression must be somewhere between belligerent and bitchy, but what the hell? "They are certainly no threat to me."

"I'm more concerned that their proximity to you may be a threat to their safety."

"What?" She blinked.

From the look in his eyes, Aaron Nash didn't like her very much, but that was nothing she wasn't used to. She put her hand on her hip. "How am I putting them in danger?"

"Not purposefully." Nash gave her another assessing stare. "Are they usually in at this time of day?"

"Yes, they are, but currently they're away on a cruise in the Caribbean."

Nash's lips curved slightly. "That's good. Do you have a key to their apartment? We'd like to check their place for intruders also."

So polite. But Hope could see determined glitter in those black depths. That was an order, not a request.

"Is this really necessary?"

Those eyes held hers. "Yes, ma'am."

She slumped tiredly against the wall. "The spare key to their place is on the fob I gave you. It has a little rainbow tag."

Nash jerked his chin to one of his colleagues, who ran up the stairs to retrieve her keys.

Hope forced herself upright and faced Frazer. "You better tell me what's going on. I want these people out of my home as quickly as humanly possible."

"I'm afraid we're not going anywhere, ma'am." Nash spoke over her left shoulder.

She ignored him and concentrated on Frazer. "Well?"

"I'm afraid Operator Nash is correct, Hope. You're to have twenty-four seven security, or you will be taken into protective custody. Orders from the Attorney General herself."

She narrowed her eyes. "You can't do that."

"You know we can," Nash stated patiently from behind her. She was beginning to hate that silky voice.

"Why? What's happened?" But she had the sudden horrible feeling she knew. "That sonofabitch did not get out of prison."

Frazer's lips pinched, and he suddenly looked tired. "A vehicle transporting Leech and three other convicts, plus two guards, was found submerged in a river late this afternoon. Police divers were able to access the vehicle, but only one man was found inside. He was dead. At this point, we don't know if the other prisoners and guards are dead or alive. Most likely they drowned, but if they didn't drown…"

"If he didn't drown," said Hope, "if Julius Leech somehow survived and escaped that vehicle, he'll be on his way to Boston to make good on his promises from the last trial."

To *rape* her. To *kill* her.

Heat coursed through her veins and sharpened her senses. She bared her teeth in a silent snarl. "Let that motherfucker try."

4

"You're not concerned for your own safety?" Aaron stared at the woman whose protection he was now responsible for.

She didn't seem fazed in the slightest that a serial killer who'd threatened her life and murdered her family was possibly on the loose.

"No." She looked at him over her shoulder. "It'll give me the chance to kill the bastard—in self-defense, of course," she added dryly.

"Hopefully, it won't come to that," said Lincoln Frazer.

"Spoilsport." Her eyes flashed like liquid silver.

Hope Harper was not what Aaron Nash had expected. Not at all.

He'd expected hard. He'd expected cold. He'd expected bitter. He hadn't expected the fiery intellect or hostile personality, nor the elegant, blonde outer perfection. Her words were chilling though when it came to her security. She showed no fear. No sense of self preservation. It sounded like she *wanted* to go a few rounds with the serial killer.

And maybe he couldn't really blame her for that.

"Do you have specialized combat training that I am unaware

of?" He kept his voice firm, suspecting she'd scent and exploit weakness like a fox scented and exploited a rabbit.

Her eyes narrowed. "I have the fury of a woman whose child and husband were cold-bloodedly murdered by that sonofabitch."

Emotion vibrated through the words, but he ignored it. His job was tactical, not emotional. It ran on logic and preparation. And maybe it ran a little on luck, but he wasn't about to admit that to a principal who was this antagonistic. He needed to gain her trust and her confidence if they were to work together effectively.

"Sometimes," he said quietly, "that isn't enough."

Something flickered in those icy depths before she looked away. "It's all I have left."

"Not true, counselor." Lincoln Fraser produced a wide smile that showed he didn't mind a little danger. "You also have the protection of the FBI."

"Whether I like it or not." The glimpse of vulnerability was gone, replaced by bitterness.

Aaron couldn't blame her for her anger, but her attitude could make his job more difficult and put his teammates at risk. He wouldn't stand for the latter. Their jobs were dangerous enough without a principal with a death wish.

Kincaid came out from the ground floor apartment. "Clear."

Livingstone came to the top of the stairs and shouted down. "Clear."

With a roll of her eyes, Hope Harper picked up her briefcase and hauled it up the stairs. Aaron stepped in front of ASAC Frazer to the obvious annoyance of the other man, but Harper was Aaron's responsibility, not Frazer's. Aaron stuck close enough to smell the faint trace of perfume, something sweet like vanilla, completely at odds with the woman herself.

She glanced behind her. "Surely Leech hasn't had time to get to Boston already?"

Aaron answered before Frazer could. It was important he develop a working relationship with this woman, regardless of her personal feelings, or his. "Depends on whether or not it was a planned escape and what sort of transportation was available to him."

"Assuming he's not at the bottom of the river."

"Assuming that," Aaron conceded.

"What about Judge Abbotsford or the jurors and any of the other people who testified against him?"

"We have another HRT team on the judge. She's at her farm in the country and is cooperating fully." He had no idea if she was or not. "US Marshal Service is informing the jurors and providing security for anyone who wants it. We'd appreciate a list of prosecution witnesses from the trial to make sure we contact everyone. We figure you can supply that faster than us going through official channels."

She met his gaze for a moment, eyes gray as the moon, surrounded by thick dark lashes, at odds with the blonde hair. "Of course."

She turned away again, and he followed her up an oak staircase that had dark wooden paneling along the wall, a plush red runner up its center.

The front door of her apartment was more solid wood with a sturdy lock. From there, up another few steps into the living room where Livingstone, Griffin, Hopper, and Cadell stood waiting.

The apartment had gleaming hardwood floors covered with several large rugs and over-sized pale gray sofas. A comfortable-looking, burgundy leather chair with matching ottoman sat beside a side-table stacked with folders. It looked as if it got a lot of use. The sash windows were large and uncovered. Snipers Damien Crow and JJ Hersh inched past him now to check out the roof and fire escape in terms of vantage points and weaknesses. The fire escape ran down the side of the building with the railings clearly visible through the windows, providing easy access for any would-be attacker. The other two snipers assigned to Echo squad had parked the vehicles and were investigating surrounding buildings for better overwatch positions, but Aaron figured they'd set up on the roof here for now.

Harper dumped her bag on the table beside the sofa. A white cat wound through her legs, meowing loudly. She picked up the cat and stroked its fur.

After a moment, the cat jumped down and ran into the kitchen.

Harper slipped out of her coat and tossed it on the back of the couch. Aaron couldn't help but admire the slim figure in form-fitting gray pants and a cream sweater.

There wasn't a lot of color around here, he noticed. Not that the apartment, or woman herself, was unattractive or unpleasant, but the atmosphere was cool professional rather than cozy. And maybe that was intentional too.

Except for that old burgundy chair…

"See." She threw her hands wide. "No serial killer lurking behind the doors. You can leave now."

"You know that's not going to happen, Hope," Frazer admonished.

"Why not?" Hope Harper was not the pushover Aaron would have wished for. "Leech isn't some highly trained superman or brilliant marksman. Seven years ago, he was nothing but a weedy nerd who got close to people because he looked harmless. I doubt he beefed up in prison." She snorted then headed into the kitchen.

Aaron bristled as he followed. Seven years ago, he'd been a weedy nerd too. He'd beefed up plenty in the intervening years.

"Seven years in prison is a long time. Best not to underestimate him, especially when he's highly motivated and suspected of killing eight people we know of." He tried to soften the bite in his tone but knew he'd failed when both Harper and Frazer frowned at him.

"Stick a couple of guys out front in an unmarked car." She sneered. "I'm sure he'll take one look at the big scary men with guns and scuttle away like the cockroach he is."

The fact she discounted and disregarded their expertise so easily pissed him off.

"And if he doesn't? If the X-ray vision of the two *big scary men with guns* in the car out front fails and Leech manages to gain access through the back garden or the fire escape? What then?"

"I have a gun in my bedroom."

He stepped in front of her, forced her to look at him. He reached out and gripped her arm loosely to make a point.

"What if he's right here in your house, when you get home from work? What if he grabs you before you can reach the gun that's up in your bedroom? Worse, what if he finds it first?"

She grabbed a kitchen knife off the magnetic strip on the wall. Held it against his Kevlar vest as they stared at one another. One hard kick of his heart betrayed his training before the organ settled into its familiar rhythm.

Temper spiked in her eyes while he kept his cool. Her pulse fluttered beneath the delicate skin of her throat. Her chest rose and nostrils flared as she inhaled rapidly before holding her breath.

He disarmed her gently, careful not to hurt her, and put the knife back on the wall. "What if he gets here first, Hope? What if he's the one with the knife?"

"Then I'll knee him in the balls and scratch out his eyes." Her eyes blazed.

"You won't have to," Aaron told her. "Because we'll be here, or you'll be in protective custody. Perhaps that would be the better option." He looked at Frazer questioningly.

Harper reached up for a can of cat food and opened it. Her hand was shaking. She scraped the food angrily into a clean bowl and placed it on the floor for the clearly starving animal.

Frazer stepped in, perhaps sensing Aaron was losing his patience and she'd definitely had enough of him. "We could really use your help with this one, Hope. If Leech did escape, we need to recapture him as quickly as possible before he hurts anyone. You can help us with that."

She rinsed the can and tossed it in the recycle bin. Put the fork in the dishwasher. Aaron could almost see her mentally counting to ten.

She dried her hands and walked away through the door at the other end of the compact room back into the living room.

They both followed.

Hands in pockets, Frazer examined the artwork on the walls and then strolled over to pick up a framed photo of a dark-haired man and a young girl with long fair hair and a wide smile.

Hope Harper stood with her arms crossed, watching him carefully. "You know him as well as I do, Linc."

"That's not true."

"Well, I fail to see how having bodyguards equates with whether or not I'll help you track him down. Of course, I'll help catch that sonofabitch. Putting him back in prison for the rest of his miserable life would be my absolute pleasure, but it doesn't mean I need protection."

"Do you think he'll come after you, ADA Harper?" Aaron asked calmly.

She shrugged before going over to reposition the photo Frazer had touched. "Any normal deviant billionaire would head straight across the border and find themselves a nice little anonymous hole to hide in." She stroked a finger down the face of the young girl and Aaron hardened his heart against the anguish that crossed her features. "But Leech isn't normal."

"Does he still write to you?" asked Frazer.

She stared toward the profiler and tilted up her chin. "Every week."

"And you read them?" Aaron asked.

She looked at him like he was an idiot. "I take great delight in making sure the warden allows them to be mailed to me and then I have my intern shred them before they even reach my desk." Fatigue tightened the outer corners of her eyes. "I like to know he's wasting his time, screaming into the void like the worthless sack of shit he is."

"Do you believe he'll come after you?" Aaron pushed again.

"Yes," Harper snapped. "But I don't care."

The statement was raw and honest and completely shocking.

Frazer looked unsurprised. Maybe he already knew how the prosecutor felt.

"We care, ma'am. You will have the protection of the Hostage Rescue Team—whether you like it or not. That motherfucker will not have the satisfaction of hurting you any more than he has already."

The line of her throat rippled as she swallowed and looked away. "It doesn't seem like I have much of a choice, does it?"

"Not really," he and Frazer said together.

"Fine. But I do not want to be tripping over FBI agents every time I turn around. You can't stay in my apartment."

"We're operators, not agents," Aaron corrected her this time. "And most of us can sleep outside the apartment to give you the privacy you need." He'd slept in worse places than the hallway of an eighteenth-century row house.

"Define 'most'?"

He grinned. "You won't even know we're here."

Her arms remained crossed, a flimsy barrier. "Fine. You can stay tonight but only because I'm too tired to argue."

Aaron was amused she deluded herself into thinking she had a choice, although she could make their time together a living hell.

Something to look forward to.

"I'm going to talk to my boss about this in the morning."

He nodded as if he was conceding the point. The AG had ordered this. Until his own boss told him otherwise, Echo squad was Hope Harper's shadow and shield.

"We *are* going to need these windows covered tonight." He pointed at the beautiful wide sash windows. "Any objections to covering the glass with trash bags?"

"Actually yes. Lots of objections. I have blinds I've been too lazy to hang, so knock yourselves out." She nodded to an inner door. "In there. Tools too. Make sure they're straight."

If she wanted to bust their balls, she'd have to work much harder than that. People who could take out a target at a mile could hang a goddamned blind. He caught Ryan Sullivan's and Hunt Kincaid's gazes. Gave them the nod to get started.

"Perhaps we could contact your neighbors and see if they'll rent their place to the FBI for a few days. Then we can set up and rest there, but still be close enough to react if necessary." They could split the team into two groups, with him straddling the two rotations and resting when time allowed. Billet a pair of operators on the roof, one on the front door. One in the transport and one just outside the apartment door.

She shot him a glance. "You think this is only going to take a few days?"

"Every law enforcement office in the contiguous United States will be on the lookout for these escaped prisoners, assuming we don't find their bodies in that river."

"I want to see the report on what they find down there," she instructed Frazer.

Frazer nodded. "Perhaps you could give us that list of witnesses from the Leech case?"

She went over to an antique bureau and opened it to reveal a printer. She caught Aaron's look of surprise that such a beautiful antique hid something so mundane.

"I often work late at night and don't always want to be upstairs in my office."

"Convenient."

She looked annoyed by his observation and turned her back to him as she pulled her laptop from her briefcase. She sat on the arm of the couch and began searching for a file.

"Do you want a bed for the night, Linc?" she offered Frazer casually.

Aaron couldn't explain the tightening in his gut. Were they lovers? He knew Frazer had a partner back in Quantico, but maybe she didn't. Or maybe neither of them cared.

"As much as I appreciate the offer, I plan to stay with another old friend tonight. Marshall Hayes and his wife, Josie."

"Give them my regards," drawled Cowboy, who was standing

on top of a stepladder holding a drill and one end of an off-white blind. Kincaid had the other end and held a spirit level along the top. "I'll drop by if I get a chance before this is over. Kids can visit with their favorite uncle."

"I'll let them know," Frazer agreed.

How the hell did Ryan know the famed head of the FBI's Forgeries and Fine Art Division well enough that the kids called him freaking "Uncle"? Aaron had no clue but would grill the guy later.

"And give my regards to Izzy while you're at it." Hope Harper gave her first genuine smile, and it was unexpectedly soft. "I'm expecting a wedding invite one of these days."

"I think we're more likely to elope than do the big white wedding thing, especially as I've trodden that path before."

"So, you asked her then?"

"Not yet," Frazer admitted.

"Better not count your chickens. Izzy's a smart cookie."

"That she is. That she is. And she could do a lot better than a man like me." But his smile was confident.

She did know Frazer was off the market. Aaron relaxed marginally. Not that it was any of his business, but things could get messy, and he didn't like messy, and he didn't like cheats.

He really didn't like cheats.

"Izzy could find a man who doesn't go off chasing serial killers at a moment's notice."

"We all have our calling, Hope. You know that better than most." Frazer sounded tired.

"Just be careful. Keep her safe."

The tension in the room throbbed with unspoken pain.

But Hope ignored it—maybe she was immune to it now—and retrieved the information they'd requested from the printer. Handed one list to Frazer and held onto the other in a power play move that had Aaron cocking a brow.

She saw his reaction and the edge of her mouth twitched in a reluctant smile. She walked over, handed him the sheet of paper.

"Make sure those witnesses are protected, Operator Nash. I don't need any more dead people on my conscience."

He nodded.

Her eyes narrowed in dismay when Cowboy started drilling.

Frazer immediately headed down the stairs to the front door, and Hope followed him out. Aaron brought up the rear, filing past the guys who stood in the downstairs hallway who quieted at their arrival.

Hope went to open the front door onto the street, but Aaron stepped in front of her. "Wait a moment."

She threw her hand up in annoyance as he spoke to the team member who was watching the front entrance from an unmarked car they'd borrowed from the Boston FBI field office.

"Clear?"

"All clear out front. Couple walking their dog in the park but no one else on the street."

"Roger that."

"Thanks for these." Frazer lifted the papers and opened the door while Aaron blocked any view of Hope from the street. "I'll talk to you first thing tomorrow. Hopefully, it'll all be over by then."

"I have court at ten." She raised her voice from behind his shoulder.

"Have a good night." Frazer shot Aaron a grin and slipped outside.

Aaron closed the door and secured it.

Hope narrowed her gaze at him and turned to survey the rest of the HRT team who all straightened.

She pulled out her cell and made a call.

Had she changed her mind despite all of their concessions? Planned to go above his head? Anger had him clenching his jaw.

"Don't panic, Larry. Everything's fine with the apartment. No, don't worry." Harper laughed, and Aaron watched the expressions move over her features like clouds shifting across a stormy sky. "I'm calling to ask a massive favor. I have some friends who arrived unexpectedly from out of town—yes, I know it's a surprise to hear I have friends."

She listened for a moment and sent Aaron a wry look to say she knew he was paying attention, and she didn't like it.

"Yes, I am aware how incredibly antisocial I am, but these people wouldn't say no. Some sort of intervention apparently." She listened again. "Well, I'm hoping this visit scares them off for good. My main problem is, I don't have quite enough space for them to all have their own rooms in my place and wondered if you would mind if they slept at yours for a couple of nights. I promise to return the favor sometime, and you can throw a party on the rooftop whenever you'd like." She listened carefully, giving the other person the chance to object.

Aaron admired the fact she didn't railroad the neighbors because he knew she was more than capable of doing so.

"Thanks. I'll change and wash the sheets, and you won't even know anyone has been there in your absence. I personally guarantee it." She smiled but her eyes were harder now. "You're both sanity savers. How's the cruise?"

She made small talk, but Aaron knew they were in. They had somewhere to set up that would help this op run smoothly. He went over to the rest of the team, and they huddled close.

"For now, we're going to split into two teams, with one on the principal at all times. Livingstone, Griffin, Cadell, Crow, and Hersh are *alpha*, Livingstone takes the lead in my absence. Alpha will take a seven p.m. to seven a.m. shift. Second team is *omega*, Cowboy is lead if I'm not around. We can billet in this apartment until the switchover. I'll overarch as needed. Get set up, and then get some rest."

Hope went to enter the apartment, but Livingstone put his arm out to stop her. "We can change the sheets, ma'am."

"I want to see what state it is in so I can make sure it's spotless for when they return."

"No need," Aaron stated. "We will make sure everything is left exactly as found if not better."

She opened her mouth to argue.

"Pretty sure HRT operators are capable of tracking down fresh sheets and using a washing machine. *I* will personally pay for any damage, not that there'll be any."

She huffed out an annoyed breath. "Fine."

It sounded like a curse.

She headed for the stairs, and this time Aaron let her go alone. She was safe enough. "Get the gear dropped off here and then someone go pick up enough food to supply dinner and breakfast. We'll set up surveillance devices overnight while the principal is sleeping. Cadell will take street duty this shift, but we'll rotate that to keep everyone sharp."

"She really get a killer off and then he went and murdered her husband and kid?" asked Seth Hopper, who still sported a tan from his recent adventures in the Arizona desert.

Aaron nodded. "Let's see if Novak can send us case files or background info. The more we know about Julius Leech the more likely we are to understand any moves he might make."

"Fucking serial killers," Livingstone muttered.

"Fucking defense attorneys," Cadell sneered.

"She's an ADA now with an impressive track record. Gave up a partnership in one of the biggest firms in the city to become a prosecutor."

"Guilty conscience." Cadell rubbed his jaw.

No one would argue with that.

"She paid a terrible price." Seth rested his hands on his carbine.

"Surely Leech isn't likely to head back to the scene of the crime to take a crack at a woman he's already hurt in the worst possible way," Griffin put in. "I'm sure a psycho like Leech would be happy at the thought of ADA Harper living a long life knowing their deaths are on her conscience."

"Plenty of people wouldn't mind having a dig at this particular attorney on both sides of the courtroom, not to mention the cops," said Livingstone.

"Why do they bury lawyers twelve feet under instead of six?" Cadell muttered. "Because deep down, they're good people."

"Look. Who our principal is and what you think of her is irrelevant." Aaron raised his voice enough to get his teammates' attention. "Our orders are to protect ADA Harper like she's our sainted mother. We protect her whether we like her or not. We protect her whether the risk is high or low. *No one* is getting past us. While she's under our protection, we will treat every situation as a high-risk security operation. If nothing else, it'll be good practice for the FNGs."

Griffin and Kincaid.

They were experienced FBI agents but newbie operators.

The slam of the door upstairs made Aaron realize with a sinking heart that Hope Harper had been eavesdropping on their conversation. Fuck.

"*Omega* get some rest, and don't leave a fucking scratch on anything in that goddamned apartment. In fact, Griffin, take photos now, before you move in. Livingstone, order takeout and save some for me because I am fucking starving. I'll stay with the principal while everyone else takes turns to eat. Let's prove we're responsible adults and not the meatheads ADA Harper obviously thinks we are."

5

Hope was shocked by the stab of hurt that shot through her when she overheard Operator Aaron Nash saying he didn't care whether his team liked her or not.

Not exactly a new or unique sentiment among law enforcement personnel but, dammit, they had no right to judge her. She didn't even want them here.

She slammed the door and ignored the startled looks of the men hanging blinds in her living room.

There was that saying about eavesdroppers never hearing good things about themselves, well, that had turned out to be accurate. She'd been hoping the FBI might reveal something about Leech that they hadn't shared with her. Instead, she'd heard veiled animosity and the fact that regardless of whether Leech turned up or not, this was a useful *training exercise* for them.

This was her goddamned *life*.

What right did they have to stand in her house and condemn her when she didn't even want them here? Goddamn it.

Hope stomped into the kitchen, opened the freezer, but the idea of cooking, even simply defrosting something and reheating it, was beyond her.

She opted instead for boiled eggs and toast.

She should have been used to the quiet whispers and accusatory glances, but these had caught her off guard. Perhaps because these men had forced themselves inside her home and they were supposed to be professionals. They didn't *know* her. This was her safe space, and she had a horrible feeling, until Leech was found, they'd be right here with her, a constant thorn in her side.

Maybe she'd go on a cruise…but her case load was heavy and never seemed to get any lighter. Then there was Ella Gibson. Ella needed her to be in court tomorrow the way Hope had promised. And the idea of doing nothing for a week didn't appeal.

What was the point?

She could travel again though, like she and Danny had done before they'd had Paige. Head to Colombia or Argentina, or maybe somewhere farther afield like Vietnam or Thailand. Explore the world and see how other people lived, people who'd never heard of Julius Leech or the naïve fool who'd foolishly defended him.

She could make it into a research trip and tie it into her next Frankie O'Malley crime novel, but she wasn't sure how a New York detective would end up half a world away when her beat was Manhattan.

Realizing she was thirsty, Hope poured herself a glass of water and drank it down in one long gulp. She wiped the back of her hand across her lips. Taking a vacation right now was a pipe dream. She wasn't going anywhere. Not until Ella's trial was finished. Not until that bastard Leech was back in prison or dead. She didn't care which.

Aaron Nash came into the kitchen with Lucifer in his arms. The cat, who usually hated strangers, writhed flirtatiously, purring and rubbing his nose against the man's black tactical vest —which was now covered in white hair.

Traitor.

"What you overheard—"

She held up her hand. "Don't bother to make excuses."

"I wasn't going to make excuses. I was going to apologize if you overheard anything that suggested judgment in any way— that is unacceptable—and to explain that we have two new members of HRT on this team and it's my duty to make sure they receive proper training on this particular op—"

"I am not an op!" She shoved the loaf across the counter and grabbed her head in her hands as if it might split wide open from the pressure building inside. She breathed deeply and then let out a long exhale.

The sudden silence made her realize the other men in her apartment had heard her lose her self-control too. Something she rarely did.

Great.

This was all simply great.

She took another deep breath. "I'm an experienced professional who receives death threats on a weekly basis. And I hate that Leech is once again influencing how I live my life when he should be locked up in a concrete cage writing letters no one ever reads. And I resent being referred to as an *op*, as if I have no autonomy." The words came from between gritted teeth. "It makes me furious, apparently. Along with the fact I haven't eaten since breakfast."

"Here." Aaron handed her the cat, and she had no choice but to take the little fur ball. "What were you gonna make?"

"Two boiled eggs and toast. I can do it," she insisted, though she was rapidly losing her appetite.

"I can do better than boiled eggs."

The man opened the fridge and pulled out green onions, cheese, milk. "How about an omelet?"

She stared at him, suddenly overwhelmed with the memories of another dark-haired man making her an omelet, taking care of her.

She'd taken it all for granted.

Every magical day. Every blissfully mundane moment.

"It's a peace offering. An apology." Nash misread her silent stare. "Go start whatever work you plan to do, and I'll bring it to you when it's ready."

Yearning tightened in her chest. Pining for a man who was long dead. All because of her. Her and a sadistic serial killer she'd gotten out of jail.

She could have kept quiet about how the cops had planted evidence. She could have turned the other way. But she'd liked to win. Needed to prove she was the best and that the concept of legal justice was more important than people getting what they deserved, than keeping innocents safe.

She was no longer an idealist. That had died along with Danny. She didn't care about legal games anymore. She only cared about putting killers where they belonged.

"You okay with onions?"

She nodded mutely. And because she could feel herself weakening in response to this man's dark good looks and easy charm—even though he wasn't Danny—she turned away and walked out of the kitchen.

The rest of the apartment was empty now, and it felt weird to be alone with this stranger. Intimate in a way she hadn't felt in years. The blinds were pulled all the way down. They looked good, she conceded, despite herself. At least she'd gotten something out of the irritating situation.

She pulled out her notes on tomorrow's case but found herself staring unseeingly at the papers.

Julius Leech was either dead or out of prison and free to enact his sick games on whoever was unlucky enough to cross his path. She hoped the former because the idea he might kill anyone else when he was supposed to have been dealt with, *punished*, was unbearable.

She didn't allow herself to think about the man often—she considered it a win for him whenever she did. Instead, she concentrated on prosecuting the cases that came across her desk, or allowing her fictional detective to punish the fictional bad guys in ways that often crossed the line. She derived a lot of pleasure

from her fictional brand of justice, so different from the letter of the law she strived to live by.

Was that wrong? Did that make her as sick as Leech?

No, because she'd never actually hurt anyone.

She wasn't sure what she'd do if she ever saw Leech again. Blood drummed in her ears at the thought. The idea of killing him, the way he'd killed Danny and Paige—a stab to the abdomen followed by a pillow over his face as she held him down...the thought wasn't abhorrent. The image didn't scare her.

And that terrified her.

That she might be like him. That he'd made her just like he was...

Her teeth clenched, and the back of her eyes heated. Even now, seven years on, she relished the idea of a little hands-on justice.

And there was that win for him again.

She jerked out of her thoughts when Aaron Nash appeared with a tray of food and a glass of white wine from an open bottle she'd had in the fridge.

She put her work to one side as the guy slid the tray onto her lap.

It looked amazing. Smelled divine.

"Bon appétit."

He was being kind.

God, she hated that.

"I don't want you here."

He paused, his dark, intelligent gaze steady on hers. "That message has been received loud and clear."

"Not enough to make a difference."

"We're simply following orders, ADA Harper. None of this is personal."

"I don't know if that makes it better or worse." She took a sip of wine. "The Attorney General is covering her ass, knowing the justice system will look weak if anything happens to a serving ADA—by a killer who is supposed to be incarcerated. Doesn't exactly engender public trust."

"Escaped convicts are never a good look. I realize this situation is not something you asked for or are comfortable with." He straightened. Those ebony eyes were soft now. Soft enough that she noticed his full bottom lip. "I will do everything I can to make sure you have the space you need in your own home."

She looked away and picked up her fork. "I prefer my own company."

"So do I." He caught her quick glance at the photograph on the cabinet. "You miss them."

She drew in a ragged breath. "Every day. Every second of every day." The words barely got past the rock in her throat.

"I'm sorry for what happened."

"Most people think it's my fault." Tears built, and she couldn't afford for anyone else to see, to witness, how utterly she'd been destroyed that day. The world saw what she wanted it to see. A strong, confident, powerful woman. A goddamned queen bitch of an attorney. Tonight, in the aftermath of learning Leech had escaped and her life had been invaded by strangers, her defenses had cracked, and emotions welled up through those tiny fissures like blood in a wound. She couldn't afford that. She had other cases to try, other people to help and other killers to convict. She wouldn't let them down the way she'd let down her own family.

This was her penance, her reason for going on.

She put the tray aside and stood, pulling that queen bitch cloak crookedly around her shoulders. "Prosecuting dangerous criminals is all I care about now. It's the only thing that matters to me. Thank you for the omelet, but if you're done, perhaps you'd like to give me that space you promised."

His jaw firmed. He obviously didn't like her rejecting his overtures of friendship or being on the other side of giving orders.

"Not a problem. An operator will be on your roof at all times until Leech is apprehended. I trust you don't mind them using the bathroom on the third floor if they need to?"

Her hands started to tremble. She needed him to leave while she could still hold it together.

"Just keep everyone away from this floor and the second floor." Her voice came out sharp, and she saw his expression flicker to dislike for a split second.

Good.

She didn't want homemade omelets and sympathy. She didn't want anyone taking care of her. She didn't want to like him.

"I'd like a spare set of keys to the building." He lifted his chin as if she might argue.

As she liked her antique doors with their hinges intact, she strode over to the cupboard by the stairs and reached inside. Pulled out her spare set that included a car key, but she didn't think he was going to abscond with her BMW.

He caught the fob she tossed. "There will be a guard outside your door. If you hear someone moving around tonight, please scream for assistance before pulling the trigger on that gun of yours or kicking one of my team in the balls. We'll mount motion sensing lighting and cameras in the outer hallways, garden, roof, and on the fire escape, and it's possible we'll need to come inside briefly to wire something. You can always call me directly if you have any concerns, but you should be safe enough with eleven highly trained operators at your disposal."

He pressed a business card into her trembling hand and then paused. She pulled away, embarrassed that he'd spotted the shakiness that defied her strong words.

"Do you need my cell number?" Her voice cracked.

He shook his head.

Of course not. He already knew everything there was to know about her. God knew there were books dedicated to her and Leech's deadly entanglement.

"Goodnight, ADA Harper."

She couldn't speak.

"See you in the morning."

She forced out a dry laugh that almost choked her. "Unfortunately."

As soon as the door closed, she sank to the floor and wrapped her arms around her bent knees as sobs threatened to rip out of her throat. She didn't let them. She cried silently. She grieved mutely.

Lucifer rushed over and butted his head against her rigid arm, and she gathered him up, one of the last living connections she had to her dead daughter and husband. Paige's kitten. Their only family pet.

Tears rushed in hot torrents down her cheeks, dripping from her face, wetting Lucifer's fur, making her hand catch as she stroked him.

She hated this. Hated the vacuum of sadness her life had become. The pall of misery she carried with her. She wished Leech had killed her on that terrible day. That would have been fairer, surely, than taking a good man and an innocent child?

The tears finally stopped, and the cat ran away as he always did when it suited him.

She smiled sadly.

She and the cat were a lot alike.

Spent and exhausted, she climbed awkwardly to her feet. She went over, picked up her dinner plate, covered it, and put it in the fridge. Grabbed the stack of files she needed for tomorrow's trial. Then she turned off most of the lights except for an under cabinet one in the kitchen and dragged herself to her bedroom. All the blinds in the house had been drawn and she stripped off, pulling on familiar flannel pajamas before sliding under the covers, hugging Paige's favorite teddy bear to her chest in an effort to fill the aching void that was now her life.

6

Julius ate his breakfast with the black woolen cap pulled low over his forehead. He was so hungry he'd *had* to stop for food. He'd needed gas anyway, so he'd risked it.

The cap disguised his features and the color of his hair, not to mention his disastrous prison haircut. The wool was itchy against his scalp, but warm, and that was pretty much all he cared about right now. Luxuries like cashmere could wait. With this snow-storm, no one noticed that he wore a hat inside. He stared out the window at the gas station across the road but also watched the TV screen and other people inside the diner via the reflection in the glass, to make sure no one was paying him undue attention.

They weren't.

It was predawn early. News of the prisoner escape hadn't hit the airwaves yet, but the US Marshals would be searching for any sign he was alive.

Sweat made his new T-shirt cling to his back, but he sipped his drink slowly, determined to enjoy every second of freedom, every minute of independence.

The food here might not be the finest cuisine, but it tasted wonderful. Crispy bacon. Buttery scrambled eggs. Homemade waffles and hot, freshly brewed coffee.

He raised his hand to indicate he was ready for the bill. He kept a pleasant smile on his face, which defied his naturally downturned features and changed his appearance considerably. He'd spent a lot of time practicing in front of what passed for a mirror in his cell. Seven years smiling at his blurred reflection, wishing he was anywhere but incarcerated in that godforsaken place.

And now he was free.

He took out enough cash from his newly acquired wallet to cover the bill and provide a decent tip, but not enough to be memorable. He drew the borrowed leather jacket together and zipped it up against the chill.

Over the years, he'd thought a lot about what he'd do if he ever got out of prison, how he'd blend in and not put a glowing sign on his forehead that screamed "helpless billionaire." He hoped he'd grasped how not to stand out—definitely a plus inside the big house. How not to be the freak everyone called him. He'd dreamed of escape, planned for it a little, but he'd never truly expected it. He wasn't about to let this opportunity slip through his fingers.

He slid out of the booth. "Thanks."

He'd always been good with his manners. His nanny had taught him that. He headed out the door. He'd parked around the side of the diner. Out of sight.

He climbed into the small sedan, moving stiffly in the aftermath of the accident. The blue jeans felt rough against his skin. It was the first time in his life he'd worn cheap denim, and he wasn't sure whether he liked it or not. However, the jeans were a massive improvement on his terrible orange jumpsuit that was still in the trunk of the sedan along with the prison guard's uniform. He'd get rid of them at the first opportunity.

He turned the key in the ignition and listened to the engine fire up. Smiled. Open-top sports cars on the French Riviera had been more his style than this nondescript gray sedan. But the

TONI ANDERSON

sedan might help hide him, whereas a fancy sports car would definitely get him caught.

Again.

He *had* to blend in. His life depended on it because he wasn't going back to that hellhole.

He looked at the full fuel gauge and felt a surge of pride that he'd managed to fill the car without looking like a total buffoon. He'd paid for gas with some of the little cash he had on his person, but it was worth it. He'd get more. It was already being organized. He'd used the previous owner's phone to make a few calls—ones that he hoped wouldn't get him thrown back in his cell.

The windshield was coated in a thin layer of frozen condensation, so he waited patiently for the engine to warm and the heater to defrost the glass. Cops could stop people if their windows weren't clear, and he didn't want to give them an excuse.

Failure to think things through had often been written on his report cards at school, but as Julius was the only person to read them after his mother and father had murdered one another, he hadn't worried too much. He was filthy rich. Rich people got away with crazy shit every damned day. However, he'd never planned to become a killer. The first time had been almost by accident. The rush had been unlike anything he'd ever experienced before. It had been better than drugs. Better than getting drunk on the most expensive Champagne.

So, he'd done it again, only better next time. Planned. Executed. To people who'd deserved it.

Oh, the *euphoria* as he'd taken their lives. The power... The supremacy... He could still feel echoes of it in his blood.

Killing the guy whose car he'd taken hadn't given him that rush. That death hadn't been punishment. It had been a logistical necessity, and the guy hadn't deserved it.

There were plenty of others who did deserve payback. Three in particular.

He thought about the people who'd written to him over the

years. Women mostly, but some men. Several had visited which had provided a nice break from the endless monotony, but could he trust them?

What drove a person to visit a stranger, a convicted murderer, within the walls of a maximum-security prison? It wasn't something he'd ever considered doing...he certainly had never expected to be an inmate of such a place.

Some of his visitors were lonely individuals whom Julius almost pitied. Many were fascinated by his crimes—reporters, authors, podcasters. Others felt the same kind of urges as he did though neither he nor they admitted to them out loud—he'd seen the excitement lighting their eyes when they asked him questions. Those were his favorite visitors. When they realized that he *saw* them. They were either terrified or excited. Or both.

For the occasional daring would-be swindler, it was about his money—after all he had no living family and billions in the bank. Most of them only visited once, the effort outweighing the reward when it became obvious Julius was no fool where his fortune was concerned and more than capable of freaking them out for fun.

He'd willed some of his assets to various charities, including the Boston PD's retirement fund—more out of a twisted sense of humor than anything else. He'd wanted to start a scholarship at Yale or Harvard or MIT, but each institution had insisted no one could know where the money came from.

Bah.

Julius *wanted* people to know he was capable of good as well as bad. He didn't expect his philanthropy to affect his chances of release, but he wasn't a cardboard cutout of a scary monster. He was complex and interesting. He was a killer, but he wasn't indiscriminate or a bully. He could be kind too. He could be a friend.

He actually had friends.

He covered a yawn. The heater was taking forever to warm up, but the glass was slowly clearing of ice crystals.

How would those same visitors feel when they learned he was free of that cage? Would they smile as openly without the protection of armed guards if he turned up on their doorstep? Would they trust him? Could he trust them?

Probably not.

The desire to unleash his base appetites was growing in the back of his mind. Rearing up like a black cloud from a volcano in a prelude to an eruption.

Which made his current freedom so utterly divine.

He hadn't figured out quite what he wanted to do with this opportunity yet. Escape, definitely. Live in luxury and enjoy his money—that would be nice. Buy a new face or simply find a place that had everything he needed so he never had to leave, and the authorities couldn't touch him. Some island somewhere... That sounded a lot like another prison, albeit a prettier one.

He and his personal assistant, Blake Delaware, who managed his affairs, had spent time discussing the idea over the years, during their biweekly visits. Not discussing breaking out, but...*imagining* what he'd need to disappear if he was magically "released."

Contingencies had been made.

The smartest plan right now was for Julius to lie low and slip quietly away when the furor died down.

Why then was he headed toward Boston?

Stupidity most likely, but he had his pride. People had said things during his trial and afterward. Things Julius didn't like. Things that weren't true. And now there were debts to pay—Hope Harper's chief amongst them.

She owed him.

The heater finally finished clearing the windshield, so he pulled onto the road, grateful that the man he'd borrowed the car from had been so well prepared for winter. Added bonus, the guy was about Julius's size and traveled with a whole suitcase full of clothing and personal hygiene products. Fate was truly looking out for him.

About damned time.

Julius tried to relax his grip on the wheel. It was a long time since he'd driven in snow, and he couldn't risk hitting anyone or going off the road. The car had sturdy snow tires and was an automatic, but it was nerve-racking especially so soon after the accident that had set him free. As long as Julius didn't slam on the brakes, he should get where he needed to go. Not that far now. Another thirty minutes or so at most.

And then he'd know.

Whom to trust.

And whom he had to kill.

7

Aaron took his first sip of freshly brewed coffee much to the delight of his sleepy brain. He'd been up half the night making sure the new electronics worked and couldn't be easily bypassed—not that Leech had any known skills in that area. Regardless, the ADA had a new state-of-the-art alarm system and so did her downstairs neighbors. They also had new fuck-off locks on all the external doors and windows.

He'd managed a few short hours of sleep while stretched out on the floor of the living room. Ryan had taken the couch. They were getting a camp bed sent over today from the local field office. Hopefully, this op would only last a day or so, but it really was a great opportunity for Griffin, Kincaid, and Donnelly—who was on Charlie squad handling the judge—to get some hands-on close-quarter protection experience in the real world. Things didn't always go to plan. Principals were usually their own worst enemy, and the ability to think on your feet and improvise was key.

His earpiece buzzed.

"Principal is on the move," Livingstone informed him via his earpiece with an edge of sardonic humor.

"Stall her. Principal is on the move," Aaron said loudly enough for everyone else to hear.

"What the fuck?" Cowboy groused, pouring his own coffee. "Isn't it a little early for roasting balls over an open pit."

"As a former rancher, I suspect you're the only one with any personal experience of fire-roasted testicles." Aaron pinched the bridge of his nose as he mentally prepared himself to deal with the woman who was bull-headed and determined, but also so full of anguish and pain he could practically taste it.

Six thirty a.m.

Omega team scrambled to finish breakfast and gear up before they took over guard duties from Alpha for the day.

"Did no one tell her what time the teams switched over?" Kincaid stuffed a piece of toast into his mouth.

Shit.

"Actually, no. That's on me." He hated making mistakes. "I didn't think she'd leave for the office before seven." Aaron swore. He'd been too busy trying to ingratiate himself into her good graces with apologies and omelets. "I'll go stall her while you guys finish up and bring the SUVs around."

He headed out the door of the downstairs apartment in time to see Will Griffin blocking the front door.

"Are you fucking kidding me right now?" Hope Harper glared at the much larger operator, clearly not intimidated.

"No, ma'am. Sorry, ma'am." Griffin looked up with relief as Aaron appeared.

Hope turned to face him, annoyance written plainly on those cool, beautiful features.

Why couldn't he be in charge of a hostage rescue mission or the takedown of a dangerous terrorist? Why did he have to oversee an op where the principal got to talk back?

"ADA Harper. Apologies for the delay. If you could give us thirty minutes, we can arrange your journey to your office."

He watched emotions race over her features. Impatience, irritation, satisfaction perhaps at catching them unprepared. Aaron had expected the surprises to come from outside, not inside, but he should know to always expect the unexpected.

"Wait." She held up a finger. Her gaze narrowed further as her eyes raked over him. "You don't actually expect to follow me around *en masse* everywhere I go today, do you? As in the DA's office? Court?"

Aaron quirked a brow. "You weren't honestly expecting us to wave you off at the door, were you?"

"Maybe?" Lines pinched between her brows. She wore a beige power suit with a cream wool overcoat that swirled around her calves. She looked both capable and intimidating. He imagined she'd be formidable in a courtroom.

"Were you planning on taking public transport to work?"

"No." Her face was perfectly made-up, despite the hour. "Out of an abundance of caution I was going to drive." Her tone was mocking.

"We'll drive you."

Her nostrils flared with impatience. "In one of your government SUVs? Do you really expect me to be able to do my job with eleven armed men underfoot?" She made them sound like toddlers. "I have victims and witnesses testifying for the prosecution and facing far greater dangers living in their communities every day—compared to the unlikely event of Julius Leech surviving that accident and making his way back to Boston to attack me."

Obviously, Hope Harper had gotten some sleep, regained some of her energy, and had definitely *not* changed her view on having the Hostage Rescue Team around.

Where was a good negotiator when you needed one?

"Firstly, you'll only have two bodyguards assigned to your person as you go about your business. The other members of a shift will be here or checking the exterior or lobby of whatever buildings you are in—or plotting various exfil routes should we need to make a quick getaway. For that, we'll need to know your schedule in advance so we can plan accordingly."

She held up that finger again and looked like she was valiantly attempting to rein in her temper. "POTUS probably has fewer Secret Service agents guarding him than I have here right now."

"POTUS has more, but we're better," Aaron told her earnestly. "And unlike the Secret Service, we've never lost one of our…clients."

"Fine. Two bodyguards it is. But you stay out of my way." Strain tightened her features as the arrogant façade slipped for a brief instant. She suddenly looked tired and pale beneath the carefully applied makeup.

"Did you sleep at all? Or eat?" Aaron frowned and took a step toward her. "You need to eat."

It had the desired effect. Her spine stiffened, and her chin lifted. "Are you going to be my life coach as well as my bodyguard, Operator Nash?"

"As required for the duration." His smile was grim.

"I don't need a nanny," she snapped.

Not a morning person. Roger that.

"I want to keep you alive, so my record remains spotless. Eating and sleeping go a long way toward survival." He kept his tone faintly amused. She was not a woman who responded well to being told what to do.

She huffed out a small laugh. "Well, if nothing else, I appreciate the honesty."

"If you don't want someone soft-soaking you then I will give it to you straight, but in return you need to listen to me—even the parts you don't want to hear."

He saw the change in her eyes. The shields lowered briefly.

"I feel like a prisoner." The words held an edge of despair. "I feel like he's winning. Even if he's dead at the bottom of a river he's winning because of all this"—she waved a hand at him and Griffin—"and when the press gets wind of everything it's going to bring it all to the surface again." She swallowed, clearly holding back painful emotion.

Her next words were spoken so quietly he could barely hear.

"Paige would have been twelve tomorrow." She looked down at the hands that now clasped her heavy briefcase. "She's been gone for longer than she was alive, and I hate that. But rather than honoring her life, her memory, I have to hide behind bodyguards from the same piece of trash who took her from me in the first place. That isn't right. It isn't justice."

The words jabbed him in the heart but didn't change the circumstances. He lowered his head, caught her gaze. "If he's alive we'll catch him, but these things can take time."

"If he has escaped, the public needs to be warned."

Which meant the media circus would definitely be out in full force. At least Echo squad wouldn't become bored or complacent.

"US Marshals will have a better idea of exactly what happened as soon as it gets light." He checked his shoulder and saw Ryan watching from the doorway. "What time do you need to be at work?"

She glanced at her watch. "I'm usually at my desk by seven-thirty a.m."

"How about you let me get you some breakfast while we give the teams time to switch over. We'll have you at work by seven-thirty, if not sooner."

She eyed him with resignation. "Fine."

Suddenly there was noise in his earpiece. "Activity out front. White male driving erratically pulled up outside the Harper residence and is now climbing the steps. He's in a hurry. Looks like he's armed."

"Quickly." Aaron maneuvered Hope into the downstairs apartment where Seth Hopper and Sebastian Black pressed her against the brick wall while others spread out to cover entrances and windows.

"Is it Leech?" he asked.

"Can't see his face."

"Take him down. Let's see what we've got."

"What is it? What's happening?" Hope asked from over Seth Hopper's shoulder.

"Armed white male on the doorstep."

"We have the suspect on the ground." There was a brief pause. "Claims he's a BPD detective. Claims he's Ms. Harper's brother-in-law."

Aaron could hear the guy yelling insults at Cadell and Hersh —the latter had come down off the roof around 2 a.m. when he'd decided they only needed one person in that position.

Aaron went to the window and stared outside at the man who was now on his feet but cuffed with his hands behind his back. His face was florid. Hair sticking up. Expression volcanically pissed.

Aaron indicated the others allow Hope to join him, though not so close as she could be seen from the outside.

"You know that guy?"

Her sigh said it all. "That's Danny's—my late husband's—brother, Detective Brendan Harper, BPD."

"You want us to let him in?"

A spark of humor lit her gaze, then her mouth dropped. "Better or I'll never hear the end of it. He has a right to know what's going on. I'll make coffee while you bring us both up to speed on any developments that occurred overnight."

8

Aaron waited for Livingstone and Griffin to escort Hope back upstairs before he opened the front door and let Cadell come inside with the extremely pissed-off detective. Hersh headed back to the unmarked car they had on the street.

Cadell and Hersh were in plain clothes so Aaron understood why a detective might be unnerved.

"Apologies for the unpleasant surprise, but the FBI are currently in charge of protecting ADA Harper." Aaron unlocked the handcuffs and tossed them back to Cadell who handed Aaron the detective's weapon.

"We checked him for a backup piece but he's clear," added Cadell.

"Give me my service weapon, you piece of shit."

Aaron held the man's angry gaze. "Like I said, for the time being, the FBI controls security around ADA Harper, and HRT protocol is for no weapons unless you're on her detail. ADA Harper wants to talk to you upstairs, so I'll hold on to your gun and return it when you leave."

Brendan Harper's eyes widened in outrage. "You think I'd hurt her? I'm the closest thing to family she has left."

"I understand that, but as I can't fully gauge all threats ahead of time, this is how we're gonna play it. If you want to leave, I'll give you your weapon back. If you want to talk to ADA Harper, I'll take you up."

Without his weapon.

Brendan Harper's eyes narrowed. "My boss is going to be talking to your boss."

Aaron pocketed the gun. "My job is to keep her safe, not to send hearts and flowers to Boston PD."

This was what he'd been trained to do, and he was confident his bosses would support his decisions.

Brendan Harper started climbing the stairs, and Aaron shot the others an eyeroll as the team went back to either guard duty or preparations. It often took time to find a rhythm during a protective detail, and sometimes having a rhythm meant you weren't doing your job as well as you might. You should never be too comfortable or relaxed. You had to expect a certain amount of variation, of unpredictability, so that potential bad guys couldn't set up an ambush at the client's favorite coffee shop where they stopped every morning for a bagel at 8:45 a.m. before heading into work.

Brendan entered the apartment without knocking and walked straight into the kitchen. Aaron followed, and found Hope engulfed in a bearhug from the other man. She shot Aaron a look over Brendan's shoulder that told him exactly how uncomfortable she was with the situation, but she didn't push the detective away.

It made Aaron inexplicably angry because he knew what it was to endure family when you'd rather be anywhere else doing anything else.

At least the smell of fresh coffee filled the air, the large pot on the burner.

He didn't see any evidence she'd eaten though. Aaron opened the fridge and put two pieces of bread in the toaster because keeping Hope fueled up would help get them all through the day.

She extricated herself from the embrace. "I guess you heard

about Leech? Is it on the news?"

"Not yet. Friend of mine from Bureau of Prisons called about thirty minutes ago. I came straight over." He sniffed. It was cold outside. The guy wore street clothes and scuffed boots. "He told me three prisoners and two guards were missing. One of them was Leech." Brendan leaned against the exposed brick wall. "Hopefully, the guy drowned in the river and good riddance."

"Well, if he did, let's hope he surfaces soon so I can get on with my life and stop running a boarding house for action heroes." Hope produced a plastic smile.

Brendan glanced at him.

Aaron kept his expression neutral. He wasn't insulted the way he was probably supposed to be.

The toast popped, and he grabbed butter and marmalade. He didn't bother to ask if that was what she liked. It was in her fridge.

"I thought I'd come over to warn you. Didn't realize the cavalry was already here. You should have called."

"And have even more people crowding me?" Hope scoffed. "You know me better than that. Unless you need protection too?"

"I can protect myself." Brendan huffed and shot a derisive glance in Aaron's direction.

Hope poured coffee into three mugs. She handed Brendan one before nodding to a mug on the work surface as if to tell Aaron that was his. A small jug of creamer sat beside it, and a sugar bowl.

Aaron nodded his thanks and pushed the plate of toast in her direction. He sipped the coffee. Black was fine.

She picked up the plate and began eating.

Brendan rolled a shoulder. "I guess I do know you better than that. Hey, why don't I move in here until they catch the animal? These clowns can take over when I go to work in the morning."

Oh boy, the guy had a healthy ego.

"Let's put that to the Attorney General and see what she says, shall we?" Aaron said dryly. "A sleeping Boston police detective versus an elite unit of highly trained operators." He shook his head, not bothering to hide his derision. "Gonna be a tough call."

Hope flashed him a quelling look as Brendan stiffened. "I doubt the situation will last long. Let's face it, the chance of Leech getting far is remote at best. He was a trust fund baby who could barely tie his own laces. I doubt he's ever used a map, let alone stolen a car."

"True. But he sure was good at killing."

Hope flinched.

Brendan didn't seem to notice and drank his coffee. "How are you holding up?"

She took another nibble of toast. "I'll survive."

"Hope," Brendan admonished. "You don't have to bullshit me."

"I'll survive," she repeated and then demolished her toast like she hadn't eaten for days.

Aaron hadn't missed the omelet he'd made last night, untouched in the fridge.

The woman didn't take care of herself. Maybe that wasn't surprising under the current circumstances.

Brendan's face creased. "Hey, you don't think Leech would go after Ma, do you?"

Hope shook her head. "I don't know. Might be a good idea for you to stay with Mary for a few days, until this is over."

Brendan scratched his head. "I guess. She could always come stay here."

"There's not really space," Hope said quickly, "and I don't want to put her in any danger. I can send her on a nice vacation if we think there's any chance he might target her." She finished the toast and placed the plate in the dishwasher along with all three mugs.

"And now it's time for me to get to work." She eyed Aaron critically. "But whoever plans to be with me inside the DA's office or courtroom needs to wear a suit jacket and at least pretend they aren't armed to the teeth."

Aaron nodded agreeably even as inside he swore. "I'll have someone go pick something up today." From a thrift store.

She looked him over for another long moment, her gray eyes full of emotions he couldn't read. "Come with me."

Curious, he followed her to the second floor of the apartment where she went into a room that looked like a sparsely furnished office.

"Hope..." Brendan's tone was chiding.

"What? I planned to donate them anyway."

She opened the door to a walk-in closet that was filled with clothes.

"But..." Brendan spluttered.

She pulled out a black wool jacket and handed it to Aaron. "Try this on."

Then she went quickly through the hangers and pulled out three more sports jackets. "I don't know who they will fit, but they will save you a trip to the store and allow me to get on with my day."

Aaron slipped into the jacket and bunched his shoulders. It fit pretty well.

"You'll also need a shirt over that ballistics vest." She tore a bunch of shirts off hangers. "Tell your team they are welcome to come up here and take anything they want or need."

"But they were Danny's..." Brendan spluttered.

"Danny doesn't need them anymore, now does he?" Hope raised her chin a notch. "As I've told you a hundred times over the years, you are welcome to go through his things and take anything you want, but you are not welcome to tell me what to do with them."

If Aaron hadn't been watching her closely, he would have missed the pain she strove to conceal. She pretended it didn't hurt to give away her dead husband's clothes, but obviously it did—otherwise she wouldn't have kept them for so many years.

"Now," she said with forced brightness. "Time to get to work."

9

Traffic had been a bitch with a fresh layer of snow making the roads slick and tempers flare. She'd taken advantage of having a chauffeur so she could once more go over the case against Jason Swann.

The FBI had spoken to security and arrangements had been made to allow her and her bodyguards quick access without going through the usual metal detectors at work, so maybe these guys would prove useful after all.

Two bodyguards shadowed her every step. In her tiny office, they'd surreptitiously checked out the small, crammed space for danger. The windows were high, and the only real threat came from being crushed by falling boxes or freezing to death if the heating went on the fritz as had been known to happen.

Hope arrived at her desk glad to see Colin had left the Du Maurier file there as requested. She slumped into her worn-out but comfortable office chair and felt a little more in control of her world.

She'd worked here as an ADA since two months after Danny and Paige died. She spent as much time here as at home. Her old boss, Jeff Beasley, had made her work a full month of severance after she'd taken all her vacation time following the murders—she hated him almost as much as she hated Leech.

She was already on her third District Attorney and liked this one better than the last two, and liked them all better than any of the partners at Beasley, Waterman, Vander & Co. She had zero desire to do the DA's job rather than her own—not that she'd ever win a popularity contest.

"Coffee is available in the break room down the hall. You can steal two chairs and wait outside—"

"One of us will be with you at all times when you are outside of your home," Aaron Nash asserted softly.

Dammit.

Unfortunately, he wasn't a pushover, proven by the fact he was still here.

"Well then," she blinked dramatically, "going to the bathroom's going to be fun for everyone."

He smiled that quiet smile of his and acknowledged, "We'll clear the room and wait outside when nature calls."

"My female colleagues are going to love that." But she suspected some of them would be more than happy to spend the time getting to know the undeniably handsome men guarding her. It was a little weird to see them wearing Danny's clothes, but her husband would approve of her actions. The clothes did no one any good hanging in the closet.

She heard footsteps and was surprised when Colin tried to enter and was immediately stopped by the other man guarding her today, Hunt Kincaid.

"You're here early," she said to clearly indicate that not only did she know the guy, but she was also expecting him.

"The DA's PA called me an hour ago and told me to be in early. What's going on?" Worry edged his tone.

Despite Nash's warning look she decided to tell her intern everything. He was going to find out soon enough anyway. "Julius Leech may have escaped from maximum security prison yesterday. These are my FBI bodyguards until he's found." She hoped that happened soon. It gave her hives not to have her own space. "Aaron Nash, Hunt Kincaid, this is Colin Leighton, my legal intern. If you scare him off, you better know how to write legal motions." Hope kept humor in her voice, but this was still a major pain in the ass.

"Hi." Colin side-eyed the armed men attempting not to look intimidated.

Kincaid stepped aside to let Colin enter and, after a signal from Aaron Nash, stepped back outside the door where he stood scanning the corridor for imminent invasion.

Hope forced them out of her mind. She had work to do, and every minute wasted was another victory for Leech. "Did you have any luck with the lab?"

Colin opened and closed his mouth, clearly struggling to catch up with new developments. "Not yet. No one picked up when I called last night. Figured I'd try again this morning."

"Call them now." Her phone rang. "Shit. That's the DA's personal assistant." Who was scarier than most cops and judges combined.

She picked up. Opened her mouth to speak. Was cut off by the order to come to the DA's office immediately. She hung up.

"You have copies of everything we might need today?" she asked.

Colin tapped his bag. "Yep."

Ella Gibson had been viciously attacked inside her own home and had been lucky to survive. She'd named a man, Jason Swann, as the person who'd assaulted her, but he denied everything, saying Ella had been drunk but unharmed when he'd left her place. That they'd argued when he'd broken up with her. The defense was going to claim that someone else had entered Ella's home and beaten her after Swann had left and that Ella had named Jason in a twisted effort for revenge. They were probably going to suggest she'd harmed herself with the baseball bat, purely in an effort to get back at him. But Hope wasn't going to let Swann get away with it. Massachusetts had a three strikes law, and Jason Swann had already been convicted of Armed Burglary and Carjacking. Hope was going for Assault with Intent to Kill and, if convicted, Swann would serve the complete maximum sentence with no chance of parole—10 years in the state prison.

Hope expected the defense to attempt to exclude various text messages and voicemail recordings from evidence. She'd subpoenaed the defendant's messages to his best buddy who was an equally unpleasant individual, and one she was certain had been involved in some way, even if it was accessory after the fact.

Bottomline, the prosecution had to prove Swann had beaten Ella after she'd dumped him with the intent to kill. It was very much a case of he-said she-said with no witnesses to the attack itself and the only blood at the scene belonging to the victim. Jason didn't deny he'd been in the house. The two of them had even had consensual sex the day before the attack. But when she'd decided to end things, Ella said Swann had changed into a completely different person. A monster.

There were too many monsters in the world, and Hope was doing her utmost to put as many of them in prison as possible.

She clenched her jaw.

If anyone needed 24/7 protection it was women like Ella, from men who couldn't handle rejection. Those men were the ones most likely to kill. People like Ella were the most likely to be murdered.

Hope checked her watch and stood. She hated going into a trial when her focus wasn't laser sharp. Ella deserved better. But Colin was an intelligent and capable intern, and one day he'd be a good attorney. But first he had to pass the bar.

"Make sure you're in court with plenty of time to spare even if I'm delayed. I don't want Ella alone. I don't want to give Swann or his cronies the opportunity to intimidate or scare her."

"Understood." Colin nodded again.

"Right." Hope couldn't delay any longer.

She headed out the door, surprised when Aaron Nash followed.

"You can't seriously think I'm in danger when I'm inside the District Attorney's office. I mean, I get that you need to be seen to be doing your job—"

"Seen to be doing my job?" Annoyance crackled through Nash's tone. "What sort of clowns do you think the FBI employs?"

Her lips twitched because she hadn't meant to insult him. "Tall ones?"

"Funny." He held the door for her, and she saw the way he scanned the offices and desks as they walked past. "A bodyguard is useless if the body he's supposed to be guarding is physically too far away to protect. Perhaps if you wore a vest…"

"I'm not wearing a ballistics vest to work." She reached her boss's office.

The DA's Personal Assistant glanced up only long enough to make Hope feel small and inadequate.

"You can go right in."

The fact Aaron Nash joined her made embarrassment crawl up her spine and a flush rise up her neck. He stood against the wall just inside the door, and she didn't get the opportunity to introduce him or say anything because the DA didn't waste time getting started.

"I wasn't sure you'd come in today, Hope. We would all have understood if you'd decided to take some time off."

"What would I do with time off?" She sat in one of his two visitor chairs. Lincoln Frazer sat in the other. "Any developments?"

"Skid marks on the road and broken guardrail suggest the prison minibus lost control and ran off the road into the ravine. If it was a planned prison break it must have gone horribly wrong when the driver went off-piste—as the Brits might say. Search teams found a deceased prison guard in the woods." Lincoln paused. "He was naked except for his boxers."

A feeling of dread clutched her stomach. "How did he die? Do you know?" Hope crossed her legs to hide her distress. She tried hard not to reveal her empathy for the victims. Empathy showed her humanity but didn't make a case. Many saw it as weakness.

"His neck was broken." Frazer picked an imaginary piece of lint off his impeccably cut suit. "Possibly when thrown from the vehicle."

"Or possibly by one of the prisoners," Hope said. "Why was he naked?"

"Best guess at this point is someone stripped him of his clothes, footwear, and weapon in order to escape the scene without freezing to death."

"That someone likely being an escaped convict."

"Most probable scenario, yes." Lincoln met her gaze with blue eyes that glittered. She realized he wasn't as calm as he was pretending to be. He knew the danger these escaped convicts posed to anyone unfortunate enough to cross their paths. "The guard leaves behind a wife and three children."

Her mouth went dry. "So now we know someone survived that crash."

"That would be my assumption." Frazer crossed his legs. He was a lot like her. Hid all sorts of emotional turmoil beneath a cool, unruffled surface. It was how they both got through the day. It was why she liked him. Nowadays.

"Presumably, the convict did not steal the dead guard's cell phone to lead us right to him?"

"The phone hasn't been traced yet, but there's no signal, and it's more likely at the bottom of the river or buried under a foot of snow."

"And no other bodies have been recovered?"

Frazer shook his head. "Marshals are working with local river experts. They've created an outer perimeter based on the flow rate. Search parties, both aerial and on foot, are working their way upstream. The person they retrieved from the wreckage was a thirty-five-year-old inmate named Michael Herbert. Incarcerated for serial rape. He was impaled by a tree branch which is consistent with an accident of this nature."

"Yikes." His victims might think his punishment was appropriate. She wouldn't judge them.

"There's a dam upstream. The authorities plan to reduce the volume of water enough so that divers can more safely attach ropes and, as soon as there's a gap in the weather, get a chopper in to lift the van to dry land where it can then be transported to the nearest forensic laboratory for proper examination. It will take some time as the weather conditions continue to be a factor."

"Is the BAU assisting the US Marshals Service in finding Leech or the others?" she asked.

Frazer interlocked straight fingers and stared at his hands. "They have their own team of analysts."

"But you worked on the Leech cases. Both trials."

"And they have copies of my notes."

She cocked her head. Lincoln Frazer had been kicked off the fugitive task force in charge of this operation. "Are you going back to Quantico like a good little boy?"

He shot her a cool look. "It so happens I have some work to do in Boston. The trial of one of the men involved in the Agata Maroulis sex trafficking and murder case is due to start soon and I thought I'd work here for a few days in case the DA's office have any queries."

That case had rocked the city both literally and figuratively last spring when sex traffickers had leveled a massive building with people inside rather than risk capture. But the Maroulis case was wrapped up nice and tight—although jury trials were never a slam dunk. Just ask Julius Leech.

"I'm sure the ADA on that case is grateful to have you available for any questions."

Frazer smirked. "As I am here, I thought I might go over any Leech files you have—both you, personally, Hope, and the DA's office. See if I can figure out where he might go if the opportunity presents itself."

Where he might run to. Who else he might target.

"Of course," the DA said quickly. "I can find you a desk somewhere."

"There's a desk in my office if I move a few files and it'll save lugging boxes all over the building." Hope glanced at Aaron, who stood silently and unobtrusively by the door. "The presence of another armed FBI agent in my office might give my bodyguards the chance to take a break or catch up on more important things."

"You are our priority, ADA Harper," Aaron Nash said. "But having ASAC Frazer onboard certainly won't hurt the cause."

"Glad to know I still have my uses," said Frazer.

"At least you don't have people following you around all day," Hope grumbled.

"I'm armed and can take care of myself."

She pulled a face and looked out the DA's window at the snow that still fell.

"The AG wants our full cooperation on this, Hope. Judge Abbotsford is holed up at her farm. I've spoken with her, and she's pissed rather than afraid."

"I know how she feels. Any indication at all that it was Leech who stripped the guard and escaped?"

"Nothing. The ground was frozen and about a foot of snow fell overnight. Zero tracks and the dogs couldn't get a scent. Marshals have made a likely perimeter and set up roadblocks. They intend to hold a press conference at nine."

Despondency swelled inside her. Worse than the fear of Leech turning up on her doorstep was the thought of the media horde, dragging out old facts and hurtful memories to boost ratings and sensationalize the story. But the public needed to know if they might be in danger.

Hope stood. "I'm due in court, so I should be safe enough. I might be twenty minutes or six hours, depending on what the defense is plotting."

"I can have Greg Ivanovich take over that case if you prefer. The defendant in his case copped a plea deal, which I agreed to in order to free him up."

Ivanovich was a hell of a good prosecutor and a bit of a shark. Hope didn't want him anywhere near the incredibly fragile Ella Gibson if she could help it. "You can't really be worried Leech will gain access to the court to attack me?"

The DA shook his head. "I doubt it. I was thinking more about the other attorneys and press ambushing you."

"I can handle myself."

"I know you can handle yourself." Her boss stared at her thoughtfully as if weighing his interests against hers.

"Do you think they can throw anything at me that I haven't heard before a million times?"

"Doesn't mean it doesn't hurt," Aaron Nash murmured from the back of the room.

Frazer's lip curled into a surprised smile as he glanced at the other man.

"I can deal with it." She held her boss's gaze. "And I'd rather do something useful than run away and hide from a convicted felon. What sort of message does that send to the criminals out there or the people we are supposed to get justice for?"

The DA leaned back in his chair. "The wrong one. Carry on with your duties for now, but don't even think about ditching the bodyguards. They stick to you like glue. You do not take any unwarranted chances. The AG was compelling in her argument with me on the phone last night. She does not want Leech to score any more victory points where you or we are concerned."

"I'm surprised she took an interest." Hope climbed to her feet. "Let me get those files for you, Linc." She shot Aaron Nash a look. "And then see how my FBI protective detail feel about walking to the court."

10

T he argument about walking to court was short-lived. While Hope Harper might be a top prosecutor, Aaron was no slouch in the logic and persuasion department.

The good news was, once Hope was safely ensconced in the courtroom, he felt secure enough to leave her under Kincaid's watchful gaze with orders not to let her out of his sight for any reason. Aaron worked outside in a quiet part of the courthouse corridor. The judge and Sheriff's Officers understood the situation and had implemented emergency exits through a side door usually reserved for people on the other side of the judicial process, if necessary. They'd also arranged for use of the court staff's private restroom.

Aaron and Kincaid carried concealed firearms, and he really didn't see Leech setting foot in a courtroom voluntarily any time soon.

But that was no reason to drop their guard.

Aaron smoothed a hand down the soft brushed cotton of the jacket he wore. It was deep navy and hid his light-weight ballistics vest and weapons. He was annoyed that he hadn't put a business suit in his go-bag, but HRT didn't often require anything so formal while on duty. It was an error he'd fix as soon as he got back to Quantico. In the meantime, he was grateful he didn't have to spend money on clothes he didn't need. Three years as a field agent meant he had suits galore. So many more than he'd ever owned when biology had been his gig. Hard to believe how many years he'd put into his studies before his world had crashed around him and he'd decided to do something a little less "geeky."

Bitterness welled inside.

The holidays had been fun.

Thank God those were over for another year.

He pushed it aside. Checked his messages. He'd used the time today to talk with various members of HRT regarding the setup they had in place and to look for any gaps in Hope Harper's security. He'd updated Novak, who'd traveled to the scene of the prison break to keep a close eye on the situation in conjunction with FBI Negotiator Charlotte Blood.

The US Marshal Service were proving prickly when it came to jurisdiction, and they outranked the FBI. But they also knew they might need the FBI's resources eventually, so they were willing to share information up to a point. That point being no sign of Julius Leech had been found, nor did they have any idea where the other two escaped felons were.

Aaron checked the news. Local and national. The media had picked up the story of the prison break and, as predicted, were abuzz with the possible danger to the public while constantly regurgitating the history between Leech and Harper.

Aaron didn't like the way they flashed photos of his principal all over the news. He especially hated the ones taken of her sobbing at her late husband's and child's funeral.

Didn't a loving mother and wife deserve to grieve in private? In one image he spotted Brendan Harper holding her up when she collapsed.

Aaron didn't particularly like the guy. Didn't matter. The detective was Hope Harper's former brother-in-law and likely to be part of this situation whether HRT approved or not.

Aaron was satisfied with the security protocols in place, but the media had started to camp outside Hope's row house which might make things trickier. Livingstone and Griffin had gone shopping earlier for the team, so they'd be self-sufficient regarding food supplies for a few days. They used the back entrance, and so far, the press hadn't spotted them. The plan was to make a very public show of strength when Hope returned home tonight. Let Leech see the FBI did not intend to let anything happen to either Hope Harper or Judge Abbotsford.

Omega team had split up. Seth Hopper and Sebastian Black were nearby with the vehicle, tuned into traffic reports and police scanners while ready to move to the court entrance at a moment's notice. Cowboy and Demarco watched the residence. Kincaid was in the courtroom, and Aaron was monitoring the corridor as well as coordinating.

He might take someone off the nightshift and add them to the dayshift if the security updates they'd made worked as designed and assuming Hope Harper stayed home every night.

Probably not a good thing to assume, although maybe she'd accommodate them while Leech was AWOL. She didn't strike him as having a death wish, although the thought of Leech sure as hell didn't freak her out the way it would most people.

Of course, she'd spent a lot of time with Leech. She knew the monster was just a man.

It was 4 p.m. now. Except for a brief break for lunch—he'd had Seth Hopper deliver sandwiches from a local deli—Hope and her intern had been busy all day with these proceedings.

Her client was a petite bleached blonde who looked like a strong wind would knock her over. The guy she'd accused of attacking her was five-feet ten-inches of wiry muscle with a dangerous glint in his eye and a nasty turn to his lips.

The doors to the courtroom opened, and people began to stream out.

Aaron stood and headed inside.

Hope was talking to her client when the defendant climbed to his feet and threw a glare at them both. Aaron was pleased to see Kincaid place himself directly between the defendant and Hope. The accused shot Kincaid a look that bounced off him. Kincaid had been a solid agent, and he was going to make a great Hostage Rescue Team operator with a little more seasoning and experience.

The defendant's lawyer put a hand on the scumbag's arm and sent him firmly down the aisle. Aaron kept an eye on the asshole and his equally dumb-looking friend.

The defense attorney smiled at Hope, a bright empty shell of a smile full of smug satisfaction.

"Counselor." The man folded his hands over an expensive-looking leather briefcase. He wore a long, camel-hair coat and an affected air of superiority. Two presumably junior associates, carrying much heavier loads stood behind the guy. Both kept their features expressionless. "I hope you forgive us for putting you through your paces today. I'm sure you weren't expecting to have to work for your measly salary."

"On the contrary, it will liven things up for what is going to be a slam dunk of a trial. I can't wait to see you in court every day while we call up character witness after character witness. I'm particularly looking forward to all the former girlfriends, not to mention Mr. Swann's own mother testifying about his violent temper."

"Your client is hardly a saint."

The young woman flinched and turned away. Hope shifted in front of her.

"My client is not on trial."

"You know better than that." The man's tone was snide and condescending.

Hope gathered her belongings then took a step closer to the guy. Kincaid was still between them and watched the man's hands.

Good.

One of the first lessons of close protection. People couldn't shoot you with their faces.

"Things must be going well at the firm if one of the senior partners is taking on *pro bono* work. Or did you run out of rich scumbags to defend and have to look further afield to make your quota?"

Obviously, they knew one another well.

The man smiled but it didn't reach his eyes. "The jury will discount the allegations as soon as they hear about your *alleged* victim's drug problem."

"Being a recovering addict doesn't mean the law doesn't protect you from violent crime. You are no less of a person because you've made a mistake. And if you are, well, you and I are royally screwed. My client, however, is a hard-working young woman trying to make a life for herself without some brainless thug attempting to kill her simply because she broke it off with him."

"So she claims."

Ella Gibson seemed to cave in on herself. The idea of putting her on the stand to be interrogated by this heartless bastard was like throwing Bambi into a wolf's den.

Aaron moved closer to Hope and Kincaid.

Hope's features were cool with disdain. "We both know he's guilty so why are you really here, Jeff?"

Jeff.

It clicked then.

This was Jeff Beasley, the lawyer who'd defended Julius Leech the second time around. When Hope had testified, and the jury had convicted.

Beasley flicked a glance over Aaron. "Hiding behind your FBI protection detail, Hope?"

"Leech threatened us both from what I remember of that day in court when you *lost*. Of course, your firm is probably still on retainer…" Hope shook her head. "Shit. Tell me he isn't still your client."

The man said nothing.

"You're here because you want to keep an eye on me. For Leech? Or for your own twisted amusement?"

"Don't be ridiculous."

"I'm not the one who's being ridiculous but you're obviously not self-aware enough to perceive that."

Beasley sneered. "You always thought you were better than the rest of us. But all you ever were was a mindless drone who could be persuaded to do almost anything if it meant career progression."

Hope went sheet white.

Aaron didn't like the insinuation this man was making.

Hope spoke to the other two attorneys. "It sounds like you're suggesting I did something unethical or immoral in return for… for what? A shitty office, an overflowing caseload? The only unethical thing I ever did was accept the cases you offered me without question. And what really sticks in your craw is that I am ten times better than you in court on any given day." She spoke to the junior lawyers again. "Whatever the salary is, take it from me, it isn't worth it. Even if he offers you a partnership, run far away from the scumbags he represents."

The two young attorneys were wide-eyed.

"Jeff Beasley continues to represent the man who was convicted of killing my husband and child in cold blood. A man I defended because *Jeff* promised me a partnership if I did so. I didn't even have to win. I just had to show up for that mother-fucker. If you think he cares about you at all, take a look at someone you love, picture them bleeding out on the floor, then picture this man defending the bastard holding the knife. That's the person you're working for."

Jeff Beasley flushed and took a step forward. Aaron put his hand out to stop him getting any closer.

"Get your hands off me." Jeff tried to brush him aside.

Aaron wasn't going anywhere. "Step back. ADA Harper is under FBI protection, and you are too close for my comfort."

"Mine too," Hope muttered.

"Hear that? You are making my principal uneasy with your aggressive words and demeanor. I suggest you step back before I have to arrest you for not obeying the instructions of a federal law enforcement officer. Step. Back. *Now.*"

Jeff Beasley quickly backed off. "I never figured you for a coward, Hope."

Hope Harper snorted. "Funny. I pegged you for a coward the moment I met you."

Aaron inserted himself fully between the bickering attorneys. "You were also offered FBI protection until Julius Leech is apprehended, Mr. Beasley. You declined, but I'm sure it can still be arranged." Aaron crossed his arms over his chest. The thought of being assigned to protect a man like Beasley was abhorrent, but he'd do it if ordered. That was the job.

Then he'd bathe in disinfectant.

He glanced at Hope Harper. He guessed they both did things they didn't necessarily enjoy because of their profession.

Beasley wasn't done. "If you think I'm hiding behind anyone in front of a jury you're as big an idiot as you look."

Aaron held back a smirk.

"Plus, I don't need underpaid FBI drones as bodyguards." Jeff took a step away and raked a derisive glance over Aaron and Kincaid. "I've hired my own protection."

Aaron glanced to the door where two beefy-looking men in black suits wearing obvious earpieces stood watching them.

Jesus. They looked like a couple of extras on a movie set.

Aaron reached out and pointed at Beasley's chest, his hand mimicking the shape of a gun. "Pretty difficult to protect you from over there." He pulled the imaginary trigger.

Beasley stepped back and swung away. The two junior lawyers scurried after him. "See you in court, Hope. Better bring reinforcements—the ones with brains rather than firepower."

Ouch.

"Well, that was fun. I would apologize, but I'm not taking

responsibility for that asshole." Hope spoke through gritted teeth as the man's coat flapped through the door.

Aaron smiled grimly. "What's that saying? *If silence be good for the wise, how much better for fools.*"

"Ha. He always did like the sound of his own voice." She fished for her sleeve.

Aaron held up her coat. "Home?"

"Is it a half day, or do the FBI work bankers' hours?"

"Ask me at midnight."

She had the grace to wince. "Sorry."

"Back to the office?" He cupped her elbow and felt a little zing of something he hadn't expected, something he hadn't felt in *years* zip along his skin. He stepped back. "We can leave through the side door."

"Fine. But we need to make a detour and drop my client home first." At whatever she read in his expression she doubled down and prepared for an argument he wasn't about to make. "I don't want her to make her way home on public transport when they could be waiting for her."

"Does she have a restraining order?"

The young woman was talking to Hope's intern as they both waited off to the side.

Hope's lips pulled back. "She has one against Swann but not his buddies." She lowered her voice. "For all the good it's worth. Maybe I should bring her home with me."

"So she can be on the evening news?"

"The press knows?" A flicker of vulnerability washed over her features. "Of course, they know. Damn. I'd hoped we'd find Leech before it became national news." Her lips pressed together and formed a mirthless smile. "Another reason to go back to the office after we take Ella home. Maybe they'll get bored after they miss the deadline for the evening news and leave my home alone."

"We can drop her off, no problem." He couldn't resist adding, "Good thing we drove, isn't it?"

11

Sylvie Pomerol stood stirring a pot of beef stew on the stove. Way back in college she'd been a vegetarian, but meeting her husband had changed that. If he didn't eat some sort of meat at a meal, he didn't think he'd been fed, and his cooking prowess was limited to the grill, so she was the main cook. He did other things to balance the scales of their lives together, but she had no desire to make two separate meals every day. Still, occasionally she'd make soups for lunch that were meat-free. Bart compensated by slathering the bread she made from scratch with slabs of butter.

She tensed as she heard a vehicle drive up then relaxed when she saw Bart jump out of the blue 1970 Ford F-250 pickup that he'd restored from a rusting hulk of steel when he'd gotten out of the Marine Corp five years ago. Security lights flooded the yard. She bit her lip then walked over and unlocked the back door.

News of Julius Leech's escape had made her nervous, but the chances of him even remembering her name, let alone figuring out where she lived when he was on the run from every law-enforcement agency in the country was small.

Still. She'd kept the door locked all day and worked remotely.

She didn't underestimate people like Leech. He was cunning and deceitful. He was also enough of a narcissist to hold a grudge, even if, ultimately, it was his own fault he'd been arrested and convicted of murder.

Sociopaths rarely saw themselves as they truly were. It was always someone else's fault, someone else was to blame.

He hadn't liked her assessment of the crimes he'd committed, nor of the profile she'd created of him that had been uncannily accurate. The fact his childhood had messed him up was no excuse. Many people had sob stories even if his was particularly tragic. His father had smothered his mother with a pillow when she'd stabbed him. They'd both died, neither of them realizing their son was hiding in the closet, watching. He'd been six.

She tasted the stew and turned the heat down to a low simmer. Bart came in the back door in his socks as he'd left his boots in the mudroom.

"Hey, there." He walked over and kissed her. "Everything okay?"

She nodded.

He put his hands on her shoulders and squeezed. "That smells amazing. I'm going to grab a quick shower."

He kissed her again and headed upstairs. She sighed with relief. Bart always made her feel safe.

A bang made her jolt. She walked over to check the window. The door to the mudroom hadn't latched properly, and the wind had blown it open. "Dammit." It happened all the time in winter when the ground shifted. She stepped outside, avoided the melting snow from Bart's boots, and grabbed the handle, pulling it closed and shutting out the bitter wind.

Her heart stopped when a hand gripped her mouth from behind and a handgun pressed tight against her temple.

"Hello, Dr. P."

Bile rose in her throat as she struggled, and the fingers clamped more firmly over her mouth and nose. She couldn't breathe, but she made as much noise as she could.

"No, you don't." Julius Leech cuffed her on the side of the

head with the heavy metal of the pistol, making her stagger and her eyes roll as she fell to her knees.

He grabbed her hand and slipped a metal cuff tight around her wrist. Pulled her arm behind her back along with the other one as she fought not to pass out. If she passed out, she was dead. Bart was dead.

Bart...

She let out a cry, but Leech slammed her head with the butt of the pistol again, this time dropping her to the floor. Then he slapped a piece of duct tape over her mouth.

Terror ran through her veins.

Oh God.

He rolled her onto her back, her wrists straining painfully from the pressure of their combined weight. His groin pressed against hers. Revulsion filled her.

"Now you get to feel what it's like to be shackled like an animal." Leech looked thinner, features more defined. But something glittered in his pale blue eyes as he looked at her. Something more dangerous than she remembered.

Had Bart heard their struggle?

She thought of her cellphone, useless in a pocket she couldn't reach. The gun in the drawer, gathering dust.

She couldn't even use her training to distract him as he'd silenced her.

He dragged her roughly to her feet, and she stumbled as her head swam.

"I've got you, Dr. P. You didn't make it easy to find you, but I've been keeping tabs for a while now. Never expected I'd get the opportunity to call on you personally. I guess you never know what life's going to throw at you." He grabbed her arm with biting fingers and pushed her ahead of him, pistol in his other hand, pointed at her head.

She had to warn Bart. In the kitchen she shoved against the table as hard as she could. Dishes rattled as the heavy wood scraped the floor.

Leech jerked her head back by her hair, and her eyes watered at the pain.

His grip tightened, and he kept his voice to a malevolent whisper. "Tut tut. Let's not ruin the surprise for Bart. You know how we unfeeling sociopaths don't appreciate others upsetting our evil plans."

The living room was empty, and they could both hear movement on the floor above.

She stumbled on the stairs, but Leech jerked her hair so hard her scalp burned.

They reached the bedroom, but rather than Bart jumping out and tackling Leech like she'd prayed, she heard him singing Bohemian Rhapsody in the shower.

She made a muffled squeal and Leech shoved her face down on the bed and sat on her back, pressing her face into the duvet so she couldn't breathe…

Please, please, someone save us.

As she heard the shower turn off and the door open, followed by the blast of a gunshot, she knew it was too late.

12

_____

Hope glanced at Aaron Nash in the seat beside her. His profile was lit by the soft glow of the streetlights that skimmed dramatically over the broad forehead, sharp cheekbones, and a fierce blade of a nose. The well-trimmed beard was the same glossy black as his hair.

The beard made him look scholarly somehow and didn't quite match her image of an FBI Hostage Rescue Team operator who were the special forces of the law enforcement world.

Feeling her gaze, he turned to meet her eyes, but she looked away, not sure why.

She'd never particularly liked machismo. Had always preferred brains over looks, nerds over jocks. Danny had been an irresistible combination of both.

Rampant testosterone made her want to hit something, which was ironic and not something she was particularly proud of.

She had to admit that as far as alpha males went, the ones guarding her hadn't been too overbearing...yet. She'd been able to do her job and, aside from that ass, Beasley, things had gone smoothly.

There was a fine line between protection and control, and one of her many flaws was her need to keep control. She'd rather face

Leech alone than be put in a box with no say in how she lived her life. Perhaps that was why she liked being the one putting violent offenders away—she could imagine how awful prison must be.

They pulled up outside Ella's crappy apartment building in Southie.

Hope squeezed her hand. She knew the young woman might be regretting her decision to hold Swann accountable, and she totally understood. "Do you have a friend who can stay with you?"

Ella's lips pinched, and she shook her head.

Hope wanted to take her home, but the DA took a dim view of getting too involved with victims. Hope didn't have space to shelter everyone she represented. Instead, she concentrated her efforts on making their cases before a jury and getting the immediate danger locked away. And she was good at it. Really good at it.

"Tomorrow, we have jury selection. It's going to be a tedious process that could take the day. I doubt the judge will want to start the trial on Thursday when Fridays are usually dark, but you never know. I'll call you when I know for sure, okay? Stay home and get some rest unless you really want to attend. Don't let that asshole defense attorney get to you."

"Easy for you to say," Ella muttered with a glance at the armed men sat in the car.

Guilt ate at Hope. The woman didn't smile as she climbed out of the car.

Hope glanced at Aaron Nash. "Will you make sure she gets inside safely?"

He looked surprised, then nodded and jogged after Ella. He came back less than five minutes later. "No one loitering outside. I checked inside the apartment and all clear. I told her to lock the door and not let anyone in."

It wasn't a particularly safe neighborhood for a woman in Ella's position but all she could afford at the moment.

Hope nodded. "I hope she listens."

What else could she do? Lock Ella up? Provide armed guards?

The hypocrisy ate at her, and she gritted her teeth.

Swann would be a complete idiot to go after Ella, but he was a complete idiot so...

Hope would make sure he answered for his crimes, but she was worried about Ella in the meantime. Fear was a great motivator—until you had nothing left to lose.

Beasley and his fleet of lawyers might delay the process, but Hope would win in the end. She was determined.

They rolled away, meandering through a neighborhood that had come a long way since the urban decay of the eighties and nineties. Gentrification had led to some of the highest real estate prices in Boston.

They weren't far from where her mother-in-law lived and where Danny and Brendan had grown up. Maybe she'd ask Brendan to swing by and check in on Ella if he was staying with his ma. But having a cop banging on the door was liable to terrify the girl too.

"She'll be okay," Nash said softly.

"Will she?" Hope wasn't convinced.

"She grew up around here, didn't she? She knows how to take care of herself."

For some reason, the comment made Hope feel judged. Sure, she came from a different part of the state and a completely different type of background. Rural. Upper middle-class. Only child. Pampered. But she knew how to take care of herself too.

It had been pure chance that she and Danny had met. They'd both attended Boston University but different programs. They had both gotten lost on their first day and had literally bumped into one another. They'd helped one another get oriented and figure out where they each needed to be and had darted off to their respective classes. But he'd written his number on her campus map in case she got lost again, and she'd called it the next day to ask if he'd found a decent coffee shop yet.

That was it. Coffee. Cake. Happily Ever After.

Until, it hadn't been.

There had never been anyone else, and she'd felt like the luckiest woman alive. They'd gotten married before they'd even graduated.

She'd been pregnant with Paige during her last year at Harvard Law, and she'd taken the job with Beasley, Waterman, Vander & Co. to help pay off her student loans.

Her throat tightened as they passed a tavern she and Danny had drunk in back in the day. It seemed like a different lifetime now. Worse, it seemed like someone else's lifetime. Someone else's memories. Someone softer. Someone kinder. Someone a lot more naive.

Someone who wouldn't rip out a throat with her bare teeth if it meant protecting her child. Someone who wouldn't sell her soul to bring her, or her dead husband, back.

They got on the Southeast Expressway and headed downtown. Traffic was thick. Roads were slick with a mix of rain and ice and general impatience.

She watched her reflection, still against the moving background. The snow had turned to sleet and water was running down the window in slow, fat rivulets that warped and distorted the lights of this city she both loved and hated. Her throat went tight at the person she saw there.

She didn't think she was the sort of woman Danny Harper would give his number to anymore. She didn't think she was the sort of woman Danny Harper would have loved.

Sadness pressed around her like a cloak.

"You okay?" Nash asked.

Another FBI operator sat in front beside Kincaid. Her intern, Colin Leighton, and yet another federal agent occupied the third row behind them.

She shivered and hunched her shoulders. "Just thinking."

"We won't let him get to you, Hope."

She huffed out a breath. "I wasn't thinking about him."

Their eyes met across the seat. Connected.

He nodded solemnly, obviously understanding the direction of her thoughts.

"Any news on Leech?" She hadn't wanted to talk about the serial killer in front of Ella. The other woman hadn't held up well today despite her insistence on being in the courtroom. This trial was going to be hard on her. Maybe Hope *should* hand it off to another prosecutor so that Jeff Beasley would crawl back into his lair, but she doubted he'd stick around for long anyway. Too *important*.

But no one else would fight as passionately or care quite as much about getting justice for Ella Gibson as Hope did. She'd visited the young woman in the hospital after the assault. Witnessed the pain and terror in Ella's eyes. Promised her the DA's office would put this guy away and keep her safe. Ten years wasn't forever, but it was a good chunk of time—a lifetime for some.

"Any evidence yet he escaped as opposed to being dead?"

Colin's rapt attention was on their murmured conversation.

Who wouldn't be enthralled by all this *drama*? He'd signed an NDA before working for the District Attorney's office, but she doubted that would stop him dropping juicy details at dinner parties.

"Nothing yet."

Where was the rat bastard?

Their vehicle took the turn onto the road in front of the DA's office and pulled up sharply.

"Wait," Aaron Nash instructed as she reached for the door.

She held on to her patience.

Kincaid hurried out of the front passenger side, and Nash climbed out and strode around to join him. The man from the back followed her out when Kincaid opened her door.

She belatedly spotted the crowd of reporters camped out near the doors and pulled her shoulders back as, one by one, their heads raised, scenting blood, and cameras were shouldered. They scurried toward her, microphones outstretched as they shouted their questions.

"What do you think about the fact Julius Leech may have escaped custody?"

"Do you think Leech will come after you now that he's free?"

She and her band of armed merry men strode quickly across the wide sidewalk toward the entrance.

She had no idea where Colin was, but she wasn't given the opportunity to wait for him.

"Will he kill again?"

"Are you scared that Julius Leech means to attack you next?"

"Is he a danger to the public?"

"No comment."

"Will he come for you the way he promised, Hope?"

"Is that why you have so many bodyguards, Ms. Harper?"

"Do you really think you should be in the prosecutor's office when you're the person who got him released at the first trial?"

Gah. They were relentless. "No comment."

"Julius Leech always maintained he was innocent. Said that you set him up."

Hope came to an abrupt halt, the hard body of Aaron Nash slamming against her as he tried to crowd her toward the door.

She pushed away, ignoring the spatter of icy rain, and turned to face her hit squad.

"Julius Leech walked free from that first trial because a Boston police detective planted evidence at the scene of one of the murders then lied about it on the stand. That same detective was later overcome by guilt and confessed before taking his own life in a tragic act. I filed a motion to dismiss based on the legal facts of the case. But let's get one thing straight for those of you who need it spelled out. Leech was not innocent. He was never *innocent*. And I helped prove that when he was convicted of murdering my family." She held back her hair that the wind had blown across her face. "I'm not scared of that sonofabitch. I *am* shocked he somehow managed to escape from prison when tying his own shoelaces was always a struggle."

"You have armed guards. Not exactly screaming self-confidence there," one man jeered.

She looked off to one side and saw a bunch of cops watching with sneers on their faces, including Lewis Janelli, the dead detective's former partner, a man who'd been investigated for his part in planting that evidence. The DA and Internal Affairs had never been able to prove he'd known the evidence was false, and he'd been allowed to return to work, bad-mouthing Hope to anyone who'd listen ever since.

"The security detail was not my idea. The DA insists if I want to work cases I need to have security."

"At least they're hot." That from a laughing female voice at the back of the crowd.

Hope brushed the comment aside.

"Do you regret it now?" This voice was more measured. Questioning without condemning. "Revealing the truth about the evidence. The suicide of Detective Monroe. The deaths of your family?"

The words pierced deep.

"Every day. Every damned day." Hope struggled to identify the speaker as rain spat in her eyes. "But I'd do the same thing if I was put in that situation again." Her voice caught, tore open a ragged gaping wound that bloomed red. The crowd went silent knowing they were about to get the soundbite they'd waited for all day. "Justice matters. Justice has to matter so people like Julius Leech are put behind bars where they belong. Cops have to play it by the book, along with the District Attorney's Office and Department of Justice. Then the system works as it was meant to work. Otherwise, we're all just paying lip service to the idea of law and order, and we're no better than the scumbags out there committing crimes."

She whirled and pushed past people to get into the building and to escape the spotlight.

Dammit. Why couldn't she have said "No comment" again like a good girl?

They skipped the metal detectors and headed toward the elevator that led to her third-floor office.

No one spoke on the ride up, but her heart pounded, and she wondered if the others could hear it.

She stepped off and followed Kincaid down the corridor. Nash and the other man were close at her back.

An older woman stood talking to the DA outside her office, and Hope's mood crashed even further. Lincoln Frazer was also there. Nash moved to her shoulder.

"It's okay." Her voice was a rough tumble of emotion. "I know her. Give us some space."

Minnie Ramon was the mother of one of Leech's female victims from the trial where Hope had represented the scumbag. During the proceedings, Minnie had been called as a witness for the prosecution, but Hope had used the opportunity to question her about her daughter's less than perfect marriage. Although Hope had been gentle, the process had broken Mrs. Ramon, and the woman had been practically carried off the stand weeping. Minnie had been admitted to a psychiatric unit that same day. Hope regretted every second of that cross examination.

She'd walk barefoot over broken glass if she thought it would help ease the pain of those families, but it wouldn't. The lack of justice regarding those murders was galling to this day.

"Mrs. Ramon came in when she heard about the possible prison break. She wanted to talk to you and waited for most of the day, despite knowing you were in court." The DA spoke smoothly.

"How are you? What can I do for you?" Hope reached forward to shake her hand, but the woman ignored it.

Embarrassment hit, and she pulled her hand back and put it in her pocket, squeezing it into a tight fist.

The light in Minnie Ramon's eyes changed, her expression filled with a dislocated kind of wonder that made Hope want to look away. "I wanted to see your face now Julius Leech is free when he should be locked up. You let that monster go once, and he killed. Now he's out there, and he's gonna come for you, he's gonna come for you because he wants you—but he's not gonna get you."

Hope opened her mouth to apologize again for the woman's plight and distress but everything after that happened in slow-motion.

The woman drew a knife out of her pocket and thrust it toward Hope's abdomen.

Nash lunged, grabbed Minnie Ramon's thin, bony wrist and jerked her arm up and away. The DA stumbled back in fright as Minnie dropped the knife and cried out in pain.

"Don't hurt her." Hope jumped forward to pull Nash off the older woman. "Don't hurt her."

Kincaid cuffed the poor woman.

Their eyes met, Minnie's not vague anymore but instead molten with hate and fury. Bile rose up Hope's throat. Then she was dragged into her office by Aaron Nash while long-suffering Minnie Ramon was pushed against the wall.

Hope's door was slammed shut. Minnie Ramon was marched away by a member of security who'd come running over at the ruckus.

Hope covered her mouth with her palm. "They need to let her go."

"She tried to stick a knife in your gut," Nash snarled.

"She needs help. She's been through hell." Hope stood there shaking. "And I'm largely to blame."

13

Aaron examined the stubborn woman to make sure she really was all right. He was furious he'd allowed a threat to get within striking distance of his principal. He was fucking pissed at himself for making what could have been a terminal error.

"They need to let her go," Hope repeated.

She looked shaken but unhurt. He needed her to snap out of the denial she seemed to be in about what had actually happened. Maybe a little brutal honesty would work.

"Look, Hope, I am no fan of defense lawyers, but I am smart enough to know that without access to a fair trial the criminal justice system becomes meaningless."

Hope lowered herself slowly to her chair, clearly freaked out. "I don't want her prosecuted."

Aaron narrowed his gaze. "Why not? You'd encourage anyone else to press charges, but when it comes to your own safety you refuse?"

"Don't you think I've done enough to that woman?"

"Leech is the one responsible."

"I grilled her on the stand. I got him off…"

"Did you?" He crossed his arms over his chest, still mad as

hell with himself for fucking up. "Downstairs you told the reporters it was the cops' fault. Detective Monroe didn't just cross a line, he pole-vaulted across the damned thing."

"If I'd sat on the email Monroe sent to me—"

"Wouldn't the Boston PD have checked the guy's email after a suicide?"

Hope looked frail all of a sudden. "Yes, but the trial would probably have been over by then. And maybe BPD wouldn't have told anyone."

"And you'd have been okay with Leech going down for murder based on false evidence?"

"No." Hope closed her eyes. "But I'm not okay with him murdering my family either." When she opened her eyes, they shimmered like opals. "If I'd *known* what was going to happen... If I'd known it was their *lives* at stake. I'd have let him rot in prison, and I wouldn't have given a rat's ass about right and wrong because they'd be alive rather than in caskets, and Minnie Ramon would have had justice for her own daughter."

Her throat worked, as she clearly tried to control her emotions.

Aaron's own throat tightened. "This wasn't your fault, Hope. You know that deep down. I know you know it." But she clearly wasn't thinking straight. He pointed through the glass into the hallway. "That woman needs to be held accountable for her actions, otherwise every Tom, Dick, and Harriet are going to think it's okay to take a shot at someone they perceive let them down. It's not okay, and if it were directed at anyone else besides yourself, you'd be the first in line to have them charged. Even if the charges don't stick. Even if they are acquitted. It needs to happen."

"She needs medical help not a jail cell." A knock on the door had Hope fishing across her desk for a tissue. Aaron opened the door.

Lincoln Frazer stood there. "Everything okay?"

"Trying to persuade ADA Harper that she needs to press charges even though she is physically unharmed."

Hope's intern, Colin, hovered in the doorway looking anxious.

"DA has remanded Mrs. Ramon into custody and plans to get her a mental health assessment ASAP. He's going to give her an official warning and issue a restraining order. The only reason he's not going for formal charges is she took that knife from the break room rather than smuggling it past security."

"Plus, the fact there's no way in hell he'd get a conviction." Hope's lips twisted. "At least she didn't come in with the express intent to kill me."

"She's been here before, right?" Aaron pushed.

"Many times." Hope's voice was ragged.

"And she probably knew there'd be a knife in the break room?"

"You'd make a good prosecutor, Nash." Frazer laughed. "But I don't think Hope wants to hear any arguments for the prosecution."

Hope waved their comments away. "You don't understand."

"She tried to stab you." How many times did he need to say it before it sank in?

"And I am sure a judge would find her mentally unfit to stand trial."

"Then let a judge decide that—"

"Let it go! Please, just let it go. You don't know how much she's suffered." Hope's eyes flashed bright with the sheen of tears.

She did understand that level of suffering though, and that was why it was so unfathomable that she refused to stand up for herself.

"I put her on the stand. I made her admit under oath that her daughter was unfaithful on multiple occasions and that her daughter's marriage was abusive to the point there were hospital visits and photographs. I cast enough doubt that some of the jury clearly believed her daughter and son-in-law might have killed one another rather than Leech being involved. And after all that, after all the pain and humiliation she endured, she never got closure for her child's murder. No one was held accountable for what happened to those six victims, and even though Leech was in prison, that matters. It really matters."

Aaron shook his head. He understood what she was trying to say, but he didn't back down. She was a menace to herself.

"That's the last time anyone gets within five feet of you unless they're FBI."

Her outraged eyes cooled to silver. "The FBI doesn't get to tell me what to do."

Aaron opened his mouth to argue, but Frazer beat him to it.

"I wouldn't bet on that. If Operator Nash recommends protective custody, then I suspect that's what you'll get. Aaron's highly respected within HRT for his cool logic. And you'll be bored out of your mind in minutes."

Aaron blinked in surprise. He didn't know the revered profiler even knew his first name let alone his rep, but maybe the guy was lying for effect.

"The AG will go along with any directives from HRT command, and HRT command will listen to their people on the ground." Frazer strolled over to the desk at one side of the room and began sliding files into a banker's box. "Mind if I take these home with me?"

Aaron and Hope glared at one another.

Finally, she looked away. "Knock yourself out."

She drew in a deep breath and let it out in an audible huff. "It's not like I run around hugging people or shaking hands. The number of people who get close to me is limited to four, five if you count poor Colin, who is only on the list because he has to be."

Her intern held up his hand in a nervous wave as Aaron narrowed his eyes at the man.

"We don't hug," Colin assured him nervously.

Hope stood and leaned against her desk as Frazer slipped on his coat. "I have another box of files at home from the first trial. If you want copies, I'll bring them in tomorrow and have some made."

"That would save me the trouble and be useful if I'm called back to Quantico unexpectedly. What happened to the letters Leech writes every week?"

"Colin?" Hope prompted.

Frazer turned to the intern who shifted his weight from one foot to the other.

"The, um, ones that have arrived since I've worked here have been shredded."

"Did you read them?" Frazer asked.

Her assistant blushed fiery red. "I was told to shred anything that arrived from Leech without opening."

Aaron noted he didn't directly answer the question.

"When did the last one arrive?"

Colin blinked rapidly as Frazer grilled him. "Last Wednesday, I think?"

"It's probable another one will arrive this week. Don't shred it. I want to read it as soon as it gets here."

"I want to read it too," Aaron stated.

Colin looked at Hope, who nodded.

"Give Frazer whatever he wants." She shot a glare at Aaron. "Both of them."

"If only Izzy was so accommodating." Frazer's tone was wry.

"Izzy is a saint," Hope huffed.

Frazer's grin sliced across his face. "Izzy *is* a saint, but definitely not a pushover. She has mellowed since we met, but she is still a former Army Captain—and, yet, she loves me." He patted his heart and gave Hope an over-dramatic dreamy expression.

Scary as hell but the guy was obviously attempting to lighten the mood.

"Must be your charming demeanor. You're staying with the Hayeses again tonight?"

"Yes." Frazer dropped the act. "Ironically, I met Marshall Hayes' wife following her own battle with a New York City serial killer. We became friends over the years."

"Well, you're a friendly guy." Hope quirked a grin that didn't meet her eyes.

"Trust me, I'm as surprised about that as anyone."

Aaron shifted against the wall.

Hope sent him a look to say she hadn't forgotten their conversation. He hadn't forgotten either.

He was glad Hope seemed calmer than she had earlier, but he didn't like how she put her personal safety last on the list of priorities. As practical and aloof as she pretended to be, she had buttons that the wrong person could easily leverage.

Leech claiming to be innocent was one of them. The way she empathized with the pain of victims, another. These were weaknesses someone could exploit to harm her, and he bet she had others. He intended to make sure no one got close enough for it to be a problem.

14

B ack at the apartment, Hope fed Lucifer and forced herself to pull out a bowl of curry from the freezer and put it in the microwave to defrost mainly because she didn't want another lecture from Aaron Nash about taking care of herself.

It felt a little weird to be alone finally after interacting with people all day. Sure, there was a guy or two on her roof and a whole bunch more squished into her wonderful neighbors' apartment, but there was no one watching her every move or following her around or waiting for her to pee, for God's sake.

She rubbed her bare arms, which were suddenly cold. She grabbed a long cardigan that was draped over the back of the couch.

She had notes to go over for tomorrow from her paralegal, whom she'd asked to dig into potential jurors. The woman was seriously good at her job, and Hope had begged the DA for her assistance on this case. Hope needed to pick the best jury she could based on their life choices and social media profiles. The defense had their own ultra-expensive consultant, but the DA refused to spring for that.

The microwave dinged, and she forced herself to stir the rich fragrant sauce and let it sit for a few minutes rather than burn the skin from the roof of her mouth, which she did far too regularly.

She poured herself a glass of wine and wandered around her home. It had been a long time since she'd felt so unsettled, so antsy. Usually, she was focused on cases or on writing Danny's books.

Of course, Leech being missing was one of the reasons she was so unsettled, plus Minnie Ramon's unexpected attack. But neither was the main one. Maybe a few hours of working would get her through the next twenty-four without her losing her mind.

She pulled out her iPad with the plot she'd been working on for her latest book. There was a murder and a crooked police officer. A massive drug bust.

The face of Pauly Monroe flashed into her mind.

She pressed her lips together. "Maybe I won't write a corrupt police officer in this one." She looked at the list of future plot ideas she had. Murder. Murder. Corrupt cop. Murder. Dirty cop. Seemed to be a theme, but she did write a homicide detective, so it wasn't like she was suddenly going to start writing about florists.

Although she liked that idea and wrote, "murder of a florist" and for variation added, "or new love interest. Florist could be a guy. A guy with a dark past who now arranged flowers."

She kind of liked the thought of introducing a hint of romantic interest. Frankie had been alone for a long time now, and Danny had said he intended for Frankie to get her Happily Ever After one day.

Hope put the iPad aside and went to pick up her bowl of curry and white wine.

At the table, she propped the tablet upright and started noodling ideas. Who was this florist? Why would Frankie be talking to a buff male florist who had dark hair, a short beard and a mysterious past?

Ex mobster? Undercover cop? Undercover cop who has been

sent to the neighborhood to look into a corrupt cop on the take…
Maybe someone had pointed the finger at Frankie herself?

Hope noodled for another hour, studiously avoiding the photo
on her living room sideboard.

At ten, she cleaned away the dishes, poured herself another
glass of wine, and went upstairs to run a bath. She soaked in
bubbles and sipped her wine, not looking at the clock and yet
feeling each second tick by in tune to the beat of her heart.

She stayed there for an hour until her skin was pruney and the
bubbles burst. She climbed carefully out of the tub and wrapped
herself in an old ratty terry robe.

She took her time drying off, pulling on flannel pajamas before
going back downstairs, dragging Paige's favorite teddy with her.
She pulled out a cupcake from the freezer and defrosted it.

Poured a third glass of wine, although there was only a half
glass left in the bottle.

She found a fresh birthday candle and some matches. Put
Paige and Danny's photo on the coffee table and pulled Paige's
baby book off the shelf. She took her time leafing through the
familiar pages. Touching Paige's baby face and tiny handprints.
Knowing a lock of her hair and two baby teeth were held in the
little pouches in the back. This practice of memorializing the
living had seemed macabre at the time, and now it was all she had
left.

When the clock struck midnight, she lit the candle and stared
at the orange glow of the flame.

She smiled at the photo of her child frozen in time.

"Happy birthday, baby girl." Hope leaned forward and blew
out the candle. "Happy birthday, Paige."

15

"**S**he's crying." Will Griffin's panicked hiss came in hot over the comms.

Aaron had been about to drop off to sleep, but he'd forgotten to remove his earpiece. Now he rolled over, then sat on the edge of the camp bed they'd set up. He pulled on his tactical pants and a T-shirt. Added his weapon holster more out of habit than necessity.

He padded out of the apartment barefoot so he didn't wake the others.

He nodded to Cadell who stood near the front door, then climbed up the stairs and found Will Griffin standing there with concern furrowing his dark brow.

Aaron took out his earpiece, and Griffin did the same.

They spoke in whispers so as not to disturb everyone. "It was all quiet until about five minutes ago. Then I heard her keening."

Aaron could hear her faintly through the door. She was obviously trying and failing to stifle her sobs.

Was the reality of the possible danger finally sinking in? Or was it simply the stress of being landed in a horrible situation? Or being attacked both verbally and physically within a short space of time?

He checked his watch and saw it was a few minutes after midnight. Then he remembered what Hope had said earlier. "It's her daughter's birthday today."

Griffin pressed his lips together as understanding washed over his features. "Those anniversaries sneak up and hit you hard some days."

Aaron knew Griffin had lost his fiancée, a fellow FBI agent, in a violent attack last year. He squeezed the man's shoulder in sympathy.

"One of us should check on her." Griffin cleared his throat. "Make sure… You know."

Part of Aaron knew it was none of his business, and yet he could no more walk away without checking to see if she was okay than he could fly to Mars. And he was supposed to be in charge here and take on the most dangerous missions. "I'll do it."

Griffin looked relieved.

Aaron eased open the apartment door and slipped inside. He headed up the short staircase, paused to see the usually perfectly attired, endlessly antagonistic Hope Harper wearing plaid pajamas, curled over her knees as she hugged a ragged teddy bear to her chest.

The smell of candle wax hung in the air, and he spotted the little cupcake on the table next to the photograph. A book lay open on the couch beside her.

His heart clutched.

She looked so alone.

He walked over and touched her back. "Hope."

She stiffened but didn't look up.

He knew she heard him. Knew she recognized him, but she didn't pause her tears.

Dammit.

He sat and drew this usually prickly woman into a tentative embrace. The same embrace his own mother had given him when the girl he'd loved had dumped him for his younger firefighter brother and then married the fucker.

That pain had wrecked him. Changed the entire course of his life. But it must be a fraction of what this woman experienced every day since a killer had targeted her family.

Rather than pulling away, she cried harder.

He gathered her to him and leaned back against the sofa and ignored the weird sensation he'd felt each time he touched her. It was probably part of the bonding process. His being responsible for her safety whether she liked it or not. Or maybe because he was beginning to see through the carefully constructed outer defenses, the castle walls, the cannon, the portcullis, all hiding a wild sea of tumultuous emotions and a vulnerable center.

Not cold and heartless.

Fierce and empathetic.

Strong and determined.

Damaged and hurting.

Her tears soaked into his T-shirt, her blonde hair rested beneath his chin, catching in his beard. Her warmth seeped into him, and he wished he could do something other than sit here in silence.

Say something profound.

Act in such a way that he could take away the hurt.

But he didn't tend to put himself out there emotionally any more than Hope did. And what could he say that hadn't been said before? Sorry for your loss? It's not your fault? How many times must she have heard those words? But how often had she allowed herself the quiet comfort of a human touch?

Rarely, he imagined.

Eventually, she stopped weeping and pulled away. "Oh boy. I'm so sorry. I didn't mean to cry all over you."

He gave her a lopsided smile. "I wanted to check on you. It was a risk I had to take."

She wiped fingers under both eyes. Her face was blotchy and her eyes red, but Hope Harper would never look less than beautiful with those sharp cheekbones and wide mobile mouth.

"It's always a toss-up between birthdays, anniversaries, and Christmas as to which day sucks the most."

"You always do this?" He indicated the candle, the cupcake, the baby book.

She pressed her lips together. Nodded.

He reached over and picked up the book. Eased through a couple of pages. "She was beautiful. You were a beautiful family."

Her smile was watery. "Love creates a wonder all its own."

A tight knot formed in Aaron's chest as he thought of his brother and his ex, now expecting a baby. "I guess it does, sometimes, when two people feel the same way about one another."

Hope's gray eyes flashed with keen intelligence that was a hallmark of the woman.

"Are you married, Aaron?"

It was the first time she'd used his given name.

He shook his head, smiled ruefully. "And thankfully no longer in love."

"What happened? Or shouldn't I ask?"

He opened his mouth to fob her off or maybe outright lie like he did with everyone else, even his closest friends. But Hope lived her life with all her heartbreak and worst decisions dangling in the wind, naked for everyone to see.

Lying would be a coward's way out.

Aaron had never been a coward.

"We were both fish biologists studying on a remote island in French Polynesia."

Hope's eyes went wide because studying fish was a long way from working for the FBI.

"I know it's probably not what you expected to hear." He smiled. "We fell in love, got engaged, and I took her home to meet the family. She promptly fell head over heels for my younger brother who was, and still is, a firefighter. Turned out she preferred the buff, sexy version of the Nash brothers more than the geek."

Hope drew back and blinked. "So, what? You went all-out on buff and sexy in an attempt to win her back?"

The fact she thought he was buff and sexy made him smile inside. He shook his head. "That ship had definitely already sailed. I couldn't stay in my PhD program after she dumped me. Couldn't bear seeing her every day. And the scientific community is small and tight-knit, and everyone knows one another." He gave a bitter laugh. "Now I only have to pretend I've forgiven them once or twice a year."

"They're still together?"

"Happily married with a kid on the way. Guess who was best man? The speech was a blast."

"Oh, man. That had to suck." She laughed, but it was in sympathy with him rather than at him.

"Yeah. My mom understands how hard it is for me. Everyone else thinks I'm over it. We're close, my mom and me."

"Mommas always know." Hope's voice hitched. "But why would they expect you to get over a betrayal like that? Not only your fiancée, but your *brother*?" She blew her nose on a tissue. "I never had a sibling, but I can imagine losing your brother probably hurt more than losing the flakey fiancée."

He laughed. He hadn't expected Hope to be the one to make him feel better rather than the other way around. "Yeah. Me and my brother were always close." He shrugged. "We aren't anymore."

"I'm really sorry." She touched his bare arm, and he stared down at where her pale skin lay against the tan of his.

She pulled away. Did she feel that weird kick too? Or was it all in his imagination? At least his pathetic confession had distracted her from her own immense grief.

"So, you joined the FBI out of a sense of revenge?"

"Ha. I guess. I decided to prove she'd made a mistake and that I could be the best of the best, not just a geek. But I didn't want to enlist. The FBI's Hostage Rescue Team is arguably the most elite law enforcement tactical team in the world, so that's what I aimed for instead."

"And where you ended up." Her eyes measured him a little differently now, as if he were more human to her somehow. She picked up the baby book and closed it. Ran her hand lovingly over the photograph before standing and placing it back on the mantel.

"You should get some sleep," he suggested.

She shrugged. "I won't be able to. Not tonight. Usually, I go to the cemetery first thing in the morning before work." The hollows beneath her cheekbones made her look haunted. "I'm angry that I won't be able to do that now, not without a crowd of reporters photographing it and, if Leech is still alive, maybe him finding out." She hugged herself. "The idea of him knowing how much it still hurts makes me feel sick."

"You don't want him getting off on your pain, I get that."

She hugged herself again. "Do you want some tea or coffee? I'm going to have something."

"I should probably get some sleep."

She hid it well, but for a split-second she actually looked disappointed. She stood then and paced. "I'll be fine. Thank you for checking on me. You were very kind, and you didn't need to be. I'm probably better off alone."

Aaron didn't think that was true. He had an idea what might help.

"Get dressed."

Her eyes flashed to his. "Why?"

"I doubt there are any reporters outside right now. Let's go pay your respects to your family."

She blinked.

"If you want to?"

Mutely, she nodded and dashed up the stairs while he rounded up the troops.

16

Hope wrapped her coat more firmly around herself. Despite the warmth of the car, she felt cold inside. She always did on Paige's birthday, a day that bonded both mother and child for eternity, even when one of them was no longer living.

Being held by Aaron Nash earlier had felt strangely wonderful and incredibly self-indulgent. She didn't usually let her guard down, but they were stuck together for the foreseeable future, and he'd caught her at a low point.

It seemed surreal looking at him now. He looked like a warrior going into battle rather than someone who'd let her cry all over his T-shirt.

She needed to pull it together.

She didn't have the luxury of public grief, not any longer, not after that first awful week and then, later, the funeral when all she'd wanted to do was climb inside with them and be buried alive. Maybe it was knowing he was a professional who wouldn't leak the information to the press. Or maybe it was some innate level of trust.

Aaron Nash struck her as honest to the bone. She hoped he hadn't lied about the former fiancée to garner sympathy, but she doubted it. It was a little too personal of a sad story.

She could imagine how hurt Danny would have been if she'd been stupid enough to fall for Brendan after she and Danny became engaged. It would have gutted him.

She glanced again at the lean profile softened slightly by the trimmed beard. She wasn't sure what to make of Aaron Nash. He certainly wasn't who she'd expected when he'd first turned up on her doorstep giving her orders.

A yawn hit her. Boy, she was tired.

She had a full day in court tomorrow—today now—but voir dire wasn't that strenuous, and her paralegal had done most of the hard work. Some things were more important than sleep. Visiting her daughter on her birthday meant everything to Hope, and she was so grateful Aaron had suggested this clandestine nighttime visit.

It took a little more than twenty minutes to get to New Calvary Cemetery in Mattapan as there was no traffic on the roads and these men drove at high speed despite the icy conditions.

They avoided the city center, drove south-west on Harvard Street then left into the cemetery itself. A large, black wrought-iron gate blocked their way. The two SUVs drew to a halt, engines running.

She'd forgotten that the cemetery might be closed this time of night and leaned forward to tell them she'd climb the low stone wall—it was hardly a barrier—and walk to the burial plot.

Aaron raised his hand to ask her to wait a moment, obviously listening to the earpiece he wore.

One of the men climbed out of the second vehicle and made short work of the lock. Hope winced at the laws they might be breaking, but they were the FBI, and she was going to let them deal with the fallout and plead the fifth if asked.

The gates opened, and the SUVs pulled inside moving in a tight, fast formation. She felt as if she were in a thriller movie rather than living her own life.

If only this were make-believe.

"Where to?" the driver asked. He was a big guy named

Livingstone. His eyes were a brilliant green and generally, whenever he looked at her, hard with disapproval.

But Hope didn't need his or anyone else's approval. "Section 23. Far south-west corner."

The few inches of snow that had fallen that evening had melted from the roads, which now looked like black ribbons in the moonlight.

The silence became unbearable, which was ironic for a woman who lived alone except for her cat. "Danny's mother chose this place. She's a devout Catholic."

She shivered because she hated to think of her daughter and husband in that hole in the ground, but she'd needed to give his mother a say in things, a role to play. Burial had been important to Mary Harper, and she visited here every week. Hope had barely been functioning at the time.

"If I die, tell them to cremate me. Spread a little of my ashes on their grave, and toss the rest in the ocean or use it as fertilizer."

Aaron eyes glittered in the reflection of the moon. "You aren't going to die."

Hope gave him a tight smile. "We are all going to die."

"Not on this op—" He cut himself off. "Not because Leech may have escaped." He changed the wording, but it was a useful reminder that despite his kindness, she was an op. Not a friend.

She pressed her lips together and looked away. The driver pulled to a stop, and the other car hung back a little. She had *four* bodyguards with her. Two more had stayed behind to monitor the house.

They began to open their doors.

She closed her eyes. Curled her fingers into fists. "I'd like to do this alone."

They all paused. Waited for Aaron's decision.

"Birdman, walk a perimeter. Livingstone and Cadell stay behind the wheels. I'll accompany Ms. Harper from a short distance." His black eyes met hers across the seat. "That's the best I can do."

"Thank you."

It was enough.

She clutched the small pot of pansies she'd bought a week ago, before this thing with Leech had kicked off and her only concern had been the weather. She pushed open the door. Aaron followed her out. The frigid wind cut into her exposed skin. The snow had stopped for now, but there was more forecast.

She led the way, feeling oddly exposed and not as present or in the moment as she wanted to be. Maybe it was the wine, or the crying jag.

Or maybe the fact she usually did this alone.

The snow and sodden grass soaked her boots and the bottom of her jeans, freezing her toes. She wove through the headstones, careful not to step in the soft indents of the graves themselves. It was impossible to read the names at night, but she knew where she was going.

She arrived at the third grave from the end. Second row from the bottom. Blew out a breath and stood in the darkness as the icy air kissed her face. Peace surrounded her as she absorbed the quiet, and let it soothe her tortured soul. Her heartbeat slowed.

This wasn't about Leech or the FBI. This was about a little girl who never got to grow up.

What would her daughter have looked like now with her blonde hair and Danny's bright blue eyes? Beautiful. So beautiful. What would she have wanted for her birthday? Probably a cell phone or maybe a puppy.

Instead, Hope made a yearly donation to the children's hospital in her name. Would she have had a best friend? Definitely. No lonely, awkward middle school years for her baby. Would she have liked sports? She'd been a fast runner as a kid, so maybe she'd have been an athlete like her daddy.

Would she have had a brother or a sister by now? Hope liked to think so. Her mouth went dry at the thought of the child who'd never even got to exist. Leech had killed them all that day.

Hope allowed herself to remember Danny on the day Paige

had made him a father. So handsome and hands-on. They'd both cried when Paige had arrived, tears of happiness because they'd been so full of joy.

Their lives together had been short, but they'd been almost perfect. The ache of being left behind was still strong, but it wasn't an open, festering wound any longer—at least, not most days. The real trouble was she didn't know who she was without her family. Queen bitch attorney. Secretive best-selling author. Widow. *Woman*?

She wasn't sure about the latter.

The years stretched endlessly in front of her, and she flinched away from what she saw there.

She touched the headstone and then crouched to place the pot of pansies beside the evergreen wreath Mary had put there at Christmas. The plant pot rocked unevenly.

Mary and Brendan both left flowers and trinkets here regularly. Hope turned on her flashlight to clear a space and froze.

Things had been scattered around the grave like garbage. Only the wreath, her pretty pansies, and a knife that glistened dark crimson rested against the white marble. Plus, an envelope with Hope's name printed on the front that was propped against the unyielding stone. She leaned closer. Someone had smeared something that looked a lot like blood over Paige's and Danny's names.

Fury rose up and engulfed her. She wanted to scream.

"Aaron," she gritted out.

He stepped forward. "What is it?"

"You're going to need to call in a crime scene unit."

17

An hour later, Aaron stood inside the tent that had been erected over the headstones to protect it and any evidence from the elements. The presumptive test had come back positive for blood, and Aaron hoped to hell it wasn't from a new human victim.

Lincoln Frazer wore his usual business attire along with a black woolen overcoat, plus Tyvek booties and surgical gloves as he crouched carefully near the grave marker.

Aaron had sent Hope home with the others and told her to get some sleep. Whether she obeyed or not, whether she could forget enough to rest, was doubtful, but he didn't want her here when the press turned up, which was probably happening right about now.

Frazer lifted the envelope and carefully used a scalpel to slit it open. A tech from the local field office held open two evidence bags and Frazer used sterile forceps to remove what looked like a photograph. He placed the envelope in one bag and the photograph in the other, sealing them both.

The profiler came over to him and showed him the image. It was of Hope crying at the funeral seven years ago. On the back was written, "Your Turn Next."

Aaron did not like the direct threat against Hope.

Frazer handed the sealed bags back to the tech to preserve the chain of evidence. Then the ERTs moved in to start processing the scene. Although he and Frazer were both trained to collect physical and biological evidence, Aaron wanted this done quickly and efficiently by experts. He didn't want any mistakes. And he wanted that gravestone washed clean and sparkling before the sun rose.

He and Frazer headed outside to give the techs the space to work, removing their protective gear and placing it in the garbage sack provided.

"Serial killers often visit the graves of their victims—I remember that from your lectures at the academy." Aaron stared at the smattering of houses that surrounded the cemetery.

"I should have insisted on cameras being set up here and on the other graves." Frazer sounded pissed too. "Something I intend to have remedied shortly."

Too late for that here, now, and they both knew it. Leech would be a fool to return to this scene if he truly valued his freedom. They'd wasted an opportunity.

Julius Leech, Reggie Somack, and Perry Roberts had shot straight to the top of the US Marshal's 15 Most Wanted Fugitives list. But the USMS's refusal to use FBI's resources, notably Lincoln Frazer, smacked of interdepartmental politics and personality clashes. Aaron didn't care about politics. He only wanted Hope—his principal—and the general public, safe.

Frazer's lips pinched. "I didn't think he'd play games at this point."

"You thought he'd skip the country?"

"Assuming he's alive." Frazer nodded. "That or move in for the kill on whoever is unlucky enough to be on his hit list."

"You think Leech has an actual list of people he wants dead?"

"I'm sure of it." Frazer tapped the side of his head. "Up here as they didn't find anything in his cell. He's had years in maximum security to hone his grudges." The man blew a big breath that clouded the frosty night air. "He never taunted the cops or victims' families before though."

Aaron turned to face the man. "You don't think this was Leech?"

Frazer shook his head. "Might be a disciple or someone trying to freak out Hope."

It had worked. "Dangerous?"

"Potentially," Frazer acknowledged. "I'll let you know how potentially after the techs analyze the blood to see if it's human or not, which will be shortly." Frazer shrugged. "Whether it's a copycat serial killer or another version of Minnie Ramon I can't say yet. They could simply want Hope to suffer but not want to put themselves at risk."

"One of the other victims' family members?" Aaron hated that idea. He wanted to arrest people who were intrinsically evil. He didn't want to have to arrest people who were twisted by grief and making poor choices—but he would. Hope was grieving, too, and rather than lashing out she'd dedicated her life to serving the criminal justice system.

What did she have to do to atone for getting Leech released before people forgave her? What more did she have to lose? Especially when it had been a cop's fault for planting the evidence and then suddenly feeling guilty enough about it to confess before he took his own life.

Something about that whole scenario smelled off to Aaron. He wanted to read the police reports for himself.

One of the evidence techs came out of the tent carrying a field test. "The blood isn't human."

Aaron breathed a sigh of relief.

Frazer said nothing.

"We'll analyze it and attempt to pin down a source. Given the quantity, I'd guess cow or pig. Probably obtained from a local butcher."

"People can walk in and order a pint of blood?"

Frazer's lip twitched. "You can buy anything you want if you know where to shop."

A point that had been brutally demonstrated last month by a serial killer who'd auctioned his murders online. A killer who'd murdered one of Aaron's colleagues in cold blood and doomed another woman to widowhood.

The tech nodded and went back to work.

"Takes a certain mindset to desecrate a grave," Frazer said thoughtfully. "Especially a child's grave."

"Did they know it was Paige's birthday and that it's Hope's habit to visit here on anniversaries? Or was the vandalism itself enough for this person and the rest is a happy coincidence?"

"I think whoever did this wanted Hope to see it and for it to inflict suffering. But they must also know the chances were pretty low given Leech is unaccounted for and she's under FBI protection. I'm surprised you allowed her to come out here at all."

Aaron grimaced. "It was my suggestion."

Frazer raised a brow.

"I found her crying in her living room. She'd lit a candle on a cupcake for Paige's birthday, and she was going through old photos." Losing a kid had to hurt. "Said there was no way she'd sleep. Said she usually visited the grave today but that she wouldn't because of the press being around to take photos. Didn't want Leech getting off on her pain should he see it. I thought a quick trip in the small hours would avoid any fuss."

How wrong he'd been.

The wind rattled the branches of the nearby trees. Local cops manned the perimeter, and he could see the news vans stacking up along the fence.

"The UNSUB could have counted on the press seeing the grave and splashing those images all over the news. Hope wouldn't be able to miss them then."

Frazer nodded. "Quite possibly. The fact someone left a dagger speaks to theatrics which was never really Leech's style."

"Didn't Leech use a letter opener to stab his victims?"

"Correct." Frazer looked impressed.

"So, like you said, this probably wasn't Leech, but one of his fans or one of Hope's enemies. Either way, it doesn't make our job any easier." Not that it mattered. Aaron would do the job regardless. Nothing would physically harm Hope under his watch. Psychological damage was harder to defend against when the blows kept coming from all directions.

Frazer had a calculating gleam in his eyes that Aaron could make out in the glow of the klieg lights. "She seems to like you."

Aaron frowned. "What?"

"She isn't a woman who opens up to strangers, nor does she generally cry in people's presence—not since the funeral."

He shrugged. "I guess she was caught off guard by the situation."

"Hope Harper is rarely caught off guard. She likes you. See if you can use that to make her stay safe and stop taunting the bastard."

Use it? How the hell could he use it? "You're referring to what she said to the press last night."

"Paraphrasing what I saw on the news—I'm not scared of the asshole, but I'm surprised he escaped given he's an incompetent moron."

"She wasn't exactly handing out olive branches." Aaron's laugh was a bitter bark of frustration.

"Can't blame her, but no need for her to recklessly taunt him into coming after her either."

"You think that's what she was doing? Deliberately taunting him?"

"Absolutely." Frazer nodded. "She would rather he focus on her than anyone else."

Aaron pressed his lips together to stop from cursing. Then he scanned the nearby cops. "That police detective, Janelli, was there last night, the one who was investigated after Monroe killed himself." Aaron nodded toward the grave. "Seems like the sort of thing a vindictive cop might do."

Frazer did a similar perusal of the patrol units. "I've spoken with him in the past. He has never varied from the story where he saw Detective Monroe legitimately collect that evidence from the scene."

Anything else would have gotten him thrown off the force.

"If he wasn't dirty, he has to harbor some serious resentment for being suspended and his reputation being tarnished. And for losing his partner." Aaron shifted his weight to his other foot. He needed to get back to the house and go over the latest development with the team. "Enough motive to have his whereabouts last night checked, perhaps?"

"I can't officially request that information."

"If the DA's office requests the information or Internal Affairs is brought in, there will be renewed antagonism against Hope, and these are the people she has to rely on in court and to protect her when we leave." Aaron held Frazer's gaze. "Alex Parker could check into it. I know you guys work a lot of cases together. Get him to work this one for us."

Frazer's lip twitched. "You notice a great deal, Nash."

"I pay attention."

"An underrated quality." Frazer paused. "I'll ask Parker to look into Janelli. If he agrees, I'll pass on any relevant information he discovers."

That was something anyway. "Want a ride back to where you're staying?"

"No, thanks. I borrowed a car from my hosts."

Aaron spotted a gleaming BMW sitting behind his black Suburban. "How does Ryan Sullivan know the Hayeses?"

Frazer shook his head. "Not my story to tell."

"Guess I'll have to beat it out of him."

"Just when I thought you were different from the other HRT louts."

Aaron gave the guy a shark's smile. It felt good to think about something other than a serial killer targeting someone under his protection. "We all enjoy inflicting pain when the situation demands it."

"Sadists."

"What are friends for?" He lowered his voice. "I don't like the way attacks against Hope are escalating."

"I don't either," admitted Frazer. "I don't like the idea of her being harmed."

"Were you and she ever…?" Aaron let the question hang in the air even though it was none of his business.

Frazer gave him a look he couldn't decipher. "That's an interesting question, Operator Nash."

He ground his teeth. That wasn't an answer. "Might be important to the op."

Frazer unlocked his car with the fob and pulled open the door. "Hope Harper is an incredibly attractive woman who, I guess on paper, is exactly my type." He kept his voice down, both of them aware of the uniforms nearby. "But she was never interested in anyone except her late husband, and I never thought of her as anything except a wickedly smart attorney and a grieving widow and mother. Until recently, I didn't think she'd ever be interested in anyone else ever again."

That made Aaron frown. "What happened recently? Is there someone I need to know about?"

Frazer simply smiled at him and slid into the car, shaking his head. Backed up and drove away.

What the fuck happened recently?

Aaron opened his door and slid into the heated seat of the SUV. Didn't matter. No one was getting close to the fierce but vulnerable woman he'd been tasked with keeping safe.

Especially not Julius freaking Leech.

18

At 6:45 a.m., Hope heard the knock on her door. She padded over to the top of the hallway, leaned over the railing. "Come in!"

She hadn't slept much, but she'd showered and at least felt as if she might make it through the day. She wasn't about to let some asshole desecrating a sacred place destroy her. Instead, she'd let the act fuel her anger and strengthen her resolve.

She'd called Brendan on the way home and told him what had happened. And, yes, she was using her personal connections, but Danny was Brendan's brother and Paige his niece, and they'd both been victims of a vicious murderer, which fell under his professional remit as a homicide detective. Add to that the Catholic outrage, and maybe someone would actually catch the sick sonofabitch who'd done this.

But it wasn't Leech. It was too sloppy. Too risky. Leech considered himself refined and sophisticated. Seven years in maximum security might have blunted some of those fine edges, but she didn't think so.

Aaron Nash looked up as he opened the door, but his dark eyes told her nothing. The other man, Will Griffin, stood outside the door. She sent Will a nod, feeling guilty for the fact he'd been standing there half the night.

Aaron's brow creased with concern as he came up the stairs. "Did you get any rest?"

"No. Did they find Leech yet? Or the bastard who vandalized the grave?"

"Not yet." Interest sparked in those midnight eyes. "Why do you think it wasn't Leech who vandalized the grave?"

"Not his style. And not his choice of murder weapon." Her stomach clenched. So many things she didn't want to remember kept forcing themselves back into her brain. "Tell me it wasn't human blood on the headstone."

Aaron followed her into the kitchen where the percolator bubbled on the stove. "Previously frozen pig's blood."

"Thank God for that." Good news. Although not for the poor pig. She slipped her arm around her middle. She couldn't have borne it if someone else had been murdered. "Is it all over the news?"

Aaron nodded, and a rock settled in her stomach. "But no pictures. Crime scene techs cleaned the site up before they left."

Relief washed through her, surprising in its ferocity. Her gaze flashed to his. She'd planned to call a company as soon as she was notified the scene was released. "Whom do I thank for that?"

Aaron said nothing.

Their gazes locked briefly, but she had to look away. This man had held her last night while she wept. He'd seen enough cracks in her armor to make it harder to pretend she was unaffected by small acts of kindness. "Thank you."

Aaron shrugged. "They're the ones who did the work."

But he'd asked them to. He'd understood what it would have done to her to see her family's headstone smeared with blood on the news—today of all days.

She didn't know what to do with her hands, so she pulled mugs out of the cupboard. It wasn't often she felt awkward in her own home. Whom would she be awkward around? The cat?

She forced the feeling away. "What was in the envelope?"

"A photograph of you that had been printed out."

"And annotated with 'Die Bitch' or something equally imaginative."

"Close enough."

She didn't want to know. "Did they find any other evidence?"

"They lifted some fingerprints. Might have DNA on the envelope. Collected all the items, except the pansies. They plan to courier everything first thing to the National Laboratory marked priority. You have Frazer to thank for that."

Frazer wanted Leech back inside as much as she did. He wouldn't want her gratitude, but he had it. "I'd like to prosecute whoever did this, so let's hope they were stupid enough to leave something identifying behind." She opened the fridge and pulled out cream. "It's one thing going after me. It's something entirely different going after my family."

"Talking of Frazer." Aaron's voice firmed. "He thinks you used your statement to the press last night to deliberately taunt Leech. To get him to come after you."

Hope pulled a face. "Assuming he's out there, better he comes after me than someone who doesn't have twenty-four-hour protection."

"Your twenty-four-hour protection detail are flesh and blood people too."

The breath whooshed out of her. She hadn't thought of it that way. She hadn't really thought at all. She'd lashed out in the moment.

"While it might be a ballsy move to provoke an escaped serial killer, I'd rather you didn't put my team in the line of fire without discussing it with us first."

Shame filled her. "You're right. I didn't think. I'm sorry."

"I know you'd never deliberately endanger anyone." His eyes softened. "If there comes a time when we know Leech is alive and decide to lure him someplace, we'll control that scenario."

Hope's spine stiffened. "That doesn't mean you get to *control* me, Aaron."

"I don't want to control you, Hope." He stared at her for another long moment, apparently seeing through her words and her sharp tone to the fear that lay beneath. "I am simply trying to keep you alive."

He'd pressed one of her hot buttons, and she'd reacted with a reflexive snap. "Sorry." *Again.*

"I can take it. Look, in a week's time this will seem like some distant dream."

"Promise?" Her lips quirked, but she realized with sudden insight, she'd miss this man. A little. Maybe she wasn't as antisocial as she thought. Perhaps she was finally ready to emerge out of the dark hole that her life had been for so long. She flinched away from the idea. There was safety in grief. She didn't have to put herself out there as anything except a capable attorney, or a grief-stricken widow, or a mother who'd lost her child.

It wasn't ballsy to provoke Leech. It was effortless.

People living their lives like it wasn't the end of the world, that was ballsy.

"Every law enforcement agency in the country is looking for Leech and the other two escaped convicts. If they *are* alive, they won't get far." Aaron touched his earpiece a second before she heard feet pound on her stairs.

His dark brow rose. "Apparently, your brother-in-law is here again and is still not a fan of handing over his weapon."

"I bet." She grabbed another mug and poured three cups of coffee, just like she had yesterday morning.

Aaron tilted his head. "You don't seem surprised. Does he come over every morning?"

"Not every day but often enough. Neither of us sleeps well." She waved away the explanation. It didn't matter. "I actually prefer the morning visits."

Easier to escape with the excuse of work than when he came

over for a drink in the evening. As Brendan was pretty much her only visitor, she shouldn't be so critical.

"I called him on the way back from the cemetery. That way I didn't have to tell my mother-in-law about what I'd found but had him do it instead. Mary would want to know straight away. Even at that time of night, she'd want to know. I expect she'll be along to put everything to rights as soon as Brendan gives her the all-clear." Hope could do it, but Mary would do it again, regardless. It gave the woman a focus, a purpose. A bit like being a prosecutor did for Hope.

She added cream and sugar to Brendan's mug. Milk to her own and left Aaron's black the way he'd taken it yesterday.

"And that way you get the Boston Police Department doing their own little investigation even if the FBI has taken over this particular crime scene."

"It can't hurt." Hope shrugged as she took a sip of the strong brew. "I can usually finagle information out of the Feds if I need it."

"Frazer."

She shrugged. "And Marshall Hayes. We're friends. I first met him as a defense attorney, but he's forgiven me. That's one of his wife's paintings above the fireplace. Josie and I bonded over serial killer experiences—not that we ever speak about them." *Like* Fight Club. "Unfortunately, Special Agent in Charge Salinger of the Boston Field Office is not a fan of mine. In here," she called out as she heard the door open.

Brendan strode into the kitchen and drew up short at the sight of Aaron leaning casually against the counter.

"You okay?" He ignored Aaron and walked toward her with his arms wide.

She held her coffee in front of her to prevent the full-on hug and accepted a side squeeze. "I could have done without this added drama, but I'm fine. Tired, but fine."

He helped himself to the coffee she'd made for him.

"Scene's all cleaned up. Press never got a single photograph."

Hope didn't miss the fact that, while he didn't directly claim responsibility for the act, he didn't give kudos where it was due either. Danny had idolized his older brother but hadn't been blind to his flaws. Neither was she.

"Any word from BPD? Were you able to find any traffic cam footage or eyewitnesses?" Hope inhaled the scent of caffeine and her brain cells perked up.

"Uniforms canvassed the area but nothing. They plan to go back tonight in case they missed anyone." Brendan scratched his head. "Not exactly a hive of activity even in the daytime. We'll take a look at traffic cams. If Leech is in town, we'll get him."

"I doubt it was Leech."

Lucy ran through with an accusing meow. He'd been asleep upstairs and was obviously worried he'd missed breakfast. Hope squeezed a pureed treat into a small dish then placed fresh kibble in his food bowl.

"Whoever it was, they're gonna pay," Brendan said angrily. "No one gets away with that."

"What about Janelli?"

Brendan made a noise. "He'd never do that to me."

"He'd do it to me," she said dryly. "Could pass it off as a prank to his fellow officers."

"He wouldn't do that to *me*," Brendan insisted. "He's Catholic too. And don't go saying anything like that where other people might hear you. Christ, the whole fucking department will think you're crazy."

Hope flinched but hid it behind another sip of coffee.

Brendan scrubbed his hand over his face. From the luggage he packed under his eyes, she doubted he'd gotten any more sleep than she had.

"Don't forget to let me know if they find anything," Hope reminded him.

"Sure."

"How is Mary holding up?"

Brendan grimaced. "She went to early mass, which will help."

"Did you stay with her last night?"

Brendan sniffed and nodded. Checked his watch. "Promised to pick her up and take her over to the cemetery before my shift starts. My lieutenant okayed me being a little late on account of being up all night."

"If only the judge in my current trial was so amenable." She didn't mean it though. She needed to get out of her home and out of her own head. Today of all days, she needed to work. "What about the Back Bay murder?"

"We closed it. Got an ID on the guy from the CCTV footage. We hauled him in, and he confessed after twenty minutes sweating in the box."

"Good news. Saves us all some time and effort and the taxpayers a lot of money."

Brendan shot Aaron a look from under his brows. "I hear the Feds are no closer to catching Leech and the other two escapees than they were yesterday."

She hated the thought that the system had failed to protect people the way it was supposed to. She was part of that system. They all were. "Presumably the marshals are checking in with his former acquaintances and seeing who he communicated with while in prison?"

"Presumably." Aaron blew the top of his coffee then took a sip.

She cocked her head. "You're not telling me everything."

"The USMS is in charge of the operation," the HRT operator said somberly. "Ask Frazer if you want more details."

Brendan sneered and turned away.

Hope wanted to push Aaron for more information, but she knew he wouldn't say anything in front of Brendan. He had integrity. Or maybe he didn't trust either of them. And why should he? His job demanded carefully guarded secrets and self-restraint. As an attorney, she understood and admired that.

"Forecast is for more snow." Brendan sniffed again and brought her attention back to him.

"Make sure Mary wraps up warm before she heads to the cemetery. The last thing we want is her catching a cold."

The woman was thin as a whippet and time had worn her down. Time and grief. At least she had her faith.

Brendan put his mug in the dishwasher, and Aaron followed suit.

"We still on for Sunday lunch?" Brendan shot her a look.

Hope gave a sharp bark of laughter. "Seriously?"

"We shouldn't let Leech dictate how we live our lives."

Just family, apparently.

"Sunday lunch?" Aaron's eyes were sharp with questions.

"Sunday roast at my ma's. Feds aren't invited." Brendan puffed out his chest.

Damn, he was annoying. It was a good thing she had to love him.

Aaron cocked his head as he looked at her, his expression clearly asking, "Will you tell him, or shall I?"

"If Leech is still on the run, we may need to reschedule."

"They can sit outside and watch the house. It's a couple of lousy hours at most."

"We can do a walk-through of the house and set up a perimeter," Aaron suggested.

"That'll look like a mob family dinner for Christ's sake."

"I'm not leaving my principal without protection—"

"She'll have protection. Me." Brendan was on the tip of his toes, going nose-to-nose with the much larger federal agent, banging his chest with his pointer finger for emphasis.

Aaron shoved the guy back. "Stay out of my face, Detective. This is not up for debate."

Brendan looked like he might take a swing. Hope doubted that would work out well.

"If Leech is still on the run, why don't you and Mary come here on Sunday? I'll cook roast beef and Yorkshire pudding. I think I can remember how." Not that his mother had ever appreciated her cooking.

Brendan looked comically taken aback. Hope never entertained. Even when Danny was alive, he was the one who'd cooked.

Aaron narrowed his eyes thoughtfully.

"It's Brendan and his mother. I'll order the groceries in." She shrugged. "Seems easier all around." Maybe she'd make enough for the men protecting her too. A show of appreciation even though she resented the Attorney General for insisting they be here.

It wasn't like they had a choice either.

Aaron pulled his lips to one side as he considered. "We can make that work."

Brendan's mouth curled, but thankfully he didn't say anything more.

Hope put her mug in the dishwasher and closed it. "Okay, then. Time for me to head to work."

"A little early for court." Aaron straightened, looking alert.

You'd never have known he'd been up all night.

"I need to go into the office first. I want to make sure Minnie Ramon is okay after her night in the cells."

"What's this?" Brendan demanded.

"A woman pulled a knife on Hope in the DA's office."

"I thought you were supposed to protect her?" Brendan blustered.

"Which is why Mrs. Ramon is currently in custody and Hope is unharmed," Aaron stated.

Hope rolled her eyes. "Enough, Brendan. I don't have time for a dick-measuring contest."

She went into the lounge, gave Lucifer a final stroke, pulled on her beige winter coat, and then slipped into her tall brown leather boots at the door.

She went to lift a banker's box, but Aaron beat her to it.

"These are the files Frazer wanted?"

She nodded.

"I'll get one of the team to make a couple of copies if that's okay? Before court. I'd like to read through everything too. Give me a better idea of the sort of person Leech is."

"Knock yourself out." It would save her time, and Colin had other things to do. She grabbed her briefcase.

"What's in the boxes?" asked Brendan.

"The FBI want to go over any files I have from the first trial to look for any possible places Leech might go or people he might seek out for help."

"That motherfucker is probably in Canada by now." Brendan followed them both out of the apartment.

Hope was not comforted by that thought. She didn't want Leech to be free. She wanted him punished or dead.

She nodded to Will Griffin on the way out. "I hope you get more sleep than we managed last night."

The man smiled, and his very attractive face lit up. "I hope so too. Stay safe at work today, ma'am."

"Call me Hope. Ma'am makes me feel old enough to be your grandmother."

"Hope." Griffin nodded.

She smiled. Despite the weirdness of the situation, she had the impression that some of these people genuinely cared. She wasn't simply a job or an *op*. She wasn't only a former defense attorney who'd messed up and gotten her family killed.

She was a human being with feelings and thoughts on how she got to live her life.

She hated that it mattered.

19

Aaron spent most of the day in a drafty hallway reading transcripts of the first trial. Lunch was brief, and they used one of the side rooms to eat and strategize. According to Cowboy, who was in the courtroom today, jury selection was a blood bath of epic proportions as Hope and Beasley fought it out like Apollo Creed and Rocky Balboa.

It crossed Aaron's mind that Jeff Beasley might have motive to hurt or unsettle Hope, and the perfect way to do so was to have pig's blood thrown on her family's headstone. He could easily have hired someone to do it too.

Aaron had texted Frazer with the suggestion hours ago but hadn't heard back from the guy. He'd since occupied himself with the witness testimonies from Leech's first trial and was right now reading about the detective who'd later killed himself.

Boston police detectives had initially questioned Leech about the crimes because the guy's fancy Maserati was spotted parked near the first two murder locations—proving Leech was not exactly a towering genius. Monroe's partner the first time he'd questioned Leech had been one Brendan Harper.

How had that gone down at family dinners?

By the time of the third double-homicide, Detective Monroe had been paired with a rookie detective named Lewis Janelli.

The used tissue had been the only biological evidence that had directly linked Leech to the crimes, and Hope had gone after them at length in an attempt to pour doubt on the item.

What are the chances of a murderer who'd been careful enough to wear a ski mask, gloves, and a condom suddenly leaves behind a used tissue at the scene? Rather convenient for the cops, don't you think?

She'd pushed both Monroe and Janelli on the stand, and the junior detective had lost his temper on more than one occasion and been reprimanded by the judge for it. But she hadn't shaken the veteran detective Pauly Monroe's story. Not one jot.

According to Monroe, he and Brendan Harper had interviewed Leech in his expensive mansion in Beacon Street. Hope hadn't directly accused the cops of doing anything illegal, but she had established both men had been alone for a short period of time in Leech's house while Paul Monroe had used the bathroom, thus allowing the jury to draw their own conclusions as to the opportunity they had to illegally gather evidence. Another attorney from the firm, not Hope, had cross-examined Brendan Harper, but he'd been unshakeable when it came to that first visit to Leech's house. Brendan had taken every opportunity to remind the jury that Leech had been holding a letter opener for most of the interview—a letter opener that was similar to the weapon used in the murders, a letter opener sharp enough to kill. Brendan claimed he'd been nervous for his own life because Leech gave off such "creepy" vibes.

The defense had objected. The judge had overruled.

On balance Aaron figured the prosecution had found enough circumstantial to go with that one piece of biological evidence to make it likely the jury would convict Leech of the six homicides and three rapes, plus all the other associated crimes. All until the night before closing testimony when Pauly Monroe appeared to have a crisis of conscience and had emailed his boss and Hope to confess he'd lied on the stand and that he'd taken the tissue from the Leech mansion and dropped it at the next murder scene while no one was looking.

Then he'd shot himself.

Which no one had anticipated.

The guy had had a drinking problem which had come to light after his death. His blood alcohol levels had been almost nine times the legal driving limit. Aaron was surprised the guy could type at all when he'd been that drunk.

Hope had moved for a dismissal based on the lack of any physical evidence and the fact BPD had demonstrated clear bias against her client along with willingness to perjure themselves on the stand, which put all the circumstantial evidence in doubt.

The judge had agreed and granted the motion. Leech had walked free.

Six hours later, he'd brutally murdered Danny and Paige Harper in their own home.

Aaron rubbed the back of his neck. Didn't make sense to him, but then he wasn't a vicious sociopath.

While he understood the animosity from Janelli and some of the other local cops toward Hope, the fact was BPD had self-sabotaged and blown the case. Leech walked free because of a crooked police officer and a lawyer who understood her job.

Could Leech have somehow gotten to that detective, hacked into his email, staged his suicide? Leech had plenty of money. Perhaps his assistant—a man who still worked for Leech, apparently—had organized a hit. But there had been no evidence of a struggle. No suggestion of foul play. And Monroe was an armed, veteran cop on his home turf.

Aaron wanted to see those police files too.

His cell buzzed. Cowboy texted they were nearly done. On cue, Beasley's goons arrived, mirror-like shine on the shoes, black suits, visible earpieces. They stood on the other side of the courtroom doors from where Aaron sat, scowling at anyone who got within six feet—because *that* stopped bullets.

Aaron tucked the file away in the small pack he'd brought

with him and stood. Five minutes later the doors swung open, and people streamed out, clearly happy to be done for the day.

Jeff Beasley swept out and away, footsteps ringing out on the tile floor. His color was high, and his eyes glittered with rage. Four assistants scurried in the wake of his bodyguards today.

Aaron headed inside the courtroom and heard Hope's laughter ring out as Ryan Sullivan regaled her with some story. As he got closer, Aaron realized it was about the armed standoff they'd attended last December in Washington State when Payne Novak had stripped naked to retrieve the body of a man who'd been shot.

"Novak figured that if the people inside of the compound knew he was unarmed they wouldn't shoot his skinny white ass."

"A bit of a risk, surely?" Hope sent Aaron a quick glance.

"Bat shit crazy," Ryan agreed. "But it worked. And he got the girl in the end, too, so I guess it wasn't as cold as I remember."

Aaron gave Ryan a quelling glance. Ryan only grinned.

Hope and Ryan had a lot in common, Aaron realized. Both had lost spouses they loved, albeit under wildly different circumstances. They both still grieved deeply, but Ryan managed to find oblivion in the arms of countless women.

Not that he'd seen the guy with anyone except Meghan Donnelly recently. Cowboy and the first ever female Hostage Rescue Team operator had been paired up in Maine last week on an undercover op as fake boyfriend and girlfriend. Meghan had somehow managed not to shoot the guy even though he spent most of his time deliberately provoking the people he liked most. Aaron wondered if Ryan had spoken to their colleague Grady Steel yet, but figured Grady needed at least another week to cool down.

"How'd it go?" he asked.

"Great, thanks to my secret weapon here." Hope indicated the woman next to her.

Aaron turned his attention to a shorter woman who had blue-black hair and brown skin and ruby lips that shone with gloss.

"I'd say we are more than holding our own." She stuck out her hand. "Aisha Rashi-Gardner. Hope's paralegal."

He shook her hand, allowing himself to relax slightly. They were in a guarded building after all—another op popped into his head from mid-December, when White Supremacists had stormed another courtroom and HRT had been tasked with taking it back. Livingstone had broken his arm that day.

He watched the bailiff, who clearly wanted to lock up and go home.

Hope packed up her belongings and Colin, the intern, hovered in the background as he waited for his next instruction. He looked tired too. Apparently, no one had gotten any sleep last night.

"Unfortunately, as the defense made such a meal of the process, we are not yet finished with jury selection." Hope shot a quick glance around the nearly empty room. "However, the fact Beasley has to come back tomorrow gives me a certain perverse pleasure."

"Me too. No amount of money could entice me to work for that asshole." Aisha's eyes widened as she realized what she'd said. "I didn't mean—"

Hope patted her arm. "I agree. At the time, we needed the money, but more importantly I needed job security. Making partner was supposed to enable me to spend more time with my family, but we all know how that turned out." Her voice was understandably rough.

"I am sorry. I sounded like a judgmental bitch." Aisha squeezed Hope's hand.

"Don't be. I feel exactly the same way now." Hope swung her coat around her shoulders, and Aaron held it while she fished for her sleeve.

Cowboy shot him a look.

What?

The other man pulled a knowing expression which Aaron ignored.

It was always something with that guy.

"Can we offer you a ride, Aisha?" Hope offered.

Aaron held onto his patience. Apparently, they were becoming a taxi service, but it stopped them being too predictable—until that too became a habit to be used as a weapon by the wrong person.

"Not today, hon. My man is meeting me for an early anniversary dinner at some fancy restaurant."

"Lucky you. And happy anniversary."

The woman's expression sobered, perhaps remembering that Hope no longer celebrated anniversaries. "See you tomorrow. We're going to get the best jury imaginable."

"I have a great imagination," Hope warned.

"So do I." Aisha grinned. "Along with a mile-wide vindictive streak. See you at nine tomorrow in your office. I'll ride over with you, especially if we get more snow as forecast. I'll see what else I can dig up in the meantime."

Aisha headed out the main door while Aaron led the four of them to a side entrance and out through a winding corridor and down a staircase where armed guards manned the exit. Outside, the SUV waited at the curb. Cas Demarco, one of the snipers, was behind the wheel this time. Seth Hopper held the door.

They climbed inside. Ryan hit the backseat with the intern.

"Back to the office?"

Hope shook her head. "I wish, but my adrenaline is crashing, and I'm suddenly feeling wiped."

Colin peered over from the backseat as Demarco peeled away. "You can let me out. I'll walk."

"We can drop you at the DA's office," Aaron assured him. "It's on the way."

"Okay. Thanks." The young man settled back for the short ride.

Hope opened her mouth to ask a question, but Aaron's cell buzzed. It was Frazer.

"Any news?" asked Aaron.

"Roberts and Somack were spotted trying to break into an

outdoor store in Oakham in the early hours of this morning."
Frazer sounded tired too.

"Oakham? Where the hell is Oakham?"

Hope stared at him intently.

"Small community about thirty miles west of the crash site,"
Frazer explained. "They couldn't get inside without setting off the
alarm and then got spooked. They stole a truck out of a nearby
driveway instead."

"Are the police in close pursuit?"

"No police station in the town—I'm surprised it had a store, to
be honest. Sheriff's deputies were busy helping with the manhunt
farther east, but the USMS have transferred most of their
manpower around Oakham now and have an APB out on the
stolen truck."

"Why am I only hearing about this now?" asked Aaron.

"No one informed me until lunchtime. I was driving out this
way anyway so continued to Oakham and spoke to the shop-
keeper myself."

"No sign of Leech?"

"No sightings of Leech," Frazer confirmed.

Hope met Aaron's stare, and he shook his head. She looked
disappointed.

Who wouldn't be?

Demarco pulled up in front of the DA's office that was thankfully devoid of reporters today.

"Hold on for a moment," Aaron told Frazer.

They watched Colin Leighton alight and hurry toward the
building. Aaron pulled the door closed, and Demarco immediately drove away.

"What aren't you telling me?" Aaron pushed.

"Let me send you a photograph. I want to know what you
think."

Aaron looked down at his cell phone at the image of Reggie
Somack and Perry Roberts attempting to pry open a door with a
piece of sheet metal.

Hope brushed her hair out of her face and leaned over to peer at his screen.

It took him a second.

"Ah. Shit." They both wore their orange prison jumpsuits and handcuffs. "I was kind of hoping they were the ones to strip the prison guard."

Hope's lips compressed into a thin line.

Frazer continued. "But the marshals didn't think to inform me of this. I obtained that photo directly from the guy whose store Roberts and Somack tried to rob."

"Do you think the marshals understood the implications?"

"They must," Frazer muttered sourly. "Novak is the one who let me know something was up, though they weren't talking to him either to begin with. Charlotte Blood got it out of them."

"She knows how to talk to people. It's her job."

Charlotte was a negotiator and a damned good one.

"If Novak and Blood weren't on the ground with USMS, how long until they'd have told us Leech wasn't drowned but had actually managed to get hold of a guard's uniform, not to mention his sidearm?" Frazer's words were coated in anger.

Aaron wanted to punch someone. "We're prepared for Leech. So is the team on the judge."

"But what about everyone else?"

Aaron didn't have an answer to that. "Did Parker discover anything useful about that other thing we discussed?"

Traffic was heavy this time of day. His gaze scanned the surroundings for potential danger.

"The subject's phone was at his house all night."

Aaron didn't know whether to be glad or sad. The idea of a cop vandalizing a headstone was abhorrent but at least it would be a known enemy. "Thank him for verifying."

"I don't think he's done yet. I'll let you know if he comes up with anything useful. I have to go. I want to check on a forensic psychologist I know who helped us during Leech's trials. She didn't want extra protection. Husband's a former Marine. Said she was safe enough. But she didn't pick up when I called this morning."

Aaron didn't like the sound of that. "Let me arrange backup."

"I'm five minutes away from her house in Lincoln, and it could be as simple as her turning her phone off for work, but if you don't hear from me in thirty minutes call the cops." Frazer hung up.

Aaron looked at Hope in the deepening gloom of the late afternoon. Her eyes were haunted as she stiffly hunched her shoulders.

Aaron fought the urge to wrap his arm around her and give her a comforting squeeze. He didn't want to turn into Brendan Harper with unwanted physical interactions. He needed to remember this wasn't personal. It was professional. HRT didn't spend millions of dollars training operators to hug people. That was what friends were for.

But Hope didn't have any friends…

Fuck.

"Why can't they find him?" she asked quietly.

Aaron shook his head. He didn't know.

20

As soon as Frazer pulled up at the house on the outskirts of Lincoln, Massachusetts, he knew something was off. Sylvie Pomerol lived a few short miles from where the first shots had been fired in the Revolutionary War. She was a small, thoughtful woman in her early forties who took her job seriously and traveled all over the US to present expert testimony and perform assessments of various crimes and criminals.

Trees encircled the property and gave it that secluded forest feel that had never appealed to him. Too many boogey men hid in the woods. Too many shadows. He and Izzy had found a place overlooking the Potomac that fed his love of openness and her love of the water.

This place gave him the creeps.

Dead leaves rustled on the branches. The breeze, which held the serrated edge of the Arctic, made his eyes smart. He removed his Glock from the holster and circled around to the back of the property, shoes immediately soaked by two inches of snow that had fallen in the past few hours.

Maybe that was what bothered him. No footprints in the fresh snow. And no vehicle in sight. No lights on inside the house, and no smoke coming out of the chimney.

Didn't have to mean anything. Sylvie and her husband may have decided to go away after all. Frazer hoped so. But the hairs on his nape quivered, and he had long ago learned to listen to his instincts.

He shone his flashlight around the house but saw no sign of anyone being here.

He decided to try the back door. He knocked first and called out, "Sylvie? It's Lincoln Frazer. I wanted to make sure you were okay."

He tried her cell again, and a stab of something bleak moved through him when he heard the ring tone coming from inside the house.

He called out again then dialed Aaron Nash who was currently closer than Novak or the HRT team who guarded the judge. Parker would have been useful right about now, but he was busy helping one of his best friends prepare for her wedding to SSA Quentin Savage.

"You find her?" Nash answered.

"I'm at her house, but the lights are off. No one appears to be home, but I can hear her cell ringing inside."

"Give me the address," Aaron instructed. "I'll call the local office."

Frazer sent him his location. "I'm going in."

"Leech could be there."

"That would be lovely." Frazer wasn't foolish enough to underestimate the guy, not when he'd murdered so many and had so little left to lose, but Frazer was a well-trained professional and catching serial killers was his job. "I'll keep the line open, but backup might prove useful."

"Already being requested."

Frazer smiled a little. He liked that about the Hostage Rescue Team. They didn't need point-by-point instruction or hand holding.

He slid the phone into his pocket and pulled on a pair of surgical gloves so as not to disturb evidence should a crime have been committed here. Assume the worst—that was his mantra. He tried the doorknob, but it was locked. He used the butt of his weapon to break the glass in the small pane closest to the lock. Pretty crappy security, but this door only opened into a mudroom. He reached through, flicked the lock and walked inside.

His shoes crunched on the broken shards of glass. Was Leech here? Was Sylvie alive?

He hoped she wasn't standing behind the door ready to put a bullet in him because she heard someone break into her house.

He pulled his flashlight from his pocket and called out again. "Sylvie. It's me, Frazer."

No reaction. No sense of predatory anticipation either.

Frazer tried the door into the main house and was disappointed to find it unlocked. Sylvie was smarter than that.

He braced his Glock on the wrist that held the flashlight and entered the main house, moving quickly away from the danger zone as he swept his light across the kitchen.

Signs of someone about to eat dinner—bowls on the table, bread and butter on the counter. An empty packet of ham. Milk and cheese left out of the fridge on the side. He touched a finger to the saucepan of stew on the stove.

Stone cold.

Frazer flicked on the light switch, glad when it came on. The fewer shadows for danger to lurk in the better. The smell of over-ripe bananas soured his stomach, but he pushed the sensation away, along with the memories of another woman's kitchen.

"Sylvie? It's Assistant Special Agent in Charge Lincoln Frazer. We had a meeting?" If Leech was here, he already knew Frazer was in the house. But if the husband was here then hopefully, he'd be less inclined to shoot first and ask questions later.

Best to clear the house and pray his instincts were off.

He stepped into the dining room and then into the living room. Nothing.

An office was on the other side of the staircase and a glance inside showed it had been ransacked. A computer was on. The screensaver active.

Ice formed inside his veins. He knew exactly what he was going to find upstairs now. He turned on lights along the way, led with his gun. He saw the soles of their feet first through the banisters.

A man and a woman lay on the floor, side by side.

Frazer had to clear the whole house before he could check them for signs of life, but that initial glance told him they'd been dead for a while. He cleared the bathroom and the other bedrooms. Methodical. Thorough. He wasn't about to let Leech leap out on him with a gun or a knife and leave Izzy as grief-stricken as Hope.

He was mindful of the fact it was a crime scene and avoided getting too close to either Sylvie or her burly ex-Marine husband. He avoided the blood spatter on the carpet and only touched what he had to, no handles where possible, using his gun to turn on the lights.

Scrawled in bright red, presumably lipstick, across the bathroom mirror was "*I have feelings, Dr. P.*"

Leech.

Cowardly bastard.

Frazer pushed the victims out of his mind and did the job, cleared everywhere except the tiny attic and crawlspace—he'd let junior agents deal with those. His instincts and senses, plus the lack of tracks in the snow told him Leech was long gone.

He lowered his weapon and put the flashlight back in his pocket. He pulled out his cell. The call was still connected.

"Two dead on scene. Sylvie and a man I have to assume is her husband judging from the tattoos. I cleared most of the house. No one else is here. I'll need a full team of agents from the local field office. I'll inform the marshals, but this will be our crime scene."

"You're sure it's Leech?"

"I'm sure." Frazer took a few photos from different angles, the last one focusing on the hands. He went into the bathroom and snapped the image of the lipstick on the mirror. He sent two images to Nash, knowing he'd understand the significance of the pose.

"So, Leech or a copycat," Aaron said quietly.

"Yes." The word tasted like acid on his tongue. "Someone shot the Marine though. That's new."

"What if the marshals decide they don't want us investigating the murders?"

"Then I'll use all my influence to persuade them otherwise. In the meantime, let's just say I'll wait ten minutes or so before I make that call to them. I'll check the garage and outbuildings first, like a pro."

"Watch your back..." There was a hesitation. "Should I call you Frazer or sir or something else?"

Frazer scoffed. "I think we can dispense with the formalities. I have a feeling we're going to be spending a lot more time together over the next few days."

"Well, shit."

"Yeah. Absolute total shit."

"Should I tell Hope?" asked Aaron.

Frazer considered for a moment. He wanted to say no, but then she would lose faith in them, and he needed her trust. Plus, if anyone could handle the truth it was Hope. She'd withstood worse.

"Tell her but delay it for as long as you can. And then sit on her if you have to, to stop her coming out here. Do me another favor and call Novak and the team guarding the judge. I seriously doubt Leech will risk going after anyone who has bodyguards, but let's get the word out."

"I'm surprised he went after a Marine."

"Me too." And Frazer didn't like surprises. "I'll come to the house as soon as I finish here."

"Roger that."

They hung up.

Frazer took a video of the scene and then walked back through the house, recording the whole time. In what was presumably Sylvie's home office, he nudged the computer mouse with his gun. A news website loaded on the screen, a photograph of Hope as she stood outside the DA's office, eyes blazing.

Headline read, "Heavily guarded ADA Hope Harper claims to be unafraid of escaped serial killer, Julius Leech."

Frazer sighed. Well, she'd certainly gotten the man's attention. Not that it had ever been in doubt.

He headed through the living room where everything appeared undisturbed. Had Leech caught one of them in the kitchen, Frazer wondered. Probably last night judging from the congealed state of the stew and stale hunk of torn-off loaf.

Probably pulled his gun on them...

Didn't feel quite right.

The Marine had been naked.

Frazer pictured it in his mind. Maybe the Marine gets home from work, Sylvie has dinner ready while he cleans up? Leech sneaks in the back door and catches Sylvie in the kitchen. Holds a gun to her head as he forces her upstairs. Shoots the Marine in the bedroom.

Yeah, that sounded more like a Leech scenario. Still cowardly.

Had they not taken the threat seriously? Maybe not. The house was in her husband's name. And she took great care with her online security, assuming that would prevent the people she helped convict from finding out where she lived. But Leech had billions of dollars and nothing better to spend it on. Frazer bet the guy and his personal assistant, or whatever the hell Blake Delaware was, had compiled a full history on everyone involved in Leech's conviction.

Frazer texted Izzy to reassure himself that she was okay and to warn her and her sister Kit to take extra care. He wasn't too worried, but it never hurt to be cautious. And while Leech might have money, Frazer had something better. Alex Parker. The cyber-security expert had helped him disappear when it came to where he lived or might be at any given time. Any links to Izzy and Kit had also been carefully erased as had their online data where possible. Kit was a college freshman, so it wasn't perfect, but the young woman liked to avoid the spotlight where possible nowadays.

Frazer headed outside to check the shed and the garage, removing keys off the hook inside the kitchen. He tromped through the snow knowing more was forecast and that was going to complicate processing this crime scene—it already had—but he didn't find anything of note, just a couple of empty vehicles.

Had Leech taken one? If not, what was he driving? Was he alone? Where had he parked?

Frazer finally made the call to the marshals, knowing that despite the fact he'd gotten a lead on Leech—while they'd argue against that being a definite—the USMS wasn't going to be happy with him.

Not his problem.

But Leech was his problem. Leech was very much his problem.

One he intended to solve.

21

Hope grabbed a large casserole that she'd ordered in frozen from her favorite French restaurant over the holidays but had never gotten around to eating. She defrosted it in the microwave for ten minutes before covering it with tin foil and placing it in the oven on a low heat. It was way too much for one person but would get her through the rest of the week, and probably Saturday, saving her the effort of cooking until she had to dust off her skills for the Sunday roast.

While dinner slowly warmed, she sat at the large dining room table which was only ever used by her but filled the space nicely. She opened her email which she hadn't even looked at yet today. Her eyes were gritty with fatigue, but she wanted to stay up as long as she could. Otherwise, she'd be awake in the middle of the night. And, for once, she'd dearly love to sleep eight solid hours.

She deleted hate mail without bothering to read it. She didn't allow that kind of negative energy into her life. She had enough of her own. She did the same with requests for comment from reporters, though yesterday's soundbites had given them enough fodder to leave her alone for a few days.

She slumped with her elbow on the table, resting her head on her hand. Was that why someone had poured blood over Danny and Paige's gravestone? Because of her big mouth? Was it, once again, her fault?

Probably.

Leech had very much started this war, and, while she'd eventually won with him being incarcerated, the battles she'd lost along the way hadn't made it worth it. Especially now that the man was once again free to terrorize.

She pushed thoughts of him aside. She had work to do.

The jury selection was going in the prosecution's favor so far, although there were a couple of potentials who didn't have a lot of online history, and that worried her a little. She called Ella to check that she was okay, but the woman didn't pick up. Hope followed up with a quick text saying today had gone well but they were still in the process of jury selection and not to come in unless she really wanted to.

Ella worked at a fast-food joint where the pay was as terrible as the coffee, but they were allowing her the time off she needed for the trial. The fact Hope had gone to visit the manager to help realign his sympathies and moral code was their little secret.

At 6:30 p.m. a reminder dinged on her cell phone to tell her to go water her neighbors' plants.

Shoot.

Larry and Enrique had given her a detailed demonstration on each of their plants, which they treated like children. Keeping her promises to them was the least she could do.

She checked the casserole, but it was still cold and would take at least another half hour to heat through. She increased the heat a little and headed downstairs.

Seth Hopper stood outside her door. They'd both had a long day, she realized with another pang of guilt. Hopper had unusual hazel eyes that held a patient kindness she appreciated. A pair of sexier, darker eyes flashed into her mind, and she blinked in surprise.

It was shocking to think of Aaron Nash, or any man, that way.

"Ma'am?" Hopper straightened away from the wall, his face a picture of concern.

She held up her hand. "Don't worry. I'm going to the apartment downstairs to water the plants."

Seth glanced behind her as if searching for a hidden adversary. Then gave her a nod and followed close behind her until she reached the ground floor.

"I think I'll be safe enough from here. I'm only going into the apartment, which I believe is full of your teammates."

"Then I'm definitely going to be your backup."

She laughed as he'd intended.

Ryan Sullivan stood near the front door and gave them both a grin. "Pizza arrived if you want some. You better knock first unless you want to catch anyone naked though."

He sent her a wicked grin that didn't quite reach his eyes. She had a read on him now. He used his glib humor as a deflection mechanism the way she used her prickly armor. She wasn't sure which was more effective, but people probably liked him better.

She knocked as instructed then opened the door that led into Larry and Enrique's almost unrecognizable living room. She stopped dead. Aaron Nash was stripping off the shirt he'd worn in court today. He was all lean, ropey muscle and broad shoulders, and had the most mouth-watering spine she'd ever seen. A small school of fish swam their way across his right shoulder blade and down.

He turned around and caught her gaping at him like a guppy.

Hope didn't remember the last time she'd felt that telltale quiver in response to a handsome man. There'd only ever been Danny.

"I, ah, sorry. I did knock."

"Not a problem. What can I do for you?" He pulled a black T-shirt over his head and made all that tantalizing flesh disappear.

"Hope?" His tone shifted to concern. "Are you okay? Did something happen?"

"No. No. Not that I know of." She blinked out of her trance. "I need to water the plants."

"We can do that." He attached his weapon to his belt but didn't put on the ballistic vest that was draped across the cot set up in front of the marble fireplace.

Cot…

"No." She frowned. "I need to do it. Larry and Enrique gave me an hour's worth of instruction, and I promised I'd take care of them. Even though my horticultural prowess is usually limited to washing lettuce."

She did have a cactus at work, a less than subtle gift from her last intern. "I won't be long."

She went into the combination kitchen/dining room, which was larger than hers, and found the fancy watering can already full. She went to the sink and added the natural plant food the couple used. It smelled like dead fish, so she added a fraction of what they'd suggested because surely nothing would die in the two weeks they were away.

The operators were arranged en masse around the dining table, which they'd covered with a thick cloth to protect. Several boxes of pizza, which smelled hot and fragrant, were laid out in a row, with some still sealed in an insulated bag to keep warm—for those still on duty, she realized.

Her stomach rumbled. At least she had her casserole to look forward to.

She started at the back of the house. Each plant had a name she hadn't bothered to memorize, but Eliza and Judy were hard to forget. Two massive monsteras that lived either side of the window seat that faced the garden terrace and had the most natural light.

She headed back into the kitchen to refill the watering can and check the herbs which grew in a hydroponic system. All the plants that lacked enough natural light had their own special full spectrum lamp. She frowned. That probably made the apartment very bright during the day even with the curtains closed, but the men here hadn't unplugged the lights.

The dining and living rooms were crammed with bags of equipment. The bedrooms were even more cluttered, though the space was tidy, beds made. They were obviously using the same bed, so whoever wasn't on duty had a space to sleep. Shame welled up that she was all alone in her five-bedroom apartment and these men, tasked with her protection, whether she—or they —liked it, were packed in like sardines.

She finished watering the plants and went back to the kitchen. Refilled the can and placed it in the allotted space alongside the food for next time.

Aaron Nash watched her as the other men finished dinner.

She cleared her throat. "I've changed my mind about the accommodation arrangements."

Everyone stiffened, clearly expecting the worst. Aaron frowned and looked around, as if searching for property damage.

"Some of you can sleep upstairs."

"We're fine right here," Aaron said quickly.

"I insist." She shook her head. "I have the space. As long as I have the main floor where I can work undisturbed, there's no reason you can't all have your own bed."

Aaron opened his mouth as if to argue.

"This is not up for discussion." She used her hostile witness tone.

"We don't want to impose," Will Griffin spoke up when Aaron appeared stumped for words.

"You're willing to take a bullet for me, but you won't sleep in an empty bed I'm freely offering because you 'don't want to impose'?"

"We know you value your privacy."

To cry alone at midnight.

The fact they all probably knew felt strangely liberating.

"Last night was difficult, and I always knew it was going to be difficult. It will be difficult again next year." They'd tried to ease her pain with a dead-of-night visit to the cemetery, but they all knew how that had ended. Still, she was glad she'd been the one to find the vandalism rather than some stranger. And she was even more glad the scene had been processed and evidence collected, and everything had been wiped clean again so no one else could witness the ugliness that had been inflicted.

"I can't pretend to know how you work, but the rooms are available if that gives you a little extra space." She gave a wooden smile. "If you don't want to use them that's fine too."

She wouldn't argue. She'd made the offer. She certainly wasn't going to beg, but she wanted them to know the offer was sincere.

"I'll take you up on it if it means I don't have to sleep on another couch. I'm about done with sofa surfing," Ryan Sullivan drawled from the doorway.

"Thank you, Hope. We appreciate it," said Will Griffin.

A warm feeling spread through her chest. "Good."

"Hope." Aaron followed her to the door.

She raised her hand to ward off an argument, but he trailed her anyway.

"This isn't about the beds."

She glanced at him sharply and noticed everyone else was suddenly busy doing other things. Avoiding her gaze.

A knot formed in her throat. "Leech?"

Aaron nodded. "Let's go upstairs and give the teams the opportunity to finish eating and switch over."

She wrapped her arms around herself as she forced herself tiredly up the stairs. *What now?* Her apartment smelled of garlic and chicken, but she feared she was about to lose her appetite.

She turned to face him. "Tell me quickly. Don't try to soften the blow."

Pity twisted his features. "It looks likely that Leech murdered Sylvie Pomerol and her husband in their home last night."

Her knees went, and she dropped to the couch. "I don't understand. Sylvie knew better than anyone how dangerous Leech was. What about her protection?"

Aaron sat beside her. "She refused protection. Her husband was a former Marine, and she went to great pains to cloak where she lived."

"He found her anyway." Questions peppered her mind. "How? How did he do that when he's on the run from prison without money or a computer. He must have help. Did they question his personal assistant, Blake Delaware? He could have supplied information."

Those black eyes of his were warm with compassion. "I'm not in charge of the investigation, but I assume he's been questioned by the marshals and will be questioned again following these murders."

"Did you call Frazer—"

"No. Frazer called me. He's the one who found them."

The breath went out of her, and she sagged against the couch. "Shit."

"He's on his way here."

She felt his eyes on her as she stared at the ceiling, probably waiting for her to break down again. Part of her wanted to. Wanted to rage and grieve, but that wouldn't stop the bastard.

"I need to contact every person on that list of witnesses at the trial again and warn them. Make them listen."

"News of these murders hasn't been released yet," he cautioned.

She narrowed her eyes at him and leaned forward, insulted. "I won't tell them about Sylvie or her husband, *Operator Nash*. I know how to do my job."

He leaned forward. "I know you know how to do your job, *ADA Harper*. And I know how to do mine." His gaze glanced off her lips for a fraction of a second, belying his harsh tone. When their eyes locked again something shifted between them.

Because she felt it too.

This underlying pull of physical attraction. The most alien

feeling on the planet, and yet familiar too. Something normal and even ordinary. Something basic and elemental like a riptide or a tornado. Something she'd never expected to feel again.

His tone softened. "I also know you're not as tough as you like to make out. Not that you aren't tough," he added quickly, "but you're human too."

Something dropped away from her then, and it scared the ever-loving crap out of her. She covered it with humor. "Don't tell anyone. My reputation will be ruined."

He took her hand, and she jolted in shock. "Let someone else make the calls, Hope. Let the FBI and the marshals do their jobs."

He gently squeezed her fingers, and she felt the touch down to her bones.

"We've got you. He isn't getting anywhere near you."

"It's not me I'm worried about."

That admission didn't make him look happy, but she'd been honest with him from the start. She wanted Leech to come for her. The fire that lit her from the inside, fed by the pain and fury in her soul, welcomed the chance to confront him. Leech couldn't hurt her anymore. But she'd sure as hell like to hurt him...

Her cell phone rang, and she used the moment to separate herself from this man who somehow felt like too much and at the same time not enough. The edgy feeling tipped her off balance.

How was she expected to think straight with everything that was happening?

She picked up her cell, and a photo appeared on her screen.

She thrust it away but not before the naked bodies and glazed staring eyes imprinted themselves on her brain.

She dashed to the bathroom. Aaron shouted after her then swore.

She heaved until there was nothing left in her stomach except bile.

Tears stung her eyes.

Leech had sent that to her.

She hadn't read the message, but the bodies themselves were

enough of a reminder of all the reasons why not to get emotionally involved with anyone—it hurt too much when you lost them. She couldn't go through that kind of pain again. No one should have to go through that sort of pain ever.

She didn't think she'd survive next time.

22

Aaron stared at the image on Hope's cell phone screen, and even though he wanted to go after her and make sure she was okay, first he needed to attempt to trace the call.

He contacted Frazer. "Someone sent Hope a photo of the latest crime scene."

Frazer swore. "I'll call Parker. I'm almost there, but maybe he can get a trace started."

"Don't bother. I just realized it was sent from Sylvie Pomerol's number."

"He must have sent a delayed message. Given himself time to get away. I'll call Parker anyway. We should put a trap 'n trace on Hope's communications if she agrees. Leech might contact her again now he has her personal cell number. I need to get a copy of the information on Sylvie's phone and her husband's because Leech had access to that too." Frazer swore again. "I don't understand how he's been able to evade authorities for so long."

"Me neither."

"Is Hope all right?"

Aaron heard the toilet flush. "I'll let you know when she stops throwing up."

"Take care of her, Aaron. She's suffered enough. I don't want her to have to go through all this again."

"Affirmative."

She came out of the washroom as he hung up.

"You okay?"

She shook her head. Her cheeks were chalk white. Lips bloodless. "I don't understand. I really don't understand how someone like Sylvie was caught off guard. She was such a careful person. Was it definitely Leech and not some copycat?"

"I don't know any more than you do, Hope. Frazer is five minutes away. Do you want some herbal tea or a glass of wine before he gets here?"

Her eyes looked lost as she hugged herself. "My heart wants wine, but my stomach says tea. There's some chamomile in the cupboard."

He went into the kitchen and put the kettle on to boil. When Lucifer wound his way between Aaron's legs, he grabbed a can of food and scraped it into the cat's empty dish.

He checked the oven and turned down the amazing smelling casserole that was starting to bubble.

A knock on the door had Ryan Sullivan, Hunt Kincaid, and Seth Hopper stepping inside and making their way upstairs, carrying bags of gear along with the damned camp bed.

Hope forced a smile from where she sat on the couch with her knees drawn up under her. "Top floor has two rooms and three beds. Help yourselves to sheets and towels from the linen closet."

You'd never know that minutes before she'd been throwing up in the toilet except maybe for the fact her eyes were a little red.

She powered through it. Carried on. Ignored the pain or hoped no one noticed.

She thought of herself as unsociable, but Aaron didn't think that was necessarily true. She kept herself isolated, but not because she didn't like people. Any idiot could see once you got past that prickly outer layer, she liked people just fine. Maybe she needed mental space—he could relate. Or maybe she was still punishing herself for her perceived mistakes.

"Thanks for this, Hope," Ryan said. "I, for one, appreciate it. Don't worry, you won't even know we're here. Stealth is our middle names. We'll set you up, Nash." He waved the camp pillow at him and grinned.

The joys of being in charge. Aaron got the freaking camp bed again.

Still, having his own space for a couple of hours would help get his brain on straight. No doubt he was attracted to his principal. Worse, she'd noticed, which made him feel like the lowest form of plankton. Even though he'd never do anything unprofessional or act on that attraction, he didn't want Hope to feel wary around him. He was better than that. She deserved better than that.

And no way in hell did he want his teammates to suspect anything was up with him. Being trusted to be in charge, to lead this elite group of men, was a privilege. One he did not intend to fuck up.

"That was generous of you," he said as the guys headed upstairs. "Offering us your spare rooms."

"Oh, please. They're there. May as well get some use. I'm sorry I held out for so long. I was a bitch when you arrived even if you did steamroll over my objections."

He crossed his arms and noticed her gray eyes flicked over his bunched biceps.

Put it away, Aaron.

"I guess we both like being able to get on with our jobs."

Her smile was strained. "I guess. I feel bad that I made it harder for you and your men at the start."

"We were strangers who gave you bad news and invaded your life. Your reaction surprised me because I thought you'd be more scared of Leech. I wish you were."

"Put the two of us, weaponless, in a room together, and I don't mind my odds, which is probably not what you or the world wants to hear."

"The world?" He certainly didn't want to hear it.

"They want me to be the weak, weeping woman, and while I seem to have the weeping part down, I still want to beat Leech to death with my bare hands." Her color was back. "I should have let Brendan do it on my front lawn all those years ago. I'd have gotten him off with a temporary insanity plea."

"Immediately after the murders?"

"Yeah. Paramedics were still working on—" Her voice hitched and stumbled. "They were trying to save Danny. Paige was already gone. I just hadn't accepted it then."

Rather than distracting her, he'd reminded her of the worst day of her life—again. The kettle boiled, and he headed into the kitchen, poured the tea and let it steep—giving them both the chance to regain their composure. He added a little cold water to the mug from the tap and tossed out the tea bag. He walked back through and saw her standing in front of the family photograph.

He held the mug out. "Careful, it's hot."

Their gazes collided as their fingertips brushed. Her pupils widened, and his breath locked in his chest. He stepped away. Moved to the window to ease the blind aside and check the street outside.

Hope wouldn't look at him twice under normal circumstances, but these were far from normal. She wasn't out of his league, she wasn't even playing the game. He recognized damaged when he saw it, and who the hell was he to think he could in some way make her feel better? No one could fix what she'd been through.

No one.

Especially not him.

Last time he'd lost his head over a woman, he'd been devastated when it hadn't worked out. He'd always feared his brilliant former fiancée had been too good for him, and he'd been proven right in the end.

Hope was staring at that beloved photograph again. He knew

true love when it socked him in the face. What he saw on hers was deep and abiding. And he was done playing second fiddle to anyone, even a dead guy.

And didn't that make him feel like a selfish prick?

But he couldn't afford to develop feelings for Hope. She was his principal, nothing more. He was allowed to *like* the person he guarded. She was allowed to *like* him. They weren't allowed to lust.

Not at work. Not on an op.

Focus and objectivity made him a damned good operator. He refused to be less than his best. Not to mention her life was in danger. She might not take the threat of Leech seriously, but the man had murdered at least ten people. Aaron wasn't about to underestimate him.

The silence grew taut.

Thankfully, Frazer arrived and rescued him from the sudden awkwardness.

The profiler sent them a grim look. "Where's the phone?"

Hope nodded toward the table where she'd left it.

Frazer went over and studied the image. "I want permission to set up a trap 'n trace on your number and email accounts in case Leech tries to get in touch again."

"Assuming it was Leech."

"It was Leech."

"How do you know? It could have been a copycat."

"Because scrawled across the bathroom mirror in lipstick was 'I have *feelings*, Dr. P.' and I doubt a copycat would feel quite so personally attacked by what Sylvie said during his trial."

Aaron watched Hope draw in a long breath, and realized she was about to argue.

"I can't let you have full access to my phone and email. What about witnesses who try to get in touch with me or confidential conversations?" She shook her head.

"Hope, we are trying to protect you." Aaron gritted his teeth. "You might not care if you live or die, but other people do."

"I never said I didn't care—"

"Close enough."

Frazer broke in. "Do you want us to sign an NDA? I can do that. Your data won't be seen by anyone outside of the BAU except for the consultant I use—who is better at keeping secrets than anyone I know. None of us have any desire to spy on you, Hope, nor to re-traumatize victims or sabotage cases."

"It has to be with the understanding you don't read anything unless you think it's from Leech. And no accessing information prior to today. And nothing regarding current cases—"

"We don't want to snoop, and we're on the same side now, remember?" Frazer dragged his hand through his hair looking more agitated than Aaron had ever seen him. "I don't want to find you the way I found Sylvie Pomerol this afternoon. She was confident she could deal with the threat of Leech too. She was wrong."

Hope hunched her shoulders. "Fine. But whoever you trust with this better be reliable."

"I trust them with my life and honor."

"Well, then," she sniffed. "If your *honor* is involved, they must be really good."

Aaron smirked.

The woman was a bulldozer, but at least she had a sense of humor.

Frazer texted someone, presumably Parker, to set up the monitoring of Hope's communications. Then he wrinkled his nose. "Is that food I smell?"

Hope nodded. "You can have it."

Frazer shrugged out of his coat. "I haven't eaten all day."

Aaron moved into the center of the room and addressed Hope. "You need to eat something."

She banded her arms over her stomach. "I can't think about anything except getting that bastard behind bars again."

"The only person who wins by you not eating is Leech. You need to keep up your strength for that hand-to-hand combat I have no intention of letting happen."

Her lips twitched which made him absurdly pleased with himself.

"Not eating weakens you. Eat, even if it is simply as a source of fuel rather than something that smells excellent."

His own stomach rumbled. Frazer came through with three steaming bowls and placed them on the table. "Where are the spoons?"

"I better leave you two to it. I can grab some pizza downstairs." Aaron did not want pizza. Not when the smell of fine French cuisine made him drool, but he didn't want to overstay his welcome.

Hope caught his arm. "Stay. Please. There's plenty, and I know you want to discuss the case with Frazer. We may as well do that while *fueling up*."

Aaron nodded slowly. "I could eat."

He caught Frazer's interested expression but ignored the man.

She released him. Rolled her eyes. "I'll get the spoons that the world-famous profiler couldn't track down."

"Bring some bread if you have any."

"Yessir."

Aaron walked over and sat opposite Frazer as Hope brought out three spoons and a loaf of sliced bread.

"Tell us what you found," Hope ordered.

Frazer shook his head. "Afterwards."

"What did the marshals say?"

Frazer blew on his spoon. "That I had no right contaminating their crime scene."

"They wouldn't even know there was a crime scene without you," said Aaron.

"And the FBI will be taking back said crime scene shortly as the marshals have other priorities, but they wanted to flex their muscles first." He rolled his eyes.

"Who did you piss off in the marshal service?" asked Hope.

Frazer smacked his lips together.

The food *was* delicious and made Aaron's stomach growl in appreciation.

"I believe it stems back to an incident after the mall attack in Minneapolis now you mention it."

Aaron remembered. "Couple of marshals died at a safe house."

Frazer nodded. "They were good agents, but I had a few things to say about USMS protocols in general, and one of the people who possibly overheard me say those things might have been Joshua Hague."

"POTUS?" Aaron exclaimed.

"Possibly overheard?" Hope snorted.

"It wasn't deliberate."

"Oh, please. Save it. You're not above a little manipulation, and we all know it."

Frazer had the grace to shrug. "Perhaps. But combined with one of my agents taking off with two of the marshals' protectees, BAU-4 hasn't exactly been the USMS's best bud this last year or so."

"How did Leech track Sylvie down?"

"I don't know," Frazer confessed. "I asked Alex Parker to see if he can figure it out."

"The same person who you want to set up a trap 'n trace?" asked Hope.

Frazer nodded.

"Sounds like he does more work for the FBI than most FBI agents. Why don't you just hire him?"

"The FBI can't afford him."

"Maybe Sylvie Pomerol shared her address with a friend or a colleague who wasn't as careful?" asked Aaron. "You two both had it?"

Hope nodded. So did Frazer.

"Perhaps she wasn't as good at hiding her location as she thought."

"Other people are usually the weakest link, and he had the

resources to track it down years ago. And now Leech potentially has everyone in Sylvie's contact list." Frazer sounded pissed.

"Including this address?" Aaron did not like the sound of that.

"I doubt it. I always give out my work address as a contact." Hope played with a piece of chicken. "But considering the press already quoted me as living in a 'grand apartment overlooking Bunker Hill Monument,' I don't think I'm hard to find. Plus, his assistant could have easily followed me home one day or hired someone to do it. Or hacked the utility company. Maybe that's what happened with Sylvie. Have you questioned Blake Delaware yet?"

"I have not. I assume the marshals have in connection to Leech's current whereabouts, but as we already discussed the marshals aren't sharing with me."

"Is there anything to stop me going over there right now and asking Delaware a few questions?" Hope's eyes glittered.

"Aside from eleven highly trained HRT operators?" asked Frazer.

Her jaw visibly clenched.

Aaron shot Frazer a look. "If you want to go over there, we can notify the team for an after-hours trip. No guarantee the guy will see you or is even there, but we are game. We'll take you wherever you want to go. You aren't a prisoner. You know that."

The fight went out of her as he'd hoped it would and she sagged a little in her chair. "I just want to know people are doing their jobs—especially the marshals."

"Leech getting out means this assistant might have to actually do some work—and risk going to prison himself if he's caught aiding and abetting a fugitive." Aaron finished his bowl of food.

"Assuming the escape wasn't planned, and the accident scene suggests it was simply that, an accident, then Blake Delaware would have been as surprised as we were at his boss suddenly being free. That doesn't mean they were unprepared." Frazer glanced at his watch. "I don't know what the marshals are doing, but *I* have people searching for any property Leech or Delaware or any of their companies purchased or own or rent. Mind if I have seconds?" Frazer rose to his feet.

"Go ahead."

Aaron watched Hope nibble on her food. When she caught him, she pulled a face. "I'm trying."

He nodded. "I know you are."

"Maybe you can teach me some hand-to-hand combat moves." That came out of nowhere.

From any other woman it might have sounded like a come on.

Not from Hope though.

Aaron cleared his throat. "I can teach you some basic self-defense. I can get a couple of the guys, and we can play out several scenarios in the evening or on the weekend."

Hope's brows furrowed. "I'd like that. I don't know why I didn't think of it before. I could be a black belt by now."

"Perhaps because Leech was incarcerated?" Aaron suggested lightly.

"Still."

Frazer came back with another brimming bowl, his expression suspiciously blank. "I think that sounds very sensible, Hope. Aaron was top of his class out of the academy."

"You looked me up?" Aaron asked in surprise.

"I like to keep my eye on promising new graduates. I thought you'd apply for the BAU for sure."

"Saving that for when I can't keep up with the rest of HRT." Which would be a cold day in hell.

Frazer shot him an amused look. "Perhaps you can join us with our walkers in a few years' time, assuming we have any vacancies."

"I don't like the idea of sitting at a desk all day." And hated the idea of being pigeonholed as an intellectual.

"It keeps getting better and better." Frazer rolled his eyes as he dug into his second bowl. "I'm surprised I can climb the stairs. We do get out of the office sometimes as you might have noticed. I even workout on occasion, although I'm not as ripped as you gym rats from HRT."

"Well. Feel free to compare six-pack abs." Hope batted her eyelashes.

Aaron grinned, and Frazer laughed.

Hope put on more coffee.

Aaron figured she'd be better off having a nightcap and hitting the sheets. If he said that to her, she'd probably have two cups and stay up until midnight. He was definitely getting a handle on her personality and figuring out her contrary nature. For some reason, that realization made him sad. Probably because he'd leave soon and none of it would matter anymore—all the more reason not to get involved.

23

Aaron and Frazer cleared away the plates into the dishwasher while Hope made decaf coffee.

"Are you ready to see the video I took of the crime scene?" Frazer asked finally.

Her stomach rolled. "Video?"

Aaron glanced at her. "Is that a good idea?"

She swallowed. "Frazer thinks I might see something that I recognize as a message or something, don't you?"

The profiler nodded. "But I also understand if you don't want to watch it. It's not pleasant."

Hope's mouth went dry. She'd seen a thousand crime scene photos. Sometimes she felt numb. Sometimes they dropped her to her knees. But Sylvie had been a friendly acquaintance with whom she'd worked on many occasions. How could seeing the scene of her murder be anything except horrific?

"I want to catch this bastard. If he left me a message, I want to know."

Frazer set up his laptop and phone on the dining room table, and they all sat back down to watch, Frazer and Aaron on either side of her, bolstering her courage.

"To set the scene, when I arrived the snow was undisturbed,

and there were no vehicles in sight. No sign of activity in the house. I hoped Sylvie and her husband had gone away for a few days. I called Sylvie's cell and heard it ringing inside. The door to the utility was locked, but the inner door into the house was not."

"Did he take a vehicle?" asked Hope.

"Nothing that was registered to Sylvie or her husband."

"So, he has to have a car or SUV."

"Or someone is helping him," Aaron suggested.

"State police have been compiling records of stolen vehicles since the prison minibus went missing. They are being followed up, but nothing has flagged in the system near Sylvie's home yet."

They watched the video through once in silence.

Hope shivered. To see a woman she knew and liked, lying on her bedroom carpet touching her husband's hand in such a familiar way made her heart shatter. It also made rage build. She didn't dare let it show.

"Play it again."

Frazer started it over, and she felt Aaron's gaze on her rather than the screen. She ignored his concern.

They got to the bathroom scene and those words scrawled in red across the mirror.

"Stop it there." Aaron pointed. "Can we get a comparison on the handwriting between the mirror and the back of the photo planted on the grave? We must have Leech's handwriting on file somewhere."

"We do. Let me check the files." Frazer pulled his laptop toward him.

"Don't bother. I have some letters here." She climbed to her feet and walked over to her large walk-in cupboard near the front door.

"I thought you said you had them all shredded?" Aaron didn't sound pleased.

She smiled with amusement. "That was after he was incarcerated for what was supposed to be life."

The HRT operator came up behind her and reached over her to

help remove a banker's box that was high up on the top shelf behind a basket of winter gear. He didn't touch her, but his nearness made heat rise in her cheeks. That flash of awareness earlier had ignited something inside her.

"This one?" His voice was soft. Eyes wary.

"Yes."

He carried the box back to the dining table.

She stood where she was, near the cupboard door. "I should warn you that that box contains copies of all the evidence and court documents from Leech's last trial, including autopsy photographs." She swallowed tightly. "I haven't looked at them and would appreciate care when searching through to retrieve the letters he sent me during the trial itself." Acid churned in her stomach. "I have no desire to see those images. Ever."

She wasn't strong enough for that. Everything else, but not that.

"Why do you have them here?" Aaron's brows bunched in disapproval.

"They are part of the case against him. I needed it to be complete even if I never looked at it again." She shrugged. "Maybe it's my training, or maybe I kept it in that box and locked away as a way of dealing with it." Put it in a box and pretend not to think about it. Sounded about right.

Frazer drew off the lid.

She couldn't move. "Letters are in their own manilla folder."

Frazer found them easily and pulled them out.

"Did you read them?" Aaron asked.

"I read those ones. In case he incriminated himself."

"Did he?" Aaron asked.

She shook her head. "Kept going on about how he was innocent and how he'd never hurt a child—as if that meant it had never happened." She couldn't believe Leech was free to once again destroy lives.

Her hands clasped together, but she couldn't let go.

Aaron put the lid on the box and placed it on a chair out of sight. The box was a reminder as to what had happened, but as trauma filled every space in her body, she couldn't understand why seeing it again, thinking about it again, affected her so much.

Perhaps she *had* been recovering from what had happened seven years ago. And now Leech was out again.

She walked over to the table as Frazer removed a handwritten letter and spread it out.

They all stared hard at the screen and letter.

"The 'f' in 'feelings' is the same as the one here in 'defend.' And the overuse of punctuation, plus the giant 'I' fits with Leech's sociopathy, right?" said Aaron.

Frazer nodded. "The writing on the mirror definitely sounds like Leech. Whining about himself after the rape and murder of two innocent people in the next room."

She pressed her lips together as emotions wanted to rush her.

"The way the words on the back of the photo from the grave have the first letter capitalized like in the title of a book is different. Plus, we have the word 'next' here and here." Aaron pointed out two examples. "I know it's not an exact science, but the way the letters are joined looks different."

"They are written seven years apart and under wildly different circumstances, but I'm leaning toward the letter on the headstone being written by someone other than Leech," Frazer mused. "I'm waiting on the analysis of the photo to see if we have the printer identification serial number, and then we can hopefully trace that to a location."

"What's the delay?" asked Aaron.

"Too many crimes, not enough crime techs. I already called and updated the director on the latest murders. She said she'd send a memo to the head of the lab tonight. Now that we suspect Leech is alive, they should start work on this tomorrow at the latest."

"Would Leech have had time to kill Sylvie early last night then drive to the cemetery to vandalize the grave?" Aaron asked.

Frazer pinched his chin. "It's only thirty minutes away by car.

But I can't see him doing it. I can't see him going from a rape and double homicide to smearing pig's blood over a headstone. Or risking his freedom for something so mundane and beneath him."

"Substitution because he couldn't get to Hope?"

Frazer cocked his head. "He'd gotten to someone on his list which would have made him buzz like a cattle prod. I would have expected him to crawl back into his hole and savor the experience while he prepared for the next one."

"Who else is on that list do you think?"

"I'm honestly not sure. The judge, the jury, Beasley and his team, the lab tech who found Danny's blood on Leech's shirt and testified in court. Presumably Brendan for beating the shit out of him."

Hope's mouth went dry.

Frazer forestalled her panic. "I've arranged for everyone to be contacted again and reminded of the danger Leech poses. That included your brother-in-law and his mother. BPD will have a car parked outside her house until they catch Leech."

Relief swelled through her. The thought of Leech hurting Danny's mom was unbearable.

"Is the business with the headstone an accomplice or sympathizer?" asked Aaron.

Frazer shook his head. "I'm not sure yet, but as soon as we identify and locate that printer, we'll be paying someone a visit."

Hope picked up one of the letters Leech had sent. "He definitely has help from someone and somewhere to stay. Or he has killed someone and is living in their house and using their vehicle. But he had to get there from the scene of the accident..." She looked up. "The FBI need to interview Blake Delaware because if anyone knows where he is, it'll be that sleazeball. The guy manages Leech's whole life, although he wasn't the sole signatory on the business accounts back in the day. I guess Julius wasn't quite as naive as he pretended some days."

Frazer looked irritated, though not with her. "Now we have this new murder investigation I can push for more surveillance—

but both Leech and Delaware would know it's likely Delaware will be watched. I don't think they'd communicate using any known means."

"Leech could have contacted Delaware from someone else's phone before we even knew he was free," Aaron said. "You should see who called Delaware in that time frame. We might find a lead."

Frazer glanced at him sharply. Hope had a feeling Aaron had suggested something he hadn't thought of, which probably didn't happen very often.

"Smart," Hope commented.

His gaze flashed to hers. "Not really."

She found herself smiling. He really didn't like being called out on his intellect. His former fiancée had done a real number on him.

"I have asked for records of all his visitors going back two years," said Frazer. "One of them might be helping him."

Hope shuddered. "Why would anyone help that monster?"

"Not everyone believed he was guilty." Frazer smoothed his hand over the paper. "Some people believed someone else murdered Danny and Paige and set Leech up."

She looked away. She'd played a part in that too. In exposing the police corruption, she'd undermined the second case against Leech.

"Could this Delaware guy have ordered a hit on Monroe? Staged the suicide with the note to get the evidence dismissed and his boss released?" asked Aaron.

Hope jolted. "The prosecutor made those same noises after I made my motion to dismiss, but they had zero evidence. No witnesses. No evidence of a struggle. Leech and Delaware both looked equally stunned by the turn of events that day."

"Who was the prosecutor on that case again?"

"Steven Foggerty. He left the DA's office and moved to Florida after the trial. Private practice. He was no fan of mine, so I'm glad we don't have to work together. I assume someone notified him about Leech getting out?"

Frazer nodded.

"I'd like to take a look at that police report on Monroe's death. Can you get it for me?" Aaron asked Frazer.

Her fingers strangled one another as disquiet filled her.

"The more I know about everything that happened back then the better prepared I am for any curve balls. That's why I'd like your permission to read your files from the second trial." Aaron's dark eyes bored into her.

He didn't need permission, not really. How could she say no, even though she desperately wanted to? "Just keep the photographs out of my sight. Maybe keep the box in the bedroom."

"I can do that," Aaron said quietly. "Let's watch the rest of the video and see if you notice anything else."

Frazer pressed the play button, and this time she saw Sylvie's office, trashed, and the monitor with a photograph of her standing in the sleet last night.

Had her bitter words provoked Leech into killing again?

Frazer read her mind. "He would have done it anyway. You know that."

"What about Janelli?" Aaron sipped his coffee.

Frazer frowned. "His cell phone was at his house last night."

"You tracked his cell? How did you get a warrant?" asked Hope.

Frazer gave her a pithy look. "I don't know what you're talking about, counselor."

"I won't be involved in illegal surveillance."

"Oh, please. It's not Watergate," Frazer scoffed.

"You said yourself you thought he could have vandalized the headstone, but Brendan wouldn't even consider it, let alone raise it with his boss. The only way we could get an expedient answer is by doing a quick check on his whereabouts," Aaron said firmly. "Anyway, I wasn't talking about Janelli being the vandal. I meant about him being a possible Leech target. You said he never wavered from the story that he saw Monroe pick the tissue up at the crime scene."

Frazer moved one shoulder. "Monroe could have easily planted it without Janelli seeing. Then deliberately put it in an evidence bag in front of the rookie. Janelli was probably telling the truth as he saw it."

"According to the court records," Aaron insisted, "Leech called Janelli a liar when he was on the stand."

"That's right." Hope rubbed her brow. The decaf wasn't enough to hold up her eyelids. "Judge warned Leech, said one more word and he'd be held in contempt." She shuddered then. She'd touched Leech's arm. Told him to calm down, that she'd deal with it. And she had. "Should I call Brendan and tell him to warn the guy?"

She didn't like the detective, but she wished him no actual harm.

Frazer shook his head and checked his watch. "I'll call his captain to tell him Janelli should take the threat seriously and see if they have anything to share while I'm at it." He put the hand-written letters back into the file folder and slid them across the table toward Aaron, who placed them carefully inside the box and replaced the lid.

Hope stared at Frazer and remembered something else. "Hey. You forgot someone on your list."

"Who?"

"You. Who's watching your back?"

24

F razer started to gather their mugs.

"Don't worry. I'll get that." Hope took the cup out of Frazer's hand. "You go on back to the Hayeses and remind them to be cautious too."

Aaron, in turn, took the cups from her hand. "Both of you go to bed. I'll take care of clean up. I want to check in with the guys before getting some sleep of my own."

"A man who does housework. Surprised you're still single." Frazer slipped into his coat.

"Maybe I like being single." Aaron narrowed his eyes. No way the profiler didn't know his pathetic story or that his ex-fiancée was now his sister-in-law.

Frazer gave him a wry look. "Most of us do, until suddenly we don't."

"Leave Aaron alone," Hope admonished. "Plenty of people prefer to be alone. Nothing wrong with that."

Frazer looked like he wanted to argue but changed his mind. Instead, he forced a grin. "You're correct. Funnily enough I seem to remember Leech *didn't* want to be alone. He said he wanted to find the right woman and settle down but could never find anyone who really understood him."

"Because he's a murderous asshole?" Aaron's lip curled.

"People say things on the stand that make them appear 'normal' by society's standards. Didn't Sylvie say he was recreating his 'family' with each murder?"

"Yes. His father was a philanderer, and his mother caught him cheating with Julius's nanny in their bed. They fought, and he tried to smother her with a pillow. She grabbed a letter opener that happened to be in reach and stabbed him with it. He managed to finish the job before he bled out. What neither of them probably realized is little Julius was hiding in the closet and watching the whole thing. Apparently, he told the police who spoke to him later that he'd thought his parents were asleep."

Aaron didn't want to feel sorry for Leech, but he could sympathize with the child he'd been.

"He never admitted to the murders, so we don't know why he chose his victims, but Sylvie believed he was punishing people for what he saw as their sins, and I agreed with her," Frazer explained. "I do think he's truthful about wanting someone in his life to share things with." He looked down his nose at Hope. "He had a crush on you during the first trial."

Aaron watched the remaining color drain from Hope's face, leaving her the shade of skimmed milk.

"Do you think he might have found someone while in prison?" asked Hope.

"I'll check those visitor logs and cull out any repeat females before I go to bed. See what the analysts can discover overnight."

"If they're not suspects, they could be potential victims." Hope covered a yawn.

"They should have thought of that before they went and attached themselves to a serial killer," the profiler said testily.

Hope crossed her arms. "Yes, well, people say the same about me."

Frazer winced. He also looked ready to collapse on his feet. Aaron wasn't far behind.

"I suppose they do. Apologies. As you know, it's easy to

become cynical in this job." Frazer covered a yawn. "Prison is a harsh environment for anyone, let alone a privileged man of wealth. I can see him having a few pen pals at the very least."

"Enough to have fallen in love?" Hope wondered.

"Leech doesn't have the capacity to love," Frazer stated baldly. "He thinks he does though, so maybe he is with someone who is hiding him. Someone who thinks they love him?"

"You'd have to be pretty fucking weird to pick a monster as a love interest." Aaron knew it was common for people to attach themselves to the incarcerated, but it didn't make sense to him. "Who wants to hang out in max security for date nights?"

Frazer laughed. "You're talking to a man who regularly visits psychopaths in prison."

"No comment on your weirdo status." Hope crossed to the top of the stairs as Frazer headed out the door. "Goodnight. Sorry you had a horrible day."

Frazer grimaced. "It could have been worse. Remember, your calls and texts will be monitored, so no sexting unless you want an audience. If Leech reaches out, stay on the line for as long as possible, but if you can't bear to listen to whatever he's spouting simply put it down and walk away." He looked over at Aaron. "Take care of her. Don't let her out of your sight."

"Where exactly would I go?" Bitterness laced her words.

Aaron nodded to Frazer. "I'll have one of the team escort you to your car."

Frazer opened his mouth to argue but glanced at Hope and seemed to think better of it. "Right. Thanks."

Aaron followed the guy downstairs and handed out some instructions, including having Cadell follow Frazer back to where he was staying. Good practice for both of them. Then Aaron checked everyone was in position and there was nothing he needed to be concerned about right now. Another three inches of snow had fallen and, aside from some earlier snowmen action in the park across the road, all was quiet. He went back upstairs. Thankfully, Hope had gone to bed.

He put all the dishes in the dishwasher and turned it on. Washed out the coffeepot.

Then he grabbed the box with the case files, turned off the lights, and headed upstairs. The guys had set up his camp bed in the office where the old clothes lived. He closed the cupboard door. He didn't want to see reminders of Hope's family, not tonight, not when he planned to read in detail about their murders.

Aaron put the box on the floor and turned on a lamp that sat on the large desk beside a nice iMac. Bookshelves lined one wall. He peered closer but rather than the law journals he expected, the books were all focused on criminal procedure and writing fiction. Then he remembered her late husband had been an author.

He cleaned up in the guest bathroom. Hope had left her door ajar, and he figured it was for the cat. He'd stripped down to his briefs when a scream shattered the quiet air.

He grabbed his SIG and dashed into Hope's bedroom, forming a firing stance.

Hope stood in her plaid pajamas dancing on the spot and pointed at the bed.

A large house spider sat on the pillow, all eight eyes pointed in his direction.

Aaron lowered his weapon, feeling like an idiot. Cowboy and Griffin burst in and then stood there in their sleep pants with their weapons drawn. Now that the threat of danger was over, Aaron's heart beat like thunder. Not that Hope looked reassured by the presence of three highly trained operatives in her bedroom.

"What's going on?" Cowboy's brows were sky-high and if he said anything about Aaron being in his underwear Aaron was going to kill the man and dump the body in the river.

"Spider." He looked at Hope. "Do you have a glass?"

She darted into the en suite bathroom.

"Alpha team are going to be pissed they missed out on this excitement." Cowboy lowered his weapon. "Three of us in our underwear in Hope Harper's bedroom. Mind if I bounce on the bed to seal the moment in posterity?"

Aaron glared at the guy. "Why don't you suggest a pillow fight while you're at it?"

"Well, that wasn't the kind of bouncing I had in mind, but I'm game if you are." He wiggled his eyebrows to add to the delivery. Then he grinned as Hope came back into the room drying a glass with a hand towel. "I think you've got this handled, Professor. We'll leave you to it."

Aaron rolled his eyes and took the glass from Hope's fingers, ignoring the brief zip of connection. He placed the glass quickly over the eight-legged beast and trapped the poor thing inside.

"Postcard? Thank you card? Anything like that?"

She strode to her briefcase, pulled out a file folder, removed the contents and handed the cardboard to him.

"Here." Her hands shook as she quickly backed away.

He slipped the card under the glass and flipped it over so the spider fell to the bottom. "Voilà. Let me dispose of this guy some where it'll be happier, and you can get some sleep."

"Outside. Maybe throw it onto one of the flowerpots on the roof."

"I'll find him a spot."

"Outside," she insisted.

"Outside," he promised.

"Thank you." Her cheeks were flushed. Embarrassment? Or something else...

"You're welcome. Glad to finally be of service." He told himself he didn't flex his hard-earned muscles to show off his six-pack abs, but he was a liar.

"Goodnight, Aaron." She laughed then. "I'm sorry. I didn't mean to scream. Reflex. I'm usually on my own, and no one hears me. Thank you for dealing with it."

Aaron shook his head as he left and headed up the stairs. The woman was willing to go hand-to-hand with a man who'd ruthlessly killed ten people now, but a two-inch arachnid reduced her to a quivering mess.

Damned if he knew why that made him smile.

25

A s they drove past the courthouse the next morning, Hope spotted reporters crowded around Jeff Beasley, who appeared to be feeding them soundbites. Jason Swann stood behind him looking like everyone's favorite grandson. Swann wore a suit today. His lank hair had been cut respectably short. He was clean-shaven, sober expression on his rat bastard face. Obviously, Beasley had taken advantage of what he knew would be sensational press coverage in the wake of Sylvie's and her husband's murder to work on his client's public image.

"Pull up out front."

"Hope—"

"My client is not losing this case because Beasley gets unlimited face time on the news. Stop the car." She went to pull the door handle.

"Pull over," Aaron instructed, grabbing onto her arm, and holding her firmly in place. When she tried to jerk away, his grip tightened. "We do this my way or not at all."

She should feel angry at being manhandled, but for some reason she didn't. There was an inherent physicality involved with such close proximity. These men took their job seriously. So did she.

"Hopper, with us. You're in the courtroom today."

Ryan Sullivan drove, and a man called Sebastian Black was the other operator in the car. She didn't know him as well as the others.

"Black, with us until Hope is all the way inside. Then meet Cowboy around the back of the building."

She went to move.

His hold never wavered. "Wait."

The strength in those fingers made her feel strangely exhilarated.

Seth Hopper and Sebastian Black both exited and came around to stand in front of her door as Aaron finally allowed her to get out. He followed close as a shadow. The SUV sat at the curb, presumably waiting until she was safely inside the building. But the chances of Leech coming here were miniscule. She was in more danger of slipping on the ice.

"Find me a place slightly above and to the right of Beasley. I want to talk to the press."

"Yes, ma'am." Hopper arrowed through the crowd like a snowplow.

Hope tucked herself into his and Black's slipstream, which also protected her from the brutal wind as they climbed the steps and headed to the front entrance.

The men cleared a space for her and even though Beasley was still talking, reporters began to turn toward her and jostle for position. Then they began firing questions.

"What can you tell us about the deaths of Sylvie Pomerol and her husband, Bart Tranter. Is it Leech?"

"Have there been any sightings? Do you know? Are the marshals telling you anything? Anything at all?"

"Have any of the escaped convicts been sighted since yesterday morning?"

"Did you hear the body of the second guard had been pulled out of the water?"

She exchanged a look with Aaron, but he shook his head. He hadn't known either.

"Did Leech throw blood on your husband and daughter's gravestone?"

"Is he in Boston?"

She looked up and spotted Ella Gibson hovering at the back of the crowd standing beside Colin. The young woman looked terrified, and her intern looked as if he was doing his best to calm her.

Hope raised her finger for quiet. "I am deeply saddened to hear about the deaths of the prison guard, and of Sylvie and her husband, Bart. Dr. Pomerol was a respected Forensic Psychologist and a great asset in any courtroom. More than that, she was a kind and decent human being, and I think we can all agree that the person who killed her is not."

She could feel Aaron's disapproval of what he'd see as baiting and what she saw as telling the truth.

More questions were fired at her, and she watched Beasley out of the corner of her eye. He had an arm on Swann's back and started to harp on about his client's battle to prove his innocence in the aftermath of the "Me Too" movement.

So sad. Too bad.

"But Leech isn't the only monster on the streets." She shot Beasley and Swann a pointed look.

"Any idea where Leech might be hiding out?" A reporter from the Globe yelled out.

Stupid question but a great segue.

"I do not." Hope gave a wide smile and swept her hand toward Beasley. "But perhaps Jeff might know where his client is currently residing. Presumably he's still on retainer, Jeff?"

She muttered "blood money" under her breath as she turned and left him to deal with the media outcry. She hoped they ate him alive.

Inside the building, Aaron led her to one side of the metal detectors, and they quickly bypassed security and strode toward the courtroom where she could see Aisha waiting outside the doors. The paralegal had called earlier and told Hope to meet her here instead of the DA's office. Hope was sure the woman had anticipated the media scrum and wanted no part in it.

Colin caught up, breathing hard.

"Where's Ella?" asked Hope.

"She went home."

"Good. She's not needed today. May as well save her sanity, and, no, you don't get that luxury in this job, I'm afraid."

"I for one am ready to help kick some defense attorney ass," Aisha said when Hope reached her. She leaned closer. "Don't let the bastard get you down."

Hope nodded and found herself searching for Aaron before she headed inside. He caught her gaze and gave her a smile that knocked the breath out of her lungs.

"That is one fine-looking man," Aisha muttered under her breath.

You should see him in his underwear.

Aisha smiled dreamily. "First time in twenty years when I wish I wasn't happily married."

Hope shot her an amused glance.

The light in Aisha's eyes was pure kindness as she whispered, "He's not looking at you like that because he's in charge of your security, you know."

Hope's mouth went dry as she looked over her shoulder again to find that dark intelligent gaze had turned quizzical, probably wondering why she kept staring at him like she'd never seen him before.

Seth Hopper stepped behind and blocked her view, so she turned to look where she was going.

Even the idea of being attracted to Aaron was preposterous.

Wasn't it?

It had been seven long years since she'd been with a man and that man had been her husband and only lover. She wasn't even sure the parts were in working order anymore. She really wasn't sure she wanted them to be.

She forced her mind off the puzzling concept of sexual attraction. She had a court case to argue, and there was a serial killer on the loose.

But she knew better than anyone that life was short. Just as she also knew that as soon as Leech was captured, Aaron would be gone and that would be the end of that. For the longest time, that would have suited her perfectly. But suddenly, she found herself wondering what it might be like to kiss a man like Aaron Nash. What it might be like to have sex with a man like Aaron Nash.

The idea was intriguing. Tempting. Terrifying.

"All rise for the Honorable Judge Erica Penton."

Hope pushed all the other thoughts that swirled around her aside and suppressed a smirk as Beasley arrived late, looking disheveled. He apologized to the judge before taking a seat with his entourage.

He sent her a glare.

Seth Hopper leaned forward and murmured, "Want me to take care of him for you later? Back alley? Me and Cowboy can make the guy disappear like that." He quietly snapped his fingers. "No one will ever know."

The gleam in his eyes told her he was joking.

"Oh, baby," Aisha murmured. "You sure know how to sweet talk a woman."

Hopper grinned. Colin smirked.

Hope suppressed a laugh. "I'll bear the offer in mind."

Then she got down to work. She looked at her legal pad and saw the numbers Aisha had circled, the ones she'd put a cross through, and the others who remained neutral.

She considered the list, stood. "Your Honor, I'd like to question juror number eighteen." A young man in his early twenties. No radical opinions on social media, in fact he seemed pretty inclusive and tolerant. Aisha had gone back further and dug up a few comments on posts after the exoneration of a quarterback in upper New York State last year for a series of brutal rapes. His overwhelming sympathy for Drew Hawke's wrongful conviction could bias his opinion in this case. Research didn't always tell the full story. Voir dire would help ascertain which side he was really on.

They settled in for another long day.

26

A aron met Frazer outside the courthouse.
He opened the Beemer's passenger door and peered inside. "What's up?"

He held back a shiver. He wore nothing more weather-resistant than a brushed cotton sports coat, and it was freaking cold outside. His raid jacket was in the back of the SUV.

Thankfully, the reporters had abandoned their positions to file their stories rather than freeze their asses on the courtroom steps. They had what they'd come for. Hope had thrown Beasley and his firm to the wolves, and the guy had been livid.

Aaron wasn't sure provoking a man like that was the best way to stay safe, but why should Hope hide under a rock while others did and said as they pleased? That was patriarchal bullshit if ever he saw it.

"I've decided to pay a visit to a woman called Eloisa Fairchild. Followed by Blake Delaware, Leech's man of affairs. Thought you might come with me so I can get a second opinion on their reactions—assuming Hope is safely ensconced in court?"

"Who is Eloisa Fairchild?" Aaron ran his hand over his chin. He'd let himself grow a short beard a couple of weeks ago and couldn't decide whether or not he liked it on his face. It was potentially useful for work, so he'd left it for now.

"An old friend of Leech's who wrote to him regularly in prison and who also visited him occasionally. She's old money. Marshall Hayes—who is also old money—says the Fairchilds kept Eloisa pretty much secluded at various international schools around the world as a child. Then the parents and only son died in a plane crash, and Eloisa inherited three hundred million at age nineteen. Marsh says she went a little wild for a few years and then withdrew from society again. Nobody knows why. Perhaps she simply grew out of it. I believe she's worth talking to."

"Trying to figure out how one 'withdraws from society' in this day and age? Did she move to Idaho? Build herself a cabin in the woods?"

Frazer grinned. And people said he didn't have a sense of humor. "I think she stopped going to parties and sending holiday cards."

"Bitch."

Frazer smirked. "I'm more interested in her relationship with Leech. Do you want to come with me, or shall I go alone?"

Aaron checked his watch. It was ten-thirty. Hope wasn't due to finish until this afternoon and even if she did wrap up early Hopper, Black, and Cowboy were more than capable of escorting her safely to the office or home. The fact he wanted to be with her personally every minute of every day was an urge he needed to quash.

"Sure," Aaron agreed. "Especially as you're a potential target too."

Frazer rolled his eyes as Aaron slid into the passenger seat. He boosted the heat.

"Let me tell the others." He used the comms which were just within range and told the team at the courthouse he was going with Frazer for a couple of hours and to contact him on his cell immediately if Hope finished early or anything happened.

After the message was acknowledged, he pulled out the earpiece and tucked it away.

Frazer pulled the Beemer back into traffic heading west toward Cambridge.

"Any hits on people who contacted Delaware after the crash?"

"As it happens, yes. A cell belonging to a man named Graham Burns called Delaware on Monday afternoon. Two twenty-five p.m. The signal bounced off a tower near the Wachusett Reservoir not far from the scene of the accident."

"Have you told the marshals?"

"I tried." Frazer's voice vibrated with suppressed anger. "The guy in charge didn't pick up."

Aaron shook his head in disbelief.

"I left a message telling him I had pertinent information and to call me at the earliest opportunity."

Aaron could imagine the tone Frazer had used. The chances of his call being returned was nil. The lack of cooperation between the federal branches was costing them time and, in this case, that could mean lives.

"Analysts at HQ are setting up real time monitoring of Delaware's electronics—we have a warrant. They'll be ready in about forty minutes. I want to see who he calls after we leave."

"And we kill time by interviewing this Eloisa Fairchild person first?"

"Why not?"

They headed south on Storrow Drive skirting the southern banks of the Charles River. Despite the frigid temps, people walked and cycled along the esplanade. The water was the color of tarnished steel. The sky heavy with the threat of more snow.

"Thanks for the escort home last night, by the way. Unnecessary, but I was touched by the concern."

"Cadell owes me twenty. I bet you'd spot him. He said you wouldn't." Aaron shrugged. "I want to catch this guy. If you're a target, then you're also a potential lure."

"Nice to be useful."

Aaron voiced something that was bothering him. "What happens if this isn't over by next Wednesday?"

Kurt Montana's memorial service was scheduled for noon on February 10.

"If the marshals still haven't caught Leech by the end of this weekend, I'll talk to the FBI director and recommend she request that USMS take over full-time protection duties on Hope and the judge from Tuesday onwards."

That idea sat sourly in Aaron's gut. He didn't want to leave Hope's protection to someone else, which didn't make any sense. She was a job. A job he admired and respected and possibly wanted to taste from tip to toe, but still just a job. And there was no possible way he'd miss the memorial service for the man who'd turned him into one of the best damned operators in the country. More than that, despite Montana's gruff demeanor, the guy had been a friend.

Frazer cleared his throat. "You might not realize, but Kurt and I knew each other for many years. He thought very highly of you. I mean, he thought highly of all the people under his command, but I know he was particularly impressed by you."

"For a geek, you mean?" Aaron pushed aside the ingrained resentment. "Do you think we'll ever find out what happened in Africa?"

"We still have FBI investigators on the ground there..." Frazer hesitated.

"What?"

Frazer glanced at him. "This hasn't been made public—"

"Tell me," Aaron demanded.

"Traces of Semtex were found on some of the luggage."

The air rushed out of his lungs. "Semtex?" The plane crash hadn't been a tragic accident. It was an act of terror. Anger burned through his veins. "Was Montana the target?"

"I don't know, but I intend to figure it out."

"I'd like to help."

Frazer shot him a considering look. "I'll bear that in mind."

"Do you know what he was doing over there?"

"I have my suspicions, but no. I don't *know* for sure what he was doing."

"Ackers knows. Krychek too."

Frazer nodded but didn't say anything else.

They were silent for the rest of the journey. Frazer turned down Kent Street and pulled up in front of a large, red-brick house with a dark slate roof.

They climbed out and headed through the front gate, up the shallow steps, past the low privet hedges and mature trees, to the wide, red front door. Naked branches rustled in the brisk breeze. The place had the look of an old Victorian schoolhouse or orphanage and for some reason gave him the creeps.

Frazer rang the bell.

Aaron watched the windows and saw a shadow move behind the sheer drapes.

"Someone's home." He inclined his head to the window.

Frazer rang again.

They heard the deadbolt turn and the door swung open. A woman probably in her late twenties stood there, eyes darting nervously over them as Frazer held up his credentials.

"Eloisa Fairchild? FBI. May we come in?"

"FBI? Why? What's happened?"

Frazer gave a quizzical smile. "Aside from a good friend of yours breaking out of a maximum-security prison, you mean?"

"Ah." Twin spots of color stained her white cheeks. "Julius. Of course."

Aaron wondered why else she thought the FBI might be on her doorstep.

"Come inside." She opened the door wider to let them in. "Have there been any developments?"

"No," said Frazer. "I was wondering if he'd contacted you since he escaped?"

She shook her head. "Of course not."

Aaron followed Frazer inside but kept his palm on the butt of his pistol as he did so.

When Frazer didn't elaborate further, Eloisa led them hesitantly into what was probably considered a parlor with a small fireplace and flowers on the table near the window. The curtains were green velvet.

"Have a seat. Can I get you some tea or coffee?" She had an oval face and straight, fine, shoulder-length mid-brown hair. Her eyes were blue and her mouth thin. She wore beige slacks and a white shirt and heavy cardigan.

"No, thanks." Frazer took an uncomfortable-looking armchair that matched the curtains. He sat opposite Eloisa while Aaron stood near the window. "Beautiful place you have here. You live here alone?"

She pulled a face. "It's been the ancestral family home since the Fairchilds moved to America and made their fortune—before the U in the US."

"How did your family make its money, originally? Do you mind if I ask?"

The woman gave a startled laugh. "Are you interested in a history lesson, or do I owe the IRS taxes I'm not aware of?"

"Simply curious." He crossed his legs. "It's a lot of house for one person."

She cocked her head. "Yes, well my parents and brother had the misfortune to die so we can blame them for the emptiness—or perhaps blame the makers of the jet they were on." Her fingers played with the nap of the velvet.

"I'm sorry for your loss."

"It's been ten years now. I still think about them every day. I'm told they wouldn't have suffered. They would have all simply dropped off to sleep and probably died before the aircraft crashed into the ocean when it ran out of fuel." Her eyes had a faraway look. "They never located the wreckage. For years, I was convinced they were going to be found on some remote island

and come back home. All very Amelia Earhart." Her mouth drooped. "I'm sure you didn't come to hear about that."

"It must have been difficult for you." Frazer encouraged her to go on.

Eloisa nodded. "It was. I went off the rails a little but…" She shrugged as if to say, "what can you do"?

"How long have you known Julius?"

"Since after my parents died—I was nineteen. He was very kind." She gave a soft snort. "I know it's hard for people to reconcile the 'dangerous killer' we hear so much about with a man who gave me advice on how to deal with grief and manage my finances, but Julius was never ever anything except a gentleman to me."

"Why did you drop out of"—Frazer shot a glance at Aaron—"polite society?"

"Polite society isn't really very polite." She shifted uncomfortably, then picked up the chain around her neck and nibbled the gold locket she wore.

She seemed nervous, but was that natural disposition when questioned by federal agents or having something to hide? Aaron wasn't sure.

"I discovered the more time I spent playing in the rich party scene, the less I liked myself. Then I got to a point when I realized I didn't have to go to parties or meet people simply because my parents would have expected me to. I could stay home. Or travel. I could do it on my own terms, not anyone else's."

She dropped the locket. Her hands twisted together.

"What did you and Julius correspond about while he was in prison?"

Her eyes sharpened a little at that. "Anything and everything. We were both lonely and it passed the time."

"And when you went to the prison itself?"

She wrapped the burgundy cardigan closer around herself. "Honestly, I don't remember."

"Why did you go?"

"I was curious. And he told me he was bored and lonely."

Aaron watched her carefully.

"It was a small thing to visit once or twice a year." She shuddered. "I didn't enjoy the experience. Too grim. Too dangerous. The smells, the security, the way the other inmates looked at me."

But she'd gone anyway.

She grimaced. "I found it distressing, but I knew it meant a lot to Julius, and I wanted to give back a little of the kindness he'd shown me. I wrote every week or so. I hope that gave him some comfort. He really didn't enjoy being locked up there."

Tell it to his victims.

"Did he ever discuss plans to escape?" asked Frazer.

"Wouldn't that make me an accomplice? Should I call my lawyer?" She laughed and raised a brow.

"If you actively conspired to break Leech out of prison or aided him after his escape, you could face serious charges." Frazer's tone was easygoing, as if amused. Aaron knew the guy was anything but. "If you'd rather your lawyer join us, then we can take this conversation to the FBI's Boston Field Office."

She considered the idea then shook her head. Tucked in her chin. "He never spoke of breaking out, but certainly he wished to be free. He spoke mainly about the things he wished he'd done and the things he wished he hadn't done and what he wanted to do if he ever had the chance again."

Frazer leaned forward. "Is it possible to read his letters to you? We have yours to Julius from the Bureau of Prisons."

Her expression stilled. "Then you'll know that I tend to go on about the sad state of the world and my latest disasters in the kitchen. But I'm afraid I didn't keep his correspondence to me. I'm not a fan of clutter."

Aaron crossed his arms and raised a skeptical brow. She was lying. She had to be. Who would throw away letters from a so-called friend in prison when they lived in a house the size of most condominiums? Hopefully Frazer could get a subpoena before she destroyed any potential evidence—but on what grounds?

"Might I ask what was top of his list of things he wished to do if he ever got out?"

Aaron watched her throat ripple as she swallowed.

"He always wished he'd started a family." She shifted. "He believed that if he'd had a family, he wouldn't have…"

"Murdered eight innocent people?" Aaron decided he got to play bad cop in this scenario.

She angled her head to look at him, spots of color appearing on her cheeks again. "*Been arrested.* He always maintained his innocence."

"You don't actually believe that, do you?"

The glare she sent him had those hairs on his neck tingling. Obviously, she'd convinced herself Julius Leech was innocent.

"What about the two people he murdered last night?" Aaron asked.

"Is there proof two people were actually murdered?" she scoffed. "Or is that another media stunt?"

"As I found the bodies and one of them was a friend of mine, I can say unequivocally that, yes, there is proof." Frazer leaned back in his chair, but Aaron could tell he'd lost some of his thin veneer of civility.

She clasped her hands together. "Not to be rude, but why should I believe you?"

Not to be rude?

Frazer pulled out his cell and found an image. Turned the screen toward her. "How is that for proof?"

She went pale and flinched. Then her lips firmed. "How do I know they aren't actors?"

Frazer stilled. "Actors?"

"Crisis actors," she insisted.

"Ah." The word was drawn out.

Aaron rolled his eyes. *Whacko.* "Would you like a trip to the morgue to prove it?"

"Oh please, I am not so easily fooled. You could take me to the morgue and show me any two bodies. I wouldn't know this woman or man from Adam. The whole thing could be an elaborate setup—"

"For what purpose?" Frazer had more patience than Aaron could summon.

"To make Julius appear to be some monster. To get rid of two people the government wanted dead?"

She'd fallen well and truly down the QAnon sinkhole.

"Perhaps the government staged Leech's escape because they wanted to kill off a bunch of people and it was easier to blame a convicted serial killer?" Aaron suggested with sarcasm. "Maybe the 'deep state' is holding *poor* Julius somewhere while committing crimes in his name."

She stiffened her spine. "It is not out of the realm of possibility."

His lip curled. *Jesus.* People were stupid.

Frazer shot him a warning look, so he closed his mouth before he said anything that would definitely get them thrown out.

"Are you sure you haven't heard from Julius since he escaped?"

She tilted her head so she appeared to be looking down her nose. "No. He hasn't called me."

"I should probably remind you it's a felony to lie to an FBI agent."

She blinked at that. Pursed those prim lips. "Perhaps I should call my lawyer, after all."

"No need. We're leaving. Thank you for seeing us at short notice. Sorry to disturb your morning."

A floorboard creaked overhead.

"My dog," Eloisa said quickly.

Frazer smiled. "I love dogs. What kind?"

"A Maltese."

"Are you sure there's no one else in the house?" Aaron pushed.

"My housekeeper, but she's in the kitchen."

"Would you mind if we searched?"

She laughed lightly. "I would mind very much."

"You aren't scared?"

She tilted her head and eyed him like he was the weird one. "Let me see you out."

Aaron led the way. He glanced at the fancy hallway and staircase and wondered if Leech was in that room on the floor above. He desperately wanted to run upstairs, find this guy and end this thing. The fact he wouldn't get to see Hope anymore was irrelevant. She'd be safe, and he'd be back in Quantico, doing what he loved.

At the door, Frazer handed Eloisa his business card. "In case Julius contacts you. If you're right and he's innocent, then the sooner we have him in custody the more likely he'll make it out of this situation alive."

"So he can rot in jail." Her expression was bitter as she looked at the card.

"There are all kinds of prisons, Eloisa." Frazer ran his gaze over the grand interior of the old house.

"Some might say living in denial of obvious truth is a prison cell built with walls of ignorance," Aaron added without any subtlety at all.

"But who controls the narrative? History is written by the victors, and the truth isn't always as it appears," Eloisa said firmly.

"Truth matters," Aaron insisted. "The earth is round. The Holocaust happened. Those two people were murdered last night by Julius Leech. Wearing blinders because the truth doesn't suit your purpose is no different than being a flat-out liar."

Eloisa's eyes widened, then she blinked and looked away.

"It can be hard to distinguish the truth. You're correct about that." Frazer spoke quietly. "But one thing I know for sure is that Julius Leech is dangerous. He might not harm you, but that doesn't mean he won't hurt others. Please be careful."

They left.

Aaron climbed into the car feeling eyes on him the whole time he was walking away. "I don't understand what happened to independent rational thought."

Frazer smiled. "Some believe being rational comes at the expense of their intuition."

"Because these people are *so* intuitive?" Aaron shook his head. "Given the complexity of the human brain isn't, it possible to be both?"

"You don't need to convince me."

"No. I realize that." Aaron stared at the house as Frazer pulled away. "Think Leech was hiding upstairs?"

"What, you don't believe Eloisa Fairchild has the only Maltese in history not to run downstairs and yap at visitors?"

Aaron laughed. "Call it my intuition, but something tells me Miss Fairchild was not being a hundred percent truthful with us."

"Leech could be there. Unfortunately, right now he could be any-bloody-where. I'll have a deeper dive done on Fairchild and request surveillance on her from the local office. I wish the BOP had found her letters to Leech."

"Why'd you lie?"

"To keep her honest and on her toes. The fact she looked surprised makes me think he promised to get rid of them which also begs the question why? What is it they don't want people to know?"

Frazer's phone buzzed. He checked the text. "Analysts at SIOC have finished setting up the monitoring of Blake Delaware's electronic and email communications. Ready to visit Leech's old home?"

"Bring it on."

27

Julius Leech's house was a four-story brownstone on Beacon Street that had neat black shutters and a glossy black front door with an ornate brass lion head knocker.

"This guy Delaware gets to live in Leech's house while his boss gets an eight-by-ten concrete cell for the rest of his life? And Leech pays the guy to do it? Nice life if you can get it." Though Aaron couldn't imagine reporting to a man he despised.

"Leech needs someone on the outside he can trust to manage his properties."

"Why not simply sell up?"

"Another of those 'old money' habits—holding on to property. Plus, the man has a billion dollars in hedge funds and financial investments. Even after he was made to pay damages to the victims' families in civil court, it barely dented his holdings. He doesn't need the money so why would he sell the house he considers his home?"

"Hanging on to the illusion he might have a life to go back to one day?"

"Exactly." Frazer nodded.

Aaron eyed the well-kept building. "I can't see this Delaware character doing anything to jeopardize living this luxury lifestyle on someone else's dime."

"And therein lies his problem. I suspect Delaware doesn't much want to join his boss in prison, so if he aids Leech's continued evasion of the authorities, it could end badly for him."

"But giving Leech up to the authorities would mean he'd probably lose his cushy job. He's stuck between a rock and a hard place."

"Let's see what happens when we squeeze." Frazer stepped forward and knocked on the door.

"Is this the same house where Detectives Monroe and Harper interviewed Leech after the second double-homicide?"

"Correct. Leech's Maserati was spotted near both murder locations, and the detectives followed up."

"Unbelievable."

"They were convinced Leech was their guy after he held on to a letter opener during their questioning. But every piece of evidence that linked the crimes to Leech was circumstantial."

"You don't think he was innocent?" Aaron couldn't disguise his incredulity.

Frazer's gaze was flinty. "Leech is a killer. I just don't know if he acted alone."

Aaron frowned. The door opened to a lanky man with sandy blond hair cut in a short, conservative style. He had tanned skin and a bright white smile. His blue eyes widened. "Can I help you?"

"Mr. Delaware?" Frazer flashed his badge.

"Ah, the FBI. I've been expecting a visit since news of the accident."

Accident was an interesting term to describe the circumstances.

"May we come in?"

Aaron followed Frazer inside and looked around the grand foyer with its black and white checkered marble floor.

"No one's been to see you?" Frazer said.

"A US Marshal came by on Monday night. Told me to call if Mr. Leech made contact, but unfortunately, I haven't heard from my employer." Delaware led the way into a large room with all white walls and dark furniture that created an otherworldly decor. Delaware sat behind the desk that was placed in front of an ornate cast-iron fireplace with a white marble mantel, a fire burning in the grate.

"Would you have expected him to contact you in an event such as this?"

Delaware steepled his fingers. "I would, yes. I'm sure he's confused and scared after what appears to be a terrible vehicular crash."

So, they were going with a dazed and confused defense? Might have worked if Leech hadn't murdered Sylvie Pomerol and Bart Tranter in their home night before last—assuming Delaware wasn't another member of the tinfoil-hat brigade.

"You believe he's still alive?" asked Frazer.

Blake Delaware clasped his hands together. "I certainly hope so."

Aaron checked out some of the fine antiques dotted around the room, probably worth a small fortune. Of course, he hoped so.

"Would you call yourselves friends?" Frazer sat in an uncomfortable-looking chair.

"I wouldn't presume to call myself a friend of my employer, but we've worked closely together for many years. We are certainly friendly."

"I remember at the first trial, you looked almost disappointed when Leech was released."

"Ah. I thought your face was familiar. The profiler from the Behavioral Analysis Unit." Delaware eyed Frazer differently then. "I was in shock. We all were. Joyous shock, but still it came as a complete surprise for Mr. Leech to suddenly be released after having been denied bail all that time."

"He was relieved?"

Delaware looked at him with easy humor. "Wouldn't you be?"

"Certainly. He wanted his freedom?"

"More than anything."

"And yet a few hours later, Julius Leech went to Counselor Harper's home and brutally slaughtered her family."

Delaware drew himself up. "That's what he was convicted of, but he always denied it."

"He denied the other murders too."

Delaware's eyes darted to the side. "And he was acquitted of those crimes."

"Not acquitted. The case was dismissed," Frazer corrected the other man.

As far as Aaron was aware, the DA's office had never pursued anyone else for the murders.

"Where were you immediately after the trial?" asked Frazer.

"Mr. Leech told me to take the week off. I'd been in court every day and been working non-stop for months. He said he didn't need me. I was at the airport on my way to the Caribbean when I received the call about the new murders and his beating and arrest." He gave a small humorless smile. "Needless to say, the vacation was canceled."

"I'm sure you made up for it afterwards," Aaron said tightly.

"What about the night before? Where were you then?" asked Frazer.

Delaware pulled another face. "Hmm. Probably here. It was a difficult period. Most of my friends had dropped me, so I didn't spend a lot of time socializing."

"Anyone who could verify that?" Frazer asked.

"Like I said, I was alone at that time."

"No alibi."

"For what? If I'd planned to commit a crime, I would have arranged an alibi." The smile looked more strained now. The conviviality force. "I'm curious what it is you think I might have done?"

Frazer ignored the question. Aaron knew he was referring to the death of Detective Monroe. Maybe Frazer didn't like the suicide verdict any more than Aaron did. "What do you know about Julius Leech's friends?"

"Mr. Leech's friends?" Delaware stared down at the desk. "Most of the people who claimed to be his friends dropped him like a stone during the first trial."

"Not everyone though."

Delaware looked up. "No. Not everyone."

"Anyone who visited him in prison?"

Anyone who might be harboring him now?

Delaware's expression grew amused. "The FBI must have access to all this information. Why ask me?"

"We have access to names and dates. We don't know the nuances of personal relationships."

"I suppose you don't, but I don't necessarily know the nuances either. I don't know exactly who visits him in prison aside from a few people he's mentioned. Myself—I go every two weeks except in January. My wife and I—"

"You're married?"

"Yes. We met two years ago and married a year ago this coming April."

"And she's okay with you working for a convicted serial killer?" Aaron found it hard to believe.

Delaware glanced between Aaron and Frazer. "I told her from the beginning. She was a little concerned, especially as Mr. Leech wanted me to live in his homes as part of the terms of my employment, but she came around."

This was why he was single. He didn't understand women.

"We have our own quarters." Delaware made an impatient sound. "My wife wanted to be able to decorate her own living space."

"What's to stop you living in the whole place and decorating however you want. Leech would never know."

"My integrity?" Delaware arched his brow.

"Not sure how you maintain personal integrity when working for a convicted child killer," muttered Aaron.

"You could have quit. Why didn't you?" Frazer asked Delaware who'd started to sweat.

He pursed his lips. "Is it wrong that I feel a strong sense of loyalty to my employer?"

Before they could open their mouths to reply he continued. "I know that probably seems absurd to you. Maybe he did kill those people. I saw all the circumstantial evidence the police presented —but then that one detective who'd been so vehement on the stand admitted to lying…and then killed himself. Well, it raised a lot of questions."

Had this man orchestrated Monroe's death? If so, he was a hell of an actor.

Wood cracked on the fire. Delaware jolted. "Julius Leech was never a monster to me. He was never loud or mean or violent. He was always more than generous to me and the rest of the staff. He still pays the butler and the cook, neither of whom work anymore. They both moved away, but Mr. Leech provides for them because they'd been in his employ for many years and the chances of them getting another job at their age under the circumstances… He treated everyone more than fairly."

Everyone except the people he stabbed and raped and smothered to death.

"He's obviously generous with his money," Frazer agreed.

Aaron bet Frazer would be investigating the cook and the butler next and any properties they might own.

"It's not only about the money." Delaware raised his hands and looked around. "Who else would manage his affairs? Some soulless corporation or entitled suit who doesn't mind skimming a little off the surface?"

"What does it matter if he's locked up and never getting out?" challenged Aaron.

"But he is out," Frazer said softly, "and now it matters a great deal."

Sweat beaded on Blake Delaware's temple.

"You ever skim money, Blake? Just a little here and there?" asked Aaron.

Was he scared of what his boss might do if he found out? He certainly wasn't voicing any sympathy for the victims.

Delaware shook his head but didn't meet their eyes. "Mr. Leech is more than magnanimous with regards to my salary and bonuses. Not to mention I live rent free and use his transportation wherever I want to go in the world. I save most of what I earn."

"You must be very grateful to the man," said Frazer.

"I am very grateful."

"And I suspect you'd do anything for him—and to protect your lifestyle."

Blake Delaware jutted out his chin but said nothing.

"Has Julius Leech attempted to get in contact with you?—and before you answer let me remind you that lying to a federal agent is a felony offense."

Delaware swallowed, but he wouldn't meet their eyes now. "Not as far as I am aware."

Frazer crossed his legs and appeared to admire the polish on his shoes. "Do you know a man called Graham Burns?"

"I don't think so." Delaware frowned.

Frazer reeled off the cell number. "Are you sure?"

Delaware paled. "It's not a number I recognize, but I do receive wrong number and spam calls from time to time. Who is Graham Burns?"

Frazer shrugged. "No matter. Would you mind if we searched the premises?"

Delaware put down his pen and leaned back. "Considering everything the government has put Mr. Leech through, I think he'd have many objections and want me to say, 'get a warrant.'"

"I can talk to Hope Harper about doing exactly that."

At Hope's name Delaware's eyes narrowed, and he opened his mouth as if to say something.

"Blake?" A woman knocked on the open door and poked her head inside. "Is everything all right?"

She had curly hair and rosy cheeks.

Delaware stood. "Melissa. These men are from the FBI."

"Have you found Mr. Leech yet?" Her eyes were round, and she sucked in her lips.

"Mrs. Delaware?" Frazer stood and shook her hand as he introduced himself. "We offered to conduct a search of the premises, but your husband wants us to get a warrant."

Her hand went to the front of her neck where a chunky gold necklace rested. "You don't think he's here, do you?"

"He's not here, Melissa." Delaware sounded resigned.

"Then why don't you let them search, Blake? I don't understand."

Aaron hid a smile.

"Because Mr. Leech wouldn't want me to."

Her eyes were wide and imploring. "Well, if he's not here, he won't know, will he? What harm can it do?"

Exasperated, Blake threw his hands up. "Fine. Search the place. But Julius Leech is not here, and you're wasting your time. Not to mention mine."

"And managing the affairs of a serial killer is so much more important than catching one and keeping people safe," Aaron muttered.

"Did he really murder two people yesterday?" Melissa asked.

"Technically, the day before yesterday," Frazer answered.

Melissa's eyes shot to her husband. "You swore he wasn't dangerous."

Blake's expression turned pained, and he looked away. "I don't think he is."

"Then why did the murders begin again after he got out of prison?" she asked.

Finally, a person who was logical and not blinded by Leech's polite manners and endless supply of cash.

"I can't say."

"Can't or won't?" Aaron poked.

Melissa's frightened gaze shot to her husband. He stood and

walked over to her. Took her hands in his. "Julius Leech isn't a fool. Why would he come here when he knows the FBI will be questioning me and watching the place?"

She bit her lip again. "I would feel safer after having the FBI look around. Just in case."

"Of course." He clasped her shoulders and gave her a squeeze. "Shall we start from the top and work our way down? Or from the ground floor up?"

"Let's do ground up." Aaron swept his gaze over the room. No hiding places. "And if you two could stay here—"

"But—"

"Less chance of someone being accidentally shot that way." Frazer smiled cheerfully.

Melissa grabbed her husband's hand. "We'll stay here until you're finished. There's a garage and a pool house."

Blake's expression grew pissed. "Any damage, and I will be billing you. Trust me, you can't afford to break anything in this house."

Aaron and Frazer left the room.

"Ever get the feeling some people value property more than human life?"

Frazer smiled. "Every damned day."

They cleared the Delawares' apartment first, a cozy two bedroom with a large kitchen and comfy living room. But it struck Aaron that they were more caretakers of a museum than living in a real home.

They were quick but thorough as they worked their way through the outside buildings that were largely empty, the enormous kitchen, dining room, up the stairs to an informal den/library combo that Aaron wanted for his own. They reached what had to be the master bedroom on the third floor.

Aaron and Frazer checked the giant walk-in closet. It was weird seeing all Leech's clothes hanging there, neatly pressed. Not a lick of dust anywhere.

"It's as if they're expecting him back any moment." Aaron shook his head.

"A week ago, I'd have said that's a preposterous idea. Now I'm not so sure."

"Do you think he's here?" The guy could have some sort of bolt hole in a wall or floor like a miniature safe room. In a house this size, it would be almost impossible to find without the right gadgets.

"Mrs. Delaware didn't look too excited at the prospect of her husband's boss coming home."

"I can't say I blame her."

Frazer felt along the walls as if looking for a secret compartment. Aaron checked out the massive en suite bathroom with its huge whirlpool tub and walk-in shower.

"I don't understand." Aaron checked out of the window at the back of the property with its narrow garden and pool. "I mean, *really* don't understand. The guy has got everything he could ever want, and he sacrifices it all because he gets a taste for killing?"

Frazer quirked a brow as they moved to the next room. A guest bedroom. The bed was stripped.

"Murder has never been restricted to the poor or needy."

Aaron frowned. "I didn't mean to suggest it was. Just the guy had everything money could buy. Why couldn't he be satisfied?"

"He didn't have what mattered the most."

"What was that?"

"He didn't have someone who loved him."

Aaron's chest tightened. "So he started killing? Because people didn't love him enough despite his obscene wealth?"

"I think he started to kill because the victims represented his parents in some way—and they hadn't loved him enough not to murder one another."

"And once he started, he couldn't stop?"

"Some people get a taste for it." Frazer shrugged. "It's why I have a job."

They cleared the rest of the house including an attic that was as clean and spotless as everywhere else. They headed down the beautifully crafted stairs and heard raised voices coming from inside the office.

"Trouble in paradise?" Aaron suggested.

"Apparently."

Melissa Delaware opened the door and stormed into the foyer. She spotted them and stopped abruptly.

"The house is clear, Mrs. Delaware."

She crossed her arms high over her chest. "Call me Melissa. And, thank you."

Blake Delaware came to the office door, looking harried. "No one hiding in the attic?" His tone was sarcastic.

Frazer ignored him. "What happens if Leech dies?"

Blake shook his head as if to clear it. "I assume I will have to find a new employer, although I'd be in no rush."

Melissa put a hand over her abdomen. "We're expecting a baby. Blake will have plenty of things to keep him busy with or without running Mr. Leech's affairs."

"Does Julius Leech know about the baby?" asked Frazer.

"No one knows." Blake pursed his lips and shook his head. "It's early days. We haven't even told our families yet."

Melissa Delaware's lips pinched with worry.

Frazer nodded. "Who holds the will?"

"That is held by Beasley, Waterman, Vander and Company."

"Do you know what's in it?"

Delaware shook his head.

Frazer stared at him for another long moment. "Get in touch with us the moment you hear from Leech. Aiding and abetting an escaped convict will earn you prison time, and that certainly won't look good on your resumé or be good for your baby."

Delaware nodded, but his eyes didn't connect with theirs, and his wife's face looked stricken.

Aaron rolled his shoulders as they left the house. "Why do I feel like I need a shower?"

"Because you have a rigid moral code and a fixed idea of right and wrong. The idea of working for a man who has murdered ten people in cold blood is abhorrent to you."

"And not to you?" Aaron scoffed.

They walked toward the shiny Beemer. "Some might argue working for the US government is no better."

"Come on. That's not the same thing."

Frazer smiled. "If you say so."

"Would you honestly be employed by someone you know is a stone-cold killer?" Aaron frowned up at the heavy clouds.

"I would never work for a man like Leech, and I can't see leaving my current employer for a few years yet—assuming they want to keep me." Frazer's eyes were icy cool as they met his across the top of the car. "Satisfied?"

Aaron grunted.

"Maybe you should ask yourself why you are so offended by me observing you have a rigid moral code and a fixed idea of right and wrong."

"I wasn't offended." Aaron climbed into the vehicle, appreciating the heated seats. But perhaps he was lying. "I guess I don't want to be seen as boring or incapable of nuance."

"Are you boring and incapable of nuance?"

"No."

Frazer stared at him. "Whatever she did to you, you have to know that she was the problem, not you."

Aaron grunted again, hating that the profiler knew too much about him.

Frazer smiled, and Aaron realized the other man had neatly deflected the conversation away from himself and his own "nuances."

Aaron's phone buzzed, and he pulled it out of his pocket. "Uh-oh, I need to get back to the courthouse."

28

Hope read police reports until her eyes bled. The lab work had come back on the Du Maurier case, but it was inconclusive, so the technicians had requested time to run more tests. She heard laughter in the corridor and looked up to see Sondra Wu flirting madly with Seth Hopper as he stood on duty outside her office door.

Frazer read case files at her other desk with a focused concentration she envied.

They still weren't done with jury selection because Judge Penton had suddenly taken ill after lunch. Despite the fact tomorrow was a Friday and usually reserved for hearing motions on other cases, the judge had decided to complete jury selection instead.

Aaron Nash came into view and her breath caught. She didn't know where he'd been and hated the fact she was curious. Sondra turned her coquettish laughter on the tall, dark, and handsome operator.

Hope gritted her teeth.

Sondra's giggling irked her today in a way it didn't usually. She was a solid prosecutor. Smart as a whip, fearless, but empathetic. Pretty too. Vivacious. *Young*.

Aaron's dark eyes met Hope's through the glass.

A mix of relief and excitement uncoiled inside her.

It felt a lot like madness.

She looked over at Frazer and found him watching her. "What?"

"Nothing."

Aaron tapped on the door and poked his head inside. "Ready to go home?"

She glanced at the clock on the wall in surprise. "Six thirty already? Wow. Time sure flies when you're having fun."

A yawn took her by surprise. It had been a heck of a week. "Any updates?"

Aaron crossed his arms and leaned against the door jamb. The sight of him made her mouth go dry. She'd forgotten what lust felt like.

"Marshals are still concentrating their main efforts on Somack and Roberts as they were spotted again, this time on foot. They have several BORTAC teams and state agencies helping in the search area and have hopefully narrowed their whereabouts to within a twenty-mile perimeter. They're being hampered by the weather as it's proven impossible to get eyes in the sky to run thermal image searches. No sighting of Leech yet."

There had been no sightings period of the serial killer whose face was all over the news. How was that even possible?

"No cameras in the vicinity of Sylvie Pomerol's home so needless to say they didn't pick up anything," Frazer told her.

"Leech has to be staying somewhere. Why can't we find him?"

"We have surveillance on the faithful assistant and another one of Leech's friends—Eloisa Fairchild," Frazer added.

Hope remembered an awkward young woman from the start of the first trial.

"And electronic surveillance on a few other likely candidates of people he might reach out to. We're searching for any links to properties within a fifty-mile radius of the state where Leech could potentially be holed up."

"Who did Delaware call after we left?" Aaron asked from the doorway.

She lifted her brows. She hadn't realized they'd paid Blake Delaware a visit.

"His lawyer."

Aaron gave that smile of his that said he wasn't surprised. Christ. She shouldn't be mooning over a guy. She was no better than Sondra, just a lot less secure about her own appeal.

"Think the wife's fear was genuine?"

"Delaware is married?" she exclaimed.

"With a baby on the way," Frazer said dryly.

She blinked.

"And I believe so," Frazer answered Aaron's question. "I checked into her background and didn't find any red flags. All indications are that Blake is a loving and supportive husband."

"Then he must be crapping his pants right about now." Aaron shot a look over his shoulder toward one of Sondra's high giggles.

"Especially as for all Delaware's supposed 'integrity,' Alex Parker found several hidden bank accounts in the Caymans and Isle of Man." Frazer lowered his chin. "He found several more he believes could belong to Leech. Maybe Delaware set them up at Leech's request?"

"Can we cut them off?" Hope closed the files on her desk with a snap.

"Better to keep our eyes on them for any activity. It might lead us to him eventually." Aaron dragged his hand through his hair.

Hope made a noise she hoped was interpreted as frustration. "Someone is helping him. That's why we can't find him. He's in someone's house with his feet up, planning his next murder and his ultimate getaway plan. Did he kill the other prison guard, do you think?"

Frazer shook his head. "Looks as if Humphrey Byron was killed when the van tumbled into the river. He didn't have any water in his lungs."

So he didn't drown.

"He was fully clothed. It appears likely he released the prisoners before the van took its final plunge."

"He died a hero." She blinked away the moisture that tried to gather in her eyes.

"He died in the line of duty," Aaron agreed. "Both guards did."

Frazer looked unimpressed, but he was always difficult to read. "After the crash, it appears Somack and Roberts went one way, Leech another."

"He couldn't even make friends in prison." Her tone was bitter. She couldn't help it. Leech had considered her a friend. He'd said so on the stand. If killing families was how he rewarded friends, no wonder people steered clear of him.

"We suspect he somehow got ahold of Graham Burns' cell and vehicle. According to his family, Burns was moving across country to start a job in New York City, but no one has heard from him since Saturday when he set off. We have a BOLO on the vehicle."

"You think this Graham Burns is dead?" A knot of anxiety settled in her stomach. That would make three people he'd murdered since he'd escaped. Three they knew of.

Frazer met her gaze. "I'll be very surprised if he's not."

"Any success pinging his cell?"

"Not yet." Frazer shook his head.

"Leech has been lucky so far. It won't last forever," Aaron stated firmly.

But she wasn't feeling it. Leech was still out there, defying the odds—killing people.

She felt Aaron watching her as she pulled on her winter coat. It was unnerving how hyperaware of her own body she'd become. As if she'd had a growth spurt and had to concentrate on each move because she no longer fit her own skin.

She contemplated taking files home but decided against it. She was tired, and if she decided to work, she could start writing her next book. Deadline was nine months out, but she liked to turn in projects early.

Being anonymous, she didn't have to do any public appearances, but she did have to do the writing and edits. She'd hired someone to update her website and social channels through her agent—Danny's agent—who was pretty much the only person who knew Hope's secret identity, aside from Brendan.

She closed her laptop and put it in her leather briefcase.

"Want to come back to the house for something to eat?" she asked Frazer. He'd be the buffer she needed to stop making a fool of herself.

He rubbed his eye sockets. "No. Thanks. I'm going to spend another hour here before taking my hosts out to dinner. You are welcome to join us."

Her lips kicked up at the sudden tension in Aaron's body. Going out to dinner would be a pain in the neck for her team of bodyguards even if it was with two other FBI agents. It hit her then. "What if we don't catch him?"

"We will," Aaron said firmly.

She blinked. "What if we don't? He could get on a private jet and end up in another part of the country—another part of the world…"

"If he was going to do that, he'd have done it before he killed Sylvie and her husband." Frazer twisted his neck to the side as if working out a kink.

"He has an agenda." She was high on that agenda. "HRT can't guard me forever."

The two men exchanged a look she couldn't read.

"You won't be left unprotected." Aaron's dark eyes bored into hers.

But they all knew Aaron didn't make decisions when it came to HRT's deployment. Suddenly, she couldn't hold his gaze. The idea of him leaving left a hole inside her, and that hole scared the crap out of her because it was a faint echo of another pain she was all too familiar with. But the knowledge also prompted her to think about taking a chance. Not anything serious. Serious was for the young or people who weren't inherently broken. Even the idea of anything serious made her crave a stiff drink. But something fun? Something frivolous? How enticing was that?

She still needed that stiff drink.

"Maybe you could show me a couple of those self-defense moves tonight. Just in case." She should probably go to a gun range and practice her marksmanship too. Even if she didn't have bodyguards, she wouldn't make it easy for that bastard. If she was going down, she'd take him with her.

"We can do that." Aaron didn't look happy at the idea.

So much for that spark of attraction she thought existed between them.

She rolled her eyes at herself. "Goodnight, Linc."

"Goodnight, Hope. Try not to worry."

She snorted as she headed out, unsure where Colin had gotten to. She'd sent him to do a few searches earlier, but maybe he'd gone to grab some dinner or cram in some revision. She nodded to poor Sondra, who was, apparently, being let down gently after asking Seth Hopper out on a date.

Hope felt for her. It was a brave thing to put yourself out there.

"Did you tell her you're already seeing someone?" Aaron asked when the three of them were alone in the elevator.

Seth Hopper nodded.

"Who is this lucky person?" Hope was amused as pink filled the other man's cheeks.

But he remained closemouthed.

Aaron grinned and looked suddenly younger. He stage-whispered, "Only the daughter of VPOTUS."

Hope was shocked. "You're dating Madeleine Florentine's daughter?"

Seth Hopper said nothing, but his eyes glittered as he shot a look at Aaron.

"I hope you voted for her mother's party."

One side of his mouth curled up, but he continued to hold his silence.

Hope frowned as a memory niggled her brain. "Wasn't she involved in some incident in the desert recently...?"

"We can't talk about ops." Aaron filled the suddenly taut silence. "But hopefully that reassures you we won't be spilling any of your secrets either."

And she had plenty of secrets she didn't want revealed.

Hope stared thoughtfully at Seth Hopper as other implications hit home. He'd been involved with Madeleine Florentine's daughter during or after an official operation. The idea of her maybe stealing a night of passion with Aaron Nash wasn't completely out of the realm of possibility.

She knew it was against the rules. She knew that he'd leave, but for the first time in seven years she actually wanted to give in to this desire that had stirred inside her. She wanted to take a risk. Except, she was scared. She didn't even know what she was scared of.

Him rejecting her—or him saying yes?

She liked him. She didn't want to look like a complete idiot if she'd misread the signals. Nor did she want to lose this new friendship. It had been a long time since she'd let anyone into her life. Now she found herself caring about not only Aaron, but all the men who found themselves guarding her from that asshole Leech.

So much for not liking testosterone.

They practically dripped with it.

The drive home was short and filled with taut silence. It had been a long week, and everyone was frustrated by the lack of sightings of Leech. These guys had to be bored out of their skulls on this assignment regardless of the teaching opportunities.

They arrived back at her house, and she was grateful it wasn't still snowing. Parents dragged tiny sleds up the small slope in the park opposite. Paige had adored the snow. A pang of longing tore through her chest, and she turned away.

The SUV parked right outside her house. Seth Hopper and Sebastian Black flanked her as Aaron followed closely behind. Ryan Sullivan led the way and opened the door.

Once inside, the door was locked behind them, and everyone relaxed a little.

"Good day at work?" Kincaid grinned at her. He'd been assigned home base today.

A reluctant smile tugged at her mouth. "Yes, dear. How about you?"

"Well, when I was a field agent I had to cope with bioterrorists and anthrax attacks." He cocked his head. "Now I'm on the Hostage Rescue Team, and watching the mailman drop off a delivery was the highlight of my afternoon."

Hope felt her mouth drop open. "That sounds…terrifying." She wondered if she could use the idea in her next book.

He shot a look over his shoulder. Lowered his voice. "Griffin lost his fiancée during that case. She was a great agent. A good friend."

Ice shot through her veins. She understood that pain far too well. "I am so sorry."

Silence filled the air for a long moment before Ryan raised his nose and sniffed loudly. "Is that Livingstone's special chili I smell?"

Kincaid nodded.

She could smell it too, and her stomach grumbled audibly.

"We can send a bowl up. He made enough to feed us all for days, but it's spicy," Kincaid warned.

"That would actually be wonderful." She had a little casserole left over, but that would save until tomorrow. "Thanks. Anything that involves me not cooking sounds divine."

She felt strangely alone when she dragged her feet up the stairs one tired foot at a time and Aaron stayed where he was. She was safe here. They had gadgets and men all over the place. Leech wasn't about to jump out of a helicopter onto the roof or knock through from the neighboring building or anything.

She pulled off her boots at the door, tossed her coat on the back of the couch and smiled as Lucifer came rushing down the stairs, crying like he'd been left alone for days.

Somebody had missed her.

She picked him up and let the cat bump her face with his. "Hello, pretty." He didn't have much patience for cuddles and squirmed free, making a rush for the kitchen as he meowed loudly. Hope followed.

"You still have kibble. Not good enough for you now, huh?"

She grabbed a can of wet food out of the cupboard and scraped it into Lucy's bowl. The cat ate like it was a contest.

"You only want me for housekeeping. As soon as a few good-looking hunks appear you're all over them for attention."

"Talking to your cat?"

Hope jolted in horror as Aaron appeared in the kitchen doorway. Nothing in his expression suggested he'd heard her words, but heat climbed her cheeks.

"Second sign of madness?" Her voice sounded strangled to her own ears.

He laughed. "I figured we'd run through a quick self-defense lesson before we eat."

She felt her eyes bug. "I, oh, er—"

"Can't back out now, Hope. I have Seth and Black up here ready for action."

She heard the rumble of furniture being moved and felt oddly relieved that they weren't alone because as much as she was tempted, the idea of seducing this man suddenly seemed ridiculous.

She looked down at her work clothes. "Should I throw on yoga pants or something?"

He shook his head. "Let's keep this real world because something tells me you don't often go out in your yoga pants in February."

Ha.

"In fact, let's start with you in your coat. Grab your keys."

Hope did as she was told and felt silly standing in her living room with these three super-fit guys pretending she could fight any of them off if they truly wanted to hurt her.

"The first thing to remember is use your voice as both a warning and a signal to others that you need assistance."

"Oh, I can do that."

"People don't always remember in the moment. Fear paralyzes their vocal cords, and their lizard brain takes over."

"My lizard brain is a shouty bitch."

Aaron's laugh caught her by surprise, but he sobered. "Okay, we're gonna start with the hammer strike. Hold your keys in your fist. Watch these two for a demo."

She clutched the keys and felt stupid.

Seth and Black stood facing one another. Seth pretended to attack the other man and Black held up his clenched fist like he was using a hammer. He brought the fist down hard toward Seth's pretty face, pulling the punch at the last moment.

"Hit *hard* repeatedly. Scream, and as soon as it is safe to do so, get the fuck out."

Aaron stood in front of her and held his hands up. "I'm going to come at you from the front. You practice hitting me."

He took a step forward and grabbed her shoulders. He smiled as she stared at him stupidly. "Get your hand up, and strike at me before I grab you. Try it again."

He stood back and then lunged at her, and she brought her clenched fist down against his shoulder.

She froze, worried she'd hit him too hard.

"Good. Again."

They did it several times over, and she managed to get her hand up and in motion without too much effort.

"Keep your weight on your front foot and put some force into it if this happens for real."

"Can I do it to Jeff Beasley next time I see him in court?" Her heart raced a little.

"You know the answer to that better than I."

Being a lawyer and all.

"Well, damn."

"Next." Aaron stood back. "What are the vulnerable places to go for if someone attacks you?"

"On a guy? The balls."

Aaron took a step back and grinned. "I'm going to let Seth demonstrate this one."

"Chicken." The guy stepped forward. "But don't really hit me in the nuts because I don't want to cry in front of the guys."

Aaron helped her get into a fighting stance. It felt weird to feel his hands touching her even in a perfunctory way.

"Feet apart, weight on that stable front foot. As soon as he steps toward you, you bring that back leg forward and kick him between the legs. And then move out of range as fast as possible as he topples to the ground. You don't want him to take you with him."

He helped her get the rhythm of the kick by demonstrating beside her. "Practice with both legs when you have time. It's a simple movement but very effective if you connect."

They practiced a few times, Hopper catching her ankle when it got a little close to his pride and joy.

She grimaced. "Sorry."

The guy smiled. "No problem."

"Move in closer now," Aaron indicated.

Seth grabbed her shoulders.

Hope froze.

"You're okay, Hope." Aaron's voice slid over her. "If you're in this position, it means you're too close for a decent kick. Best use a knee to the groin instead. Then twist away to the side as he falls. Lose the coat if it means getting away. Let's practice without connecting."

They did so several times until she felt confident enough to grab onto Seth's T-shirt before twisting away.

"The other places with a lot of vulnerability are the throat or eyes."

Hope's stomach lurched at the idea of sinking her fingers into anyone's eyes, but she had to remember if she ever needed to use these moves, she'd be fighting for her life, and she didn't intend to lose.

"Let's try this one. Flex your wrist. Dominant hand." He took her arm and patted the heel of her hand. "Use this."

He moved her into position as Black watched from the couch.

"Jab upward to the nostrils or under the chin."

Black got up and demonstrated on Seth. Seth pulled back before being hit.

"Now you try it." He curled his fingers as if to say, "bring it on."

It felt empowering to do this, to learn how to defend herself.

Nobody mentioned the fact Leech had a gun or liked to use a sharp implement.

She balanced on the balls of her feet and then twisted, throwing her hand toward Aaron's nose. But she misjudged and expected him to jerk away and was horrified when she connected. He spun away and swore, holding his face.

"Oh my God! I'm sorry. So sorry."

Hope was even more mortified when Seth handed Aaron some tissues because he was bleeding.

Aaron swore again.

Seth and Black both started laughing, but it didn't ease her guilt.

Seth's cell dinged, and he checked it. "Sorry, I have to take this." He headed upstairs at a jog.

"Are you okay, Aaron?" she asked. "Let me get some ice."

Sebastian Black began to move the couches back into position. "I think that's enough fun for one day, but tomorrow we should work on what happens if someone grabs you from behind."

"Okay…"

He didn't seem bothered about the fact she'd smacked his colleague in the face.

Aaron headed into the kitchen, and she followed him.

She dug into the freezer drawer and pulled out some ice. Wrapped a clean dish towel around it. "Hold it against your nose. Don't worry about the cloth."

His eyes were watering. Blood smeared across his upper lip.

"I am so sorry, Aaron. I thought you were going to move."

"I thought you were going to pull the punch." He sounded amused rather than angry.

"I did pull the punch. I'm not very good at judging punches, apparently." She couldn't believe she'd made this man's nose bleed. And her with her secret little fantasies of seducing him. Giving him a nosebleed was much more in her wheelhouse.

He held his head over the sink, but the bleeding had slowed to a slight trickle.

"This was a terrible idea."

"Are you kidding me?" He looked at her as if she'd lost her mind. "That was fantastic. You fucking nailed it. And me."

Hope wrung her hands together. "Despite my reputation, I'm not a violent person. The idea I hurt you, anyone…"

He caught one of her hands, and the touch of his warm fingers made something catch inside her chest.

"Don't let this put you off. In a real fight, don't pull your punches, and remember it's you or it's him. Only one of you will walk away, and the odds are in his favor because he doesn't mind causing pain." Those dark eyes of his held hers. "What you did when you hit me meant I couldn't see or think for a few seconds, and that would give you valuable time to get the hell out if it were a real-life situation."

She heard footsteps come into the living room and dropped his hand, taking a guilty step back.

He gave her a quizzical look then shifted his attention to Ryan, who carried two giant bowls of chili.

"Coming in hot." Ryan slid them onto the kitchen counter.

"I was about to head downstairs—" Aaron began.

"Wasn't sure, so I fetched two bowls. Alpha team are officially on the job now, and the actual *alpha* team are eating." He winced at Aaron's swollen nose. "I heard Hope clocked you. You look like you need a drink. Almost makes me feel sorry for you, and then I remember what happened Monday and find myself losing all sympathy."

Aaron narrowed his eyes at his colleague. "You deserved Monday."

"What happened on Monday?" asked Hope.

"Pain and humiliation with a hint of sadistic satisfaction." Ryan winked at her and then turned and walked away.

29

Jeff Beasley sneered impatiently at the gum someone had spat out in the dark, filthy, narrow little alleyway. He edged his handmade Italian leather Oxfords out of the way. A flyer for a local bar with live music wedged itself under a bulging bag of rancid garbage, fluttering in the frigid wind coming off the stormy Atlantic. The smell of dog excrement permeated the air—the perfect allegory for his shitty day. He shivered inside his camel-hair coat, furious at being forced to take such a risk, furious at the inconvenience, furious at being kept waiting—especially in such a disgusting locale.

The scent of pizza drifted from a nearby restaurant and reminded him he was supposed to pick up dinner tonight to save Fiona the effort of cooking and give him an excuse to be late. Again.

He texted her, grateful he'd remembered before he was likely to be bitched at.

She texted back that two of the kids had friends over so to double up the order.

He sent her a thumbs up emoji. He didn't spend much quality time with his family, but with three teens in the house, he was okay with that. He loved his wife, and socially she was an asset, but their sex life had taken a dive over the past decade or so. Rather than rock the boat, he owned a small downtown apartment where he had those needs met by women he could pay by the hour and who kept their mouths shut. Unless he wanted it otherwise.

He smiled.

He hadn't had the opportunity to visit the apartment this week for obvious reasons. Too many eyes on him at the moment. And no one could know about this meeting. His career would be over if the DA's office found out. The bodyguards thought he was still at the office, and he didn't have long before they started tracking his phone. Ridiculous under the circumstances, but he had to at least pretend to be terrified of Leech.

He snorted.

As if that guy was anything other than a pathetic loser. It hardly seemed fair that people like that had so much money and the rest of the population had to earn their paycheck. Jeff was rich by anyone's standards, but he worked hard for his money while the likes of Leech and his ilk were fed gold milk from their mother's teat.

A scuff of a shoe alerted him.

Jeff Beasley whirled in the darkness. "This is madness. What the hell do you want? You know we can't be seen together."

Shadows surrounded the other man, his features hidden beneath the hood of a sweatshirt.

Jeff shuddered as a wave of apprehension crept over him. Or maybe it was the sushi he'd had for lunch. He was working his way up to a peptic ulcer, but when the hell did he have time to take care of himself?

Never, that was when.

Leech's escape was another spanner in the works of his life. A complication he didn't need.

"I couldn't risk the phone." The man stepped closer.

Jeff moved forward so they could speak without being overheard. Something sharp slid into his stomach and was jerked upward at a vicious angle.

He couldn't breathe as the blade was withdrawn and then plunged again, once, twice, three more times.

What...

He collapsed to the grimy garbage-laden ground. The man shoved him backward, and Jeff fell against the damp wall, banging his head and making it ring.

He opened his mouth to call for help, but nothing came out except the blood that bubbled on his tongue.

The man rifled through his pockets, removed his cell and held it up to Jeff's face to unlock it. A moment later, the light off the screen highlighted Leech's angular chin, full bottom lip. Revealed the pitiless glint in those pale blue eyes.

"I guess I'll no longer be needing your services." The smile was cruel.

Pain consumed him. He was going to die. He couldn't believe it. He was going to die here in the grime and the shit. He was going to die, and Hope Harper was going to get the last laugh.

30

Aaron watched as Hope reached up to pull a bottle of red from a wine rack.

"I don't know about you, but I need a drink. Is Ryan always like that?"

"A jackass, you mean?" Aaron grimaced, thinking about the stunt Ryan had pulled on Grady Steel last week. He'd taken his usual overprotectiveness and ramped it up by a factor of a thousand. And he'd totally deserved the ass kicking he'd received on Monday. "Pretty much."

He washed his hands and face in the sink. His nose still throbbed. Hope had caught him at the exact right spot to make his eyes sting and nose bleed. He was grateful she hadn't broken it, and he hadn't gushed blood all over her cream rugs or pale gray couch.

He dabbed the tissue against his upper lip some more, but the wound had clotted, and he could breathe properly.

He took the cloth and tossed it into her washing machine that was in a small utility room off the kitchen. "Want me to run it?"

"Sure. Feel free to throw your T-shirt in too."

He stilled as his imagination kicked into overdrive.

A nervous laugh followed. "That, ah, sounded a bit dubious. Sorry, I meant—"

"I know what you meant." Unfortunately. "My shirt's okay, thanks." He smiled because anything that made Hope laugh a little was a good thing. He programmed the washer. She'd probably throw the cloth away, but he liked to clean up his own messes.

When he came back, she'd taken her chili bowl and glass of red wine and set up in the dining room. She looked so alone sitting at that big table all by herself.

Even though he knew he shouldn't, he found himself picking up the bowl Ryan had brought for him and setting it down beside her. "Mind if I join you?"

"Be my guest. Help yourself to wine."

He watched her take her first spoonful of food as he sat down. He opened his mouth to warn her that Shane Livingstone's idea of spicy was some people's idea of hell.

She blinked, and her eyes started to water. "Oh boy. He wasn't kidding about the heat. Want a glass of water? I'm getting one."

"Sure. Thanks." What he really wanted was a tall, cold beer, but that could wait until he wasn't on duty, which at this rate would be never.

"How is Judge Abbottsford holding up? Do you know?"

"I know Charlie squad have a bigger perimeter to deal with that involves four acres of woods. And there are livestock to take care of." Romano was bitching good-naturedly that Echo squad had drawn the easy assignment. Except Charlie didn't have to deal with the DA's office and court, not to mention reporters every damned day. "Judge is safe enough but sounds like she's a little pissy at the delay in recapturing Leech."

"I know how she feels." Hope placed two glasses of water on the table.

Aaron ate a spoonful of chili and felt his tastebuds explode. It was good though. Livingstone took great pride in his recipe and claimed it had several secret ingredients. Aaron was always happy to taste test for the guy. He knew Shane made a milder version that he supplied to Grace Monteith and her kids.

Grace was the widow of one of their teammates who'd died last month.

Aaron hoped she was doing okay with most of Gold team away from Quantico. She'd lost her husband on the first day of the new year when seven months pregnant. She also had two other kids plus Grady Steel's new rescue dog to take care of. Grady usually pulled his weight, but last week he'd been shot by an old KGB agent, so he had a good excuse.

Kincaid's fiancée, Pip West, had been taking the rescue for a run every day. The people still at Quantico would rally around and make sure Grace had the help she needed, but still Aaron felt bad. It was Gold team's responsibility, their honor, to take care of her the way Scotty would have wanted. He made a mental note to call her later.

He realized, belatedly, that Hope hadn't had that sort of support network. She'd walled herself off instead. The sadness of it hit him all over again.

She'd almost finished her food, and her color was better now than it had been when they'd first arrived back here this afternoon. The self-defense training—while rudimentary—had definitely helped. Nothing like beating up grown men to take your mind off your troubles—in his experience anyway.

He spotted several shelves of hardback books by an author he really liked. Multiple copies of some of the books.

"You must be a big fan." He nodded to the books, but she frowned in confusion. "Frankie O'Malley."

"Oh." Her lips formed a perfect circle, and he found his imagination flaring.

"Yes. Yes, I am." She swallowed. "Kind of."

He tilted his head. "What do you mean? Kind of."

She looked at him then quickly away. "Nothing."

He stared at the books again and thought about the writing

craft textbooks he'd spotted in the office upstairs where he was sleeping. "You wrote those books."

"What?" Her mouth dropped open, and her eyes grew wide in shock.

"And if you're planning to deny it you need to work on your poker face."

She closed her mouth and took a sip of water. Fanned her cheeks which were now bright red. "No one has ever guessed before. I mean, Brendan knows because…well, that's a whole 'nother story."

The more Aaron knew Brendan the less he liked him. He shouldn't let his personal feelings show though. Brendan was her family by marriage, and she obviously cared about the guy. The fact some of Aaron's feelings might stem from some juvenile form of jealousy was something he'd take to his grave.

She inhaled a big breath. "Can you keep it a secret?"

He leaned back in his chair. "I am the soul of discretion."

She put her spoon down, and her hands played nervously in her lap. "I've never told anyone. Ever."

He felt a glow of satisfaction at her confession. "You never told anyone you're a talented bestselling author?" But he didn't understand. "I thought your late husband was the writer?"

"He was." She nodded quickly. "He wrote under a pseudonym. The first three books are all his. I helped him plot and was his first reader, but they are all Danny's work. He had the first ten books in the series all mapped out. He was halfway through book four when Leech…" Shadows crossed her features. "When that sonofabitch murdered him. I couldn't bear for the story to be unfinished, so I worked on it in the evenings. The alternative was losing my mind to grief, so there was that. After the story was finished, I sent it to his agent and told him what I'd done. I never expected them to want to publish the book." She shrugged. "It went from there."

"And no one ever suspected?"

She picked up her spoon and took another bite of chili, licking her lips. "I don't think so. People knew Danny was a writer from an earlier set of books he published under his own name. They didn't do so well, and he sold the Frankie O'Malley books under a pseudonym that he kept anonymous for that reason. The first book was optioned for a movie"—pride filled her voice—"but it never happened."

She had a faraway look in her eyes as she ran a finger up and down her water glass. Then picked up her wine instead and took a large swallow.

"At some point, he would have revealed himself as the writer, but I think he was so focused on getting the books out there. Getting them right. He didn't want to jinx himself."

She looked sad and vulnerable again under the bright lights.

"Writing was a kind of therapy for me." Her eyes flickered. "I could happily kill a few bad guys and get my on-paper revenge." She smiled suddenly. "You can bet your ass Frankie is going to knock someone out using the heel of her hand."

"Glad my pain can be of use to the arts." He took a sip of water. "It was a heel palm strike, by the way."

Her eyes shone as she grinned. "Good to know. Thank you. And, again, sorry."

He wiped his mouth with a napkin. "How did Brendan figure it out?"

"Oh. God. In typical Brendan style, he pitched a fit when he heard Danny's book was being released because he knew Danny was only halfway through writing it when he died. Brendan and I both advised Danny on police procedural and legal stuff. Brendan rushed over here the way he does sometimes and told me he was going down to New York to 'talk' to the publisher." She rolled her eyes. "Told me to threaten them with legal action or else he would. I had no choice but to tell him the truth and swear him to secrecy because by then, they'd offered me another contract." She shrugged and Aaron found himself distracted by the outline of her lacy bra visible through her cream blouse.

He cleared his throat and covered the way his skin heated by eating another spoonful of chili. "I think it's remarkable. I'm genuinely a big fan."

"You read them?"

He nodded.

She laughed self-consciously and blushed a little. "It feels weird that anyone beside my agent or Brendan knows." Her eyes widened and her eyes shot to the bookcase. "Do you think the others will guess?"

"They might. Kincaid's fiancée is a writer too. She was a journalist before." He caught the look in those worried silver moon eyes. "They won't say anything. You can trust us, you know."

"It's been a long time since I trusted anyone."

He reached out and took her fingers in his. Squeezed gently.

She swallowed but didn't withdraw her hand. In fact, she held on tight.

Suddenly, they were staring into each other's eyes, and he didn't want to look away, and he didn't want to destroy this fragile moment by asking her what she wanted or what any of it meant.

He was in charge of her *protection*.

Nothing else should be on his mind. Not how good it would be to undo the silky buttons on her blouse. Not finding the source of that sweet vanilla scent. Not the thought of her hands on his feverish skin.

Footsteps on the stairs had him quickly withdrawing, but those questions pressed down on him.

He looked across as Seth Hopper entered the room. "Everything okay?"

"Yeah. Fine." His eyes scanned the two of them sitting there together.

Fuck.

Aaron hated what he didn't see in the man's blank expression. "Ryan brought us some chili. You want me to go fetch you some?"

Seth shook his head. "I was thinking of going for a run before I eat, but the weather sucks. Do you think your neighbors would mind if I used the running machine in their apartment, Hope?"

"They wouldn't mind. They're lovely people, and I'm going to have to find them a suitable gift for when they come home next weekend. Maybe a Mercedes."

They all laughed, knowing she was joking.

Aaron wanted to believe this would all be over by then, especially as they needed to be out of here by Tuesday night, for thirty-six hours at least.

But Leech wasn't some madman running around in the woods. He had resources and people who'd help him evade the authorities. Aaron hoped local agents had Eloisa Fairchild staked out tonight because he was convinced someone else had been upstairs in her house earlier today. Someone with two legs, not four.

Maybe Aaron should go for a run. Get rid of the unsettled itchy feeling that plagued him.

Seth tipped his head in thanks and took a step back. "I'll grab my gear. Thanks again for the use of your bedroom. A little privacy is a wonderful thing."

"How is Zoe?" asked Hope.

Seth looked surprised.

Aaron raised his hands in denial.

"What, you think I can't google the name of the Vice President's daughter?" Hope backed off at Seth's obvious discomfort. "She's pretty. And I promise I won't tease you anymore."

Seth's eyes glinted. "Maybe you'll get to meet her someday."

Hope's wide mouth pulled to one side. "I don't run in those circles."

"Neither did I." Seth sent Aaron a loaded look before he jogged away to get changed.

Aaron ignored the guy. Reminded himself this was a job, and that job meant no fantasizing about the principal naked. She wasn't going to be interested in a guy like him. Not really. He pushed back his chair. Collected the empty dishes as he stood.

"I'll rinse these and return them downstairs. Let you get on with your evening."

"Thank you for that. You have been the best houseguest I've ever had—you've also been the only houseguest I've ever had." She looked a little embarrassed by her attempt at humor. She cleared her throat. "I have no exciting plans for the evening." She hesitated. "If you wanted to stay, that would be all right..." She looked away, clearly unsure of his reaction.

His pulse gave a little skip, but he calmed himself down. Hope wasn't the sort of woman to be hitting on a guy like him. "I'd be happy to stay, but I need to go talk to the guys. And then I want to read some more case files before I get some sleep."

"Of course. Of course, you have work to do, and you must be exhausted." Uncertainty, and what looked like disappointment, flashed over her features.

Had that been a come on that he'd completely misread? He'd opened his mouth to say something that would probably get him fired when her cell rang.

She reached over to where it lay on the table. Pulled a face. "Sleazy Beasley. I wonder what he wants."

Aaron turned away to give her the illusion of privacy even though he was listening to every word.

"What can I do for you, Jeff?" Her gasp had him turning. "Aaron. Quickly." She hurried toward him and showed him the screen.

It was dark but he could see Jeff Beasley slumped against a white-painted brick wall, his face contorted with pain.

She fiddled with the volume.

"Is it a video call or a video message?"

"I don't know. A call I think."

He touched his finger to her lips and caught her gaze to remind her whoever was on the other end could hear them too.

Eyes massive, she nodded.

"Jeff, can you talk to me? Are you okay?"

The videographer pulled back slowly until they revealed a pool of blood spreading over Jeff's white shirt.

"Jeff, where are you? Can you tell me?"

The man's eyes flickered briefly.

Aaron moved away out of earshot. Called Frazer. The man picked up immediately despite probably being in a fancy restaurant. "Jeff Beasley has been attacked. Someone is sending Hope a video call of him right this very second."

"I'll call Parker. See if he can track down the position. The call will be being recorded."

Aaron looked over to Hope, whose face was stricken.

"They hung up. But I think I know where Jeff is." She hurried to the door to pull on her boots.

"Where?"

"Downtown. An alley near his firms' offices. I'll show you."

"I'm not letting you get anywhere near potential danger, Hope."

Her eyes glinted with fire as she turned to him. "He's still alive. And I'm not asking permission."

"Anything?" he asked Frazer.

"Not yet. Parker is heading to his computer to triangulate, but it will take time now the UNSUB has hung up."

Hope had pulled on a black puffer jacket. He could force her to stay here, but he'd lose any trust he might have built, and she'd hate him for it.

Rule number one. Never get emotionally involved with a principle.

Hell. He'd smashed that one into a thousand tiny pieces.

He pulled the comms unit from his pocket and put it in his ear. "Alpha team. I want both cars brought around front immediately. Possible victim downtown, and we are going to check it out."

He strode down the stairs and found everyone in motion.

Livingstone shot a surprised glance when he spotted Hope. Dropped his voice for Aaron alone. "We're taking the principal to a possible active crime scene?"

"She thinks she knows where he is, and frankly, that's the best we have right now in terms of locating the vic."

"It's an alley near Beasley's offices, but I can't remember the exact address. I'll know it when I see it." Hope sounded genuine, but he wasn't so sure.

He went into the downstairs apartment, grabbed his ballistics vest and raid jacket.

"Ryan, I need a couple of your guys on duty here until we get back. The others get some rest while you have the chance. It's gonna be a long night."

31

Hope gnawed at her thumbnail until the skin was raw as worry carved at her insides. They were flying across the North Washington Street Bridge, Shane Livingstone driving scarily fast, cherry lights spinning, sirens blaring—the second SUV close behind.

"Take a left then first right down Prince." They drove through Little Italy. This whole area was full of Italian restaurants and cafés.

"Beasley, Waterman, Vander and Company have a building on Hanover, not far from Paul Revere's House. I think he's somewhere east of there."

"Are you sure you don't remember the exact name of the street?" Aaron sounded like he didn't believe her.

"It's been a few years since I visited this part of the city." Things might have changed. "I might be wrong, but there was something about it that seemed familiar…"

God, what if she *was* wrong, and Beasley was bleeding out on a sidewalk somewhere else?

"Show me on my cell where you think it might be." Aaron pulled up the map of the area on his phone.

She leaned closer, brushing against his arm, fighting the

awareness that was so completely inappropriate under the circumstances.

"I think it *might* be on Fleet." She pointed to a gap between buildings. "There. I think it might be there or somewhere along that street. The wall behind Jeff had flaked white paint over red brick. I think that's the place where I've seen brick like that." But it wouldn't be the only place in the city…

She watched Aaron text Frazer the location they were headed to and then tell Griffin the address so he could program the SatNav for Livingstone who was driving.

"Why call me?"

Aaron's lips firmed but he remained silent.

"To taunt me. To say, 'you're next, Hope, but while you're hiding behind bodyguards, I'm picking off the low hanging fruit.'" Her eyes went wide. "Jeff had bodyguards too. Where are they?"

Aaron shook his head.

Hope didn't like Jeff Beasley, but she didn't want to see him dead.

Less than fifteen minutes since she'd gotten the call, and they were pulling up in front of a manicurist that was closed for the day.

"Yes. Down there." Hope pointed and went to get out of the vehicle.

Aaron clamped his fingers around her arm. "Stay here. Beasley isn't my responsibility. You are."

She opened her mouth.

"No arguments, counselor. Stay here with Livingstone, or we all go home."

She glared at him knowing a man was possibly nearby bleeding to death. "Just go. And be careful."

Aaron and Will Griffin joined Ford Cadell and JJ Hersh on the sidewalk—men who'd been hostile strangers to her only a few days ago. Now she knew bits and pieces of each of them. The idea of any of them being hurt while protecting her was unacceptable. They headed down the alleyway and out of sight.

She called Frazer, but he didn't pick up. She felt so useless. The sound of sirens pierced the air.

Her cell rang. It was Aaron.

"We found him."

"Alive?"

"Yes. But he's in bad shape."

Flashing lights strobed the buildings around them. "Ambulance is almost here."

Livingstone moved the car a few feet along to make room as patrol units rolled up along with the EMTs.

All of a sudden, she was thrown back to the day Danny and Paige were murdered. Her daughter's blue-tinged lips. The slight rise and fall of Danny's chest. The faintest elusive flutter of his heartbeat. Catapulted into the overwhelming fear and terror and sheer helplessness of not having the skills needed to save them.

An invisible steely hand gripped her throat, and she couldn't suck in oxygen. Her body shook and her hands went numb. Her vision turned black along the edges.

"Hope. You're okay. You're having a panic attack. Just breathe." Livingstone's voice was a deep hum in the background as he twisted to face her. To calm her because she was losing her fucking mind.

She nodded and looked out the window, and saw Leech smiling at her from the gloom of an alleyway across the road. At first, she thought it was a flashback. A memory of the smile he'd had on his face as he'd watched her family dying. But he wasn't wearing a suit this time. He wore a wool hat and a jacket over a hoodie, the hood pulled low, casting shadows over his gaunt features.

She fumbled with the door, but the locks clicked shut.

"Nash said to wait here—"

"Leech! Leech is over there!"

"Where?" Livingstone spun around.

"The guy in black." She fought with her seatbelt. "Shit, he's gone. You have to let me out. He was over there, goddammit!"

She tried the door again and then struggled to lower the window, but that was locked too.

Livingstone was talking into his comms, and she saw Aaron, Griffin, and Cadell come running.

"Let me out of here." She started swearing, and Livingstone finally unlocked the doors as Aaron opened it. He slid inside, forcing her back across the seat.

Hope jabbed her finger toward the alley. "Leech was right over there watching us."

"I didn't see him." Livingstone's tone was concerned.

She glared at the guy.

"You're sure it was him?" Aaron opened the window to look.

Hope grabbed him by the shirt, pulled him nose to nose. "You don't forget the face of a man who violently slaughtered your family."

"Griffin, Cadell, check out that alley. Shane, let's see if we can pick him up coming out the other side. Crow and Hersh stay in position," he told the second car.

Livingstone took off, cruised around North Street, then up Lewis.

She peered out the window and the others did the same. Up ahead she saw a figure and pointed. "There! That's him." The man was walking briskly away from them, head down, hands in pockets. Livingstone sped ahead, and Aaron jumped out and had the man on the ground before she could take a breath.

She followed, ignoring the shouts that told her to stay inside the car. She heard running feet as Griffin and Cadell caught up with them. Excitement surged through her as Aaron pulled the man to his feet and spun him around.

A rock hit her stomach. It wasn't Leech.

32

"I'm *so* sorry. This isn't the man I saw." Hope whirled around clearly searching for the serial killer.

Aaron exchanged a look with Livingstone, and the guy shook his head. He didn't believe Hope had seen Leech at all. Aaron let Griffin deal with the innocent passerby, who'd probably pissed himself.

"Hope." He caught her shoulders. "Let's get back in the car."

She whirled on him then, her eyes wild. "I saw him. You have to believe me."

"I do believe you, but he's not here now, and we need to get into the car and find out how Jeff Beasley is doing."

That snapped her back into the present, and she nodded and hurried to the SUV.

Once they were all inside, they drove around the block in time to see an ambulance pull away, sirens blaring.

"Wait here." Aaron jumped out as he spotted Frazer and caught up with him. "Is he still alive?"

Frazer's mouth pinched. "Barely. They doubt he's going to make it."

"Parker or anyone else have any luck tracing the call?"

"Yes, but you're already here. It came from Beasley's cell,

253

which was found near the body." He pulled an evidence bag out of his pocket. "I'm going to drive it to the nearest lab and get it analyzed for fingerprints and DNA overnight before I courier it to Parker and see if he can find anything on the phone that he can't get from the cell company or tower records."

"Hope saw Leech watching the scene. She's pretty strung out."

Frazer's gaze sharpened. "It wouldn't surprise me at all if Leech hung around to watch the show."

"We searched for him, but we didn't pursue immediately. The guy we grabbed wasn't Leech, but Leech could have gotten away or slipped into one of these buildings."

"She may or may not have seen him." Frazer's gaze scanned the shops along the street. "I wonder if any of them have security cameras that may have captured Beasley before the assault. Did he meet Leech willingly—he is his client, after all—or was he attacked by someone else?"

"Why would someone else call Hope?"

Frazer's gaze met his. "It's all connected, I have no doubt of that. But where are his bodyguards? Would Beasley really have met the guy alone?"

"Meeting with an escaped convicted killer would mean instant disbarment if anyone found out?"

"Yes, but I'm sure Beasley could spin it that he was trying to get the man to turn himself in. As lucrative as Leech is, I doubt Beasley would risk his license for one man."

Aaron spotted a jeweler's shop a few buildings down. "Some of these places will have security footage. But I can't help canvass. I have to get Hope home. She shouldn't be here at all."

Frazer nodded. "I'll call the Boston SAC. See that he puts agents on it immediately. This is an FBI case even if I have to pull strings." Frazer was a pro at pulling strings. "We need to go to Beasley's office and question his assistant. Seize his appointment book and monitor his email and texts, although the law firm will fight us every inch. Is Hope all right?"

Aaron thought of the despairing look in her eyes when she

thought they didn't believe her. Shook his head. "I don't think so."

Frazer swore.

Aaron looked up at the windows that overlooked the street. People stared out at the activity. Plenty of possibilities that someone saw something.

"If Beasley survives, how will he live with the irony it was Hope who saved him? And how will she live with the irony she managed to save a man she loathes but not the people she loved?"

"It's a hell of a thing," Frazer agreed. "I'll call as soon as I hear about Beasley's condition and go to the hospital after I've dropped the cell with the crime lab."

"Leech is keeping a lot of people very busy."

"I'm pissed it's gone on this long."

Aaron nodded and walked away.

Inside the SUV, there was a tense silence. Hope was ghostly pale, and her jaw clamped tight. Arms crossed tight around herself as she stared out the window at the patrol cars.

He wished he could pull her into his arms to comfort her, but she was angry and aloof. "Frazer's going to call when he hears anything about Beasley's condition—"

She twisted to face him. "We can't go to the hospital?"

He shook his head and watched her spine straighten as if preparing for a fight. "Look, we can go and hang out all night in the public waiting room if you like. Get in the way of the medical staff. Tire out the team. Put you in potential danger from either Leech or the likes of Minnie Ramon. Or we can be sensible and wait for news. Get some rest. It's not like you're family. They won't tell you anything."

She exhaled with a shudder. "I hate it when you throw logic and reason at me."

He suppressed a smile. That was the Hope he knew and...*liked*.

Yeah. Best not to think about it.

"Logic and reason. That's why we call him the Professor," Livingstone joked, but his eyes in the rearview were worried.

Aaron gritted his teeth. He wasn't feeling logical or reasonable when it came to Hope. Not anymore.

Hope's fingers gripped one another. "He has a wife, Fiona, and three kids who must be teenagers now. I can only imagine—" She cut herself off and ran her hands over her face.

She didn't have to imagine. She'd experienced this exact situation herself.

"Can you have someone pick them up and drive them to the hospital?"

He texted Frazer to ask agents from the Boston Field Office to do just that. Without a dedicated task force, Frazer was the de facto contact point and team leader—whether he liked it or not.

"Done." He reached out and touched her arm. She was trembling beneath the down. "You okay?"

She inhaled a juddering breath. Nodded. "Just a normal Thursday night. Let's head back like you suggested. I need to call the DA and update him."

Livingstone didn't wait for more permission than that. He pulled into traffic. Aaron checked the back window and saw the other SUV follow, Damien Crow driving.

Hope fished out her cell and called her boss. The conversation was long and heated. They were drawing up outside her home by the time she hung up. The shadows under her eyes looked like bruises under the harsh streetlights.

He was about to open his mouth and say not to worry, that they'd catch him, but her glittery gaze caught his.

"Don't," she warned.

He shut his mouth. Dammit.

Once inside, Hope went straight upstairs, and he stood and watched her go. Then he went in to brief the team and Novak about this latest development.

Could Leech have been watching them downtown? Where had he disappeared to? Who was hiding him? Had Eloisa

Fairchild left her house tonight? Was Leech thumbing his nose at them, staying at his Beacon Street mansion with the Delawares providing cover?

Aaron had an idea. "Hey, Shane, JJ." He waved Livingstone and Hersh over to him. "Do we have the handheld radar with us?"

Livingstone nodded.

"I want you guys to go check something out for me. No one else needs to know."

33

Hope dragged herself upstairs and, once inside her apartment, kicked off her boots.

She walked into the kitchen and poured herself a tall, cold glass of water, drank half, then rested the cool glass against her brow. It had been a long time since she'd suffered from a panic attack, but then again, it had been a long time since she'd experienced a day like today.

The memory of Jeff Beasley's haggard features. The blood on his shirt...

It was too shockingly close to how she'd found Danny.

On top of the murders of Sylvie and her husband, it was all too much. She closed her eyes and blew out a long breath. She decided to head straight to bed. She still had court in the morning even though there might be a slight delay to the trial. But as Beasley wasn't doing the legal leg work, she doubted it. She felt selfish for thinking about the trial, but Ella Gibson's wellbeing was on the line too. The longer Jason Swann was walking around free, the more danger Ella was in.

Hope squashed the guilt by reminding herself how Beasley had made her work her full months' notice when she'd quit the firm. She'd walked away with a lot of money following a settle-ment and nothing in her heart except hatred and despair.

Maybe it wasn't Leech who'd stabbed the guy. Maybe it was one of his many dissatisfied coworkers or clients, and they'd used Leech's escape as a cover to get rid of the man. But that would mean she'd only imagined seeing Leech on the street tonight and that she really had lost her mind for a few minutes back there.

She didn't want to believe that. She needed to believe in herself if nothing else. What else did she really have? But she was tired and anxious after a week of little sleep and high stress. She needed some rest. She switched on the under-cupboard lights. Lucy was asleep on the couch, and she thought about stroking him, but he looked so content she didn't want to disturb him. A king in his kingdom, overlord to one.

She headed to her bedroom and shut the door to get changed even though she usually left it open for the cat. She didn't want an audi-ence should one of the guys be heading down the stairs. They moved more quietly than the resident feline. She stripped and climbed into the shower to wash away the acrid scent of sweat and fear.

For all her tough talk, she'd almost passed out back there tonight, and that was simply because a man she didn't even like had been stabbed—and the memories it had evoked.

She'd wanted so desperately to get out of the car and grab onto Leech—to catch him and put him back inside the box he so richly deserved. To rot. To wither. To die.

She wanted to see him punished. She wanted to see him suffer. She wanted him to hurt even a fraction of how much she hurt.

And it would never be enough.

She'd always known prison would never be enough for him to atone for what he'd done, but it was all she could ask, except in the dark shadowy places of her soul where she wanted much, much worse.

But she wasn't the monster. He was.

She rinsed the conditioner out of her hair and turned off the tap. Wrapped herself in her soft bathrobe before quickly blow-drying her shoulder-length hair in the mirror.

She ran through her nightly skincare routine. Her eyes, probably her best feature, looked stormy and dark. Nose too sharp, mouth too wide for true beauty. But she had seen attraction on Aaron Nash's expression more than once. And suddenly she was thinking of something other than Leech and death and grim recovery as the only life path.

Desire uncoiled inside. Layered with guilt and the knowledge that Aaron technically wasn't allowed to get personally involved with someone he was supposed to be protecting. There were rules. Hell, with most government organizations even the rules had rules.

But he wasn't alone on this assignment, standing guard with his rifle night and day. There was a whole team of people on the job. Ten other men in an around-the-clock circle of protection. And she wasn't some poor victim who'd asked to be saved. She was the woman who'd helped convict that motherfucker in court, and Leech was one of many scumbags she dealt with on a regular basis. She was part of the same justice system Aaron was part of. Effectively they were on the *same* team.

And they hadn't given her a choice.

So, while this attraction might come to nothing more than the quickening of a pulse or the flaring of pupils in an unguarded moment, she at least intended to be ready for whatever scenario might come her way. She wasn't some wilting wallflower, and while she might not be that sexually experienced, considering the fact she was thirty-seven years old and had been married and conceived a child, she remembered the basics.

She pulled out her favorite scented body lotion and smoothed it all over. If nothing else, she was going to smell great tomorrow.

She felt better, she realized. Thinking about something other than Leech always felt good. And she knew it was nothing more than physical desire, but it was another win over the serial killer who'd for some reason declared himself her nemesis. Leech had stolen her sexuality as well as her family, she realized now.

This thing with Aaron was the perfect distraction. She wouldn't allow herself to get emotionally involved. She refused to be devastated when he left. She was immune to all that. Losing the man she'd loved had almost destroyed her once, and Aaron was a man whose job dared things to kill him on a regular basis.

She swallowed hard at the thought of it.

She was not about to risk going through that kind of heartbreak again. Ever. But for the first time in many, many years she wanted a man in her bed. And she wanted that man to be Aaron.

She hadn't heard him come upstairs, so she climbed into bed and pulled out her tablet, intending to read case notes. Instead she opened the latest thriller series she was hooked on.

She was asleep in under thirty seconds.

34

It was almost midnight by the time Aaron finally made his way to Hope's apartment. The guys had come back and reported that Leech's home was surprisingly empty whereas there were indeed three people in the Fairchild mansion, one in a room near the kitchen, and another two upstairs, one who looked child-sized.

He'd called Frazer. According to him, Eloisa's live-in house-keeper had a six-year-old son, so chances were they were the other people in the house.

Cancel the dawn raid.

Hope had gone to bed. All the lights were off except for a thin strip under the kitchen cabinets that he suspected she left on for them so they weren't disoriented—which was sweet, especially considering how strung out she'd been tonight and the fact they were supposed to be elite operators, not little kids scared of the dark.

He grabbed a glass of water and headed silently up the stairs. Hope's room door was shut, and the light was off. He hoped she was getting some rest. The strain of the past few days was starting to tell.

He resisted the urge to knock on her door to check on her. The last thing he needed to do was disturb her rest or put himself in temptation's way.

She'd invited him to spend the evening with her. Had she meant hanging out watching TV? Or had she meant…

Nah.

If only.

He shook his head and walked into his room. That was his overactive imagination at work and the fact he hadn't had sex since the dawn of time. Plus, the fact he was absolutely attracted to the woman, and it wasn't simply her blonde good looks. Her grit, her drive, and the fact she struggled so hard not to be a nice person. It made him smile when it shouldn't affect him at all.

He stripped off his holster, comms, shirt. Tossed them on the desk and pulled out his phone which he plugged in to the charger. He grabbed sleep pants and a towel and headed for the shower. He scrubbed himself clean and, afterwards, quickly dried off and headed back to his room.

The shower had woken him up, and he paced for a few minutes, checking for updates from Frazer or Novak.

Beasley was still in surgery. His odds were poor.

The man's "bodyguards" had been under the impression the guy was in his office when it turned out he'd snuck out via an interior door and secretly left the building.

Aaron sat on the side of the camp bed, which creaked ominously under his weight. He spied the gaming chair at the desk and decided that looked sturdier and more comfortable for reading, so he picked up the box that held the files from Hope's family's murders and set it on the floor beside the desk.

He started with the police reports, which described the Harper home scene as chaos and severely compromised by EMTs and cops after almost everyone in the local vicinity traipsed through it. He read the interview detectives had done with Hope while she was at her mother-in-law's house in Southie, raw with loss. The interviewing officer wasn't particularly sympathetic. In places he was downright cruel, describing Hope as robotic and uncooperative.

Then Aaron read her written statement of how she'd come home after making partner at her law firm only to find the two people she loved most in the world, dead or dying. He felt sick thinking about it. And how Leech had been Johnny-on-the-spot.

Occam's razor had been applied.

Next, he read Leech's statement taken from the hospital bed that Brendan Harper had put him in. Leech's nose had been broken and his one cheekbone shattered. Though under arrest Leech had stayed in the hospital until his surgeries were finished, BPD covering its own ass despite having twenty witnesses to say Leech resisted arrest.

Leech claimed that he'd received a call around 5 p.m. inviting him to dinner at Hope Harper's home. He claimed he thought they were friends after spending so much time together over the previous four months. He'd planned to give her a massive bonus, maybe pay off her mortgage in gratitude for all her hard work. When he'd arrived, he claimed Hope had answered the door and pushed past him and then waved down the EMTs. He'd had no idea what was going on. He described how she'd had blood on her hands, clearly attempting to incriminate her rather than himself.

He recounted how she'd begged the EMTs to revive her child. *Begged*.

According to phone records, Leech had indeed received a text with the dinner invite and Hope's address. The text had come from a burner that had never been traced or recovered.

Hope swore under oath she hadn't texted the guy.

Was it possible that Blake Delaware had texted Leech before he'd left for the airport and then destroyed the phone to give Leech an alibi? Leech had gotten away with murder before. Perhaps he'd gotten cocky.

It was technically possible that Hope had texted Leech from some unknown phone and used the release of the suspected serial killer as a scapegoat to murder her husband and kid, as Leech's lawyers had claimed at one point. But most people didn't commit murder to get rid of an unwanted partner, and certainly not a beloved child. Divorce existed for a reason. The murder angle only made sense if you were comfortable taking someone else's life. The way Leech was comfortable.

The last thing Aaron looked at were the autopsy photos, and even though he'd been in law enforcement for six years and there wasn't much he hadn't seen, the red petechiae in Paige Harper's blue eyes about shattered him. He flicked through the photos quickly. The girl had not been sexually assaulted, which was a small mercy. Leech often said to anyone who'd listen that he didn't hurt children. A lot of pedophiles said the same thing. They *loved* children. They'd never harm them. The kids liked what was done to them. They enjoyed it. They instigated it. Mutual pleasure or momentary weakness—Aaron had heard it all, and it turned his stomach.

Danny Harper had been a fit, good-looking guy. The autopsy had revealed scrapes on his knuckles and a bruise on his jaw. The single stab wound just below the ribs had led to massive internal bleeding, but he'd taken his time to die—in slow increments, all the while knowing his daughter was dead beside him and his wife's life was about to be completely blown apart.

Hope had admitted they'd argued the night before over her representing Leech.

The ME hadn't been too clear on Paige's time of death. It had been a warm afternoon, so the body hadn't cooled much. Danny had died on the operating table.

Aaron knew that part of Hope's guilt would lie in the belief that if she'd gotten home earlier, if she'd skipped the celebrations at her firm, even though she was the guest of honor, she might have prevented the attack, or she might have arrived home in time to at least save her husband. He didn't know if he could have coped with half of the pain she'd endured. It made his fiancée's betrayal look like a fly in his beer.

And that wasn't quite accurate because the betrayal had wrecked him, but the comparison was stark. But Aaron would rather his ex find happiness with his brother than end up on a slab. No contest. No fucking debate.

The cat began scratching at Hope's door. He hesitated a moment but didn't want the meowing and scratching to wake her if she was asleep. The woman deserved some peace. He closed the folder and went silently into the hall to let the cat inside. He had his hand on the doorknob when it opened.

Hope stood there in a pretty blue silky sleep shirt that barely reached her knees. Her face was pale, eyes dark and haunted.

Lucifer darted inside.

Aaron's heart thudded. He opened his mouth to explain about the cat when she reached out and put her hand around his wrist. Tugged him until he took one step, then another. Once inside the room she closed the door and ran her hands up his bare chest, up to his collarbones.

She stood on tiptoe and brushed her lips over his. "Aaron."

His resistance crumbled. He pulled her to him and crushed his lips to her, devouring that mouth of hers which had slowly been driving him mad with lust. She tasted like toothpaste and smelled like summer. He wrapped his arms so tightly around her body it was as if he was worried she might try to escape. Instead, she wriggled closer and sank her hands into his hair. The material of her shirt was smooth as satin and stirred his senses. Their tongues tangled as his hands greedily roamed the soft curves. Need rose up inside him. Damn, he wanted this woman.

A noise on the street jerked him out of the moment.

He pulled away, breathing hard. Caught her hand to stop her touching him.

The silky material clung to the hard peaks of her breasts. He desperately wanted to see her naked but knew if he did, he'd be lost. "This is wrong."

But God help him nothing had felt this right in years.

She blinked, a look of hurt entered her gaze.

"I want you, you know I do, but if anyone finds out, I'll be reassigned back to Quantico." And have his ass justifiably kicked. She was off-limits no matter how much he desired her.

"And your perfect service record will be blotted." She ran her lips over his jaw, reaching up to nibble his earlobe in a move that almost brought him to his knees. "No one has to know, Aaron. I won't tell anyone."

"I'll know." He thought about how upset she'd been earlier. "I don't want to take advantage."

The word *liar* screamed through his veins.

"I think I might be taking advantage of you." She smiled at him then, a smile full of womanly knowledge. She didn't look vulnerable or lost right now. She looked like a siren. She slid her hand slowly down his stomach and then wrapped her fingers around the hard length of him through his pants—a part of him that clearly had not gotten the off-limits message.

He gritted his teeth as sweat broke out on his brow.

She kissed him and swallowed his groan, touching him, stroking him, making him shudder with need.

"Couldn't we have one night? One night where no one but us has to know?" Her gray eyes were dark in the moonlight.

Would one night really be so terrible? He knew Novak and Charlotte Blood had gotten together during that Washington op. And Seth had definitely been getting busy with Zoe during their escape from the drug cartel. The idea of missing out on this connection with Hope... Of always wondering what it would have been like...

He didn't think she'd ask him again if he said no tonight. He didn't think she'd give him a second chance.

"Wait here." He carefully eased open the door and went into his room, grabbed his Glock, his cell, and his comms in case something happened he needed to know about. He dug into his wash bag for a strip of condoms everyone on the team carried for reasons other than sex with the person they were responsible for protecting. But, fuck, Hope wasn't the average civilian. She was in the trenches, and she wasn't scared of Leech or dependent on Aaron for anything except overseeing her security detail. The team were so good they could do the job blindfolded.

He couldn't stand the idea of not taking this chance to *be* with her.

He closed his door and slipped quickly into Hope's room. She stood by the window stroking her cat and turned as he came inside. He turned the old-fashioned key in the lock with a quiet snick.

The cat jumped down and ran under the bed.

"I thought you'd changed your mind," she said softly.

He walked toward her and closed the drapes. Showed her what he had in his hands. "Getting supplies."

Her eyes went wide, and her lips curved. "I hadn't thought that far ahead, but I am grateful for your preparedness. Not sure how my head of security would feel about sending someone out for condoms at this hour."

He didn't want to think about being her head of security right now. He placed the gun, phone, comms, condoms on the table beside the bed.

"You only have to ask anyone on HRT, and they'll have condoms tucked away somewhere."

She coughed out a laugh.

"Not because we're all having sex every five minutes." It had been so long for him he didn't even remember the last time. Well, not the last time that had felt amazing, anyway. Encounters had become mundane, going through the motions because his body wanted it, but his mind hadn't been engaged, and definitely not his heart. "They're useful in survival situations for carrying water."

Hope pulled a face. "Have you drunk out of one?"

Aaron grinned at the image that evoked. "No, but I would if I had to."

She wet her bottom lip, and like that, he was hard as stone.

"We don't have to do this though, Hope. If you've changed your mind—"

She grabbed him and pulled him down by his hair to kiss his mouth with a clash of tongue and teeth.

He hesitated only a moment before resting his hand on the slippery material that hugged her body. He smoothed his hands up and down her sides, the side of his thumb brushing the side of her breasts. She quivered as he tasted her mouth. He pulled her against him, let her feel what she did to him.

She moaned, and it was the hottest sound he had ever heard.

She smelled like vanilla ice cream, and he wanted to lick every inch to see if she tasted like it too. He lifted her, and she surprised him by circling her legs around his waist and pressing her center against his rigid cock.

Sweat burst out of his pores. He was never gonna last. He was going to embarrass himself and leave this woman, who he guessed hadn't had sex with anyone in all the years since her husband had passed, disappointed and unsatisfied.

To hell with that.

He eased her down onto the bed.

He was an elite operator who ran marathons for fun in his spare time. He had no intention of disappointing this woman, but he needed to start running the show.

35

Aaron laid her on the bed and then quickly stripped, revealing a lean and muscled body that made her mouth water. He followed her down onto the sheets. The weight of him pressed between her thighs felt wonderful.

Her alarm clock combined with the city lights through her thin curtains provided enough illumination to see by.

She watched his eyes heat to inky black as he took her in, leaning on his elbows. He kissed her, tongues tangling, lips exploring, the taste of him filling her senses. It had been so long that the need for him ripped through her and made her muscles clench. She wanted this. She couldn't believe he was here or that she wanted him this much. She needed him, before he changed his mind or came to his senses.

Before she did.

He surprised her when he pulled away, lifting her nightgown to reveal her abdomen and matching panties. A friend who lived in the UK had sent her the clothes along with a subscription to a dating app a few years ago. She'd never worn them. Never looked at the app. She didn't even know why she'd kept the nightclothes —until now.

He inched down the bed and licked her through the silk,

zeroing in on her clit without effort. She jolted in surprise. He pressed down harder with his tongue, and her back arched up off the bed. He took advantage of the move by sliding his hands under her ass and lifting her to his mouth. His tongue slid down the side of the panties before he pulled the thin strip of material to one side. He found her center, sinking deep and making her toes curl as the air evaporated from her lungs.

The bristles of his beard and the warm breath on her most sensitive skin made her cry out but he quickly pulled away.

"As much as I want to hear you scream in pleasure, the slightest noise will have this whole house on high alert and the guys rushing in here to save you."

She laughed quietly even though she was appalled by the notion. She whispered, "Are we having stealthy sex, Operator Nash?"

"We are having covert, stealthy sex. Hell, we are having *black ops* sex, and if anyone finds out I will have to kill them." He reared back and dragged the scrap of silk down her legs before tossing it aside. "But I can't seem to help myself."

He crawled back up the bed and his mouth was on her, inside her again, driving her higher and higher. She kept the noises inside because no way did she want to get Aaron in trouble, nor did she want anyone else to know their business. Everyone thought they knew everything about her.

This was private.

Very private.

And, *oh my God*, Aaron Nash knew his way around a woman's body. She tried to hold on, but he pinched her nipple between two fingers and then licked her hard while his fingers filled and stretched her. She rocketed so quickly over the edge she had to bite back the cry that caught her completely by surprise as she shattered into a billion particles of stardust that shimmered through her body.

She grabbed his hair and pulled the dark silky strands between her fingers.

"Come up here for a moment, soldier."

He crawled up her body but stopped at her breasts, stretching the material of her nightgown tight across her nipples before sucking on them with his hot mouth, gently scraping them with his teeth.

"Oh, my God," she whispered. The wet material rubbed the hard beads of sensitive flesh, driving her mindless with lust, and she didn't know what to hold onto to ground herself. "You are so good at this. Did you take classes somewhere? Is that what you're a professor in?"

She loved the flash of a grin he gave her. "No, but I appreciate the performance eval."

"Keep it up, and you'll get an A-plus."

His smile turned grim around the edges. "I'll do my best."

She ran her hands over his shoulders. "I want you inside me, Aaron."

He reached over and snagged a condom off the side table, and she grabbed it out of his hand and tore open the packet, reaching down to sheath him.

She widened her legs, and he positioned himself against her before holding her gaze as he slowly eased inside.

Her nails dug into his back, and she wrapped her legs around him, pressed her heels into his ass as he slowly filled her up.

It felt incredible.

He rocked forward, trapped her head between those large hands of his and held her gaze as he filled her again, and again, and again.

"You're beautiful." His words matched his expression, and they scared her a little.

She hadn't expected to feel the intensity of this quite as keenly as she did, but it had been a long time and marked a lot of firsts. It would be stranger if she wasn't knocked off balance and disoriented by the experience.

It was just sex, but sex was an intimate act, which was why it was such a betrayal when the trust was broken.

She tilted her pelvis to take him deeper still. He groaned softly, nuzzled her neck, her ear. His hand found her breast, and his fingers found her nipple, stroking it, playing with it, finally pinching it until her back arched again, and she exploded into convulsions of pure ecstasy.

He waited for her to come down again, to float back to reality, before he carefully rolled them over so she was on top.

The snow outside made the room so bright she could see every perfect inch of him.

"I don't know if I can do that again." Her voice was a murmur in the velvet darkness.

"Try." His black eyes challenged.

She nodded, then began to move, cautiously at first, then with more confidence. This position gave her all the control but also meant he was as deep inside her as it was possible to be.

She'd forgotten how good it could feel.

He dragged her nightgown up over her head and tossed it away. The desire in his eyes grew feral. The clench of his jaw tighter.

His hands gripped her thighs as she rode him. She went slowly at first, cautious until she found her rhythm, then faster, harder, feeling the need build higher again, the expectations and anticipation coiling inside her. On and on, driving him, driving them both with utter absorption in this connection, this want. And then he wrapped his arms around her so she was immobile as he thrust deeper and harder, and she felt the ripples of his release set off another orgasm as her muscles spasmed around him. Afterward, she lay sprawled across his chest, unable to move, her muscles lax and sated.

He rubbed his hand over her back and nuzzled her neck.

She wanted to thank him but that might sound weird.

A light came on his phone, and he reached over and grabbed it, still inside her.

She went to move away, but he gripped her to him. He read

the phone screen and put it down again. Reached for the condom before letting her ease away.

He rolled up and went into the bathroom. She heard the tap run for a while as if he were washing up and the toilet flush before he came back.

She supposed she should cover herself, but instead she lay there on the bed, completely naked. She wanted him to see her. She wanted him to want her again. She didn't want reality to crash in on them yet.

His eyes latched on to her naked body.

"Something important you need to do?" she murmured.

"Novak said the marshals think they have Somack and Roberts cornered in a small wood not far from where they were last spotted."

She moved up the bed. "Does that mean you have to leave?"

He looked uncertain for a moment. "I can't sleep here, Hope. Not tonight. Maybe when this is over—"

"I wasn't thinking about sleep, Aaron." This wasn't about the future. This was about the now. She bent her knee and watched him swallow.

"Do you *have* to leave right now?" She ran her hand down her front.

He huffed out a breath. "I admire your confidence in my abilities."

"Lie down." She patted the sheet. "Let's see if I can help."

He stood there for a long moment and then finally lay down on the bed. She stretched out in the other direction and started by kissing the delicate bridge of his left foot. He jerked softly, clearly ticklish. She worked her way up to his ankles, his strong calves, figuring out the muscle and bones that made up this man. Suddenly, he grabbed one of her ankles and dragged her across him, way up the bed until he could once again feast with his mouth, and she discovered the astonishing recovery power of a virile man.

36

An hour later, Aaron sat up.

"Now I really have to go." As much as he wanted to be here, he couldn't stay. If he was caught, he was fucked in an entirely different way. The idea of being sent away in disgrace and someone else being put in his place to command Hope's protection team burned a hole through him. That would happen if his superiors suspected he was personally involved with the principal, and it didn't get more personal than naked sixty-nining on the principal's bed.

She ran a hand over the tattoo on his back, her fingers a gentle caress. "Fine. I like your fish by the way. They're *hot*, as the kids would say."

He turned and grinned. "I like every inch of you. And now I have to get my ass out of here before I fuck you again and my dick falls off because it hasn't had this much action in years."

She looked intrigued rather than put off. "We wouldn't want that."

He stood, found his sleep pants. Pulled them on. He grabbed the Glock, cell, comms and stuffed the latter two items in his pocket. He left the sole remaining condom on the bedside table.

Was that optimism for a repeat performance? Probably. Would

he be that lucky? He doubted it. Would he be that stupid? *Absolutely*.

He kissed her, then walked to the door.

"Aaron," she said softly.

He turned.

"Thank you for tonight."

Was that a thank you for tonight, let's do it again sometime? Or a thank you for tonight, and now we're back to being professionals who don't get to see one another without our clothes on?

He didn't know what she wanted and couldn't ask. He didn't want to look desperate. If she wasn't interested in anything more, he'd look like a love-sick moron. If she was…he'd look like a love-sick moron.

He wasn't opening himself up to humiliation. He'd had enough of that for a lifetime and got to choke more down every time he went home to visit his family. Better to keep his mouth shut and enjoy the moment. He eased open the door. The cat ran through, and when Aaron stepped out his insides turned to ice as he spotted Cowboy coming down the stairs.

The other man paused for a moment but said nothing. His eyes narrowed.

Aaron pressed his lips into a thin line. He wasn't ashamed of what he'd done, but he still knew it was wrong and, fuck, he did not want to be thrown off this op.

"Careful, buddy," Ryan murmured as he headed downstairs.

Ryan giving him advice on his sex life was rich. The guy fucked any woman willing and available. But it didn't mean the warning wasn't valid, so Aaron shook off the red-hot fury that lit up inside him and buried it beneath a little common sense. He *was* being careful, but not careful enough, apparently.

Why the hell was Ryan up and about at 2 a.m.?

Aaron grabbed a towel and hit the shower again. He wanted Leech caught. He wanted Leech back in prison so Hope could get on with her life. And he'd love to see her when this was over, but he hadn't missed the fact she'd cut him off when he'd mentioned the future.

Maybe this was simply a case of forced proximity leading to two horny and attracted humans doing what horny, attracted humans generally did? There was a population crisis for a reason.

And while the likelihood of this going anywhere was small, he could afford to be a little patient. Hope had been through hell. The fact he was her first lover in years made his chin come up. A week ago, they hadn't even met. This thing between them was moving at warp speed, and a little "careful" was not a bad thing.

Especially if this was simply a casual hookup for Hope. A way of getting back in the saddle. He didn't want his heart broken again. Who the hell would? And now he needed to thrust the nagging thought of a possible relationship with his principal out of his head because he had work to do to keep her safe.

No way was he letting anything happen to this woman. Not now. Not ever. Even if what happened between them tonight was the end of it. He wasn't about to screw that up. Not when her life and the lives of his teammates were on the line.

37

Hope woke up late, showered, and came downstairs a little after seven. She didn't see Aaron anywhere and didn't know whether to be disappointed or relieved. The sex had been stupendous. Scream-from-the-rooftops ridiculous. She wanted to walk around grinning like an idiot, but she had promised she wouldn't tell anyone, and she didn't need to verbalize her orgasm-fest to give the game away.

She put on the coffee pot she'd filled the night before. She was going to have to invest in one of those industrial-sized expresso machines sooner or later, but this ritual gave her a little thinking time in the mornings while she waited for the water to boil.

Her cell rang, and she braced herself for some new grotesque image or video, but it was Brendan. The guy must be tuned into her coffee addiction.

"Hey."

"What the hell happened with that jerk Beasley last night?"

Hope jolted at his tone. "Someone stabbed him. Why?"

"I heard you were at the scene."

"I received a call from the scene with a video of him injured. Thought I recognized the place but couldn't remember the exact location, so I went with the FBI to try to figure it out. Is he still alive?"

"Fucker croaked on the table."

She sucked in a shocked gasp.

"I thought you didn't like him?"

"That doesn't mean I'm glad he's dead!"

"Save your sympathy for someone who deserves it. The FBI have a lead yet?" Brendan's cynicism was on full display. That's what years on the job did to some people, but it didn't necessarily make for a better cop.

She heard someone talking in the background.

"Look." She didn't bother to hide her annoyance. "I just woke up. Believe it or not, the FBI don't brief me on cases in the middle of the night." She pictured Aaron in her bed last night wearing nothing more than some very sexy ink. She wouldn't mind being briefed at any time under those circumstances.

Lucifer started to cry for food, and she pulled down a Churu treat, making a mental note to resupply the groceries, especially with this stupid dinner coming up. She could order in from a restaurant, but Mary would sniff disdainfully and pick at her plate as if Hope were feeding her rat poison.

She heard someone in the background again. "Is that Janelli?"

"Yeah." Brendan "We're at a homicide."

"Did he ask you to call me?"

"No, for the love of God, will you quit it with the guy."

She jerked away, stung by his tone. "Do you tell him to quit it when he goes after me, Brendan, or would that go against the bro code?"

She looked up and saw Aaron leaning against the kitchen doorway, watching her with those inky eyes. He moved like a ghost. They all moved like ghosts, and she realized they probably deliberately made noises so she knew they were around.

Emotion welled up and caught her by surprise. Desire twisted with something else, something light and bubbly that frothed in her stomach like Champagne and made her feel lightheaded and possibly nauseous. She felt like a giddy, nervous teenager experiencing her first crush. Her mouth went dry. What was wrong with her?

This wasn't a crush. It was a fling. An *affaire du jour*. It wouldn't last. She wouldn't allow it to be anything more than that.

"I have to go."

Brendan had been speaking, but she hadn't caught the words. She reached up and pulled down two mugs.

"I'll see you Sunday." Brendan clearly expected a reply.

She said nothing, simply waited for him to apologize for trying to boss her around or hang up. He hung up because pride was bigger than his ability to admit when he was being an ass.

She put her phone on the counter and went to grab milk.

Aaron took a step forward as she opened the fridge door and cupped her cheek. He leaned down to kiss her in a move that made her want to absorb him on a cellular level.

He pulled away. Leaned his forehead against hers. Smiled. "Morning."

She wanted to wrap herself around him and hang on. It scared her, but then what did it matter? She'd take the little they could have. Enjoy the warmth and the sex and be sad when he left. She knew he wouldn't stay, and she had no intention of letting herself care too deeply. It wasn't worth the pain.

But a slightly dented heart?

Maybe that would do her good, prove she was still a human being rather than the brittle, isolated woman she'd let herself become these past few years. She didn't want to become even more like Brendan than she already was. She had her moments of acrimony and cynicism—it would be a lie to pretend otherwise. But she wasn't an embittered cynic. Not yet anyway.

A noise in the other room had Aaron stepping back.

"Is that coffee I smell?" Frazer.

"In here." Hope pulled down another mug. "Good thing I always make plenty." Usually, she drank a cup at home and then filled a massive travel mug for work. It was possible she drank way too much caffeine.

Frazer came inside, and Lucifer immediately ribboned through his legs then dashed across to Aaron as if to make sure he got in his man quota for the day.

She'd had her man quota for the day, she thought with a slightly hysterical inner laugh. She poured the coffees and left them on the counter for them to add their own milk and sugar.

The first sip flooded her tongue and stirred her sleep-deprived brain cells. "Brendan informed me that Jeff Beasley died on the operating table. Is that correct?"

Frazer nodded. "Around 5 a.m., but in the ICU not on the table. I would have called you sooner, but I was driving to the UPS office, and I figured some of us deserved some sleep."

She hoped she wasn't blushing but kept her gaze firmly averted from Aaron. "You were up all night?"

He nodded.

"Do you want to catch an hour's sleep here?" She thought about her room and the state of the sheets and the smell of sex she was sure would be flashing like a huge neon sign above the bed.

Just got laid.

It was great.

She could quickly change the sheets and open the window, or he could sleep in one of the other beds.

Aaron shot her a glance as if he read her thoughts.

"No, thanks. I'll muddle through."

The thought of Lincoln Frazer "muddling" anything was laughable.

"The local field office went through security footage from various businesses in the area last night and managed to find some of Jeff entering the alleyway."

"Who was with him?" Beasley certainly hadn't stabbed himself.

Frazer pulled a face and showed them both a grainy still on his cell. "About five minutes after Beasley arrived someone else followed him into the alley. Looks like a male. Medium height and build. Hood pulled so low over his features and the quality so poor we can't make a positive ID. I'll send it to you when the techs have finished cleaning it up, but it's next to useless."

Aaron cursed.

She took another sip of coffee. "Do you think I saw him last night?" She framed the question casually while staring into her mug.

"Yes," Aaron stated immediately.

Fierce relief swept through her. Maybe that's why she'd jumped his bones.

"Probably." Frazer shrugged, unrepentant in his need for proof. "Unlike the marshals who haven't spotted a goddamned thing. Apparently," he went on, "they've somehow managed to lose Somack and Roberts again."

"Where's Tommy Lee Jones when you need him?" Aaron took a deep slug of coffee and the sight of him leaning against her counter in black pants and a tight T-shirt, a lethal-looking handgun strapped to his side, struck her forcefully. The man was absolutely gorgeous. Built. Handsome. Smart. And, for a short time, hers. She looked away because Frazer didn't miss much, and she didn't want to jeopardize Aaron's career or the chance of a repeat performance that she was hoping for tonight by giving their secret away.

"I think the marshals stacked the odds by going after those two in the hopes of an easy win—two out of three ain't bad and all that, but they have failed miserably. As far as Leech is concerned, presumably, they are relying on hearing from the public to find their starting point, but instead they're finding the bodies left in his wake. They have alerted all airports including the private ones and all the ports and border crossings, north and south." Frazer rubbed the bridge of his nose. "I think they're reluctant to remind people of the hunt for the Boston Marathon bombers."

Hope shuddered. That had been another truly horrific few

days for the people of this city. "Any actual evidence that might point to where he is?"

"Not a damned thing except your possible sighting. Delaware and his wife booked a hotel room last night."

"Do you have eyes on the guy?" Hope asked.

"No. Boston Field Office have a team on the house but not the man. Apparently, they can't afford to watch everyone." Frazer sipped his drink and made an effort to sound understanding. The creases around his eyes suggested he really was exhausted.

"An odd time for a vacation especially when you own one of the nicest places in town," she said thoughtfully.

"Minus the serial killer aspect. His wife did seem pretty spooked when we spoke yesterday," said Aaron.

Hope snorted. "She must be more intelligent than I imagined." She finished her drink and put the cup in the dishwasher.

"Our consultant is tracking Delaware's phone. Not as good as eyes on the man himself but better than nothing. He's still downtown—or rather the phone is still downtown."

Aaron took Frazer's empty mug and added it to the dishwasher along with his own.

She loved the way he cleaned up after himself and tried to take care of her, even if it was only because of his job.

"What are today's plans?" She tried to infuse positivity into the general doom and gloom.

"Looking further into Jeff Beasley's last few hours and days. Waiting on evidence. Waiting on a warrant to search Eloisa Fairchild's home. We know she lied to us about being alone in the house. I'm ninety-nine-point-nine percent sure that she lied to us about having kept her letters from Leech which I want to read because they might contain clues. If he's with Eloisa, we'll catch him—but I sincerely doubt it unless she has a high-tech panic room we don't know about—a possibility given that she's rich and paranoid. If he's not there but staying with another friend, hopefully the FBI raid will make them nervous, and Leech will be forced to move."

"So we have a better chance of spotting him." Which hadn't happened so far. "Did my weekly missive from Maximum Security arrive yet?" she asked.

"I haven't seen it."

"I'll remind Colin. We've been pretty busy with the trial, plus he's cramming for the bar." She checked her watch. "I better go. I want to head into the office before court."

Aaron frowned. "You think the trial will continue as scheduled?"

Hope nodded. "The judge wants to get the jury sworn in so people can get on with their lives. As sad as it is"—and it was sad for his family—"Jeff Beasley was only the mouthpiece of that crew, and now that he's dead, I suspect the firm will give less weight to Jason Swann's case. Jeff took the case either for spite or at least to get the same airtime as I did while his more famous client was unaccounted for."

"Would Beasley have knowingly met with Leech, do you think?"

"Oh, yeah." Hope nodded. "He wasn't scared of Julius. He was contemptuous of the man." He was contemptuous of everyone. And now he was dead.

"He could easily have underestimated the danger." Aaron crossed his arms.

She began to unconsciously mimic Aaron's stance and forced herself to stop.

"You saw him. He was a braggart and a bully." Hope did not like to speak ill of someone who'd died less than three hours ago. "I need to send a card to the family and see if there is anything I can do."

"That's more than Beasley would have ever done for you."

"Oh." She stretched her neck to the side. "I'm sure his assistant sent a card."

"Did you read them? The cards?" Frazer raised a brow.

Hope blinked and looked away. "I honestly don't remember."

Frazer's expression seemed to say "exactly," but it wasn't the point.

"I'll send one of the team to pick up a card." Aaron yawned.

She suspected he'd been up all night, too, probably to counteract the guilt he'd feel for breaking FBI rules.

"Are you coming with us to the DA's office?" Aaron addressed Frazer.

"Yes, but I'll drive myself." The senior agent shot a glance between her and Aaron. "You two are getting along a lot better than you were a few days ago. I haven't heard a single argument this morning."

Hope narrowed her eyes at the man. "It's early yet."

"Hmm." His expression turned thoughtful.

Hope ignored him and the heat that started to climb her cheeks. She was a grown woman and didn't need anyone judging her—but since when had that stopped people? She strode out of the kitchen and grabbed her coat, hat, and boots, feeling a little like a gladiator preparing for battle.

38

L eech paced the confines of his new prison. Ironic that freedom had turned into a bit of a drag. The New England winter was cold and dank, and he wanted to be away from it, feel the sun on his flesh, sand between his toes. He had one more score to settle, and he wouldn't rest until he'd taken care of the woman who had lied about him, disparaged and insulted him, both on and off the stand.

Who said he didn't know how to follow through?

He'd taken a risk last night, but it had been worth it in the end, especially when he'd seen her face in the back of that SUV. He'd also known it had been time to run when her eyes had widened as they'd locked onto him. He'd enjoyed sprinting through that alley, heart pounding at the thought of her bodyguards in pursuit. Then he'd driven calmly away without anyone spotting him.

He'd felt *alive*! Which was one thing he never felt in prison.

He didn't like being betrayed by people he thought he could trust. Nor did he like being called names or labeled by people who only wanted him for his money. He wasn't that scared little boy hiding in the closet anymore. He was the monster under the bed.

He picked up the hunter's knife he'd found in the drawer. Ran his thumb over the tip and felt the sting of the edge. A droplet of blood bloomed, ruby rich.

He sucked his thumb. He imagined Hope's silky blonde hair spread out on a pillow. He imagined a single drop of blood marring the white satin. Eyes, the color of a frozen moon, staring sightlessly up at him.

He did want to see Hope suffer. To regret. To repent and to beg his forgiveness. And then he'd slide this blade right into her heart.

Right into her goddamned soul.

39

Aaron was once again sitting in the hallway of the court building where he'd spent most of the past week, currently reading the files on the Monroe death investigation. The main thing that struck him as off about the whole situation was the fact the email had been typo free when the man had been sailing three sheets to the wind. The explanation was probably that Monroe had written and even scheduled the letter to be sent before he'd drunk all the whiskey. And the whiskey had been a way of lowering the barriers and dulling the pain of what he'd planned.

Monroe would have lost his job for sure if he confessed to perjury, but he wasn't that far from retirement. He might have been forced to do some prison time, but a guy like that—thirty-five years of service and not a single blot on his record? On a charge like that? His lawyer would have gotten him off with diminished responsibility and community service.

Why kill himself? Especially when the guy had been a devout Catholic.

It didn't sit right.

Aaron spotted Detective Lewis Janelli. Monroe's partner at the time of his death loitering in the hallway.

Aaron slid the file back into his pack and shouldered it. Then he headed for the detective.

"What can I do for you, Agent…?" The guy looked Aaron up and down with a slight sneer to his upper lip.

"Nash." Aaron introduced himself. "Detective Janelli, right?"

"That's right." The detective's eyes danced all over the place, not meeting his. "You're on Hope Harper's security team. Right?"

"That's right."

"They found any sign of that asshole Leech yet?"

"You think I'd be sitting here if they had?"

The guy laughed. "I guess not."

"Why're you here? Testifying?"

Janelli jerked his chin in a non-answer.

"I was reading the files about Paul Monroe's death."

Janelli's eyes widened at that. "Oh, yeah?"

Aaron watched the detective's expression tighten. "He didn't seem like the kind to kill himself."

Janelli clenched his jaw and then looked away. "I never figured he did that to himself."

"You found him?"

"What was left of him."

"Must have been rough."

"Yeah." Janelli stared down at the tiles and scraped his shoe over the worn surface. "He was late for his shift. I went over there because he'd been hitting the bottle pretty hard." He rolled his shoulder. "Never expected to be scraping him off the walls." He shot a look at Hope's courtroom.

Bitterness twisted his features. "It was all that bitch's fault."

"Harper?" Aaron frowned and settled in. "She was just doing her job, right?"

"Huh." Janelli threw back his head and sneered. "Sure, if you believe her bullshit."

Aaron had read the trial transcripts. And media reports. She'd done her job.

"She went after Pauly like he was the goddamned serial killer. Tripped him up. Made him doubt himself."

Aaron flashed his eyebrows. "He never wavered from his story on the stand."

"Because it wasn't a goddamned story. It was the truth!"

A sheriff's officer looked over at them and frowned. Aaron sent him an apologetic nod.

"You're saying Monroe didn't lie on the stand? He didn't plant that evidence?"

Janelli's cheeks flamed red. But he looked uncertain suddenly. "I don't know. Not anymore. I thought I did… What I do know is no way Pauly Monroe blew his own brains out, and no fucking way would he have copied that bitch on the email where he confessed all. He hated her." Those dark brown eyes glared at the door again. "I hate her."

"Easy, Detective."

"Ah, don't worry. I won't do anything to hurt her. Brendan would never forgive me. He's got a thing for his former sister-in-law, although he'd never admit it."

Aaron thought so too. Hope seemed oblivious. "You and Brendan Harper are partners now?"

"Yeah. He's a good guy, despite his family relations. A good detective. Knows how to get results." Janelli scuffed his shoe against the smooth floor again. A nervous tic? "He was with me the morning we found Pauly. He'd been on a stakeout all night, and I bumped into him when I was mouthing off that Pauly was late again. He's the one who said we should take a drive over. Sober Pauly up enough to ride a desk for the day or get him to call in sick. Keep the captain off his back. The trial had done a number on the guy."

"Do you think Monroe truly believed Julius Leech killed those six people?"

"Oh, he knew Leech was the right guy." Janelli's lips pinched into a bloodless line.

"You think Monroe decided the ends justified the means to get a conviction?"

"Maybe. He probably figured he could confess to Father Jamieson and say a few Hail Marys and all would be forgiven. Anything to get the guy off the street because we all knew he was guilty." Janelli glared as if sensing Aaron wasn't as sympathetic as he appeared. "I mean, what happened the minute Leech was cut loose? What happened the minute Leech escaped from prison?"

People died.

Aaron nodded. "I don't think anyone regrets Leech's release more than Hope Harper."

"Whose fault was that?" Janelli sneered again and patted the butt of his gun. "Maybe she'll get a little extra this time around too."

Aaron had Janelli up against the wall and was relieving him of his service weapon when the security guard raced up.

"The detective threatened ADA Harper, and I want him out of here. Unless he's taking the stand, I want him banned from the courthouse."

Janelli was shouting now, vibrating with rage. Aaron let the sheriff cuff him while he removed the magazine and the bullet in the chamber from the guy's gun and handed it back to Janelli. He didn't have the authority to confiscate the weapon or arrest the detective. Not without proof the guy had intent to act on those threats, but he could sure as hell draw attention to his attitude, and he wasn't about to pretend it was cool.

He gave the guard the bullets. And wished he could have hit the bastard but needed a little moral superiority. Plus, he couldn't afford to be thrown out alongside Janelli.

He watched Janelli get escorted down the corridor. The detective was yelling, his hatred of Hope palpable. Aaron had no doubt he'd have happily smeared blood all over Hope's family's headstone and reminded himself to checkup on where the evidence from that was.

He texted Cowboy, who was sitting inside the courtroom—

and Aaron had definitely done that deliberately, so Ryan had less time to run his mouth to the rest of the team. Told him to watch out for the little prick. Then he got a call from Frazer to inform him they had the warrant in hand to search the Fairchild mansion and did Aaron want to join them.

He thought about it for exactly two seconds and told the guy to pick him up. He needed to move, and he wanted to see exactly what Eloisa Fairchild was hiding.

40

Hope spent a boring day going between the DA's office and the courthouse. As she suspected, the judge made a statement about how upsetting the news about Jeff Beasley's death was, but also impressed on the lone lawyer sitting at the defense table that it was time to get the jury seated.

The young attorney was a junior associate with minimal trial experience.

Aisha kept her promise to help get Hope the best jury she could wish for.

When it was finally over, Aisha whispered, "I would high-five you if I didn't think the judge might disapprove."

Hope smiled. Ella had insisted on coming in today and it was good she had the chance to see them having a good day in court. Hope knew she was worried about Jeff's murder and how it might affect things. But now they could move on from the bullshit and get on with trying the meat of the case.

"Do you want a ride home, Ella?" asked Hope.

Ella flashed a look across to where Jason Swann was staring sullenly at his lawyer, who was pretending not to notice. She bit her lip. "I wanted to visit a bookstore. Buy something for my mom's birthday next week so I can mail it."

Hope opened her mouth to say they could do that first when she heard Ryan Sullivan clear his throat behind them.

She glanced at him and saw something in his eyes that expressed disapproval of the idea.

But she was in charge here—

"I can take you," Colin said cheerfully. "And then see you get back to your place."

Hope exhaled. "Excellent idea. Remember, you don't need to be here every day, but it would probably help as often as you can." She didn't expect it to take more than a few days because Jason Swann was not a nice guy. Hope surreptitiously opened her wallet inside her purse and pulled out a hundred-dollar bill. She pressed it into Colin's hand without Ella seeing. "Take a cab."

At least this way the DA wouldn't find out she was babying her client.

She shot Ryan a look, and he nodded curtly. He hadn't been cracking jokes today. In fact, he was strangely quiet. Did he know about her and Aaron? Was that why she was getting the silent treatment? Was it disapproval that furrowed his brow?

The others started to pull on jackets and coats ready to leave, but she leaned over. "Are you okay? Or is something the matter?"

He blinked at her in surprise. The smile he sent her seemed genuine if a little worn around the edges. "Concerned about one of my coworkers. She's burying her father today. I texted this morning but didn't hear anything back."

"I'm sorry."

He nodded and looked away. "She'd tell me to butt out of her business, but losing a parent is hard."

Hope nodded. "Mine passed very close together. I felt anchorless for a long time after. Still do."

Ryan nodded. "Yeah. My dad was larger than life and my mother a force of nature." He pressed his lips into a thin line. "You never expect to lose them, and then one day they're just gone."

She knew he'd lost his wife to cancer, so there wasn't much she could teach this man about grief.

"Did you text her again?"

Ryan pulled a face. "Nah."

"Why not?" Her eyes widened.

"Don't want to interfere. Today of all days."

"You *like* her."

Ryan's face lost its humor, and his jaw firmed. "I work with her. She's off-limits."

You keep telling yourself that, sweetheart.

The guy was irritated she'd figured it out. "I won't tell anyone."

One brow arched slyly. "Not even Nash?"

So he did know what she and Aaron had done last night.

The others had stood and moved away, milling, and waiting to say their goodbyes.

She leaned closer to Ryan. "Please don't say anything to anyone. It won't affect me but—"

"You *like* him." He sounded surprised.

"No." She looked away, not the only liar in the room. "I don't want to screw with his career, not when I was the one to drag him into my bedroom last night."

Ryan's gaze was intent on her features, eyes full of unspoken thoughts. Finally, he stood and casually leaned forward. "Don't break his heart."

"It was sex." Her low tone was sharp. "Trust me, I'm not the lovable type." She shook her head, admitted, "Even the thought of falling in love is…"

"Scarier than any serial killer." His expression changed then. "Other people don't get it." He stared into space. "The idea makes me want to puke."

He looked lonely rather than liberated though.

Hope didn't want to think about the future. Not right now with Leech on the loose and her world turned upside down again. She had enough to deal with, and she didn't even know if she and

Aaron would get the opportunity to spend another night together, let alone anything else.

She didn't want anything else. Remember?

"You should text this work friend of yours again. Make sure she's okay."

His eyes went hooded then, and he shook his head. "Nah. She's with her family. I'm sure she'll be fine."

41

Lincoln Frazer felt a buzz run through him as he led agents from the local field office up the steps to the front door of Eloisa Fairchild's mansion, Aaron Nash at his side. He rang the bell and could almost write the script of what came next.

Eloisa opened the door and eyed the crowd of feds on her doorstep. "What is the meaning of this?"

Her prim outrage pierced the cold quiet of the morning, but the surprise sounded staged. She knew this was coming. She was expecting them.

One of the local agents moved past him to present the warrant.

"Think she got rid of everything incriminating?" Aaron said out of the side of his mouth.

Frazer grunted.

That was the trouble with waiting on the law, but he didn't have the luxury of any covert B&E activity with his two best go-to people busy on other things. He could probably have requested TacOps, but that would have made it official and then he'd have still needed the warrant.

"Let's see what she missed."

Frazer stepped over to where Eloisa stood reading the paperwork. "You might want to call your lawyer, Ms. Fairchild."

She pressed her lips together, and her eyes glittered. "I would if he hadn't been murdered last night."

Interesting.

"You realize Julius Leech is a suspect in Jeff Beasley's murder."

Her eyes flashed. "Julius didn't murder Jeff."

"How do you know? And where were you between 6 and 8 p.m. last night?"

Her smile was mean. "Why don't you ask the FBI agents you had watching the house? Or did they fall asleep on the job?"

Frazer gave the field agents the nod to get started. They knew what they were looking for—any correspondence from Leech, including any cell phones or computers or gaming platforms. But first they had to conduct a thorough search of the premises, including any possible wall or floor cavities big enough to hide a man.

She looked down at the piece of paper. "You can't seriously be taking my cell phone? How am I supposed to contact anyone?"

"You don't have a landline?"

"Who uses landlines anymore?"

"Spammers and con artists?" Aaron offered.

Eloisa's eyes sparkled at that.

The operator looked different this morning somehow. Less tightly wound. Frazer wondered if Hope had anything to do with that. He'd certainly noted the energy between them and encouraged the connection. As long as it didn't compromise Hope's safety, he didn't care—and he didn't see how having an armed man in her bed could make her more vulnerable to Leech or others.

Unless there was an imbalance of power or abuse going on, Frazer wasn't interested in who was sleeping with whom. He didn't exactly play to the letter of the FBI's rulebook—not that people generally appreciated that.

He was more concerned with getting a friend over the worst day of her life. Maybe Aaron Nash was the guy to do it? Or maybe they'd break each other's hearts—what did he know? He could only hope they had the sense to figure it out without destroying each other in the process.

He used his experience and knowledge to help predict or decipher human behavior, but add sex or God help him, *love*, into the mix?—that twisted logic and defied reason. There was nothing sensible about his feelings for Izzy. Nothing rational about how he'd react if anything bad happened to her.

He started as he realized Eloisa was staring at him pointedly, clearly waiting for an answer while he was busy woolgathering like some first-year theology student.

"If you cooperate, I will see that your cell phone is cloned on site, and you can retain it for use."

She tilted her head to one side, her fine hair dancing with static. "That sounds as if you're doing me a favor and yet, as I've done nothing wrong..."

"You know the deep state, Ms. Fairchild," Aaron said wryly. "Always wanting to control you. If not nano-machines in your veins, it's FBI raids on your cell phones."

"Which, as you monitor them anyway, makes turning up on my doorstep moot."

"And, yet, here we are." Frazer was fast losing his patience. "We have the warrant, Eloisa, don't make us arrest you for defying it."

"Oh, I'm sure you'd enjoy that, however, I'm not defying anything." She turned to calm down another woman who came running toward her. The housekeeper.

"It's okay, Cerise. The FBI are looking for evidence we're sheltering poor innocent Julius." She turned back and sent him a look that was probably supposed to be coquettish but came off as creepy.

Dear God, he missed Izzy and wanted to get home.

The housekeeper nodded and disappeared back into her domain.

"Anyone else in the house?"

She shook her head.

"You're sure?" He narrowed his eyes.

"Yes."

"And what about your dog?"

She frowned in confusion and then pulled her lips to one side. "I was watching him for a friend."

"We might need the name of that friend." Frazer had warned her lying to the FBI was a felony offense.

"Of course." Eloisa's expression was blank.

"Where are your safes located?" he pushed.

She examined her nails which were bitten to the quick.

"Don't pretend you don't have at least two on the premises. We know who installed them. I will find them. I'd hate to have to tear them out to take them into evidence."

Her gaze flew to his, and she held up her pointer finger. "Firstly, I want to call the lawyer's office. As much as I hate disturbing them when they are mourning their colleague, I want legal representation present." Her smile didn't reach her eyes. "To protect my interests."

"Your interests? Or your son's?" Aaron asked out of nowhere.

Frazer blinked.

"How do you—" Eloisa's mouth stalled. "I don't have a son. Cerise has a son. You must mean him?"

"Why was Cerise's son sleeping upstairs last night? Why not in her apartment?"

She gaped at him. "He... I... We have lots of room."

Aaron crossed his arms over his chest. "So why doesn't Cerise sleep upstairs too?"

She looked as if all the energy had been drained out of her, but she wasn't done trying to lie. "How do you know she doesn't?"

Aaron gave her a humorless smile. "Call it a hunch."

Eloisa clasped her hands together and sucked in her lips. "Let's discuss this inside."

They followed her into the parlor again, but Frazer was seeing the situation through a new lens now. He'd known Aaron was smart, but he hadn't appreciated how perceptive he really was.

She closed the door firmly as if that would help keep her secrets.

A child made all the oddities fit together a little more cohesively.

"Why did you want to keep your son a secret?" Frazer asked softly.

She spun to face him. "Samuel is Cerise's son. We're very close, and I often let him sleep upstairs." Her forced laugh was supposed to be bright and cheerful. It reeked of desperation.

"How does he feel when you pretend he's not yours?" Aaron watched her with pitiless eyes.

Her fingers clenched into useless fists.

"Does Leech know?" Frazer leaned casually against the mantel.

She lost every ounce of color then. Her bottom lip vibrated visibly before she lowered herself carefully to the ugly green velvet chair. Rather than denying it this time, she went with the other option rich people used when their backs were against the wall. Litigation.

"If word of this gets out, I will sue the FBI for every penny they have, and I will make it my personal mission in life to make sure you are both demoted—"

"That's not really how it works," Frazer cut in. "Letters of censure can be added to our personnel files, and we can obviously be fired." He held her haughty gaze. "But not for doing our jobs. Not when a suspect is lying to us. And"—he ran his fingers across the cool marble—"I think you'll find my friends are more powerful than your friends."

She looked furious, and he suddenly understood why.

He sat across from her, braced his elbows on his knees and leaned forward. "We have no reason to release any information about your son, Eloisa, I promise you that. As long as he's safe. As long as you haven't handed him over to Julius Leech—"

"No! No. I would never do that."

"For all your protestations of Julius's innocence, you don't trust him with his son?" Aaron prompted.

"I don't believe he's a killer." Her chest heaved as if she was running. "But I don't want Samuel to have to carry the weight of Julius's wrongful conviction. It's not fair on a little boy."

"Is that why you didn't tell Julius he fathered a child? Because you didn't want him telling the world? The boy stands to inherit a fortune."

"Money isn't always a positive thing." She wrung her hands together. "Julius and I had a bumbling drunken one-night stand not long before he was arrested. It didn't mean anything. It just happened. I was four months along before I even realized I was pregnant. I'd been so upset about Julius's arrest I wasn't really paying attention to anything else. And I had sex with another man I was seeing around the same time, but I took precautions with him." She squeezed her hands tight between her knees. "I knew it was Julius's baby." She blinked away what looked like tears. "I contemplated having an abortion, but I was shocked to discover I actually wanted the baby. Wanted the chance to be a mother. I decided to wait until after the trial was over to tell him, sure that he'd be found innocent. And I was delighted when he was released." She put a hand to her head as if she was in pain.

Hiding a secret this big would give anyone a headache.

"I spoke to him on the phone after his release, and we arranged to meet for lunch the next day. He was beside himself with relief."

"In the meantime, he went to Hope Harper's house and killed her family."

She shook her head. "I don't believe that."

Frazer could understand now why she so vehemently rejected the idea that Leech was a sadistic murderer. It had nothing to do with the facts and everything with not wanting her son to have a serial killer for a daddy.

"Where is your son now?"

"I sent him to stay with friends who are heading to the Hamptons for a short vacation. They have a boy around the same age. Cerise dropped him off this morning."

"You trust them?"

She nodded, stiffly, then bit her lip.

"You didn't want to risk Julius arriving on your doorstep and seeing the child, knowing you'd lied to him all these years."

Her eyes flared wide in fear.

That was it.

"Have you spoken to him since he escaped?"

She looked away and finally nodded. Then she covered her face and released a sob. "I offered to drop some money for him, and, and"—she hiccupped—"I left it in a car in the woods near Harrisville. Cerise picked me up in a rental—she didn't know why I was leaving the car there."

The housekeeper must be an idiot if she didn't suspect—or keen to keep her job.

"I didn't want him coming here and seeing Sammy."

She started sobbing uncontrollably, but Frazer wasn't feeling particularly sympathetic.

"Please don't arrest me. If you do, the press will figure out about Sammy, and Julius will find out I lied to him."

"You're scared of him."

"Yes," she snapped, eyes suddenly earnest. "Yes, I am. It's the one thing he said he hated beyond all reason. People who lie."

Frazer raised an unimpressed brow. If Eloisa hadn't helped Julius Leech, Sylvie and her husband, not to mention Jeff Beasley, might still be alive.

"I want to know exactly where you left that car. I want to know what the model and registration is, and I want access to every letter he ever sent you. And then, if you fully cooperate, I'll talk to the DA's office about trying to keep your son out of the spotlight after his mother confessed to aiding and abetting a wanted fugitive, not to mention lying to the FBI about it."

Eloisa drew in a shocked breath and covered her mouth as if she only then realized the seriousness of what she'd done.

Aaron straightened from his position near the window. "I'm sure the DA will understand, After all, if anyone comprehends your fears regarding your child's safety, it will be ADA Hope Harper."

42

It took ninety minutes to drive to the exact location in Harrisville that Eloisa Fairchild had marked on the map. It took another ten minutes of driving down little used nearby tracks to spot a small dark gray sedan parked along the side of the road near a hiking trail.

"Same make and model Graham Burns drove, but different plate." Aaron pointed out to Frazer, who was driving.

They pulled up a short distance away.

Frazer called in the license plate, and it came back to a Toyota Camry not a Chevy SS.

They both got out of the Beemer and walked toward the other car. Frazer handed him a pair of surgical gloves.

They walked around the vehicle slowly, careful to avoid any tracks in the snow and frozen earth. Frazer took photos with his cell from multiple angles.

"Door's unlocked," Aaron noted.

"Probably hoping it would be stolen."

Aaron nodded and eased open the door, avoiding the vague indented footprints that led from it. It had snowed since the person, presumably Leech, had dumped the car. Frazer placed a quarter on the ground and took more photographs from various angles. He obviously believed this was the car they were looking for. So did Aaron.

Aaron reached inside and popped the trunk. They both walked to the rear of the car. The orange jumpsuit and the brown of the prison guard's uniform were instantly visible.

Frazer took more photographs.

This was definitely the right car.

The profiler reached inside and gently pulled the heavy jacket back to reveal the pale face of a young man who'd been in the wrong place at the wrong time.

At least the cold weather had held decomposition at bay.

"Graham Burns." Sympathy welled within Aaron's chest followed by anger. "Think Eloisa Fairchild will believe this evidence?"

Frazer's mouth thinned. "I think she'd find a way to convince herself Leech was innocent even if he stabbed her with a letter opener."

"Are we about to ruin her kid's life?" Because Aaron didn't mind Eloisa paying for breaking the law, but he had a hard time condemning a child.

"I'll talk to the DA. If we can get her full cooperation, maybe we can use her to help catch this bastard. Spring a trap."

"At least we know what he's driving."

Frazer shot him a glance. "We know what he was driving yesterday."

Aaron swore. Checked his watch. "You call it in and organize evidence recovery techs to get out here. I'll see if I can get a local cop to guard the scene in the meantime. I need to get back before Hope leaves work."

Frazer's eyes gleamed at the mention of Hope's name, but Aaron ignored him. He took another long look at the young man who'd been murdered and dumped in the back of his trunk like so much garbage. *This* was who Leech really was. Not the mansion or the private jets. Not the wardrobe full of fancy suits or protestations of innocence. He was death and destruction and egocentric self-gratification. And perhaps Eloisa Fairchild had been right to deceive him, because who would want that man, a serial killer, as the father of their child?

Aaron stared up at the tops of the trees as the naked branches swayed and tried to keep his own fears at bay. Julius Leech wanted to kill Hope, a woman Aaron was starting to care deeply for.

He strode to the BMW suddenly anxious to get back to her side. Frazer locked up the other car while Aaron called the local police department. He didn't have time to waste, but Graham Burns deserved the respect of being guarded, being watched over and protected in death.

Aaron thought about Burns' loved ones and how they'd never get the chance to say goodbye, and of Hope's overwhelming grief at the loss of her family. It hit him with sudden insight that he could no longer hang on to his lingering resentment about what had happened with his brother and ex.

Life wasn't perfect, and it was surely too short to hold grudges, especially if it meant *him* missing out on occasions that had always been important to him.

Look at Leech and his twisted need for revenge because he couldn't let go of perceived wrongs. Or Minnie Ramon blaming Hope for simply doing her job.

It was exhausting.

His brother and sister-in-law were blissfully happy and, however Aaron had felt about it at the time, he was over it now. Done. Finished. And the last thing he wanted was to go to his own grave with this lingering resentment haunting his soul. He wanted his brother back even though it would never be exactly how it had been before. He wanted the chance to know his new niece or nephew because he loved kids and wanted his own someday. He wanted the cousins to be friends. He desperately wanted to be free of the stinging resentment and *hurt* and to accept what had happened, not just as a cross to bear but also as a blessing, a lucky escape.

It wasn't as if he still loved his ex. He didn't. He really didn't.

And, although it wasn't exactly the same kind of situation, Hope had found a way to coexist with Brendan despite their issues. She clearly set boundaries, and the relationship was far from perfect, but she'd found a way to make it work.

He was tired of living in the past. It was time to put it behind him and truly forgive. He needed to move on while he still had the chance.

43

"**E**lla get home safe?" Hope looked up as Colin came into her office.

"Yep. I even mailed her mother's birthday gift for her." He pulled out some cash and tried to hand it over.

"Keep it." Hope waved him away. "I'm grateful you could go with her."

He cleared his throat. "Talking of mail..." Colin pulled an envelope out of his suit pocket, placed it on the desk in front of her.

She recognized Leech's neat handwriting, his expensive stationery with his initials, an elegant gold scroll, stamped in the corner—which he must pay the prison warden for the privilege of using.

She didn't want to read it, but Frazer wasn't here, and neither was Aaron. She needed to check if Leech had written anything that might point to a planned escape or to a place where he might hide. She could ask Colin or Hunt Kincaid who stood at the door to read the letter, but she didn't want to appear scared of Leech. She refused to let him affect her.

She checked her cell for a text from Aaron but there was nothing. Had they discovered anything at Fairchild's house? They'd been gone for hours.

Because her communications were being monitored, she could hardly call and ask him if he was okay or tell him Ryan Sullivan knew where he'd spent some of last night.

Or ask him if he wanted to do it again tonight.

She sighed.

She didn't like the way she kept looking for the HRT operator whenever she heard a door bang or footsteps approach. She didn't appreciate the way he snuck into her thoughts when she was supposed to be concentrating on something important.

She pulled out her wooden letter opener that was shaped like a fish. She'd bought it from a market in Malawi during a trip she and Danny had made one summer while undergrads. Her fingers shook as she sliced through the top of the letter but not because of Leech.

It was because she was thinking of the man she'd loved, whose life Leech had extinguished without a second thought. A man she would love until the day she died. But something about her grief had shifted recently. She silently acknowledged the fact without delving into the why.

She felt Colin watching her with interest and glanced up. She didn't want a witness to this act. "Did the lab ever get back to you about the fibers from the Dutton case?"

Collin's brows beetled. "I thought I sent you that?"

She shook her head. "I didn't receive anything."

"Fibers were a match between the apartment and the ones found on the body, but the carpet is cheap and commonplace."

"Still—"

Colin gave her a wide smile and held up a hand. "*However*, the pet hair was also a solid match."

She grinned back. "Yes! We're gonna nail that bastard to the wall. Can you resend the report?"

He checked his watch. "Of course."

It was almost six. "Do you have plans? It can wait until tomorrow given it's the weekend."

Colin looked surprised, and she couldn't blame him. She usually wanted things done immediately, but she was being reminded this week that other people had lives.

She thought about staring deep into Aaron's eyes when he'd been buried inside her. Maybe that included her. Scary thought.

"Only cramming for the bar. I'll send it before I head out." He nodded and backed away, obviously disappointed she hadn't opened the letter and read it in front of him.

Some things were private though, and she guarded what she could. Not the content, but how it affected her. She wasn't a lab specimen. She wasn't open to being analyzed.

She heard footsteps coming down the hall and Kincaid turned away from whatever Colin was saying to him and nodded in acknowledgment.

It was Aaron. She knew from the rhythm of his footsteps and the way Kincaid straightened.

The little dance her heart did inside her chest made her fingers curl.

It was lust. And the novelty of something new and shiny and bright.

That was all.

She would let go of the guilt and enjoy it for the few short days it would last. No harm. No foul. Simply pleasure.

Aaron opened the door and smiled. Her breath caught at his perfect masculine beauty. The man was stunning, and her mouth went dry at the thought of another night together.

His eyes shone darkly. "What?"

She shook her head.

His gaze drifted to what she held in her hands. He stepped forward. Jerked his chin. "What's that?"

Hope pulled a face. "Leech's letter from prison."

"Gimme." He came around the desk, his thigh brushing her

arm as he leaned closer and plucked the note from her fingers. He began to ease it out of the envelope, then his expression changed.

"Hey, Kincaid!"

The other operator rushed inside, closely followed by Colin.

"You have an evidence bag on you?"

Kincaid shook his head. "In the SUV. Why? What is it?"

"I have one." Hope stepped over to the drawer of the other desk. She didn't remember why she had these in her office, but they'd been there for years, taking up space. She grabbed one and opened it wide.

Kincaid took the bag from her and opened it for Aaron to slip the letter inside.

"What?" she demanded. "What is it?"

"Looked like a printout of a screenshot of you outside this office on Tuesday night."

"But…" Ice filled her and her bones rattled but not from cold. "But he wasn't in prison then."

"Correct." His eyes were almost black. "And there appears to be bloody fingerprints on the back."

Her legs wobbled and she lowered herself to the chair. "Could he have printed it out at Sylvie's house? But that envelope… it's his personal stationery—the same he used in prison. How can that be?"

"He somehow got hold of his stationery after he escaped. Is that enough to get us a search warrant for his mansion on Beacon Street, do you think?" Aaron asked.

Hope nodded, her skin crawling because Leech was so fixated on her that he'd written her a letter while covered in the blood of two innocent people. "It should be. Let me call the DA."

Aaron's lips were pressed tight together. "I'll call Frazer. We can drop this at the crime lab on the way back to your apartment."

She shivered and rubbed her hands up and down her thighs as her stomach dropped. "I'm sick of this guy playing his mind games with me. What did you find at Eloisa Fairchild's home?"

Aaron's eyes burned with emotion. He indicated Colin leave and closed the door on her curious intern.

"What?" Her heart sank. "What did you discover?"

He took a few steps toward her and stopped. "She admitted she gave him a car and some money. We went to the location where she left it and searched nearby for whatever getaway vehicle Leech had been using up until that moment." He dragged a hand through his dark hair. "We found the body of a young man we believe Leech crossed paths with shortly after he escaped."

He killed again.

Hope's hands shook as she tried to make sense of how anyone could do such terrible things. "Why would she help him?"

At least she could do something about that. Aiding and abetting. The wealthy were not immune to justice.

Aaron sat on the edge of her desk. "Turns out she had Leech's baby and kept it a secret all these years. Passed the kid off as the housekeeper's son."

Hope sat in shock at the revelation. *Julius Leech had a child*? A *child*? Her eyes smarted at the unfairness of it all. Leech had a child but had stolen hers away from her. The blow felt like a sucker punch to the heart.

Aaron's eyes filled with silent understanding.

She forced back the devastation scorching her. "Does Leech know?"

He shook his head.

Somehow that made it a little easier to bear. "All Leech ever wanted was a family. He said so on the stand."

Aaron nodded.

The implications hit her anew. "He can't know about this boy or that Eloisa lied to him. Not until he's safely back inside a prison cage." Or preferably never. "I'll talk to the DA."

"Frazer already spoke with him."

A sharp stab of hurt lanced her. Why had no one thought to tell her? Hearing it in person from Aaron made it a little easier to cope with, and maybe that was why. Frazer always saw more than people wanted him to.

Aaron's lips pressed together. "We're going to catch this sonofabitch, Hope."

She didn't think so. Not anymore. "Don't make promises you can't keep."

"I never do. I never do."

44

Exhausted and frustrated, Aaron arrived back at Hope's place around nine that night with Frazer in tow. After the warrant had come in, they'd gone through every cupboard in Leech's mansion, every drawer, searched for hidden recesses and found nothing except an empty safe. They'd removed Delaware's desktop computer and couriered it to Quantico. Found nothing actionable and knew little more than they'd known yesterday with the exception that he'd killed again and had more than twenty thousand dollars in cash thanks to Eloisa Fairchild. The BOLO had been issued regarding the new car he was using but no alerts yet.

Leech was a ghost.

A ghost fixated on hurting Hope.

Even though Aaron wasn't about to let anything happen to her, it nagged at him.

"Any sign he'd been back to his house at all?" Hope asked the moment they walked inside.

Aaron shook his head. "The place was empty."

"Cold as a tomb." Frazer slipped off his coat. "The Delawares appear to have skipped town."

"Who could blame them?" Hope muttered. "You're sure they aren't dead? He does have a thing for married couples."

"I'm not sure of anything at the moment except both Delawares' cell phones are at the hotel downtown, but neither he nor his wife are anywhere to be found. Mind if I...?" Frazer pointed at her drink cabinet.

"Help yourself."

"They might be out having a late dinner or at the movies. Visiting relatives," Aaron pointed out.

"Perhaps, but wherever they are we can't trace them." Frazer raised a bottle of Kentucky Owl Batch #12 to Hope, but she shook her head. The profiler poured two good measures in cut glass crystal tumblers and handed one to him. Aaron should say no but what the hell. He needed some sleep and maybe this would help. He knocked it back, savored the slide of good bourbon down his dry throat.

"Anything on the letter?" asked Hope.

"Postmarked yesterday. Mailed in the city. Printed on Sylvie's printer."

Hope swore. "What did it say? Apart from the photo, what did he write?"

"The usual bullshit. This is all your fault. Blah, blah. Reap what you sow. You hurt my feelings by calling me a killer even though I am a killer, *beotch*." Frazer tried to lighten the mood.

It didn't work.

The tension in Hope's jaw looked as if it might crack her wide open. "DNA? Fingerprints?"

"They're running it. We need elimination samples from everyone who handled it. It's going to take time to run them all."

"Mine are in the system. I can give you Colin's cell number and find out his address to arrange to collect his."

Frazer nodded. "Monday is soon enough. The primary objective is to find Leech's DNA and tie him unequivocally to Sylvie and her husband's murder, and we have that in the database."

"How did he get hold of the stationery?" Her face was pale,

hair pulled back into a short ponytail that emphasized the hollows under her cheekbones.

Frazer paced. "Maybe Delaware set up a little hide-y-hole with all Leech's creature comforts in case he ever got out. Or did a dead drop as soon as he heard Leech was free."

"Yeah, 'don't forget the fancy stationery when you bring me my escaped-from-prison supplies. Never know when I may need to reply to some urgent correspondence.'" Aaron rolled his eyes.

"I suspect they've discussed it over the years. Leech may have created his fantasy list, and Delaware put it together because when you're being paid that much to do almost nothing, why wouldn't you?" Frazer sipped his drink, clearly savoring the smooth whiskey.

"No luck on tracing property in the area where Leech might be holed up?"

"Analysts are still looking. Unfortunately, Parker is busy." Frazer pulled a face. "What with his company, family, best friend's wedding, and all my other requests he hasn't had time." Frazer bared his teeth in a shark's smile. "I should have brought Mallory Rooney with me. That would have focused his attention."

Hope looked as if she felt sorry for Alex Parker. "Delaware probably disappeared so we couldn't question him again, catch him in a lie."

"It won't be hard to prove aiding and abetting once we track down Leech and figure out exactly where he's been hiding. Whoever helped him probably didn't think to wear surgical gloves during the process." Frazer tipped back his glass.

"We found matching stationery in the mansion, but presumably Delaware orders it and sends it to Leech in prison as required," said Aaron.

"Or maybe Leech somehow snuck into his old home and out again without anyone seeing and grabbed some so he could taunt Hope," Frazer mused.

It was possible. It was all possible. Especially if Delaware distracted the team who was watching the mansion. Or if Leech wore a disguise. Even if he went around the back. One FBI team watching the front door wouldn't see a whole helluva lot in the grand scheme of things, not in that kind of neighborhood.

"We did get the printer ID on the photograph of Hope placed on the gravestone Tuesday night." Frazer reeled off an address for a commercial printing business downtown. "I'll have an agent check it out tomorrow. See if they recognize the picture or Leech or have security footage we can access."

The print shop was between the courthouse and the DA's office, close to the police department. No one in this room really thought Leech had desecrated that headstone, but they all wanted the asshole who did named and shamed.

"I can do that," Aaron offered. He didn't want it falling off the radar.

Frazer nodded.

"I hear you had Janelli thrown out of the courthouse today?" Hope looked straight at him.

Shit.

That probably wouldn't help her popularity with the cops. "He threatened you."

She waved her arms. "He's always badmouthing me and talking shit. He's never actually had the balls to act on it."

"Why doesn't your brother-in-law shut that bullshit down?" Aaron had the feeling Brendan Harper didn't mind the hostility directed at Hope. It kept her outside the fold. Out of the inner circle that the justice system relied on so much. It kept her reliant on him for information as to what was going on inside the Police Department.

Her brow creased. "I don't want to talk about Brendan right now. Bad enough he and his mother will be here for lunch on Sunday." She shuddered. Then her expression turned hopeful. "Do either of you want to join us?"

Aaron shook his head. "I'll use the time to run a few practice drills with the guys. See if we have any holes in our defense."

Frazer yawned. "As much as I'd enjoy your company, and

watching the entertainment, I'll pass. I'm hoping we will have caught Leech by then."

Hope grunted in a very unladylike manner. "I want to go to the shooting range tomorrow."

"Because of Leech?" Frazer asked archly. "Or because of the in-laws?"

She huffed out a reluctant laugh, and Aaron felt his heart ease a little. The stress she was under was extreme, but it was a good sign she could still laugh at Frazer's attempts at humor.

"No comment."

"We can arrange a trip to the FBI gun range." It would be a good opportunity for them all to put a little time in on their marksmanship.

Frazer picked up his coat. "I'll call you in the morning with any updates from the marshals—God forbid—or the crime labs."

She nodded but remained seated as Frazer headed down the stairs.

As soon as the other man was out of the door she asked. "Did you eat yet?"

"I'm not hungry." He looked at her mouth as she bit her lip. Not for food anyway.

She must have read the look on his face. Her eyes widened.

Had last night been a one-off, or was there a chance this was something more than a one-night stand?

A minute ago, all he'd wanted was to lay his head on a pillow and sleep. Now there was something he'd much rather do first. *Her.*

She walked over to the stairs and then sent him a look over her shoulder. "I'm going to get an early night, Operator Nash. I suggest you do the same."

His pulse thrummed.

He followed her up the stairs. She went into her room but left the door wide open. Then she pulled off her shirt and kicked off her pants, leaving her wearing only pretty lacy underwear that had him as hard as stone in an instant.

That was definitely an invitation.

Even though he knew it was wrong. Even though he knew it was a sign of weakness, he stepped inside. Closed the door. Dug into his pocket for the strip of condoms he'd taken out of one of the supply bags. Then he pulled her to him and lowered his lips to hers.

45

Hope woke to the delicious feel of Aaron's chest glued to her back, his arm curled around her and holding her tight against him even though she was pretty sure he was fast asleep. His short beard tickled her shoulder. His breath was warm against her flesh.

She felt incredible. Deliciously used and achy and still hungry for more. She didn't think she'd ever had this many orgasms in such a short space of time and figured her body was making up for all the lost years.

She shifted slightly to see the time. Just after two. Felt the sudden tightening of his fingers as he woke.

"Sorry," she whispered.

His arms squeezed her for a moment before letting go. "I wasn't supposed to fall asleep." He eased away from her, and cold air filled the gap.

She rolled over and grabbed his hand. "I forgot to tell you that Ryan knows."

He stood at the side of the bed looking all dangerous and moody but not surprised. "He saw me leave last night. What did he say?"

She swallowed. "Not to break your heart."

He gave a quiet, bitter laugh. "No emotional entanglements. Sounds like Ryan."

She thought about the coworker Ryan obviously had feelings for. Raised a brow. "I don't know about that."

Aaron's eyes flashed to hers. But she wasn't about to give up Ryan's secrets, not when she wanted him to keep theirs.

Aaron had pulled on his pants but didn't zip them. Her eyes traced the delicious dark trail of hair that disappeared, and, like that, she wanted him again.

She looked at the dresser where the lone surviving condom from last night's adventures still lay. She reached over and held it up. Caught his eyes in the snow-brightened darkness. "Seems a shame to waste it…"

She knelt up on the bed and let the covers fall away. Watched those black eyes narrow as she moved naked toward him. She reached up and pulled his head down for a kiss. Dropped the condom onto the duvet and slid her other hand into the open zipper of his pants. He was already hard and ready for her, and her muscles clenched in anticipation.

"Surely, ten more minutes wouldn't hurt anyone?" she murmured softly.

He swore against her lips and then again when she shoved his pants down and cupped him and stroked him until she was quaking with want. He removed her hands then surprised her by grabbing her behind the knees and flipping her back onto the bed.

She let out a muted squeak that she swallowed as he spread her knees wider and dragged her to the edge of the mattress. She watched him roll the latex over himself and then position his cock at her core before surging inside. It was all she could do not to cry out with pleasure as he filled her with one firm stroke.

"Is this what you wanted?" He drove deep, pushing her knees up and going deeper still.

It was exactly what she wanted, but suddenly she wanted more. More than his magnificent body plundering hers. More than his heat and his beauty. She wanted his mind, his protective streak, the quiet determination that verged on stubbornness. She liked him. *Really* liked him. The way he listened, the way he considered all the angles, the way he came up with intelligent, thoughtful solutions, the way he respected her even when she was doing her best to piss him off.

She watched the light play over his features as his hands held hers, pinned her to the bed. He drove into her relentlessly, his gaze holding hers so she couldn't look away, couldn't hide. Then his mouth found her breast before he slid his hands beneath the curved arch of her back and lifted her up. She wrapped her legs tightly around his hips. And she thought he'd been deep before, but now she felt bound to him, fused with him. Soldered. Melded. Saturated with Aaron Nash.

Every nerve in her body wound, coiled, tightened. His chest abraded her nipples, his body stroked her clit with each surge forward. Every inch of skin felt as if it smoldered from the lust that burned between them until, finally, the spark struck and she ignited in flame.

He captured her cry with his mouth. Swallowed the sound of her pleasure as his own body strained before shuddering against her so forcefully it almost hurt.

A delicious and wonderful pain.

He pulled away.

They stared at one another, time suspended between them, stretching their connection until it had no choice but to break.

It seemed like a lifetime.

It seemed like not long enough.

They slowly disengaged, and he dealt with the condom. She half hoped he'd climb back in beside her and realized with terrible blinding insight that she was falling in love with this man. Falling in love with this incredible human being.

Panic zipped along her nerves and exploded in her brain, obliterating the memories of orgasm and happiness. Her mouth was so dry she could barely swallow. Sweat beaded on her forehead and slid over her skin.

No. No, no.

It was impossible.

She couldn't do that. She wouldn't do that. Not ever again. Especially not when she could tell he was falling for her too. Aaron Nash wasn't the pretend type, and the truth was visible in every line of his serious face. In the way he watched her, the way he worshipped her body, the way he spoke her name.

But she wouldn't risk going through that pain again.

Leech was still out there.

What if he figured it out?

That she had stupidly fallen in love again? What if he attacked this man, *killed* him, simply because of her. The idea made her feel as if her insides were being hollowed out with razors. She couldn't bear the thought of Aaron being injured. Leech had already taken so much from her, she wouldn't let him take Aaron too.

He brushed her hair off her face. "What did you say to Ryan when he said not to break my heart?"

Oh God. Oh God. Oh God. Her heart buzzed in her chest like a wasp. Then she forced away every ounce of the feelings that paralyzed her tongue because this was the perfect way out. The perfect way to slam the door shut and push Aaron firmly away before either of them got in too deep.

"I told him not to be an idiot. It was just sex."

Aaron jerked away as if stung.

"I mean stupendous, incredible sex, but still…" She watched him steadily, knowing she was hurting him. Deliberately causing that shocked look of surprise in his eyes. Hating herself but unable to stop. It was better this way. She could already see with stunning clarity what a disaster this would be if she allowed it to continue. For both of them. And that was without Leech entering the mix. "But I don't want to put your job at risk, so we should probably stop before you get into trouble."

Like stopping would be an option if she hadn't already been fundamentally incapable of being what the man deserved?

Reflexively, she stretched out an arm to soothe him before she controlled herself. He moved away as if he couldn't bear the idea of her touch. Something inside her curled up and died, but she pushed on, knowing she had to be convincing or they'd be right back here tomorrow night, only it would be worse next time because she now understood the risk. "I'm getting a little old for sex marathons."

His smile was grim. "You seemed to be doing fine until round five." He pulled his T-shirt over his head with swift, jerky motions.

"Well," she forced out. "I'll keep working on it, although I doubt I'll find anyone else of your caliber." She wanted to tell him there would never be anyone like him again. She smothered the words. He'd get over it. She was a job, and he'd get over it. But if he died because of his connection to her, she never would.

He zipped his jeans, pulled on his boots, and swept up his weapon and cell phone from the counter. Paused by the bed.

"You know, you should talk to Ryan. If it's sex you want and you've had your fill of this particular HRT operator, he's single. Must be good in bed considering the number of women who flock to him. Hell, Black, Griffin, Crow, Demarco would all line up to fuck you if they knew it was an option, even Cadell, even though he doesn't like you much."

Inside, she flinched at each bitter word.

"Not that *like* needs to be an issue, of course, as long as everyone knows it's just sex, right?" The ice in his voice was enough to freeze the icecaps. He shook his head. "Hell, Hope, we could keep you busy for months. Taking it in turns to come in here each night and work you so hard you won't be able to walk straight the next day."

She gripped the sheets with her fingers so he wouldn't see how her hands shook.

"I'll bear that in mind." Her voice was as frigid as his. She knew she'd hurt him, and he was lashing out.

"I'll check on the condom supply before tomorrow night.

Wouldn't want to run short now, would we?" Apparently, he wasn't going to quit.

"I'm sorry, Aaron. I didn't mean to offend you—"

"Offend me?" The words were a whisper, but anger pulsed through them. "*Offend* me? I'm actually grateful for the reminder, ADA Harper. In fact, I'm beyond grateful. I *was* getting attached, I admit it. I mean you are hot and smart as fuck, which are two of my weaknesses. But you reminded me that you're missing the other vital ingredient that I value above all else."

She forced herself to ask. "And what might that be?"

"Loyalty."

She flinched.

"And friendship."

That stab to her heart felt like a blade.

"I actually thought we might be becoming friends. But I should have known better. It was 'just sex.'"

The words were whispered, but the slam of her door was not. She closed her eyes and realized belatedly that, thanks to the trauma inflicted by the former fiancée, he had some insane notion that he wasn't good enough. Her comment, intended to protect him, had probably made him feel as if he wasn't worthy of a bigger place in her life—wasn't worthy of being more than a two-night stand. Wasn't good enough for her.

God, Aaron.

That couldn't be further from the truth.

She opened her eyes and lay in the darkness staring up at the ceiling, hating everything she'd become.

At least it would keep him safe.

The knowledge brought little comfort.

46

Aaron slipped downstairs in his running gear. As much as he'd worn himself out having "just sex," he couldn't sleep. He'd end up tossing and turning and replaying the words that had seared him like a brand.

He didn't want to think about Hope or how badly he'd let down his team.

He hadn't meant to lash out, and now he was going to have to swallow his pride, grit his teeth and apologize to her for being such an ass. *He* was the idiot. He knew better, but he'd gone and done it again. Fallen for a woman who didn't actually want him.

Hell, he should be used to it by now.

He was so pissed.

Not at Hope because he'd known she was out of his league from the start. Not only that, *he* was the one with the job to do. She was the goddamned *principal*.

Everything he was feeling. Everything in his messed-up head —that was all on him. If this was a test, then he'd failed. Flunked out. *F*-fucking-minus.

He wasn't used to making errors in judgment or screwing up, but that without a doubt was what he had done ever since he'd walked into this house.

He thrust the spiraling thoughts out of his head. He needed to wear out his body to the point of collapse and then hopefully he could fall unconscious into bed and get some rest.

It wasn't snowing, and the temperature had risen above freezing. He wore layers, and a hat, and strapped his smaller backup SIG Sauer P365 in a specialized holster that fit at the small of his back.

Livingstone was on the front door and eyed him the way a parent eyed a kid who was awake past their bedtime. "What's up?"

"Going for a run."

"You know trying to keep going twenty-four seven is not the best way to manage an op."

"Do you have an issue with how I'm running this op?" Aaron raised up to his full height and stared down at the guy.

"Nope." Shane shook his head and held up his hand in surrender. "Not at all. I…" He swallowed and looked away. "I guess I'm a little overprotective of my friends these days."

Aaron blew out a long breath as the fire went out of him. Squeezed Shane's arm because he knew what the guy was thinking about, and it wasn't this op. "Sorry. I'm on edge with this asshole still being loose. How's Grace? I meant to call her earlier."

"Yael and Pip have been helping her with the kids and the dog." He rubbed his neck. "She has a hospital appointment on Wednesday after Montana's memorial service. I offered to watch the kids, but she wanted me at the hospital instead." He grimaced. "She wants me to be her birthing partner, but I don't know if I can do it."

Aaron swallowed the grief that threatened to choke him. Losing their colleague and friend was bad enough. Knowing he'd left a pregnant wife and young family behind amplified the tragedy by a thousand. "Scotty would want you there."

"I know. Yael said she'd act as support in case I'm not around when Grace goes into labor." Shane ran his hand over his face. To see the usually unflappable operator nervous cut through some of the tension Aaron was carrying. So what if he was hurting. Plenty of other people had it worse, including Grace. Including Hope.

The knowledge he'd reacted poorly sat sourly in his stomach. He'd figure out a way to clear the air in the morning then avoid her as much as possible after that. No more cozy dinners. No more intimate debriefs.

Do the job.

Avoid the humiliation.

"I can watch the kids for Grace on Wednesday afternoon. Assuming the team isn't ordered straight back here."

It would be easier to let the marshals take over Hope's protection, and he knew Gold team might get called out on a more critical mission at any moment. Although nothing was more critical to him than Hope's safety. The thought of never seeing her again burned, despite everything, despite her stabbing out his heart with her cool gray eyes and throwaway words. He'd been blindsided. He wasn't sure how to deal with that. Not to mention, the marshals weren't exactly winning any awards in the aftermath of this prison break.

"Any word from Grady?" Aaron changed the subject.

"Only that thumbs-up message on Monday night when I checked in to see if everything was all right with Brynn. He obviously managed to talk her around after Ryan's epic fuck up."

Aaron froze for a moment when he realized Ryan had spent the day in court with Hope. But there was nothing Ryan could have said to sabotage their non-existent relationship, not when Hope was only looking for a short fling. Aaron wasn't as transparent as Grady Steel when it came to displaying his feelings.

It was Hope who'd ended things before it had truly begun. Her choice. Her decision. Not Cowboy with his overprotective bullshit. Aaron should be grateful to her for doing it now before he'd gotten in too deep.

"I spoke to Romano. Krychek replaced Donnelly after she left last night to go to her father's funeral." Livingstone scowled.

TONI ANDERSON

"Romano doesn't think Krychek is telling us everything he knows about what went down in Africa."

"Not much he can say if it's classified." Aaron rolled his shoulder. The fact he knew about the Semtex and hadn't told his teammates sat badly with him. Maybe once they were back in Quantico, he'd get some of the guys around and share what Frazer had told him in confidence.

The thought of leaving Hope, of never seeing her again, felt inherently wrong.

He ground his teeth.

He had to get over this.

"I need to get out of here. I'll be an hour at most, but if the idea of me running at night makes you nervous have Griffin shadow me in the Suburban."

"Streets are icy."

"I have grips for the bottom of my runners, Mom"—he dangled the spikes in his hand "and I have no intention of breaking anything."

He sent a pointed glance at the arm Shane had broken last December.

Shane flexed his bicep. "Good as new."

"Sure, buddy, you keep telling yourself that." Aaron stretched using the stairs while Shane relayed the message to Will Griffin who was in the vehicle tonight. Then Aaron attached the grips to the bottom of his running shoes and headed out into a blast of cold air. He immediately started to sprint down the sidewalk.

It was quiet at this hour in this neighborhood. He found himself heading to the river, having spotted a footbridge from the car earlier. That would prove a challenge for Griffin but as Aaron had his smartwatch and cell on him, it should be a good exercise in tracking him down.

Aaron set a fast pace. No point *jogging*. No point giving himself time to think or brood. Get over it. He'd been dumped before and at least this one wasn't screwing his brother.

On the other side of the bridge, he crossed the road and started southwest down Causeway. He smiled grimly when the black SUV fell in behind him. Good. He headed south, feeling the incline in his thigh muscles as he passed some tall government buildings. He was headed toward the fancy place Frazer was staying on Mount Vernon Street, but that was only a mile and a half from Hope's. Not far enough to clear the crap clogging his brain. He carried on and found himself on Beacon Street, which ran for miles. He pushed the pace until sweat soaked through his T-shirt then slowed a little.

He wasn't feeling the cold yet, but if he stopped, the sweat would turn to ice on his skin.

He pushed on, past Boston Common and the public gardens. The street was a mix of business and residential with most of the large brownstones having been divided into condos. Not Leech's place though. His was still a glorious mausoleum to an unrepentant killer.

Aaron spotted the vehicle watching the house with an FBI agent inside. Stakeouts were miserable assignments, but Aaron wasn't impressed the guy had the engine running to fight the frigid temperatures.

He continued down the long straight. After five miles, he turned around and began retracing his steps. Back at the Leech place, he deliberately ran past the agent in the vehicle and dammit the man's eyes were closed now. Aaron pulled up short and jogged on the spot.

He glanced at the house. Stared harder. Was that a flicker of light in one of the upstairs rooms?

He saw it again. A flash of something coming from inside Julius Leech's bedroom. He glanced over to where Griffin had stopped nearby. Aaron pulled out his creds and tapped the gold badge on the glass, causing the agent inside to jerk guiltily awake.

The agent wound down the window. "I didn't mean to fall asleep. Shit." He rubbed his eyes.

Aaron stepped back. "Anyone supposed to be in that house?"

The agent looked embarrassed. "No. It was empty after we searched it earlier."

"Well, unless there's a ghost, I'd say it's no longer empty."

The agent climbed out of the car and softly closed the door. "I have a key to the front. I hope it's that sick bastard, Leech."

"Agent?"

"Diego Fuentes." The guy was built like a tank. "I was up all last night canvassing the Beasley murder." He rubbed his eyes. "I don't normally sleep on the job. Nash, right?"

Aaron nodded. If Fuentes was looking for forgiveness, he'd need to go elsewhere.

"Let's check it out." Perhaps Leech had decided to risk coming back knowing the Feds had recently searched the place and were unlikely to return.

Aaron took the key from Fuentes and jerked his chin toward the mansion. Griffin got out. He texted Frazer to give him the heads-up but not the rest of the team. Their job was to guard Hope. He didn't want them distracted.

Aaron crossed the road and Griffin thrust a ballistics vest at him as they walked up the front steps. He dragged it over his head then peeled off the grippers on his sneakers and tossed them to one side. He kept his voice down. "I saw a light on the third floor. Leech's bedroom."

Excitement stirred in his blood. This could be it. This could be Julius Leech's luck finally running out.

"Fuentes, take the back."

The guy nodded and started jogging to where a narrow alley cut between buildings. Aaron didn't want to lose Leech if he was here by him slipping out the rear entrance while they were searching the attic.

He pulled his weapon and quietly unlocked the door.

They slipped inside, moving in opposite directions, weapons drawn. Aaron indicated the main staircase, and they headed up on silent feet. Griffin cleared the landings while Aaron kept an eye on the stairs. Leech's bedroom was on the third floor. Second door on the left facing the front of the street. They crept forward, and Aaron smelled the scent of burning candles.

He exchanged a look with Griffin as they positioned themselves on either side of the large double doors.

He ignored the excitement that surged through him, found the gray zone where adrenaline didn't hike up his blood pressure and his heartbeat didn't waver. That's why they trained constantly—so their physiology didn't betray them in a firefight. The perpetual risk of death became a routine part of the job rather than something to worry about.

But he'd be lying if he said he wasn't happy at the prospect of meeting Julius Leech behind these doors and putting the asshole away for good. Hell, Aaron could be away from Boston before Hope woke up in the morning, safe and sound.

He twisted the knob, rushing inside, Griffin behind him before taking position in the opposite corner of the room the way they trained over and over in the Shooting House.

It took him less than a second to take in the scene. A large poster of a blonde in a pornographic position had been taped to the wall. The woman's face was Hope's, but Aaron didn't think she'd spent a lot of time naked in high heels in the desert. A dozen candles were lit beneath it forming a sort of shrine.

Aaron was all for worshiping naked women, but this scene made his stomach lurch.

Another smell hit his nostrils the same instant he spotted the blood saturating the white bedding. It wasn't just blood, Aaron realized after a quick glance. An animal had been disemboweled and displayed on the covers like some kind of satanic sacrifice.

He whirled at a noise. "FBI! Get your hands where I can see them!"

The hooded figure hesitated in the darkness and then darted away. Aaron charged after them, but they slammed the door shut and locked it in his face.

The bathroom.

He rammed his shoulder into it, once, twice, but the solid wood didn't budge.

Then he remembered there was another way out of that room. "Other door."

He and Griffin sprinted through the bedroom to find the exit wide open. "He's gone down the back stairs. Take the front."

Aaron took off after the sounds of the rapidly retreating intruder, hoping the asshole went out the back and ran straight into Fuentes' arms or doubled around to the front door to be confronted by Griffin.

No such luck. Aaron heard the mystery man's noisy progression through the Delawares' ground floor apartment and out the side door that formed the Delawares' main entrance. The cold breeze slice into Aaron as he threw himself out the door and bounced off the opposite wall.

The sound of two shots being fired was all the warning he got. One bullet smacked into his ballistic vest like a sledgehammer. The second hugged the wall and grazed the side of his head like a hot poker.

Aaron raised his gun to aim, but the figure whipped around the corner onto the front street. He wanted to keep in pursuit, but the shot had knocked the breath out of his lungs, and he could barely inhale, let alone run.

He heard footsteps behind him and raised his hand to tell whoever it was not to shoot.

"Nash?" Fuentes huffed up beside him. "You okay?"

"Yeah." He finally managed to draw in some air. "He got away."

Running footsteps told him Griffin was approaching down the thin alleyway.

"You see him?" asked Aaron.

"No. Did he hit you?"

Aaron tore off the vest and pulled up his shirt to make sure he hadn't been shot. "Hit the vest." Dead center of his chest.

He held Griffin's stare for a moment. If Griffin hadn't fetched the body armor from the SUV, Aaron wouldn't have wasted time to go get it. He'd either be dead or bleeding out right now. And his friends would once again be in mourning.

He nodded to the other operator. "Thanks, man."

Griffin made a face. "I can't believe we lost the bastard."

Aaron pushed away from the wall. "He might be hiding in the shadows. Let's go see if we can flush him out." But suddenly the smell of acrid smoke filled the air. Shit. "Call the fire department. I think the house is on fire."

47

Hope's cell rang at 8 a.m. and woke her. She couldn't believe she'd slept this late, though she'd been awake until well after four mulling things over in her head. She'd made the right choice. The threat to Aaron from Leech and the potential for pain meant getting emotionally involved wasn't worth the risk.

It was safer to be alone, and she was used to it.

She checked the screen. Answered groggily. "ADA Harper."

It was the clerk from the courthouse. "Judge Penton wants to see you in chambers this morning."

"On a *Saturday*?" She pushed herself upright and realized she was completely naked except for the scrape of a beard across the top of her breast.

A lump formed in her throat, but she forced it down. She'd pushed Aaron away, and he'd gone. No surprise there. She excelled at pushing people away. And the fact his lashing out at her had hurt so much was another indicator she'd done the right thing. They'd already managed to damage one another. Why risk more?

"Ten-thirty a.m."

It was highly unusual to receive a summons on the weekend. "Can I ask what this is about?"

"In her chambers. Ten-thirty. Don't be late."

He hung up, and she sagged against the pillows. "Dammit."

Perhaps it was to do with Jeff Beasley's death and the trial. Perhaps Jason Swann had taken a plea deal? She texted Colin to tell him to meet her there. She hoped he wasn't hungover or with someone. Next, she texted Aaron, ignoring the fact he would still be pissed with her. This was work, and he was the one who'd insisted on accompanying her everywhere. And, until Leech was caught, and Aaron went home, they were stuck together. They had to figure out a way to work with one another because no way was she going into protective custody. Not now, not ever. Nor was she jeopardizing Aaron's career.

She pulled on plaid pajamas and her coziest dressing gown and, ignoring the fact she probably looked like crap, headed down to put on the coffee.

The man on her couch wasn't Aaron Nash. It was Lincoln Frazer. And her cat was curled up on top of the legendary profiler, purring like a Ferrari.

He cracked an eyelid. "Morning already?"

"Apparently." She raised a brow, wondering why she wasn't more surprised. "What time did you arrive?"

He grunted. He was not a morning person, apparently.

She headed into the kitchen and put on the coffee. Her new role in life was coffee girl, but as long as she got the first cup she wouldn't complain.

Frazer had swung his legs down and was sitting up when she leaned on the door jamb and watched him.

"What are you doing here, Linc?"

"It seemed easier to crash here than go back to the Hayes's after visiting the hospital last night."

She frowned and went to stand opposite him. "Hospital?"

He widened his eyes. "You haven't heard?"

Everything inside her knotted.

"I assumed someone would have texted you about it."

She gripped her hands together. "About what?"

"Aaron getting shot last night."

Her legs went from under her, and her vision tunneled. The pain in her body was surely her ribs caving in.

"He's okay," Frazer assured her.

She closed her eyes and slumped back in the chair. "You should have led with that."

"He's fine. Bullet hit him in the chest, but he was wearing a ballistics vest—"

She drew in a ragged breath. If he hadn't been wearing body armor, he'd have been dead. That's what Lincoln had just told her. A few hours after leaving her bed, he had almost died, and she hadn't even realized. And nobody had bothered to tell her.

Her mouth tasted like ashes. "Who shot him?"

Frazer shook his head. "We don't know."

"I don't understand. How did this happen? I thought he was asleep in the next room." She hadn't heard him leave.

Frazer gave her a long look, and she wondered what Aaron had told him or what this astute man had guessed.

"For some reason, Nash decided to go for a run in the middle of the night and ended up outside Leech's mansion. He spotted a light inside and he, along with the FBI agent supposedly watching the premises, plus Will Griffin, entered to find a man in Leech's bedroom performing some weird ritual."

"Was it Leech? Or Delaware?"

Frazer shrugged. "We really don't know, and the chances of finding out now are pretty slim."

She frowned. "I don't understand. Why not?"

"Because Leech's thirty-million-dollar mansion went up in flames last night—from a fire caused by burning candles that surrounded a photoshopped poster of you doing impossible things on the back of a Harley, nude—or so I'm told. By the time I arrived the top two floors were engulfed, and the FBI agents barely made it out alive."

Aaron.

Griffin.

Hope sat stunned. The horror that overwhelmed her felt eerily reminiscent of losing Danny all over again. Even though Aaron was okay, had in fact cheated death twice last night by the sounds of it, the feeling of grief almost bowled her over.

That he hadn't texted her or knocked on her door to tell her he was okay hurt too. She'd done such a great job of pushing him away that it probably hadn't even crossed his mind. She was well and truly on her own again.

And she didn't like it.

She really didn't like it.

She'd have to get used to it again. Anguish filled her at the thought.

"Thank God he was wearing a vest," she managed.

"He wouldn't be here if he hadn't been. His ribs are bruised, but nothing's broken. He's one very lucky man. He's upstairs sleeping."

She wanted to run up and see for herself that he was okay and to demand that he never put himself in jeopardy again... But this was his job. Jeopardy. Danger. Hazard. These were the things he lived for. He'd probably raced into that burning building without a thought.

Worse, he'd probably enjoyed it.

Frazer left her and returned a few moments later with a steaming mug of coffee and pressed it into her hands. "I'll take him up a cup unless you want to?"

"You do it." Her voice cracked.

She swore she spotted disappointment on his face before he turned away.

Hope knew if she saw Aaron she'd break down and beg him never to do anything like that ever again. Which was bullshit. This was what he was trained for. This was what he loved.

She'd barely survived losing Danny. She didn't think she'd be able to deal with the constant fear and dread every time Aaron walked out the door.

The man deserved someone capable of living with that

constant risk. Someone who held their heart out like a gift to him and promised to cherish his in return. She'd made a vow like that before, but death had broken it. She couldn't do it again. She couldn't take that risk. It hurt too much when you were left behind.

48

They were in the vehicle heading downtown. Hope was giving him the ice queen treatment, but her red-rimmed eyes told another story.

Frazer had no doubt filled her in on the adventures last night, and Aaron wondered if she blamed herself for his middle of the night excitement or, more appropriately, blamed him for nearly taking a bullet in the head.

It was easy for him to be blasé about live ammunition as he dealt with it on a daily basis, but civilians? Getting shot at generally involved the worst day of their life.

Thankfully, the graze on the side of his scalp was difficult to see, especially since he'd pulled a black wool hat over his hair. He wore blue jeans, a black T-shirt, and a black down winter jacket he'd borrowed from JJ Hersh, leaving it unfastened in case he needed to access his weapon. Hope shouldn't be at the courthouse long. He had an errand to run along the way, and he wanted to blend in.

After getting back last night, he'd managed a couple of hours of sleep so deep it had felt like coming out of a coma when Frazer had woken him. If exhaustion had been what he'd been seeking when he'd gone out for that run, he'd certainly found it in the end.

The good news was, it only hurt when he breathed.

His ribs hadn't been broken, although the bruising made him look as if he'd gone a few rounds with the back end of a mule. Despite the cold marble floors of Leech's home, the old house had gone up like a tinderbox. The smoke he'd inhaled attempting to extinguish the fire in the elegant home—to preserve evidence more than architecture—meant he hadn't been able to stop coughing for the first hour after he'd gotten out. Each cough felt like he was being stabbed in the chest with a wooden stake.

Good times.

Griffin had also been treated for smoke inhalation, as had Fuentes, but both men were otherwise unharmed.

Aaron was furious the assailant had gotten away from him. He hadn't even seen the guy's face. But an Evidence Recovery Tech had dug a pristine bullet out of the side of the pool house. They just needed a weapon to match it to.

The other bullet had splattered into an unrecognizable mess upon impact with his breast plate. He was thinking of getting both framed.

His teammates had not been happy with him, and he'd been hearing from everyone in a litany of scolding texts like a bunch of worried mamas.

A car honked, jerking him out of his thoughts.

Hope glanced at him, and he had to fight the impulse to reach out to touch her fingers because a) she didn't want him, and b) the guys were in the vehicle too. Everyone except Cowboy and Demarco, whom he'd left guarding the house today.

"Drop me here."

"You aren't coming with us?" Hope finally met his gaze.

Was he kidding himself that she sounded like she wanted him to be with her? Probably. She'd made her thoughts quite clear yesterday, although that had been in the bedroom not about work.

He still hadn't apologized for what he'd said. God. What a

jackass. He would. He needed a minute to swallow his pride between coughing bouts.

He coughed again, annoyed with himself but unable to control the spasm.

Finally, he was able to speak. "I have something to do. Kincaid, text me when you're done. I don't know how long this will take."

Hope opened her mouth to say something, but he didn't want to hear it. Not right now. Once he had his own feelings under control, he'd find somewhere private they could talk without everyone else knowing their business.

And the real problem was they shouldn't have any private business.

He jumped out and ducked his head out of the wind. Headed down a side street to the print shop where the picture of Hope had been printed before being placed in an envelope on her daughter's headstone.

Aaron hesitated as he looked in the window. Considering everything Hope had been through this week, he'd acted like a jerk. Especially as there had never been any promises or commitment between them.

He reached for his phone then stopped. He could hardly text her or call her to admit to being an idiot or apologize when all her communications were being monitored—not without giving himself away.

He'd tell her later. When he hopefully had proof as to the identity of the vandal who'd desecrated her husband and child's grave. Maybe that would be peace offering enough.

There was an itch in his brain that the vandal and the guy from last night at Leech's house were one and the same. It hadn't escaped his notice that Lewis Janelli was the right height and build for the man who'd shot at him. And he carried a 9mm. And Aaron had pissed him off yesterday. Big time.

He pushed inside the door of the premises into a wall of heat.

Walked up to the counter. Flashed his creds at a young woman currently not serving a customer.

"I need to track down a printer." He reeled off the serial number which was linked to the machine identity code that had been printed on the image. The code was a bunch of yellow dots, invisible unless you knew what you were looking for.

She looked confused. "I'm not sure…"

"It's for an ongoing investigation. Is it possible to examine the units you have in the store?"

She looked uncertain. "I—"

"It shouldn't take long. If I can't find the right machine, I'll be out of your hair in five minutes."

Sounded great, except he knew the printer was here.

"Okay. I suppose so. Come on back. My manager went out for coffee, I'm sure he'll return shortly."

She opened the door in the counter.

But he pointed to the self-serve units. He had a feeling that's how this guy would roll. The less interaction the better.

"I'll start over there."

She nodded again. Obviously torn between complying with law enforcement and worried she was doing the wrong thing and would get in trouble with her boss.

He checked out the large copier against the nearest wall and struck gold.

The young woman joined him. Crossing her arms.

"Hey, this is it." He pulled out the copy of the warrant he had in his pocket that Frazer had given him earlier. "I'm going to need to seal this unit off until the crime scene techs can process it."

A couple of customers in the queue looked their way.

"Crime scene techs? Process it?" Her eyes swung wildly around the room. "What do you mean, *process it*?"

"If we're lucky, they can do it on site. Download the memory from the machine." DNA and trace would be useless when there were probably hundreds of people using it every day.

"Oh man, I don't know. My boss isn't going to like that."

"Jeanine?" That's what her employee tag said.

"Yeah?"

"You aren't in any trouble. None at all." He showed her the warrant again. "This means I was always going to be allowed to search the premises and I was always going to find this printer. But you cooperating with me is a really big help, so I won't shut you down even though I can. You have an Out-of-Order notice you can put on this until our guys get here?"

"Sure." She chewed her lip then dashed behind the counter and came back with a big red sign. Placed it on top of the machine. "They aren't going to have FBI or CSI on the back of their clothes, are they?" She grimaced. "It'll scare people."

He thought about it for a second. "I'll ask them to wear plain clothes."

Which suited them anyway. That way the press wouldn't be alerted to a new development in the investigation and whoever had printed that photo and probably the poster of Hope that had been taped to that wall last night—and who had, therefore, tried to murder an FBI agent in the line of duty—wouldn't get an early warning that their time was running out. The images should be stored inside this machine's vast memory.

He glanced up at the surveillance camera. "Does that thing work?"

"Yes. We keep the recordings for a couple of weeks and then delete."

"I need to check out your surveillance footage."

"Let me text Lyle—"

"You can do that, but in the meantime, let me get started on the video."

Her mouth opened to argue.

"Lives are at stake, Jeanine."

She blinked. "Oh. Sure. Come on. Follow me. But if Lyle yells at me, I might need you to defend me." She bit her lip and a dimple appeared. Was she flirting with him?

He was surprised. She looked about twenty.

"If your boss yells at you, you probably need another job." Not that that applied in his organization, but in his job a mistake could cost someone their life.

She sobered. "You're right." Then stronger. "You are completely right." She led the way into a back room and turned on the lights. "Lyle hasn't actually arrived yet today. He gets me to open up and arrives after he's stuffed his face at a diner down the street." Jeanine woke the PC then opened the surveillance app and folder. "Each twenty-four-hour period is stored automatically in a separate file. Cameras are motion activated. We're only open seven a.m. to seven p.m., so there's about twelve hours of footage per day." She scratched her nose. "Guess who closes?"

"You do. Can I get permission from the onsite person in charge to send these files to the FBI analysts ASAP?" It was probably covered in the warrants, but having her permission was good too.

She gave him a grin. "As the senior member of staff, you have my permission." Then she checked her watch. "I'll give you a ten-minute head start before I message Lyle and tell him the FBI are here. Hey, if you find any porn on that thing," she pointed at the computer, "it's not mine."

He smiled as he quickly copied the files to a secure network. Then he began fast-forwarding through them, starting on the day Leech escaped, pausing to check each face of the people who used that particular copier.

He texted Frazer that he was here and had found the machine and to send the CSI guys down in plain clothes so as not to alert the world. He also told him to get someone—AKA Alex Parker—to run the payments and see if they could come up with a credit card and a name. Of course, the guy could have paid cash.

Aaron carried on watching the footage. He could have let the techs do this, but it was personal now, and he wanted answers. He settled in to watch. Paused the footage when he heard a yell from the front of the shop. Sounded like Lyle had arrived.

He rolled his shoulders and stretched out his neck, wincing from the stab of pain in his injured chest. Not only the bruises. He thrust thoughts of a broken heart out of his mind. He'd known before it even started he wasn't in her league. He'd pretty much resigned himself to bachelorhood over the years, and that was okay.

Hope had been a blip.

Lust getting out of hand and the great sex making him think he might be in love. Ridiculous. Absolutely ridiculous. He had his teammates for when he got lonely, which wasn't often. He needed to get back in the dating pool if he was this desperate for sex.

The thought left a sour taste in his mouth.

He heard Jeanine yelling back at Lyle and felt a surge of pride. He was about to go reinforce the message about how to treat staff.

The sooner he figured out where Leech was, and whoever the hell else was targeting the woman he'd stupidly gone and fallen for, the faster he could go home and forget about the whole goddamn thing.

49

Hope strode down the familiar halls with a frosty look of indifference fixed on her features, but it did nothing to soothe her inner turmoil.

Aaron had looked tired this morning, mouth grim with either annoyance or pain. She'd wanted to go to him and ask if he was all right, but as soon as he'd spotted her, he'd turned away and headed downstairs.

What had she expected? Smiles? Laughter? Empathy? The easygoing, respectful conversation they usually enjoyed throughout the day? No. That connection had extinguished. She'd killed it.

And he'd almost *died* last night.

She couldn't get over that salient fact.

He'd almost died. And she hadn't even known he'd left the house. A stone wedged in her throat, and no matter how many times she tried to swallow it wouldn't budge.

Where'd he gone this morning?

Get used to not knowing.

And that's what she'd wanted. What she needed. Ignorance. So why did she feel as if she was already drowning in worry and frustration?

She stopped dead in the corridor as the knot inside her started to unravel. She was already in deep and even now the pain was almost overwhelming. She didn't want to go through that again. She wouldn't survive. Life was much simpler and easier when she kept to herself and lived life on her own terms. No more friendship. No more foolish optimism. She liked her own company. She liked her job and putting killers and criminals where they belonged. She liked her writing career where she got to enact whatever twisted vengeance she dreamt up. It had to be enough.

Her heart squeezed tight, and suddenly she couldn't breathe.

What she wanted didn't seem to matter because suddenly it wasn't enough. It *wasn't* what she wanted.

"Hope? Everything okay?" Seth Hopper asked patiently from her shoulder. He and Sebastian Black had accompanied her inside today.

"Yes," she snapped then regretted it as his mouth firmed and eyes went blank.

"God, I'm sorry." She dragged her hand through her hair. So much for finding her inner queen bitch attorney persona. It wasn't Seth's fault she'd gone and fallen in l—

She shook her head. No. It wasn't that. It couldn't be that. They'd only known each other a few days.

How long did you know Danny before you knew he was the one?

She pushed the irritating inner voice away. She wouldn't put Aaron in danger the way she'd put Danny in danger, no matter what she felt for the man.

"Everything okay, Hope?" Colin asked. Expression concerned.

She forced her brain to remember where they were and why they were here. "I'm concerned to be called in this way on the weekend." She took a deep breath. "You spoke to Ella, right?"

"Not since last night." He blinked at her. "Should I call her?"

He reached for his phone, but it was 10:29 and Hope didn't want to be late.

She shook her head. "We're almost there anyway. Let's see what the judge wants. Call her afterwards to check in."

They arrived at Judge Penton's chambers and were ushered into the outer office by the clerk. When they went to go inside the inner chamber, the clerk put his hand out to prevent her FBI detail following her inside.

"The judge insists security stays outside."

Seth Hopper turned his head as he calmly removed the clerk's hand from his chest. "I'm not security. I'm a federal law enforcement officer enforcing very specific orders from the US Attorney General." His voice was steely. "I intend to search the judge's chambers before I allow Hope inside. If the judge has an issue with that, she can take it up with the AG." It wasn't a request.

He muscled his way inside.

"You can be sure she will." Judge Penton's gaze narrowed, and her lips thinned as she examined the two FBI operators. "Do it quickly, and then get out."

Hope was shocked by the tone, though many judges suffered from a God complex.

It took Seth only a few seconds to complete his search of the rooms and private bathroom. The adjoining door to the courtroom was locked.

He addressed the judge. "Thank you, ma'am."

"Your Honor," the judge corrected him testily.

Hope smiled at him in reassurance. She had no idea what the judge's issue could be, but Seth Hopper didn't deserve to be dodging verbal bullets all morning.

"Your Honor." Seth's expression was unreadable as he nodded to Hope and joined Black outside the door.

Hope stood in front of the judge's desk even though the woman herself didn't sit. In fact, she walked over to the heavy wooden door and turned the lock.

Hope sighed.

Was that a power move? Seemed like it. It would be taking all of the HRT operators' self-control not to beat down the door in the next five minutes. She quickly texted the guys that everything was fine.

The judge sat. "It's come to my attention that that individual threatened to murder Jeff Beasley the afternoon before the man was killed."

"Seth Hopper?" Hope froze. "He was kidding."

"Well, it wasn't very funny, and Jeff Beasley ended up dead in an alley exactly the way as threatened." The judge leaned forward as if imparting a secret. "HRT operators are trained to kill."

Hope opened her mouth to argue. It was ridiculous. "How do you even know about that?" She stared at Colin as red stained his cheeks.

"I only told the bailiff," he confessed. "I never expected…"

"I'm disappointed that you didn't come forward with this information yourself, ADA Harper, and I can only conclude that the pressure of Julius Leech's escape played a part in your poor judgment." The judge raised her chin and looked down her hawk-like nose. "I will need to report the threat to the FBI Field Office, and they will have to investigate. In the meantime, Operator Hopper needs to be suspended—"

"Wait. No! There is no way Operator Hopper killed Jeff Beasley. He was in my house at the time of the murder." Hope couldn't believe they'd been dragged in here like this over this nonsense. "In fact, he was on a treadmill in my downstair neighbor's apartment with several witnesses when I received the call from Jeff after he'd been stabbed. It's impossible for him to have been in two places at once." The words tasted gritty on her tongue. How dare this woman question the integrity of these men?

"I still feel it is necessary to make a formal inquiry—"

"This is bullshit. He has a solid alibi that includes me. Are you suggesting I'm lying?" Hope drew herself up and raised her chin.

The judge narrowed her gaze. "I'll have you held in contempt if you're not careful, counselor."

"You are questioning my integrity, Your Honor, and that I do not appreciate. Nor do I appreciate you accusing an honorable man who has a solid alibi of such a heinous act."

Colin thrust his cell phone at Hope, and she took it in confusion. He rounded the table, hand in his pocket, and the judge looked at him with startled eyes. He placed his hand over the judge's mouth and then pulled a syringe out of his pocket and jabbed it into her thigh, pushing down the plunger.

"Colin? What the hell are you doing?" Her heart pounded. Had he lost his mind?

He held the judge still as she struggled for a few moments, looked over his shoulder. "Look at the photo on the screen, Hope."

She glanced down at the image on his cell, and her own mouth dropped open in horror.

Ella, gagged and bound to a chair.

Hope stumbled backwards and turned toward the door. Colin stepped in front of her and put his finger to his lips. "Read the caption. He wants you. He says if we don't come alone, he'll kill her. But if we do come, he'll release her."

She read the texts.

Leech. Dammit. It had to be Leech.

"He's lying. He probably already killed her." Anguish curled inside her.

"Don't say that."

"How did he get your number?"

His features twisted. "I don't know. Maybe Ella's phone? He had to know yours are being monitored."

He reached into his pocket and pulled out a small automatic pistol. She opened her mouth to scream for help, but he offered it to her, grip first.

Confused, she took the weapon, the weight heavy in her hand. The implications were not good. Colin smuggling in a weapon into the courthouse was not good. Colin having a tranquilizer in his pocket and using it was definitely not good.

Was he having some sort of mental health crisis? Had he formed a personal attachment to Ella?

"We'll both be armed. Leech won't be expecting that. We can pretend I forced you to come with me, but then we turn on him and save Ella. He says if anyone else shows up he'll run, and Ella will die."

The thought was abhorrent, but she didn't think Colin was being truthful with her. "Why do you care so much?"

Colin's eyes went wide with outrage. "Well, there's a serial killer on the loose for a start, and Ella is in danger, isn't that enough?"

Hope looked at the judge who was slumped unconscious. None of this made any sense. "You know your law career is over."

Hers would be too if she went along with his crazy plan, which she had no intention of doing.

Aaron would tell her to trust him to do his job. To rescue Ella and catch Leech. And she had. She did.

She met Colin's gaze and saw the moment he realized she wasn't going to go along with this insanity. She opened her mouth to call for help but he slammed his palm over her mouth and held her jaw closed. They struggled and she remembered she held a gun, but she didn't actually want to shoot Colin or herself. She tried to hit him with it, but Colin wrapped his other hand around her and forced her to the floor.

He was a lot stronger than he looked. The pistol was pinned underneath her and she realized with sudden clarity there was no way he'd give her a weapon with real bullets.

The warning Aaron had given her when they'd been practicing self-defense training flashed into her mind. It would be them or you, and she'd already lost the first battle.

"All you had to do was be a good girl and follow some simple instructions, but you always have to be the one giving orders. Such a fucking bitch." Colin's quiet murmur shocked her with its intensity. She'd trusted this guy, and he'd betrayed her.

Use your voice.

She struggled frantically to free her mouth, but he had a firm grip of her jaw, and she felt as if he might rip her head right off her shoulders. He used his weight to pin her before she felt a sharp sting in the side of her ass.

"Don't worry," he whispered against her brow. "I don't plan to hurt you."

She didn't believe him.

"You always say you want to confront Leech. I'm about to give you your wish, ADA Harper. Give you the chance to atone for all the deaths on your hands."

Tears welled up, but they were tears of anger. He fidgeted for a moment but didn't let up his grip on her jaw. She moaned as loudly as she was able to try to get her bodyguards' attention through the thick wooden door, but he smacked her face against the floor. Pain radiated sharply from her cheekbone. He slipped a piece of duct tape over her mouth as nausea swirled in her stomach. She deliberately calmed herself as her heart raced out of control. She was already starting to feel woozy from whatever he'd drugged her with. His weight was gone for a few seconds, and then she heard the rattle of keys. She turned her head and saw him walk back from the judge's desk.

She tried to get to her feet, but he grabbed her and handcuffed her hands together behind her back. Picked up the gun she'd lost during their struggle.

He must have brought all these things with him this morning —and because they were able to skip security they'd never been detected.

Hope was such a fool. Why had she never seen there was more going on with this guy?

Because she hadn't looked. She'd been so focused on her mission to put away the murderers and rapists that she hadn't spotted the danger lurking right beside her every day.

"Come on." He dragged her to her feet, and she stumbled slightly. If she didn't get away soon, she was in serious trouble. "Up you get."

He pushed her toward the door that led into the courtroom, forced her through it and locked it behind him.

She tried to run then, but her feet caught on something as she entered the familiar space. and she crashed hard to the ground, hitting her chin on the parquet flooring.

She tasted blood.

He went over to the exit that the prisoners used which was unmanned on the weekend. He unlocked it as she tried to get to her feet.

"Come on, Hope. We both want the same thing. Leech."

Seriously?

His hand manacled her arm. "Almost forgot." He fished in her coat pocket and pulled out her cell phone. He checked her messages and answered the text that had just come in from Seth with a thumbs up. And "We'll be about 10 min."

"That should hold them for a while." He slid her phone across the courtroom floor and closed the door, locking it and pushing her forward into the dimly lit space.

Her body was feeling more and more disconnected from her mind. She didn't know what the hell was going on, but she didn't have to make this easy for him. She sat down in the middle of the corridor.

He laughed, a tortured, bitter sound. Then he pulled out a second lethal-looking gun. "I don't want to hurt you, but I haven't spent the past seven years working my ass off to fail now."

The realization he'd been planning something all this time pierced the fog in her mind. This was clearly related to Leech. Colin had never been the trusted colleague he'd pretended to be. He'd been waiting all these years to spring a trap on her—like a spider spinning a web. She really hated spiders.

The question was why? Was he working for Leech?

"While it's a lot easier if you walk out under your own steam, I can easily knock you out and carry you. But I won't be very happy about it, and you *will* regret it later."

The look in his eyes told her to believe him, but she obviously didn't move fast enough.

He grabbed her by the hair and dragged her upright.

Pain screamed through her scalp, blinding her to anything else.

"I promised Leech I'd bring him *you*. The ten million he's paying me will make up for all the training I've wasted and help me get away."

That Colin was doing this for money burned.

"And I get to kill the man who murdered my father." He spoke mockingly as he shoved her along.

His father? She thought she'd known all the family members of Leech's victims but obviously not. So this wasn't about money. This was about revenge, which she understood much more clearly.

"Julius Leech escaping from prison was like a gift from the heavens."

Not for her, it wasn't.

"What about Ella?" The words were muffled behind the tape. Pain throbbed through her skull from the hair pulling and when he'd smacked her earlier. The drugs weren't cutting through that yet, but she knew they would. He'd obviously given her a much lower dose than the judge who'd been unconscious in seconds.

"Leech doesn't have Ella. I do. And *if* you behave. *If* you get into the car I have waiting outside without making a scene, I will make sure she is rescued. Otherwise, she'll die a slow death of starvation—assuming she doesn't freeze to death first."

The cowardly bastard. Hurting a young woman who'd already been abused.

Unfortunately, Hope could barely keep her eyes open, let alone fight him.

Regret filled her. Because the words she'd spoken to Aaron last night had been nothing more than a coward's desperate lie.

She already *loved* him. She loved him, and she'd go to her death with him thinking that what they'd had together meant nothing more to her than great sex. In reality, he was her second chance. Her gift from the universe. And she'd blown it. Now she was going to die, and he was going to be so mad. Not only had she ruined his perfect record, but she had the horrible feeling she'd broken his heart.

50

Aaron checked his watch, about to give up in frustration. He needed to get back to the team rather than go rogue on this investigation the way he was doing. Then, on screen, a man wearing a dark hoody and jacket walked through the door of the shop.

Aaron frowned. Sat up. Leaned forward.

The man wore wraparound sunglasses even though it was dark outside. Aaron was pretty sure he recognized the figure from last night.

Son of a bitch.

He watched as the guy printed first a small photograph and then a large poster that Aaron could identify even from this distance. The figure kept checking to the side to make sure no one was watching the pornographic image as it came through.

Aaron frowned. Who the hell was that? He looked familiar.

Janelli?

"Take off the glasses, dickhead." He gritted his teeth then froze as the guy dipped the shades to read the control panel.

Aaron stood up so sharply the chair flew across the floor.

He pulled out his cell as he strode to the front of the print shop. "Do not go into that room," he ordered. "It's officially part of a crime scene investigation until I tell you otherwise. I will haul you off to jail if you fail to comply."

A much-chastened Lyle nodded sullenly, but Jeanine gave Aaron a perky thumbs up as she spoke to one of the CSI techs downloading data from the copier.

Aaron went out the front door and dialed as he started to run toward the courthouse.

"What's up?" Seth answered his call.

"Colin Leighton, Hope's assistant. He's the motherfucker who shot at me last night. Do you have eyes on him?"

"Negative. He and Hope are both in the judge's chambers, and we got kicked out."

Shit.

Aaron heard Seth arguing with the clerk to open the door.

Aaron sprinted as fast as he could while still listening to the conversation. He fumbled for his comms and slipped them into his ear, dodging pedestrians and tourists alike.

Seth swore. "They aren't in the judge's chambers. Judge is unconscious at her desk. Still breathing. Must have gone out via the courtroom. Call an ambulance," he yelled at someone obviously there with him.

Aaron felt as if his heart was about to explode. They could leave via any exit. Or Colin could kill Hope on the spot—but the prick had had plenty of opportunities to do that so he must want her alive for some reason. "Kincaid take the front entrance. Seth and Black go out the rear exits. I'm going to check out the prisoner entrance."

Aaron had never run this fast in his life and his lungs were on fire. He got to the side of the building and levered himself up to look over the security wall and railings.

Nothing.

He glanced around. Across the wide busy sidewalk, he spotted Colin shoving Hope into the back of a yellow cab. Aaron pulled his weapon and ran, ignoring the way the civilians scattered in terror.

"FBI! Stop."

No clean shot.

Colin dashed around to the driver's seat and threw himself behind the wheel, starting the engine and pulling into traffic. A minivan screeched to a halt just in time to prevent a collision.

Aaron ran after the cab and spoke into his comms. "He's in a yellow cab heading north."

Aaron kept running, hoping to catch him at the next red light, but the fucker piled through, almost sideswiping a compact. Aaron aimed at the back tire, but crossing traffic and civilians in the area made it impossible to get off a clean shot.

He dodged cars that slammed on their brakes and honked their horns at him like he was a lunatic.

He pumped his legs faster, but the cab accelerated away and turned a corner. Then it was gone.

A few seconds later their black SUV with emergency lights pulled up beside him. He jumped in. Tried to catch his breath. Hopper and Black were already inside. Kincaid was driving.

"Take the next left. He's driving a yellow cab." He reeled off the license plate and cab number. He dialed Frazer. "Colin Leighton abducted Hope from the courthouse. I found him on the surveillance footage at the printers, and I'm almost certain he's the guy that shot me last night." He ignored Frazer's reaction. "I need a BOLO for that cab. Get locals to call it in, but don't attempt to stop it."

"You're in pursuit?"

"We lost him—I was on foot—but we're still looking. On Staniford Street." There were multiple tunnels or bridges or even ferries Leighton could take to get away, assuming he left the downtown area.

"I'm going to get Alex Parker on Leighton's communications. Presumably this is related to Leech?"

"That would be my guess, but you're the profiler." Aaron barely kept his temper.

"She's my friend too, Aaron," Frazer snapped. "If you don't see him in the next two minutes, get to his apartment and search for clues. Anything that might tell us what the hell is going on and why he's taken Hope. Wear gloves, but speed is of the essence. I'll get you the address as soon as I've spoken with Alex about tracking his communications."

Frazer hung up.

Aaron was shaking. So much for combat training and the gray zone. Hope's life was in the balance, and he was a wreck. The thing he was supposed to make sure never happened had happened to the only woman to get past his guard in years. Which was exactly why you did not get personally involved with your principal!

Fuck.

"We'll find her." Kincaid eyed him via the rearview.

"I messed up." On so many levels.

"You figured out Colin was a threat while we stood outside the goddamn door like a couple of morons," Seth Hopper gritted out. "You would never have let her out of your sight. This is on me."

What did it matter? Hope was at this prick's mercy until they could find her. Was Colin Leighton in league with Julius Leech? Nothing else made sense.

"Her cell phone?" Aaron asked suddenly.

Hopper handed it over. "Found it on the courtroom floor."

Shit. He should have implanted a sub-dermal tracker or something, but she'd never have gone for it. He touched the phone screen. Opened it because he'd memorized her password without her permission. Knowledge was power in their business and collecting data was pure muscle memory.

He read the messages from Colin, but there was nothing non-work related.

"We'll find her," Kincaid said from behind the wheel taking turn after turn. But there was no sign of the cab.

All the determination in the world wouldn't stop a knife attack if they were too far away to help.

"Think Ella Gibson is involved?" Hopper asked. "She and Leighton seemed tight."

"Good thought. Let's see if we can track her down." He dragged his hand through his hair then concentrated on what he did best. Looking at things from every angle. "Frazer wants us to check out Colin's apartment for clues."

The address popped through on his phone. He checked the map. "It's not far from Hope's place." But something was niggling at him. "Even if we figure out why he's doing this it won't bring us any closer to finding Hope. We know he took her, and he must have planned for that. Hopper, call Frazer."

"What are you thinking?" The guy was already dialing the number.

"Turn off the emergency lights, and let's do another trawl of the neighborhood. Don't just look for cabs. Check the driver of every car. We might get lucky." He dialed Cowboy and gave him a brief rundown of the situation. "You and Demarco take two of alpha squad and head to Leighton's apartment and search for any evidence of where he might go—be careful though." There was no suggestion of boobytraps, but Colin Leighton was an unknown factor. "Tell the rest of alpha squad to use Hope's car and to await instruction. Pack all the gear we might need for a hostage rescue." He hung up.

"What would you do if you were trying to get out of town without being seen?" asked Seth.

"Depends where I was going, but I'd have a second car that I'd have switched to already then take backroads out of the city avoiding any cameras and toll roads. Wearing a hat and glasses to fool any I'm not aware of." The same way Colin had done at the printers, except he wasn't disciplined enough not to screw up.

Aaron remembered how Hope had flopped into the back of the cab. "It looked as if Hope might have been drugged, which reduces the chances of him transferring her to another vehicle without people noticing…unless he has underground parking?"

Black checked. "Nope. Street parking at his home address at least."

"So, the fact he took her in the day suggests he might not risk changing cars, but he could switch plates easily enough and disguise the taxi number with tape or a magnetic strip, which would be my next move. Then—assuming he's taking Hope to Leech… Shit, *fuck*, they could be anywhere." He pressed his thumb and forefinger to the bridge of his nose and squeezed. *Think*. "If it was me, it would be an isolated property with some sort of building and, knowing Leech's penchant for the good life, probably a luxury home or a really nice cabin. There would be a garage—probably attached or close enough he wouldn't be seen by neighbors walking from there to the house—so he could hide his vehicle. Close to a private airfield probably. Leech doesn't want to get caught. How many of those are there?"

"About seven within a two-hour radius. Nearest is Crow Island Airpark but that's only a small strip with Cessnas and microlites and shit."

"Frazer said to tell you he's serious about that offer from the BAU when you leave HRT," Seth said, still having an open line to the profiler. He frowned. "You can't leave HRT."

If Aaron didn't rescue Hope before Leech hurt her, he wouldn't be staying with the FBI. He'd joined to prove a point. And while he loved his job, if he lost Hope then he didn't deserve to be in the elite organization. He kept his mouth shut, but from the way Kincaid eyed him in the mirror he knew what he was thinking.

Aaron checked the map, and his eyes caught the town of Lincoln. "Ask Frazer what are the chances Leech and Leighton would meet up at Sylvie Pomerol's farm?"

"He says it's possible but unlikely."

"Get someone out there anyway. Fuck!" Aaron yelled. He was

supposed to be the cool logical one, but he needed something to go on.

"Frazer has something."

Hopper passed his cell to Aaron, and he put Frazer on speaker. "Parker managed to narrow down the cell signals of Colin Leighton's phone."

Aaron frowned. The guy wasn't that stupid, surely? Not after pulling off something so complicated and clever.

"His registered phone has been turned off, SIM card removed or destroyed. But a burner that bounced off a tower near Ella Gibson's apartment at 4:30 a.m. also bounced off a tower near the courtroom around the time Leighton was in the courthouse today."

"That's it." Excitement raced over Aaron's skin. "Where is it now?"

"Near Fenway Park."

Kincaid started heading that way. Fast.

"No sirens," Frazer cautioned.

Kincaid turned the sirens off but gave a low whoop through each intersection and eased through before once again going as fast as he was able.

Aaron's skin itched with the need to move. To get to Hope and beat that motherfucker until his knuckles bled—the way Brendan had beaten Leech the day he'd murdered his brother.

He should call Hope's brother-in-law to let him know what had happened, but would the local cops help find Hope or get in their way? He wasn't sure.

"If you catch sight of Leighton, you need to follow him covertly." Frazer's voice echoed metallically from Seth's cell.

What the fuck?

"You think he'll lead us to Leech," Aaron realized.

"Don't you?" Frazer shot back.

Aaron stared out of the window as a boulder settled in his stomach. "Probably, but my mission is not to capture Julius Leech. It's to protect Hope Harper."

Something he'd already failed to do.

"Which do you think Hope would prefer? Rescuing her now and losing our best chance at tracking down the serial killer who butchered her family? Or rescuing her AND recapturing Leech and arresting Colin?"

"It doesn't change my mission," Aaron repeated stubbornly. Then he swore. "You're right. It makes sense, but I do not want the marshals or locals fucking this up, so make your peace with that. Otherwise, we will box this motherfucker in on the highway, and Leech will have to be caught the old-fashioned way. And we are not losing that cab—which we will if he realizes that burner is a liability and dumps it." He dragged his hand through his hair. "My team is in pursuit, but I'm gonna talk to Romano about using some of Charlie team and sending up the drones he has with him to follow that cab."

"Good idea. Parker has found a satellite feed we can use for the time being, but that's only in play for the next hour or so."

Aaron looked up at the overcast sky. That meant Parker had probably hacked a satellite that used RADAR technology to see through clouds.

"Can Parker send me the tracking data and the sat feed?"

"I'll ask him, but there's a delay in the feed due to image processing time which means we are always going to be a few minutes behind, but combined with the cell data—"

"Assuming Colin doesn't turn it off or toss it out the window."

"Aaron," Frazer said softly. "She's going to be all right."

"You don't know that."

"No, but I know Hope, and she's a survivor."

"Let's pray you're right." He didn't know what he'd do if Frazer was wrong. He already felt as if he were dead inside. No wonder Hope was gun shy of relationships.

Frazer hung up.

Aaron called Romano without letting himself think about Hope as anything except a missing principal. He couldn't function if he thought about how much danger she was in. He should never have let her out of his sight. Maybe he'd been kidding himself this whole time, and his ex had called it. Maybe he really wasn't good enough to call himself a Hostage Rescue Team operator.

51

Wooziness bombarded Hope as she slowly roused from a heavy sleep. Instinctively, she knew something was seriously wrong, probably alerted by the thick tape that covered her mouth. She stayed quiet and still. Her skin stuck uncomfortably to the warm vinyl of the car seat. The hum of tarmac beneath the wheels told her they were moving.

Where was she?

She blinked awake and tried to remember what had happened. The last thing she remembered was being in the judge's chambers and Colin attacking Judge Penton.

Holy crap. He must have drugged her too.

Was he driving?

Or was it Leech?

Fear lanced her, sharp claws of dread defying her usual bravado.

Her head throbbed, and the swirl of nausea in her stomach scared the hell out of her because she didn't want to die by choking. She didn't want to die at all.

Fragments of memory came back to her slowly. Foggy thanks to the drug.

She didn't dare move as she lay there, even though her arms

screamed from the tension of being restrained behind her back. She used her tongue to push against the duct tape to loosen it. She faced the rear of the seat so whoever was driving couldn't see her trying to free her mouth, but she couldn't see them either.

Out of the corner of her eye, steely gray clouds raced by as skeletal tree branches reached their bony fingers across the road.

She didn't see any buildings, and her heart dropped a little to realize they were out of the city.

Ella...

The image of the young woman tied up flashed into her brain. Where was she? Was she okay?

From her work with sex crime cases, she knew memories of what happened after the drug kicked in might never return, but certain details were starting to break through. She remembered Colin had said Leech had kidnapped Ella and he was bringing Hope to him in exchange for her safety. And Colin had given her a gun...which she'd lost during their struggle. The rest was hazy.

It was frustrating, but she knew one thing. Colin was a liar and not to be trusted.

The car's turn signal started clicking, and they took a turn off the main road. She used the momentum to roll onto her back but closed her eyes and kept her expression slack. The area around her lips felt disgustingly itchy and moist.

"Almost there, Hope. It's too bad you slept most of the journey. I would have enjoyed telling you everything."

Colin was driving.

She mentally rolled her eyes. God, how some men loved to hear themselves talk. She didn't bother to open her eyes. Let him wonder if she was really awake.

What would her bodyguards be thinking? *Aaron?* Her heart clenched. Blaming himself no doubt, but who could have predicted this? Had they found the judge? Hope hoped she was okay. Colin's maneuvers to get them into the courtroom had been cleverly done. The judge had reason to keep Hope's protection detail out of the room, but she wasn't sure Aaron would have stayed outside. Not that people had that much choice when a judge ordered something unless they wanted to end up behind bars.

After another ten minutes, she opened her eyes a slit. The trees overhead drew closer together until the branches interlocked.

Dread pierced deep. Whatever Colin planned couldn't be good.

HRT wouldn't be far behind. Aaron might be upset with her for rejecting him, but he'd be worried sick. They had lots of ways of tracking people, right? They'd find her. Somehow. She had to believe that. If she could escape and hide, the FBI would find her. She forced herself to sit up and look around.

"Ah. Excellent. You're awake." Colin sounded delighted.

Hope rubbed her face against the back of the seat and managed to unpeel the tape from her mouth. "What's going on? Why are you doing this?"

His mouth pinched and his eyes examined her critically from behind his glasses. "I could tell you, but then I'd have to kill you."

She met his glare. "Isn't that what you're planning anyway?"

"Not me. Not anymore." His voice was jolly, but his smile didn't reach his eyes. "Although that *was* my original idea."

She jolted at the depth of his betrayal, then frowned. "Did you help Leech escape from prison?"

"I did not. But I am very grateful to the good Lord for all his assistance."

"Because he's paying you?" Revulsion filled her tone.

"It isn't about the money," he insisted.

"What is it about then?"

He remained silent.

"Revenge? Admiration? Hatred? Or am I that lousy of a boss?" She almost laughed, except this was definitely not funny. "Oh, wait. I remember now. You said Leech killed your father." She gave a bitter laugh. "I'd apologize for forgetting something so important, but I guess that's what you get for injecting someone against their will with a date rape drug."

"*Shut* up."

"I thought you wanted to *talk*? Oh, wait, silly me." Saccharine dripped off each word. "I forgot. You didn't say you wanted a conversation. You said you wanted to *tell* me *everything*. The cliched evil monologue before I'm sent to my death—but no answering back or interrupting, right? Yes, sir, sorry, sir." She leaned forward and would have saluted if her hands had been free. "Did you find it too difficult to work for a woman?" She was deliberately provoking him any way she could. "Too humbling? Poor Colin—"

He took his arm off the steering wheel and lashed out toward her face with his clenched fist. She avoided the punch and latched onto his wrist like a terrier. Her teeth sank deep into the material of his suit jacket and found skin, flesh and bone. This wasn't a game. She didn't hold back. He screamed as she tore into him. He used his other hand to grab her hair and jerk her head violently. She still didn't let go even as she eyed the punch he was about to deliver.

The tree they were hurtling toward got there first, and the impact had her smashing against the back of the seats as the airbags exploded.

And then there was nothing.

52

They'd been in the vehicle for nearly an hour now, but the drones had been in the air for less than twenty minutes.

Aaron reined in his frustration. These were large machines, but the range was limited, so some of Charlie team had raced down on an interception path north of Concord and launched from a point that would hopefully maximize range in order to be the most effective.

Judge Abbotsford and her husband were in lockdown with the rest of Charlie squad, who were taking no chances that this might be some sort of distraction.

Romano called. "Drones have located the cab."

"Where?" Aaron, Seth, and Black were watching delayed feeds from the satellite and cell phone data and knew they were within a few miles of the vehicle, but that was a few miles too far in Aaron's opinion.

"Rural road called Mill Lane."

"Send me the drone feed." Aaron wanted to tear out his hair in frustration, but this was good news.

"Roger that."

"Here." Black thrust ballistic vests he'd pulled out of the cargo area toward them in the front. He followed it with carbines and ammunition. Aaron geared up while he waited for Romano to patch him into the live feed.

"Where are you?" he asked Romano.

"Two clicks east of you, but we have a river we need to cross, so make it five to the nearest bridge. Novak is about ten clicks west."

The feed came through, and Aaron felt as if his heart was being removed from his chest with chopsticks. "It hit a tree?"

"Looks that way."

"Any sign of life?"

The camera panned out, and Aaron saw a house down a lane. Smoke coming out of the chimney.

"Not that we've seen yet."

He called Frazer on Hope's cell phone. "We have the cab on the drone feed."

"I see it. Parker patched me in."

Aaron shouldn't be surprised. "Any intel on properties around here that might suggest they're being used by Leighton or Leech?"

"We're working on it."

Aaron spotted it on the feed at the same time Frazer did. A helicopter sat on a helipad in a clearing north of the house closest to the crash site.

"Can we get a closer look at that bird?" he asked Romano.

"Sending the second drone down for a closer look. Let's see if we can get a tail number on this sucker."

"Can we get air support out here?"

"I'll see what we have in the area."

"Property is registered to Camden Corp. Alex is trying to trace an actual person, but it might be some sort of shell company so could easily be Leech." Frazer spoke to someone else on another line. "Okay, from hacking Colin Leighton's cloud information, Parker has discovered that Colin believes he's the son of one of Leech's victims, the second man to die, Richard Prince. Prince abandoned his pregnant girlfriend of many years and married his younger secretary, Lynette Lombardy, whom Leech later raped and smothered to death. Colin's mother apparently told him after the first trial against Leech fell apart. Colin was eighteen years old. He immediately began pursuing a career in law."

"So, this isn't a simple payoff situation. He's also after Leech?" said Kincaid.

"He deliberately volunteered for the position of Hope's intern, so he's been planning something for a long time, and we have to presume they are both targets." Aaron was furious they'd missed it. "Whatever his original intent, right now, he's got Hope and is presumably heading for Leech. We need to prepare for an immediate hostage rescue mission because Leech will not wait or keep Hope as a hostage once he knows we're nearby. He will kill her if he thinks he's going back to prison."

"And from our conversation with Eloisa Fairchild and reading his letters, I suspect Leech will do anything to avoid going back to prison," Frazer agreed.

Romano spoke over them both. "Hold. I see movement in the vehicle."

53

———————

Hope struggled to get out of the footwell. She twisted onto her front and dragged her torso back across the gritty mat to rise to a kneeling position. From there she levered herself onto the seat and then repeated the maneuver. A glance at Colin told her he'd been knocked unconscious by the impact.

Was he alive?

She wasn't sure and wasn't about to try to find out.

Her body shook from reaction.

The engine hissed, and she could hear steam pouring out of the radiator.

The landscape around them was pretty. Rolling hills covered in snow and a small black stream running at the bottom of this valley. Smoke came out of the chimney of a nearby home. She backed up to the door and felt for the handle which opened easily. Surprised, she tumbled backwards into the road.

Ouch.

Sore, she lay half in, half out of the vehicle and had to wriggle like a caterpillar onto the rough asphalt.

Colin groaned and began fighting with the airbags.

Shit.

Urgently, she rolled and managed to get her legs beneath her, using the cold metal of the car to push against as she rose unsteadily to her feet.

Did she risk the house?

Colin had a gun, and she had to decide quickly. If she went into the forest, he could simply follow her tracks in the snow and shoot her.

She had to risk the house. She started running down the road praying that someone would drive past. She got to the end of the long driveway and paused, looking desperately around for someone to help.

The sound of the car door slamming had her starting up the drive. As she rounded the corner, she saw a huge rustic home with a large double garage/workshop off to one side.

She scurried along the edge of the lane, treading in the tire tracks, which had compressed the snow, so hopefully she left less evidence of her progress.

She needed some kind of saw to remove the cuffs. Hugging the outbuilding, she ran until she found the door. It was locked.

Dammit.

Her heart started to race as she heard footsteps crunching up the driveway. She looked wildly around and dashed into the woods behind the garage. She stood behind a large pine, held herself as tall and straight as possible while not breathing. Blood rushed through her ears, deafening her when she needed to hear everything.

Please, please, please.

"Nice try, Hope."

Her heart stumbled, and terror froze her spine. Her teeth chattered as she turned around to see Colin standing there with a gun pointed at her. Blood trickled from his nose, and he cradled the wrist she'd taken a chunk out of.

"Ah. Excellent," came a horribly familiar voice from near the garage. "Guests! Welcome. Welcome."

She shivered from loathing as well as cold. Julius Leech stood there, wearing a black cashmere sweater and blue jeans and good hiking boots. Hatred for this man welled up inside her a thousand times more powerful than fear.

He'd dyed his hair dark brown, but his eyes were the same creepy washed-out blue she saw in her nightmares.

"Come inside. I'll have someone deal with the vehicle before some Good Samaritan comes along and has to die for their trouble." His smile was colder than her breath, which frosted in the air. He raised a cell to his ear and walked unconcerned back toward the house.

She thought about running.

"Do it, and I'll kill you, right here, right now."

"You're going to kill me anyway."

"Not necessarily."

She took a half-step, but he fired off to her left.

"That's your last warning."

She drew in a deep breath to try to settle herself. She wanted to live. Really wanted to live. Without fear or regret. She wanted Aaron for longer than a few stolen nights, but she doubted she'd get the chance to tell him how much he meant to her.

"Now, Hope!"

She reluctantly followed the man who'd killed her family, her mouth getting drier and drier with each step. Walking to her death.

She headed into a mudroom and then stepped into a beautiful, modern kitchen.

Colin grabbed her from behind, using her as a shield. And forced her through into the living room which had a magnificent, vaulted ceiling.

"I want my money, Leech." His voice boomed around the room. "Put it in my account, and you can have Hope to play with however you want."

Hope sneered over her shoulder. "You are such a fraud. I knew it was about the money."

But Leech wasn't there, and she heard a curse from behind her as a gun went off, and she screamed and tumbled forward.

54

E cho team ran through the woods beside the cabin as a gunshot rang out. Charlie team and Novak were still five minutes away. Aaron refused to think about that shot or the fact Hope might already be dead. He'd watched her attempt to flee on the monitor. Watched her try to hide. Watched an injured Colin Leighton track her down in the woods and then a figure who was probably Leech come out to meet them before heading casually back into the house.

They'd parked on the other side of the rise, as close as they could get without being seen from the cabin. It had seemed to take forever to get here, and there was no time to waste.

Hope was trapped with two very dangerous individuals.

"Alpha team take the front. Omega take the back. I'm with Omega. Let's not be seen until we're ready to enter the house." He spoke quietly through the comms.

They headed into position. Chances were that Leech planned to use the helicopter that a pilot had started to warm up to escape —and that meant leaving out the back.

Seth Hopper squeezed his arm. He'd been in a similar situation a few weeks ago when Zoe had been kidnapped. "We've got this."

Aaron nodded even though his mouth felt like dirt.

"Kincaid, I need you to go secure that machine. Secure the pilot in the hangar for questioning, and then get your ass back here."

Kincaid took off without argument, and the rest of them got into their stacked formation near the back door. Seth Hopper, Cas Demarco, Ryan Sullivan, Sebastian Black and himself. Men he trusted with his own life. Men he had to trust with something far more valuable—Hope's.

55

H ope spun around and saw Colin fall to the ground and his gun skidding across the room. She froze.

He started to crawl across the wooden floor toward it.

Leech stepped out from behind the wall. There was another opening at the other end of the living room that led back into the kitchen behind the massive central fireplace. He'd circled around and shot Colin in the back.

Leech aimed the gun at her former intern, his finger tightening on the trigger to take a second shot.

"Don't!"

Leech looked at her. "Why not? He came here to kill me after he'd collected his ten million dollars for fetching you. I'm sure you'd have been next, Hope, considering he's Dick Prince's bastard."

"You killed my father, you sonofabitch," Colin ground out as he inched slowly toward the weapon.

Leech threw back his head and laughed. "If you finish that sentence with 'prepare to die,' I will be officially the happiest man on the planet."

"Fucking loser," Colin grated.

Blood poured from his wound, and Hope felt panic well up inside her. Not only for Colin but for Ella too.

Leech's smile disappeared. "I'm the billionaire whose dreams have all come true, and you're the one leaving a trail of blood across my beautiful floor. I'm not the loser here, bucko." He lifted the weapon again.

"Wait." Hope took a step forward. What she really wanted to do was to run. "Don't. Please don't shoot him. I know he's a weasel and a liar, but he's little more than a kid."

Leech raised his brows and blinked at her theatrically. "Why, Hope, is that forgiveness I hear in your tone? I didn't think you had it in you."

"Maybe," she admitted reluctantly. "Also, he took one of my witnesses, and I don't know where she is."

Colin spat blood. "Ella will die if you don't find her."

Leech's expression looked amused. "Oh, the little mouse who was beaten by her deadbeat boyfriend—"

"No," Hope corrected because what the hell? "She was beaten by an *ex*-boyfriend who as an ex should have no more influence on her life than a stranger." The term *domestic* when applied to couples who'd broken up was her pet peeve. "Were the people you murdered strangers to you?"

She figured he'd deny it again, but she needed to stall for time. The FBI couldn't be far behind, and there was no way she was using Leech's child for leverage. Thank goodness Aaron had made Colin leave yesterday before he'd told her about Eloisa's son.

Leech's expression twisted to reveal the killer he really was. "Well, they weren't friends, but trust me. They all deserved it."

She sucked in a horrified breath. Danny hadn't deserved it. Paige hadn't.

She heard the throb of helicopter rotors and optimism began to grow inside her.

"Not a rescue mission I'm afraid, my dear." Leech spared her a glance. "My getaway plan." His pale blue eyes met hers. "My reasons for sticking around are almost over."

Because she'd be dead.

"Killing me, Sylvie, Beasley, you mean? Why not the others? The judge, the crime scene techs?"

"Oh, you bloodthirsty soul, Hope. Who knew?" He held her gaze then as he gave a smile that didn't reach his eyes. "Well. I did. Obviously."

What did that mean?

She thought about all the times she'd wanted the opportunity to be alone with this man and extract her pound of flesh. In none of the scenarios had she imagined herself with her hands cuffed behind her back and him with a gun.

"If you must know," he sounded almost bored. "You were the three who told lies about me. You and the good doctor in the courtroom and Jeff to anybody who'd listen after he screwed up the trial."

"*You* lied."

"No." He tilted his head to the side. His eyes glittered. "I omitted certain truths. Not the same thing."

Semantics.

She hadn't lied on the stand but he'd convinced himself she had. She couldn't imagine she'd be able to change his mind after all these years.

Colin was inching closer to the gun. She had no more desire to see her former intern reach it than Leech did.

She walked over. "Don't worry. I'm handcuffed. I'm going to kick it out of reach." She shoved it with her foot, careful not to let the trigger catch on anything. Then moved back so she stood in front of the fireplace.

Was that a shadow she saw moving outside the window?

"Any last words?"

"Colin or me?"

He smiled. "I always liked you, Hope. Why don't you start? Leighton here bores me."

She raised her chin and swallowed. "Last words? Sure. How about I've dreamt of being alone in a room with you for years. I had planned to kick your ass for what you did to my family."

"Oh, spare me the self-pitying theatrics. It's you and me, Hope. You can drop the pretense." Leech sighed dramatically. "I didn't kill your pathetic little family. I went to your house that day because I stupidly believed we were friends."

Fury burned through her veins.

"You murdered them in cold blood!" She rushed him. He still had the gun pointed at Colin, and she took him by surprise.

She barreled into him and shoved her knee into his groin the way Aaron, Seth Hopper, and Sebastian Black had taught her. She didn't hold back but put all her force into shoving his balls into his scrawny throat.

Leech's face contorted in pain as he curled over, and she remembered what else her bodyguards—her friends—had taught her. To run. She sprinted for the back door and was brought up short in surprise as she heard an ear-splitting crack, and then men poured into the house. She froze. They streamed around her, and she flinched as she heard another gunshot.

Please don't let any of these people get hurt.

She went to whirl around, but someone took her head and pressed it against his chest. *Aaron.* She sagged against him as he wrapped his arms tight around her.

"Don't look," he ordered. "Leech definitely didn't want to go back to prison."

Her stomach lurched, and she closed her eyes as her heart thudded madly against her ribs. "Thank you. Thank you for finding me. Thank you for saving me. I knew you would."

His hand rested cool against her nape.

"I think you were already saving yourself." He laughed against her hair, but the sound was cut off abruptly as if he couldn't quite go there. Someone removed her handcuffs and placed them inside an evidence bag. When her wrists were free, she wove them around this man and held on so tight she was worried she might hurt him. She didn't care about the ballistics vest and weapons. She didn't care about the audience. Slowly her pulse calmed, and her breathing returned to normal as she realized it was over. Leech was dead. She could hear them working to stabilize Colin.

She stiffened and tried to pull away. "Oh, God. Ella is—"

"We have her." His arms tightened and his hands moved up and down her back in a soothing motion. "Alex Parker back-tracked the movement of the burner cell Colin used, which is how we initially found you. When Frazer noticed it was outside Ella's apartment early this morning, we figured she was either an accomplice or in danger. They were able to follow the signal to an abandoned warehouse near the docks, and Boston PD sent out a search party and found her bound and gagged in an old office. She was fine but suffering from exposure. They took her to the hospital for observation."

Hope gripped his vest. "Thank goodness. That poor woman." The scent of Aaron filled her senses and helped ease the terror of the last few hours.

Her fingers dug deeper into his flak jacket, and she held him to her. She didn't want to ever let go. "Even alone with me Leech wouldn't admit to killing Danny or Paige. The bastard went to his grave denying it."

"Maybe the reality of murdering a child was too much even for him."

"I'm glad he didn't know he had a son." Maybe that was cruel, but Leech had died thinking he was the last of his line. There was satisfaction in that.

And as tempted as she was to stand here and absorb Aaron's comfort, she knew he had a job to do. She was ready to declare undying love to the guy, but maybe he wanted a casual relationship. Sure he'd been upset by the "just sex" comment, but it didn't mean he wanted to jump into the deep end with her. He'd been hurt before.

Suddenly unsure, she released him and stepped back. "I hope

we get the chance to talk privately back at the house when you finish here."

He looked confused for a moment and then his expression blanked as he became aware of the other men moving around them.

He nodded and stepped away. "We'll escort you to the hospital, and I'll talk to my boss about what time we ship out."

Her eyes went wide, and agitation swept through her. She didn't want him to leave. She reached for her usual armor, but it seemed to have disappeared.

Aaron was still a man who risked his life on a daily basis. Could she deal with that? Would he want her for more than the short time they had left when she suddenly wanted a whole lot more? A *whole* lot more.

"I'm not going to the hospital."

Aaron opened his mouth to argue.

"I'll have blood drawn and photos taken here for evidence by anyone qualified to do so but I feel fine and I refuse to put myself through hours of being examined by doctors to tell me the same thing. There's blood, prints, DNA, and duct-tape in the back of that crashed cab. I have a few bruises and a couple of sore wrists but I'm otherwise uninjured."

Aaron examined her critically, staring into her eyes, searching for signs of a concussion. She smiled so he would realize she was telling the truth. "If I feel unwell in any way when I get back to Boston I will go to the ER."

Realizing she was serious, Aaron yelled. "Hopper, get over here and take some photographs of Hope's injuries."

Seth strode over to her side. "Somebody refusing medical treatment?"

Aaron's jaw flexed.

"I don't need a doctor. Just record these injuries and take a blood sample so they can figure out what he drugged me with." Hope held out her wrists for a series of shots, then turned them over for more, spreading her fingers wide. Seth angled her head toward the window to photograph the gash on her temple and bruising on her face.

Aaron scowled.

Someone dumped a heavy medical kit on the floor beside them and Seth made short work of collecting two vials of dark crimson blood. He taped cotton wool over the injection site, labeled the blood vials with time, date, plus her name. Signed them and sealed them in an evidence bag that he stored in a small cooler.

"All done." Seth nodded and backed away, taking the evidence and medical kit with him.

Aaron opened his mouth to speak, but they were interrupted by yelling coming from outside.

Her head dropped as she recognized Brendan's voice. "Uh-oh. I better get out there before he gets himself arrested."

"Okay." Aaron scrubbed the back of his head, his brown-black eyes full of regret. "I'm sorry for not protecting you—"

"What? No! You did everything right. No one could have predicted Colin abducting me from the courthouse."

"I should have."

"How? There's a difference between smart and psychic. I like the former, but I'm not sure I'd enjoy the latter." She forced a smile, but she could tell he was going to beat himself up about this. She touched his arm. "Please don't leave without saying goodbye. I need to apologize—"

"No. You don't."

"I want to explain." She couldn't say what she needed to say in front of an audience. It might cost him his job. "Promise me, Aaron. *Please.*"

He pressed his lips together and looked away. He nodded again but still didn't say the words. Instead, "You'll need to make a statement, which is gonna take some time, I'm afraid. And I have a lot to finish up here before the local agents arrive to take over."

"Don't worry about me. The danger is over. Brendan can give me a ride home."

Aaron walked her to the door. They didn't touch, and the few inches between them felt like a gulf a thousand-feet wide. She looked up before she went outside and noted all the other guys pretending not to stare.

"I'm sorry if I got you into any trouble, Operator Nash," she whispered.

"You are worth every moment of trouble, ADA Harper." He smiled suddenly—a flash of white teeth against that trim beard—and her heart double-timed in her chest.

She blinked slowly. Maybe they had a chance. Maybe he'd forgive her for the hurt she'd caused him, and she'd figure out how to deal with the constant risk of his job. After all, she realized with sudden insight, she'd survived the worst life could throw at her, and she was still here. Why not be open to the best that life had to offer?

She took his hand and leaned up to press a quick kiss to his cheek.

"So are you, Aaron, worth every moment of trouble."

Surprise widened his pupils.

She stepped outside to find Brendan and Lewis Janelli going nose-to-nose with Hunt Kincaid.

She sighed. Some things didn't change.

56

Aaron watched Hope walk into the backyard and into the arms of another man. A tiny kernel of hope that maybe they could figure something out had started to grow inside him— if he was willing to take another chance with his heart. Hope had said she liked the fact he was smart, and he knew she liked his body. Maybe rather than diminishing one aspect of himself, he should start embracing the whole.

But what if she was only looking for a little fun? Who could blame her after what she'd been through?

He wanted more.

Brendan wrapped his arm around his former sister-in-law and hurried her away. Aaron squashed the petty jealousy that squirmed free of its shackles.

Lewis Janelli stood and glared after the two of them.

"You're letting her leave with that guy?" Seth Hopper stared at him as if he'd lost his mind.

"I can't abandon the scene—"

"Yeah, you can. Fill in the FD 302s on the flight home. In the meantime, go claim your woman."

Aaron crossed his arms. "I'm not sure Hope would appreciate

being 'claimed.'" But the thought of her being his woman made something primitive rear up inside him.

Seth grinned. "You won't know until you try, will you? What d'you have to lose?"

"My self-respect. My pride. The chance to maybe grow on her over time?'

"She is gone on you, you idiot."

Aaron shot his friend a curious look. He'd thought he'd hidden his feelings pretty well this last week. "What makes you say that?"

"You see her hugging or kissing the rest of us?"

Aaron pulled a face. "She's been through a traumatic experience—"

Seth slapped the back of his head. "For a smart guy, you're being dense as a rock."

Aaron rubbed his head. "Hey."

"Go after her. We're out of here anyway. Gotta clear the crime scene. ME's en route, and Boston FO agents are five minutes away."

Aaron held Seth's eyes. "She's too good for me."

Seth's eyes widened, and he grabbed Aaron's hair and brought their heads together. "You are one of the best men I know. Don't let me hear that bullshit pass your lips ever again."

Aaron shook his head and laughed.

"She's been through a lot. She deserves someone like you, Professor." Seth scrubbed his head with his knuckles and released him.

Aaron checked his watch. "Okay, I'll drive her Beemer back to her place. Hopefully, the brass doesn't want us to fly back tonight. Once Colin Leighton is transported, leave two guys behind until the locals get here. Everyone else can head back to Hope's place to pack up."

"Understood. Air ambulance is almost here. Demarco will ride with Leighton."

"Good. Let me know his status and where he's taken." Aaron strode off and tried to stop himself from grinning.

"Hey," Janelli hurried toward him. "Can I catch a ride with you?"

He paused. "Your partner left you behind?"

Janelli sniffed. "He said he wanted a private conversation with Hope and knew she wouldn't be comfortable if I was there."

"Sure. I can drop you back." Aaron headed to Hope's Beemer which was parked in the driveway, key in the console.

"Leech really tell Hope Harper he didn't do Danny or their kid?" Janelli asked. "I heard some agents talking."

Aaron nodded. Placed his flak jacket and carbine, safety on, in the footwell behind the driver's seat. Got in.

Janelli climbed in the passenger side and admired the butter soft leather of the seats. "Nice ride."

Aaron reversed out and headed south back to Beantown.

Janelli pulled a face. "I guess I owe you an apology."

"Not me. Hope."

Janelli grimaced. "I was a prick." The furrows in his brow were deep enough to plant corn.

"Something on your mind?"

Janelli ran his tongue around his teeth. "No."

He wasn't a very good liar for a detective.

"But I got to thinking, after our conversation."

Aaron's lips twitched. "After I had you thrown out of the courthouse."

Janelli rolled his eyes. "I'm trying not to remember that asshole move—did you really think I'd attack a woman? Especially one who could get me thrown off the force?"

Aaron pulled his lips to one side. "You threatened her. I was doing my job."

Janelli moved his head to one side and rubbed his neck. "I guess. I'm used to running my mouth without anyone calling me on it, ya know?"

Aaron scowled at the guy. "You have to know Hope was only

doing her job back then. Like the judge. Why pile all the blame for what happened on her?"

Rather than looking annoyed Janelli pulled his lips back thoughtfully. "I've hated her for so long. Pauly was such a good guy, a mentor to me when I never really had one before…" He shook his head. "It was hard to lose him that way."

Aaron thought about losing Montana and knew exactly how challenging it was. "Time to let it go, at least in relation to making Hope responsible for the mistakes Pauly Monroe made."

Janelli pursed his lips. "I guess. Leech getting out got me thinking about a lot of things from back then."

Aaron frowned. "Like what?"

"Stuff that didn't add up the way it should with the benefit of hindsight and more years on the job." Janelli sank into his seat and looked uncomfortable. "I checked logs for the night Pauly Monroe died." He sucked in his lips. "Brendan was lying about being on a stakeout."

Aaron frowned. "Why would he lie?"

"I dunno." Janelli picked at a loose thread on his jacket. "Maybe it was an unofficial investigation or something he knew the captain wouldn't approve of."

"Brendan Harper doesn't strike me as the type of cop to put in unpaid overtime." Suddenly things clicked into place for Aaron and fear flooded every neuron in his body. "Could Brendan have killed Monroe?"

Janelli huffed out a disbelieving gasp. "No way."

Aaron's heart beat too hard. "It makes sense. He's Johnny on the spot the next day. Makes a point of seeking you out, and the two of you head to Monroe's house together so he can be there when you find him and check he didn't forget anything. He can also explain away any of his DNA being found at the scene."

"Why?" Janelli shifted uneasily. "They were partners for years. They were pals."

The full implications hit Aaron. "Shit. Could Brendan have

killed his own brother and niece?" He pressed his foot hard on the accelerator. Brendan had Hope.

Janelli held out his hands toward the dash clearly reading Aaron's mind. "Whoa. Slow down. Brendan's not gonna hurt her. He's obsessed with her. He wasn't very happy when he spotted her giving you that peck on the cheek back there though."

Great.

Aaron's head was going to explode. He thought they'd rescued Hope, but he'd allowed her to walk right into another predator's arms.

He shifted and pulled his cell out of a side pocket. "Call Frazer. Put it on speaker."

Frazer answered, but rather than let the guy congratulate him on a job well done, Aaron interrupted. "Listen. I have Lewis Janelli in the vehicle, and we're heading back to town, following Hope, who caught a ride with Brendan. The thing is, I got to wondering, what if Leech really didn't kill Danny and Paige Harper? What if Brendan did?" The wheels in his brain were spinning at full speed now. "What if Brendan was the detective who took and planted that material at the third crime scene?"

"He was the first detective on scene at the third double-murder," Frazer confirmed. "He'd only recently switched partners and, as he'd worked the previous murders, both he and Monroe got the call even though it was officially Monroe's case."

"Perhaps Monroe was involved or maybe he wasn't, but suddenly he's overwhelmed with guilt and threatens to tell someone, his captain—"

"His priest," Janelli interrupted. "If he started to feel guilty, he'd want to confess to his priest. Brendan often says he doesn't trust priests to keep confessions secret, and that's from a man who takes his mother to mass every Sunday."

"So Brendan kills Monroe and maybe his brother figures it out —and the only way Brendan can be sure Danny doesn't tell anyone, especially his wife who's defending the guy Brendan tried to set up, is by killing his brother?"

"I'd say it was possible," said Frazer. "And if Brendan figures out we're onto him before they get out of that car, Hope's dead because Brendan has more than an unhealthy obsession with her. He'll drive them off a bridge if he believes he's been found out."

Aaron refused to think about that. "What can we charge him with?" Leech had already been convicted of the murders.

"Leech's conviction would be overturned, which would be extremely ironic, and Brendan prosecuted." Frazer sounded as if he was typing something into a computer.

"We get him on Monroe," Janelli said angrily. "We get him for killing one of his own and getting away with it for so many years." He reached for his phone. "I'll talk to my captain—"

"No." Aaron shook his head. "What if he calls Brendan or someone overhears at the precinct? They'll warn him."

Janelli opened his mouth to argue, but Aaron raised his voice so loud it boomed off the interior. "If you touch your cell, I will handcuff you and put you in the backseat! I'm *not* putting Hope's life in danger. Don't you think she's been through enough?"

"Order your squad back to Hope's place, and make sure they arrive before Brendan gets there," Frazer ordered. "We'll take him down before they go inside the building. Do not spook him. I'll meet you there."

Aaron ignored the fear that wanted to trample his training and made the call. Suddenly, all his fears about having his heart broken again seemed petty and inconsequential. He'd joined HRT to prove himself, and yet all that really mattered was the same thing that had mattered when he'd been that geeky biologist. Love. His issue all along wasn't that he wasn't good enough, it was simply that he hadn't found the right person. And now he had, and the thought of losing her before they really had a chance together cut him into a million pieces.

"We'll get her." Janelli awkwardly tried to comfort him.

"We better," Aaron said grimly.

57

"So Leech is really dead?" asked Brendan.

"Yeah." Hope bit her lip. He was driving too fast. He always drove too fast.

"Can you slow down? The drugs have made my stomach woozy, and I don't want to vomit all over your manly muscle car."

He took his foot off the accelerator. "Your intern drugged you?"

"Yeah, to get me out of the courthouse."

"That fucking little prick." Brendan shifted and looked at her. "I never trusted him."

"Oh, come on. You barely knew him."

He laughed. "I didn't trust the sleaze ball."

She snorted. "Well, you are the only one. Most of the ADAs wanted to poach him off me. I should have suspected something was off when he volunteered to work with me."

"You aren't that bad."

She laughed and looked out of the window. "I am." But she felt different now. Despite the terrible betrayal by someone she'd thought of as a trusted colleague within the justice system, she felt lighter somehow.

"So, you and the asshole bodyguard, huh?" His knuckles stood out as his fists curled around the steering wheel.

She turned away to stare at the snowy horizon as the lightness faded. She didn't want to talk about Aaron with Brendan. What they had was special, and she wanted to guard it the same way Eloisa Fairchild had guarded the news about her son.

"It probably won't last." She squeezed her hands into fists. But she hoped it did.

Brendan grunted.

"I've spent all these years trying to atone for what happened to Danny and Paige." And she'd never gotten close. "I always thought that if I had the opportunity to confront Leech one-on-one that he'd tell me the truth." She shook her head. "He admitted to the other murders." Her eyelid twitched. "The ones where I defended him."

"Yeah, well, we all knew he was guilty." Brendan shot her a look that as plain as words blamed her for Danny's and Paige's deaths.

She swallowed.

"He's probably only after sex, you know." Brendan's gaze flicked over her form. "The Fed."

"Ha. Thank you, Brendan. I am aware of male foibles. However, as we've already had sex on multiple occasions, I don't think it's quite that simple."

Even though she'd tried to make it that simple.

The car swerved slightly.

"Slow down." She grabbed her stomach. She hadn't felt this kind of nausea since she'd been pregnant with Paige. She clutched herself. Jesus. The thought of having another child hit her like a sledgehammer.

The desire was so visceral she could almost taste it.

Would Aaron be interested in kids? She had no idea. She'd never imagined she'd reach a place where she'd even contemplate having another baby.

"Leech say anything else?"

She shook her head. "Not really. Cracked a few jokes that I'm sure he thought were witty. Colin was Richard Prince's illegitimate son."

"Jesus." Brendan shot her a look. "That was a brutal crime scene. You think the kid checked out the case file?"

She swallowed, thinking of all the files she'd kept in her office that he'd had access to. All the crime scene photos and autopsy reports. Richard Prince had died a slow, painful death. "I suspect he did." She shivered. "I need to call the DA and update him about Colin and check up on Judge Penton, but right now I don't have the energy." They were speeding toward the city limits. "Hey, can we grab a coffee or a hot chocolate? I haven't had a drink since this morning, and I skipped breakfast."

"Sure. Want food too?"

"Maybe some fries." It might help settle her stomach.

They pulled up to a fast-food joint, and he put in the order. She pulled out her wallet to pay but he insisted. She wondered where her cell phone was and felt strangely disconnected from the world without it.

They drove away again, and she nibbled on the fries and tentatively sipped the volcanically hot drink.

She put the cup into the cupholder.

"You're not serious about the guy, are you? I mean, I thought you were still stuck on Danny?"

She blinked repeatedly to clear the emotion that blurred her vision. God. He was so blunt. She should be used to it by now, but he always knew how to hurt her the most.

"I loved your brother with all my heart." But she'd finally found the strength, the courage, to feel, to live, to love again. "I think I might be ready to take a chance."

"It won't last, Hope."

Christ, if she was half as miserable as Brendan, it was no wonder no one had even asked her on a date in all these years.

She realized then how bad they'd been for one another. Each encouraging the other to wallow in failure and grief.

"Wanna go by the grave before I drop you home?" He looked hopeful at the idea.

She shook her head. "It's been a long day."

Today wasn't about the past. Not now that Leech was dead. Today was about the possibility of a future. And Aaron might not even be able to stay the night if the team were needed for another operation. At least he'd promised they could talk. Hopefully, he'd forgive her for pushing him away, and they could figure something out.

They pulled up outside her home. and it felt as if she'd been gone for days rather than hours.

"Are we still on for Sunday lunch tomorrow?"

Hope stared at Brendan in shock. After everything she'd been through this week, the fact he thought he and his mother's meal plans would rank as a high priority in her life was baffling.

"It's going to depend on how I feel in the morning." After either having sex all night or in the aftermath of the sorrow she was going to feel if Aaron had left.

"Ma is expecting—"

"I *know*, Brendan." She clutched her forehead at the leaden weight of obligation hung around her neck. "I know. Give me a little breathing space here, okay? It's been a hell of a day."

She got out and took her cup and fries. Leaned down. "I'll call you in the morning."

She slammed the door before he could answer and headed up the steps to her front door. She searched her pocket for a key, but the door opened, and she found herself dragged inside by Aaron.

"How did you beat me home?"

Rather than saying anything, he took her cup and food from her hands and then led her into her neighbors' room that faced the street. He parted the curtains, and she saw Lewis Janelli dragging Brendan out of the vehicle and pushing him over the hood of the Charger before slapping cuffs on his wrists.

She whirled. "I don't understand?"

He led her back outside in time for her to hear Janelli reading Brendan his rights.

She strode toward him. "What's going on?"

"It's not what you think." Brendan shot her a look of anguish and her heart sank.

"What have you done, Brendan?"

"Have you got the balls to tell her, asshole?" Aaron asked from over her shoulder. "Or are you going to lie to her for the rest of your worthless life?"

"What do you mean?" Dread began to fill her. She'd thought it was all over.

"It was an accident." Brendan's expression was pleading.

"What was an accident?" She found herself taking a step back.

"Danny." He sobbed then. "Paige."

Every muscle in her body froze. "What are you talking about?"

Brendan hunched over. "He figured it out. Danny figured it out. Monroe…"

She frowned. "Pauly Monroe? What did Monroe do?"

Tears streamed down Brendan's face. "Monroe was going to confess to his priest what we did."

She covered her mouth and her voice got low. "What did you *do*, Brendan?"

He pursed his lips, but it was too late.

"You killed Monroe and sent me that email because you thought everyone was going to find out it was you that planted that evidence? So you set Monroe up to take the fall, didn't you?"

Brendan looked like a wounded animal.

She took a step forward as another unthinkable truth crashed into her. "Danny figured it out."

We have to talk.

Those four little words had haunted her for years. The thought that Danny had been angry with her when he'd died had nearly broken her. And he'd known. Brendan had known all along.

"It was an accident. I swear. I went over to talk to him because he said you two had had a big fight and the news reported the trial was over. Leech was released. We started talking about Pauly and the evidence and…he knew." Brendan started sobbing. "He always knew when I was lying. We started fighting, and I saw the letter opener on his desk and…it just happened. *It just happened.*"

She started to crumple. Aaron put his arm around her waist to hold her up. Brendan's eyes narrowed.

"Paige?" Her voice broke. "What did you do to Paige!"

He flinched. "She came running in and saw everything. I thought she was at a playdate. *She was supposed to be at a playdate!*"

His anguish bounced off Hope like hail.

"She started screaming and I picked her up and tried to stop her from making all that noise while I figured out what to do about Danny, who was bleeding." He met her gaze then, beseeching her to understand. "And then, *then*, I realized I could pin it all on Leech or a copycat or someone who hated you for setting a serial killer free. And that's what you did, Hope—"

"No." She shook with ice-cold fury. "You don't get to blame me for this. Not anymore. Don't you see? *You* did it. You did it all. You're the reason the case was tossed out and Leech was released. You're the reason Danny and Paige are dead." She sobbed. "All these years, I blamed myself, and you let me. You watched me. I tried to atone for Leech targeting them because I'd defended him, but it was always you. I never want to see you ever again, Brendan. I hope you finally understand that you murdered a detective you'd been friends with for years. You killed your brother who you claimed to love, and you killed a child who idolized you. I hope you rot in hell."

She stumbled, and Aaron swept her up in his arms and swung her away.

58

Livingstone opened the door, and Aaron carried Hope upstairs to her apartment and sat on her sofa, holding her while she wept uncontrollable tears. He rocked her until she finally quieted and lay lax against his shoulder.

"I'm sorry, Hope."

He felt her swallow.

"Not your fault." Her expression crumpled. "And now I know for sure it wasn't mine either." She wiped her face. "I have all these emotions fighting inside me. I feel this incredible sense of betrayal combined with a sudden sense of freedom. People talk about a weight being lifted from their shoulders, but I've never experienced it before."

"You've had a helluva day."

"I have, but I finally know what really happened, and it helps." She sucked in a breath. "I think Leech truly believed I'd done it. I bet that's why he wouldn't stop writing to me, calling me a liar. How ironic that he went to prison for a crime he didn't commit after being released for the ones he did."

Her eyes were red from weeping, but they were starting to clear.

"Ella was released from the hospital, and so was Judge Penton.

I guess the trial might be delayed." Aaron wasn't sure about those details.

"I was so mad at Penton this morning. She had some crazy notion Seth Hopper might be involved in Beasley's murder."

Aaron drew back. "What?"

"Colin threw him under the bus about a joke he made in court. It was nothing. I explained to Penton that Hopper had a solid alibi. Leech did admit to killing the first six victims, plus Sylvie, her husband, and Jeff Beasley—for lying about him, apparently." She rolled her eyes. "Pretty sure the DA will remove me from the Gibson case whether I like it or not—but I'm thinking of taking some time off anyway."

"I think that's a smart thing to do."

"I'll speak to Ella. Hopefully, they sent a victim's advocate to talk with her."

"Colin Leighton's position in the DA's office will raise a lot of questions and concerns."

She huffed out a tired laugh. "Oh, yeah."

"I suspect we're going to find all Leech's letters to you since Colin became your intern stowed somewhere in Colin's belongings."

"Is he still alive?"

Aaron nodded. "He lost a lot of blood, but he's in surgery. Apparently, he has a good chance of making it." Presumably the guy had set up a go-bag with all the things he needed to escape the country after he'd killed Leech and Hope. They'd find it. It was only a matter of time.

Hope gripped his T-shirt. "What I said to you last night with the 'just sex' comment…"

He tried to interrupt.

"No, please let me explain. I deliberately made you think that all we had was physical chemistry because I was scared of you getting too close. If Leech targeted you because he discovered I'd gone and fallen in love with you, I wouldn't have been able to live with myself."

He held himself still, not sure he'd heard her correctly. "Pardon me?"

"You heard." She bumped his shoulder.

"Are you saying you love me?"

She smiled, and it was the most carefree expression he'd ever seen on her beautiful face.

"I do." Whatever shock she saw on his face, she misinterpreted. "It's okay. You don't have to say it back. You've given me a gift. Even if you run away screaming down the street this second, you've freed me from a prison of my own making. You made me realize I was stronger than I knew—not simply a victim but a survivor. I can't thank you enough for that."

Aaron couldn't believe what he was hearing. "I fell in love with you the moment I saw you downstairs not backing down when faced with a whole squad of Hostage Rescue operators."

"You were pretty intimidating."

"We didn't intimidate you for a second." He kissed her then because he couldn't not kiss her.

She kissed him back, and it was gentle and sweet.

Her fingers gripped him tight as if she was scared he was going to walk out the door. The fact he was going to have to at some point in the near future made him agitated.

Then she pulled back. "I need to tell you a couple of things before we continue."

Uh-oh.

She cleared her throat. "First, I'm going to find it difficult to cope with your job being so dangerous, *but* I will not try to change who you are." She ran her finger over his lips. "I happen to think you're perfect as is, so change is pointless. Instead, I will work on my own mental health and coping mechanisms."

Perfect? "My job is dangerous. So is crossing the street."

She elbowed him in the ribs.

He laughed softly. "The fact you're talking as if we may have a chance of more than 'just sex' and said that you think you love me is all I want."

"Aaron, I don't think I love you. I *know* I love you. I've only ever felt this way once before." She sucked in her lips. "Danny would have liked you, and he would have hated Brendan for what he did and for getting away with it for so long." Her eyes had that faraway look, then focused back on him. "The other thing I realized today amid all the excitement is I'd like to have another child."

A warm glow started in his chest.

"And if you aren't interested, I'll be disappointed, but I'll also understand. Parenthood isn't for everyone. But I'm going to pursue some options because a woman in her late thirties can't dilly dally. I just want you to know that going in."

Going in.

He pushed her hair away from her face and stared into those unusual gray eyes. "The fact you would consider that, with me…"

Her brow crinkled. "A sinfully attractive, astoundingly intelligent, and remarkable human being like you, you mean?" She went up on her knees to face him and ran her hand over his jaw, resting her cool fingers against his neck. "A man who is supportive, considerate, unafraid to speak his mind when the situation calls for it. A man who is thoughtful and kind and who listens even when he doesn't agree? A man who is respected by his peers, who takes care of me, be it doing the dishes or shielding me from whatever danger comes my way? Aaron, how can you not know how wonderful you are?"

The fist around his throat loosened.

Maybe in reality the problem had never been him. The fact he'd feared he wasn't good enough was his former self's reaction to heartbreak and betrayal by the people he'd loved most. They were the ones who'd been lacking in all the things that mattered. But now he wanted to thank them both—for saving him from a disastrous marriage and an even more complicated divorce.

He liked his brain—it made him a better operator. And without his intellect, he'd never have put together all the pieces of this seven-year puzzle. Hope would still be unaware of her brother-in-law's treachery.

She was watching him. Patiently awaiting a response. That Hope was talking about a future together made him feel overjoyed. He was holding her too tight. He finally managed to find the words, although probably not the right words.

"I want kids. I've always wanted kids. And the thought of being with you, starting a family with you, makes me so fucking hard I want to carry you upstairs and—"

Her eyes sparkled and what looked like relief lit her features. "What's stopping you?"

"My teammates waiting downstairs like teenage girls and the fact Frazer will be here any second. Then there are the FD 302s I need to fill out. The knowledge field agents from the local office will need to interview us all about what went down, and my boss will want an update…"

She laughed reluctantly, and then he felt the cat jump onto his shoulder and start kneading him with his claws.

He twisted. The cat jumped off and meowed for food. Hope leaned forward and kissed him. "Unfortunately for you, Lucifer and I are a package deal. How about we schedule an after-hours meeting in my room? As soon as everyone is done hassling us."

"I'd like that." He took her hand and folded her fingers and kissed them. "I'd like that very much. And you need to tell them to back off if it gets too much for you. You were drugged and abducted today and had to deal with some pretty hard truths."

She gave him a smile that lifted her cheeks. "I've seen many of my clients deal with worse."

He gripped her arms. "They didn't have me to run interference."

Her eyes glittered for a moment, but she blinked away the threat of more tears.

He sighed. "There is a small possibility we'll get called back to Quantico immediately and another we'll be sent somewhere I can't communicate with you from. But know that I will do everything I can to get out of whatever assignment it might be."

Her lips twitched. "I can wait for you, Aaron."

"I don't know if I can wait for you," he said honestly.

A knock sounded on the door, followed by footsteps on the stairs.

"I'll make coffee and feed the cat." She laughed, and he stole another brief kiss as Frazer arrived.

The man's cool gaze brightened. "Can I make mine a bourbon? I promise I'll send you a new bottle."

The man first walked over to Hope as she stood. He gave her a hug and kiss on the forehead. "I'm sorry about Brendan."

Hope shuddered as she drew in a big breath. "So am I, but I'm not wasting another moment on him. I feel sorry for Mary, but she's going to have to find a way of dealing with this that doesn't involve me."

"Good."

Frazer headed to the liquor cabinet, held up the bottle, flicked a look in both their directions. "Anyone else?"

Hope shook her head.

"I'll wait until I've made my statement, and then I'll have a double." Aaron ducked into the kitchen and pulled down a tin of the good stuff for Lucy.

"Oh, I forgot," Frazer called out. "There's a pretty brunette called Jeanine, who asked me to give you her number. She works at the printers in town."

Aaron felt his cheeks flush as he came back into the room. "Shit, I told them I'd be back to deal with the computer."

Frazer waved a hand. "Don't worry. The CSI unit dealt with it. And guess who the marshals finally caught up with?"

"Roberts and Somack?"

Frazer nodded.

"Thank God for that."

Hope rubbed her wrists, obviously sore from the overtight cuffs Colin had put on her. The fact the bastard had handed Hope over to Leech without a second thought meant Aaron had zero compassion for the guy.

"I'm going to order Chinese food for everyone. And as soon as we've written our statements, I want to thank everyone personally." Her clothes were dirty, and her face a little scraped up, but she'd come through this ordeal miraculously unscathed.

And his.

She'd come through it as his.

It felt like a miracle.

"We were just doing our jobs, Hope."

"You saved my life and gave me exactly that—hope. I want to thank all the team."

"As long as you don't get any ideas about what I said last night," Aaron muttered jokingly. A flush crawled up his neck. He shouldn't remind her what a prick he'd been.

"Now you mention it…" Hope smiled, then went off to tend to Lucy, who was still complaining about being hungry.

"Were these the ideas that prompted your middle of the night run?" Frazer admired the light through his large glass of bourbon.

"Not prompted, but they stemmed from the same source," Aaron admitted.

Frazer grinned. "Hey, Hope, will you sign one of your books for Izzy? She's a big fan."

Hope came out of the kitchen with her mouth agape.

"Did you really think I wouldn't figure it out with the books staring me in the face at dinner?"

"Uh, yes? I didn't think anyone would notice."

"Are you writing a book right now?" asked Frazer.

"I'm in the plotting stages." Her eyes flashed to Aaron. "I was thinking of introducing a romantic element to the series."

"Frankie gets her Happily Ever After?" Aaron teased.

A smile curved that wide mouth of hers.

"Come down and stay with us for a few days."

Aaron went to object, but Frazer spoke first. "You can stay too. As long as you like dogs."

Aaron looked at Hope, wondering how they were going to work out the logistics of a long-distance relationship, especially if they were going to try for kids.

Hope stared at him. Bit her lip. "I already told Aaron that I'm thinking of taking a leave of absence from my position as Assistant District Attorney so I can figure out my next move. I spent so many years going after the bad guys because I believed it was my fault Danny and Paige were murdered. I need to decide if it's still what I want to do or whether I would be happier as a full-time author."

She didn't mention wanting kids. That was their secret, for now.

Her smile was contagious. "So, I'd love to come meet your Izzy and explore the great state of Virginia. I've never been."

Frazer grinned. "You'll like her and Virginia." He looked between the two of them and seemed to realize he was possibly the third wheel in a private conversation.

"Okay, then. I'm going to go downstairs and order that food because it's probably my turn. I'll bring it and the others up when it arrives." He checked his watch. "I figure you have approximately thirty minutes to either write a report or..." He raised his eyebrows. As soon as the door closed Aaron swept Hope into his arms and carried her up the stairs.

She laughed and touched his cheek. "I'm not sure thirty minutes is going to be long enough."

"It won't be." Emotion pulsed through him as he walked into Hope's bedroom and closed the door with his foot. "It will never be enough time, Hope, but we'll make the most of every second."

"Promise?" Her eyes held his.

"I promise." And then he kissed her.

BONUS EPILOGUE

H ope looked around her usually barren apartment with no
small measure of surprise.

The men who'd guarded her night and day for the past week
were finally able to relax and have a drink. Some sprawled on
couches, others stood around chatting to their teammates. Even
off duty, each still wore at least one weapon holstered to their hip.

They probably all carried a concealed backup pistol or knife
somewhere on their body also, and she planned to search Aaron
later to find out what he was hiding, and where.

Earlier, masses of Chinese food had been delivered and
consumed. Lucy had alternated between begging for food and
attention—thankfully, no one had fed the rascal any scraps. Will
Griffin and Hunt Kincaid had led the cleanup operation, and she
had the feeling that was because they were the newest members
of the team. A bit like interns doing grunt work at the DA's office
without the back-stabby kidnapping and betrayal factor.

Aaron wasn't here.

She felt an unfamiliar pang and knew she had it bad.

He'd gone to shower, having finally finished being interviewed by agents from the local FBI Field Office. She'd wanted to
join him but was too aware of all his work colleagues in her living

room. The fact he was probably packing up his gear made her clench her fingers with anxiety, until she reminded herself they had all the time in the world to figure this out now. And all the will in the world to make it work.

Between the two of them, nothing could stop them except each other, and she refused to be the weakest link in the chain. She refused to blow her second chance at love.

Her eyes drifted to SAC Marshal Hayes and his wife, Josie, who were talking to Frazer while their three kids, Jake, Lizzy, and Max, played under the dining table, supervised by an equally excitable Ryan Sullivan.

One of the guys had put on some soft rock music in the background.

Hope smiled. It was probably bad taste to throw a party after being kidnapped, threatened by a serial killer, and discovering two men you trusted had betrayed you in the worse possible ways, but what the hell. The bad guys had finally been rounded up and exposed. She could close that chapter and leave the past behind. She was free to figure out the next part of her life.

Mary Harper had called her. She'd begged to come over and talk, but Hope had nothing left to give the woman. Certainly not reassurance that this was all a terrible misunderstanding. A mistake. A vendetta.

Naturally, Brendan had recanted his confession before he'd even gotten back to the precinct.

There were witnesses.

It had been recorded.

She *knew*.

Frazer came over, bringing the Hayeses with him.

"Good to see you, Hope. Even under such difficult circumstances." Marshal Hayes's handsome visage was suitably sober.

"As you have all suffered through similar experiences, I'm sure you understand that the horror of what happened today is balanced by relief in knowing that those bastards won't ever hurt anyone again."

"Amen to that." Marsh looked around the room, raised his glass toward the large painting on her dining room wall. "I see you have one of Josie's paintings. She has another that would look amazing right over there—"

His wife elbowed him in the stomach. Hard.

"But that one looks lovely." Marsh coughed his diaphragm back into shape.

"Thank you for buying one of my pieces. It sits perfectly in the beautiful space you have here." Josie changed the subject. "Linc says you're taking a leave of absence from the DA's office?"

"I am, yes."

"If you need any help, you only need to ask." Josie reached out and squeezed her arm.

Hope had to fight back the rush of emotion that wanted to overwhelm her. She'd been alone for so long. Her choice but still... "Thank you. I appreciate that."

Aaron walked in the room, and her breath caught. He looked like the epitome of tall, dark, and handsome, his black hair damp from the shower. He'd shaved, she realized with a start. She'd liked the beard, but she liked the smooth line of his jaw even more. He glanced around at his teammates, and she noticed the silent communication that passed between them. Everything was okay. He looked at her for that same affirmation.

Something settled inside her as she gave it to him.

Josie smiled as she noticed the exchange.

Frazer wrapped his arm around Hope's shoulders as Aaron grabbed himself a beer and then sauntered over. "She's promised to squeeze in a visit with me and Izzy. I suspect she and Aaron here might end up doing a little house hunting."

Aaron raised his brows but didn't run screaming at Frazer's meddling. "Can't wait."

He introduced himself to Marsh and Josie.

Frazer smirked. He seemed to enjoy rocking other people's boats.

Hope decided to return the favor. "So, when are *you* going to start a family, Linc?"

He almost choked on his bourbon.

He wiped his mouth. "I'm happy with a dog. Thanks."

She patted his arm. "Relax. I'm teasing."

"Not all of us are built for parenthood." He tilted his head to where the Hayes children were trying to tickle Ryan Sullivan into submission as the guy rolled about on the floor. Everyone was shrieking loudly. Ryan had placed his weapon on top of the bookshelves.

"And," Lincoln recovered from his shock at the idea of being a parent. "You forget. I'm already putting mine through college."

"Not sure that counts when they come ready baked." Hope leaned against Aaron as he stood beside her.

"That's because you've never met Izzy's sister." Pride swelled in Frazer's gaze despite his words. Hope knew he really loved the teen.

Marsh finished his drink and took his wife's empty glass. "I'd better corral the kids and get them home. It's already later than their usual bedtime."

"Want a ride back to our place, or are you gonna stay here and party?" Josie's New York accent held a slight tinge of Boston nowadays.

Frazer checked his watch. "I'll take a ride. My flight is the first one out in the morning."

"Not staying for the Maroulis trial then?" Hope commented.

"Turns out the prosecution has everything they need."

"Funny that. You and the US Marshall Service still fighting?"

"Rumor has it there's going to be a change in leadership over there." His mouth curved into a grim smile. "But don't say I said so."

They said their goodbyes, the Hayeses making plans with Ryan to catch up for breakfast the next morning. After they left, Hope found herself staring at Danny and Paige's portrait.

Aaron caught the direction of her gaze.

He was so different from Danny in many ways, and yet in others, so very similar.

He looked uncertain suddenly. "This is all new territory for me."

"For me too."

His jaw tightened. "I know you'd never have looked twice at me if—"

She placed her finger over his lips. "That's not how it works."

Aaron glanced around.

There were too many ears around for a deep conversation. Hope was terrified she was going to say the wrong thing and hurt this man again.

He took her hand, seemingly uncaring of his teammates. "Come with me. I want to show you something."

"I hate to break it to you, but I've heard that line before."

He sniggered as he pulled her across the room. They went upwards but didn't stop at her bedroom. He snagged a coat from his room, an FBI raid jacket. Slipped it over her shoulders as they headed up to the roof.

The icy wind took her breath, but Aaron steered her to the railing that faced south across the city.

He wrapped his arms around her and rested his chin on her shoulder.

She shivered and huddled into him as they took in the lights off the ocean to the west. The silence was peaceful but also building toward something. So she waited.

"I'm scared you're going to end up comparing me to him every time we have a fight and find me wanting," he admitted finally.

She turned in his embrace and reached up to cup his cheek. "Danny wasn't perfect any more than I am. He was a boy from Southie who had to balance his life with me with that of his interfering mother and"—she forced down the lump in her throat—"brother."

"You haven't met my family yet."

The idea terrified her. "I already know I'm going to like your mom. Not sure about your brother or his flaky wife."

Aaron smiled. "She's not flaky. Unfortunately, she's really fucking smart."

"Not as smart as you are," Hope corrected.

His eyes crinkled as he looked at her. "Maybe not. But smart enough to realize what we had together wasn't enough."

"Do I have to be nice to her?" Petulance leaked out.

"Worse. I think you're going to end up being friends. At least, I'm hoping that happens. If we have a baby, they'll have cousins. I'd like them to play together."

Her heart fluttered under her ribs at the thought. "It doesn't seem real. Even the possibility…"

"I know." He pulled her in and kissed her brow.

She burrowed her face into his T-shirt. "We could go start working on this right now."

She felt him laugh.

"I intend to as soon as I get the guys squared away for wheel's up in the morning."

Her fingers tightened on his shirt.

"I have tomorrow off but have to be back in Quantico by eight a.m. Monday for the team briefing."

She didn't want to lose him yet.

"Come with me."

She looked up at him in surprise. A mix of excitement and trepidation swirled inside her. "I don't know if I can organize everything by—"

"Like what?" He held her gaze. "Your caseload? If I know you, the paperwork is all ready for another prosecutor to take over. Plus, the local FBI office is still investigating everything Colin Leighton had his hands on. I doubt they'll let you back in this week anyway."

She looked around. "What about the apartment?"

"It's been here for more than a hundred years. Pretty sure it'll be okay for a week or two. I'll put both apartments back together before we leave. I'm sure we can find someone to bring in the mail and water the plants."

Larry and Enrique would be back soon.

Her mouth went a little dry. "I guess all I really need is my wallet, laptop, and cat."

"And me."

She smiled. "And you."

"Marry me."

She pulled back but didn't let go. He was serious.

"You don't have to—"

He swept her hair back from her face. Brown eyes earnest. "I want to. Maybe it's old-fashioned, but I want to."

He stepped back and dropped to one knee, holding onto her left hand. "Hope Harper, would you do me the very great honor of one day becoming my wife?"

She laughed, but suddenly, her vision was blurry. "Yes." She wiped her eyes. "Yes, I would love to marry you and begin the next adventure." She dropped to her knees onto the cold cement floor and wrapped her arms around him. Tears spilled over. "I don't usually cry this much, you know."

"This week has been a lot." Aaron tilted her chin up when she would have hidden from him.

She sniffed. "I'm so grateful to have found you, Aaron."

His lips curved into a smile just before he leaned down and kissed her.

———

Ryan slumped down to the couch cradling a beer. It was good to catch up with Marsh and Josie. Marsh was the reason he'd been accepted into the FBI Academy, although he'd managed to graduate and get into HRT all on his own. Seeing Josie and Marsh so happy with their kids reminded him of home and his own family who he needed to call.

Tabitha was eight now. In second grade and loving every

damned minute of it just like her momma had. The only thing Ryan had loved about school was the social aspect and sport. He'd gotten good grades, mainly because he was competitive and had a twin sister in the same classroom. No way was he letting Sarah beat him if he could help him. Also, because his parents had demanded it.

They'd demanded the best of each of them, and he knew he'd failed to deliver that after Becky died. His grip tightened on the bottle at the thought of his sweet wife. It was so damned unfair that the world had lost an angel. That he'd lost the love of his life. He thought about Hope finding the strength to try again with Aaron. It was admirable. Course, Aaron was one of the best men Ryan knew and would treat Hope like a queen the way she deserved to be treated. Aaron would never let her down, at least, not on purpose—but death didn't always give people a choice.

He wondered how Meghan was after burying her father yesterday and checked his phone. She hadn't replied to him.

He was concerned. The way he'd be concerned about any of the people he worked with.

Hope was wrong about her assumptions regarding that. It wasn't anything other than compassion for a shitty situation. Same way he worried about Grady and Shane, JJ and Seth. Losing Scotty and Montana had reminded them all they weren't superheroes. They were frail, fallible, badasses who bled as red as the rest of the humans on the planet.

He looked up as Payne Novak and Charlotte Blood headed up the stairs. He put his beer down and rose with a smile only to freeze on the spot when Grady Steel and Brynn Webster followed them into the apartment.

Fuck.

From the way Grady had his arm wrapped possessively around Brynn's waist, she'd managed to forgive the guy for what Ryan had said to her the day Grady had been shot a couple of weeks ago. Ryan had been trying to be a good friend, but he'd blown it in the worst way. From the glint in Grady's eye, Grady hadn't forgiven him yet.

Why should he? Ryan had fucked up.

The room went silent. Eyes watchful. Air expectant.

Ryan took a step forward and then another. He'd never been a coward—whether climbing onboard the biggest, meanest bull at the rodeo or defusing an explosive device, he knew how to man up. He just didn't know if it was going to be enough, and that scared him.

He walked over until he stood in front of Brynn and noticed the way she ducked her head and looked away, a trace of not only nerves but fear edging her gaze.

Shame filled him. "I am so sorry for what I said that day in the hospital." He shook his head as she still looked away, her lashes fluttering as if she was trying to stop tears.

Ryan hated tears. They destroyed him.

"Brynn." He took her hand and felt Grady's hard gaze, the guy watching his face like he could read Ryan's mind. "I was an idiot. I could blame the whole nerve gas situation or seeing someone I cared about bleeding out."

Grady's eyes became narrow slits as Ryan remembered all the things Brynn had endured that same day.

He let go of her hand. She tucked it away.

"It's no excuse. I know it's no excuse, but I was worried Grady was going to get his heart broken—"

"So you broke mine instead." Her gray-green eyes rose to meet his then. They weren't angry. Instead, they held traces of devastation that he was all too familiar with.

"I'm sorry. I'm truly sorry. I know I can't do anything to change the past, but I am so fucking sorry, and I was wrong to do that. If I could change it I would, but I can't." He wanted everything to go back to the way it had been before he'd opened his stupid fucking mouth. He pointed to his chin, half joking. "Take a shot at me. It'll make you feel better."

Brynn shook her head and backed up a step. Grady punched

him so hard Ryan saw that flash of white light as the room spun in that split-second it took to hit the hardwood floor.

His ears rang, and there was a shocked silence. Then Grady held out his hand, a cocked brow on his unsmiling face. Ryan reached out and let his buddy pull him to his feet.

He bracketed his jaw with his thumb and pointer finger, hoping nothing was broken. "Am I forgiven?"

Grady's eyes went shiny with what looked suspiciously like tears before he drew him in and hugged him tightly. Ryan gripped him back and closed his eyes in relief.

"You're forgiven, but I swear to God if you ever, *ever*, pull a stunt like that again..." Grady thumped him on the back a couple of times—a little harder than strictly necessary but now wasn't the time to complain.

Ryan grimaced. "I'll do my best."

Everyone started talking again. Show over.

Grady let him go and put his arm around Brynn.

"What are you doing here?" Ryan's voice came out a little high as he tried to pretend his jaw didn't hurt like a bitch.

"We left Deception Cove this morning. Needed to pack up some of Brynn's belongings and talk to the person subletting her apartment here in the city. I only realized you guys were also here when the tenant mentioned something about the FBI takedown of a serial killer nearby, so I called Novak." Grady shot a look at Brynn. "We've been avoiding the news for obvious reasons."

The fact they were both crazy in love was obvious. Ryan felt like a fool for doubting Brynn and for interfering. It wasn't up to him who got entangled with whom. It didn't all have to end in tragedy. He thought of Grace and her poor orphaned children and his heart bottomed out.

"You heard from Meghan?" Ryan asked. Grady was Meghan's partner, the two operators being part of Charlie squad.

Grady nodded. "She texted me to tell everyone the funeral went well. She plans to be back in Quantico in time for the memorial service."

Ryan ignored the sting of hurt that she'd contacted Grady but not him. He had no right to those feelings.

Aaron and Hope chose that moment to rejoin the party. Hope looked windblown and mussed and Aaron's pants were damp from the knee down. Ryan shook his head as Aaron and Grady reunited and Hope was introduced to Brynn, who'd finally removed her coat.

When Aaron made the announcement that he and Hope were engaged, joy welled up inside Ryan. Joy and that terrible lingering fear that the two of them would one day end up desolate and alone again. And maybe his problem wasn't that he understood that bad stuff could happen. Perhaps his real issue was that somewhere along the line he'd forgotten how to nurture the joy—to value it as much, if not more, than the grief. He'd let the bad feelings extinguish the good and let his fear drive his need for emotional self-preservation, and now he had the horrible feeling it was all too late for him to change.

Not that he wanted to.

He grabbed his beer and raised it not just to Aaron and Hope, but also to Brynn and Grady. He held Hope's warm gaze with a wry smile as he toasted them all.

———

Thank you for reading *Cold Fury*. I hope you enjoyed Aaron and Hope's story. Ready for the next exciting installment of the Cold Justice® - Most Wanted series?

Order *Cold Spite*…the next Romantic Thriller from *New York Times and USA Today* bestselling author Toni Anderson.

USEFUL ACRONYM DEFINITIONS FOR TONI'S BOOKS

ADA: Assistant District Attorney
AG: Attorney General
ASAC: Assistant Special-Agent-in-Charge
ASC: Assistant Section Chief
ATF: Alcohol, Tobacco, and Firearms
BAU: Behavioral Analysis Unit
BOLO: Be on the Lookout
BORTAC: US Border Patrol Tactical Unit
BUCAR: Bureau Car
CBP: US Customs and Border Patrol
CBT: Cognitive Behavioral Therapy
CD: Counterintelligence Division
CIRG: Critical Incident Response Group
CMU: Crisis Management Unit
CN: Crisis Negotiator
CNU: Crisis Negotiation Unit
CO: Commanding Officer
CODIS: Combined DNA Index System

CP: Command Post
CQB: Close-Quarters Battle
DA: District Attorney
DEA: Drug Enforcement Administration
DEVGRU: Naval Special Warfare Development Group
DIA: Defense Intelligence Agency
DHS: Department of Homeland Security
DOB: Date of Birth
DOD: Department of Defense
DOJ: Department of Justice
DS: Diplomatic Security
DSS: US Diplomatic Security Service
DVI: Disaster Victim Identification
EMDR: Eye Movement Desensitization & Reprocessing
EMT: Emergency Medical Technician
ERT: Evidence Response Team
FOA: First-Office Assignment
FBI: Federal Bureau of Investigation
FNG: Fucking New Guy
FO: Field Office
FWO: Federal Wildlife Officer
IB: Intelligence Branch
IC: Incident Commander
IC: Intelligence Community
ICE: US Immigration and Customs Enforcement
HAHO: High Altitude High Opening (parachute jump)
HRT: Hostage Rescue Team
HT: Hostage-Taker
JEH: J. Edgar Hoover Building (FBI Headquarters)
K&R: Kidnap and Ransom
LAPD: Los Angeles Police Department
LEO: Law Enforcement Officer
LZ: Landing Zone
ME: Medical Examiner

MO: Modus Operandi
NAT: New Agent Trainee
NCAVC: National Center for Analysis of Violent Crime
NCIC: National Crime Information Center
NFT: Non-Fungible Token
NOTS: New Operator Training School
NPS: National Park Service
NYFO: New York Field Office
OC: Organized Crime
OCU: Organized Crime Unit
OPR: Office of Professional Responsibility
POTUS: President of the United States
PT: Physiology Technician
PTSD: Post-Traumatic Stress Disorder
RA: Resident Agency
RCMP: Royal Canadian Mounted Police
RSO: Senior Regional Security Officer from the US Diplomatic Service
SA: Special Agent
SAC: Special Agent-in-Charge
SANE: Sexual Assault Nurse Examiners
SAS: Special Air Squadron (British Special Forces unit)
SD: Secure Digital
SIOC: Strategic Information & Operations
SF: Special Forces
SSA: Supervisory Special Agent
SWAT: Special Weapons and Tactics
TC: Tactical Commander
TDY: Temporary Duty Yonder
TEDAC: Terrorist Explosive Device Analytical Center
TOD: Time of Death
UAF: University of Alaska, Fairbanks
UBC: Undocumented Border Crosser
UNSUB: Unknown Subject

USSS: United States Secret Service
ViCAP: Violent Criminal Apprehension Program
VIN: Vehicle Identification Number
WFO: Washington Field Office
WMD: Weapons of Mass Destruction

COLD JUSTICE WORLD OVERVIEW
ALL BOOKS CAN BE READ AS STANDALONE STORIES.

COLD JUSTICE® SERIES

A Cold Dark Place (Book #1)

Cold Pursuit (Book #2)

Cold Light of Day (Book #3)

Cold Fear (Book #4)

Cold in The Shadows (Book #5)

Cold Hearted (Book #6)

Cold Secrets (Book #7)

Cold Malice (Book #8)

A Cold Dark Promise (Book #9~A Wedding Novella)

Cold Blooded (Book #10)

COLD JUSTICE® – THE NEGOTIATORS

Cold & Deadly (Book #1)

Colder Than Sin (Book #2)

Cold Wicked Lies (Book #3)

Cold Cruel Kiss (Book #4)

Cold as Ice (Book #5)

COLD JUSTICE® – MOST WANTED

Cold Silence (Book #1)

Cold Deceit (Book #2)

Cold Snap (Book #3)

Cold Fury (Book #4)

Cold Spite (Book #5) - Coming soon

The Cold Justice® series books are also available as audiobooks narrated by Eric Dove, and in various ebook box set compilations.

Check out all Toni's books on her website (www.toniandersonauthor. com/books-2) and find exclusive swag on her new store.

ACKNOWLEDGMENTS

Choosing a lawyer as a main character was one of my more challenging choices. I'm fine with making stuff up, but I'm not fine with butchering an entire judicial system unless it suits my purposes. Thankfully, one of my talented author friends, and former attorney, Leanne Kale Sparks, read an early version of the book and helped me with the basics. That said, any mistakes are mine, although I reserve the right to use artistic license where necessary in pursuit of a good story.

A hearty thanks to Dr. Ian Bouyoucos, whose experience of being a research biologist in French Polynesia sparked the idea for Aaron Nash's backstory (as far as I'm aware, during Ian's time in Mo'orea he had no fiancées or fiancée-stealing siblings).

I'm grateful for my longstanding critique partner, Kathy Altman, who has been with me since the very beginning. She's a rock! And my bestie, Rachel Grant, who gave me some fab notes to polish up the story.

I have an amazing editorial team in place. Developmental editor, Lindsey Faber, copy editor, Joan at JRT Editing, and proof-reader—the ridiculously talented Pamela Clare who provided input and commentary.

I'm so grateful to have assembled such an talented group of humans to help me produce and package my books. Huge appreciation also goes to my assistant Jill Glass, my brilliant cover designer Regina Wamba, my awesome audiobook narrator Eric G. Dove.

As always, my family supported me through the process of

writing this book. We added another black lab to the brood so now we have two crazies zooming around the place again, keeping things lively.

ABOUT THE AUTHOR

Toni Anderson writes gritty, sexy, FBI Romantic Thrillers, and is a *New York Times* and a *USA Today* bestselling author. Her books have won the Daphne du Maurier Award for Excellence in Mystery and Suspense, Readers' Choice, Aspen Gold, Book Buyers' Best, Golden Quill, National Excellence in Story Telling Contest, and National Excellence in Romance Fiction awards. She's been a finalist in both the Vivian Contest and the RITA Award from the Romance Writers of America, and shortlisted for The Jackie Collins Award for Romantic Thrillers in the Romantic Novel Awards. Toni's books have been translated into five different languages and more than three million copies of her books have been downloaded.

Best known for her Cold Justice® books perhaps it's not surprising to discover Toni lives in one of the most extreme climates on earth—Manitoba, Canada. Formerly a Marine Biologist, Toni still misses the ocean, but is lucky enough to travel for research purposes. In late 2015, she visited FBI Headquarters in Washington DC, including a tour of the Strategic Information and Operations Center. She hopes not to get arrested for her Google searches.

Check out Toni Anderson's shop with exclusive merch and offers:
https://toniandersonshop.com
Sign up for Toni Anderson's newsletter:
www.toniandersonauthor.com/newsletter-signup

facebook.com/toniandersonauthor

x.com/toniannanderson

instagram.com/toni_anderson_author

tiktok.com/@toni_anderson_author